HARRY HERON: HOPE TRANSCENDS

Book Six of the
Harry Heron Series

Patrick G. Cox

Paperback ISBN: 9781946824691
Hardback ISBN: 9781946824745
ebook ISBN: 9781946824752
Library of Congress Control Number: 2020909560

Publisher's Cataloging-in-Publication Data
Names: Cox, Patrick G., author.
Title: Harry Heron hope transcends / Patrick G. Cox.
Description: [Longwood, FL] : INDIEGO PUBLISHING, 2020. | Summary: In the sixth and final book in the Harry Heron Adventure series, Harry faces insurmountable hurdles in his quest to defeat his enemies and reunite with Mary, the love of his life and his bride-to-be.
Identifiers: LCCN 2020909560 | ISBN 9781946824691 (pbk.) | ISBN 9781946824745 (hardcover) | ISBN 9781946824752 (ebook)
Subjects: LCSH: Life on other planets – Fiction. | Man-woman relationships – Fiction | Space flight – Fiction. | Space warfare – Fiction. | BISAC: FICTION / Science Fiction / Space Opera. | FICTION / Science Fiction / Military. | FICTION / Science Fiction / Alien Contact.
Classification: LCC PR6103.O9 H377.H6 2020 (print) | PR6103.O9 (ebook) | DDC 823 C69--dc22

PUBLISHING
Our Brilliance . Your Success
WWW.INDIEGOPUBLISHING.COM
WWW.INDIEGOPUBLISHING.CO.UK
WWW.GETINDIEGO.COM

The Harry Heron Series

OTHER BOOKS by PATRICK G. COX

www.harryheron.com
www.patrickgcox.com

Dedication

The Harry Heron Series was inspired by my grandfather, the original Henry Nelson Heron, who ran away at the age of fifteen to join the British Army to fight in World War I. He and his best friend were among the casualties on the first day of the Somme battles, which saw the 36th Ulster Division almost wiped out. They survived and went on to make new lives for themselves by making use of their broad knowledge and vast array of skills to further their ambitions.

This book is dedicated to my brother Robert.

1950 - 2020

Table of Contents

HARRY HERON:
HOPE TRANSCENDS

Chapter 1

Renewed Threat

Commodore Felicity Roberts, Director of Surveillance Operations, Fleet Security, looked up as Captain Mike Frey, her second in command, entered her suite. They were aboard the *Thermopylae*, a freighter by outward appearance, but internally the ship's layout and fittings had been retrofitted so that it primarily served as an intelligence processing centre for the North European Confederation Fleet.

"What have you got, Mike?"

"The latest decrypts from the group we're monitoring. They've been in touch with the League for the Protection of Sentient Life again. They seem very keen to set up a meeting with an unidentified group—we think they're talking about that new species the Brotherhood have been getting tech from."

Felicity nodded. "Any sign they're going to meet?"

"Looks that way. They're suggesting a couple of locations outside our borders. More worrying though, is the subtext to their messages." He activated a display. "There's a suggestion they're wanting to install some sort of signal relay on ships, possibly ours. They mention delaying the build program for the new River Class as well. They may have people already working on it." He moved his hand in the air as if swiping a screen to display the second message. "I've alerted our people in the building docks and the maintenance bases."

"Thanks. This is looking more and more like they're getting ready to take over their target ministries in key administrations. Prepare the information for me in a briefing note and I'll inform the Boss by hololink." She sighed with an air of frustration. "These damned political ideologues never give up. The newscast last night had another of them spouting about how restrictions on trading technology with alien races should be lifted entirely."

He laughed. "I didn't catch that one, but there is an odd set of messages between someone at DigiMedia Corporation and the LPSL, and they all mention the same little band of politicos and their so-called research groups, though I doubt any of them know how to conduct research of any kind. Something about getting Commander Heron onto a show and manipulating the broadcast to make it look like the Fleet caused the Niburu War. The message is in response to a question about live editing, and the reply assures the questioner that it can be done. So their intent is to ensconce Commander Heron on stage in front of a live global audience, and contort his words in real time with the intent to expose him as a dangerous relic of the past—their words, not mine."

She frowned. "Commander Harry Heron? Admiral Heron's nephew?"

"That's the one—the young man who led the corvette flotilla that destroyed the Niburu queen ship." He paused. "He's a nephew of the Admiral?"

"Not really—actually he's the God-knows-how-many-times-great uncle of James Heron." When she saw the baffled expression on Mike's face, she laughed and added, "He's one of the infamous three ancient mariners who arrived here in our century straight from the year 1804 from the deck of a wooden sailing ship during a sea battle with the French. Something happened with one of our transit gates and caused a rip in the space-time continuum, or some such. I don't quite understand all that."

Captain Frey looked stunned. "Ah, yes, I remember now. That explains a lot of what I've heard about him."

She chuckled. "It's quite the story. Look it up when you get a minute. It's easier just to call Harry the Admiral's nephew and leave it at that." She paused. "Anyway, see what you can find on this LPSL business—who's behind it, who the contacts are at

DigiMedia and the LPSL—anything and everything. Send it to Commander Heron's current CO—he's on the Perisher course, I think, and then ... no, I'll contact James Heron myself."

"Will do. There's one more thing. We think the Pantheon is involved in this. Their fingerprints are all over the sudden retirements and fatal accidents, if one can call them that, among the top secretaries in several governments. Senator Samland's involved in it too. She's in regular communication with a front man for the Pantheon. So far just arrangements to meet in various places, but we need to keep a close eye on her."

"Good idea," said Felicity. "What's the Pantheon up to?"

"They're being as cautious as ever, but recently one of the Senator's rivals for a key ministerial appointment had a rather nasty and fatal accident, or so it was reported. I seriously doubt it was accidental. It had the modus of the Pantheon stamped all over it—sadistic and designed to cause maximum alarm among their opponents."

Felicity recalled a much earlier encounter with one of the Pantheon goddesses, as the female operatives in that underground group referred to themselves. "Give me the details. I think we need to assign a special team to monitor them, and I want the business with the signal repeaters examined fully."

"Private holocall for you, sir," announced the Coms Lieutenant to Admiral Heron. Normally he'd have declined the call, logged it and passed a message to his superior, but this caller had used a code word to identify her, and he knew that meant it was top priority.

James Heron hesitated, frowning. "A private message?"

"Yes, sir. The lady said to tell you, Remember Brown."

"Ah. Very well, I'll take it in my Day Cabin." James Heron strode to his quarters and activated his desk display. "Felicity, good to see you again. Business or pleasure?"

"Business, I'm afraid, James." She laughed. "Congratulations, by the way, on your promotion. Full Admiral now!" She grinned. "You've been avoiding me, I think."

"Congratulations on your promotion as well, Felicity. But if you will insist on swanning about in that freighter they've given you—even an Admiral can't drag his entire fleet across the galaxy to the places you go!"

She laughed. "True, but this way I can hear and see things some people would like to hide. Anyway, back to business. We've learned that someone wants to get Harry onto a talk show so they can attempt to destroy his credibility and promote their own agenda. We aren't sure why or what purpose it will serve, except it seems to be linked to a very quiet coup d'état attempted by stealth. We know that a takeover of key ministries in the Treaty States is underway, so we'll keep digging until we find whoever is behind it, and we have the evidence to stop it."

"Thanks for the heads-up. I'll make sure Harry is aware, and I'll alert my brother-in-law as well."

"There's more, I'm afraid. Our lovely friend of the Fleet and general pain in the neck, Senator Samland, seems to be linked in some way, and she's up to something that involves the Pantheon."

"Them again? Are they still active? I thought we put an end to them when your people took out Bast and a few of their top players in 2204."

"Unfortunately, no. We nabbed some of their top-level gods and goddesses, and several members of their support teams, but the others went into hiding, and lately they've been making a reappearance." Felicity paused. James Heron, then a Senior Captain, had played a major part in the killing of Bast and her team. "Take care, James. We don't know who they're after, but you and I could be prime targets if it's about revenge. So could members of our families."

Admiral James Heron, Commander in Chief, Allied Fleet One, studied his display. The briefing was comprehensive. The Fleet had recently encountered an alien fleet of ships that completely avoided the Fleet's attempts at contact. Clearly, the aliens were evasive and technologically advanced. Worryingly, they were known to be in contact with humanity through an unofficial channel linked in some way to the takeover of several Treaty governments' ministries.

Samland and her friends wanted to raise the issue of the Fleet having finally, and after much argument and millions of human casualties, used a Siddhiche-provided toxic agent to destroy the Niburu. The League and its supporters still maintained the fantasy that the Fleet had been guilty of starting the war, and then of genocide to end it. Politicians like Samland were merely using the

controversy to advance their own ambitions and—presumably—
to gain some advantage.

He frowned. It looked more and more as if Samland and her
cronies were attempting to revive the ideas behind the Consortium. Making a note to raise this with his well-placed brother-in-
law, Theo L'Estrange, he keyed his link.

"Adriana, ask Lieutenant Biggar to come to my Day Cabin,
please. And book me a holocall to my brother-in-law for 20:00
Dublin time, and one to Commodore Roberts in an hour."

"As you wish, Admiral. Lieutenant Biggar is here."

"Send him in."

Harry's link chirped, breaking his train of thought as he worked on
his dissertation.

"Lieutenant-Commander Heron? See me in my office at your
break, please." The College Deputy Commandant was a large
cheerful man, but like all Deputy Commandants in Training
Establishments, he was the enforcer of discipline for the student
population. His voice on the link betrayed no indication as to
whether his request to meet with Harry was to award an accolade
or issue a reprimand.

"Aye, aye, sir." Harry closed the link and returned to working on
his dissertation. It had been a gruelling nine months. The course
had attracted the nickname The Perisher because it pushed the
candidates to the extreme, exposing their weaknesses and building on their strengths, but the rigorous academic discipline prepared the candidates for promotion and command. This course
had been tougher than most, since many of the candidates had
already been tested in battle in ranks and positions they were only
now being trained to perform. That had certainly been Harry's
experience—flying by the seat of his pants, learning with boots on
the ground—practically from the day his feet landed on the hangar deck of the NECS *Vanguard* some eight years earlier, straight
from the year 1804 and the deck of the HMS *Spartan* in the midst
of a sea battle with the French.

Harry was having to scramble to make up lost time in his
coursework because he'd agreed to film a documentary with Alisdair Montaigne, host of the *Montaigne Show*, about Harry and
his friends Ferghal O'Connor and Danny Gunn. The making of
the documentary had been quite enjoyable in one sense. 'Monty'

Montaigne had proved to be meticulous in the shaping of it, and the research had been accurate. Even the most difficult part—the abuse they'd suffered on the planet Pangaea at the hands of the Johnstone Research Institute—had been done with great sensitivity.

Harry'd had some reservations about how much the documentary would reveal of his and Ferghal's ability to connect to any AI network in proximity to them, but thankfully that was not fully revealed or discussed.

His feelings regarding Alisdair 'Monty' Montaigne were less clear. Montaigne obviously regarded him as a friend, but Harry preferred to keep a little distance between them. They'd had a few encounters onboard the *Prins van Oranien* during the Niburu War, but that was about it. Harry considered Monty an acquaintance, but there was certainly not enough between them to claim friendship. He didn't dislike the man; it was more a question of familiarity, and Monty tended to be overly so.

As he saved his work and secured his files, Harry wondered what this summons from the Deputy Commandant was about. Had he offended some instructor with his forthright approach? He thought of the documentary then pondered his live appearance on Monty's television show afterward. That was probably it. He'd been warned and briefed on how these shows could be manipulated. That must be the reason for this summons.

"Commander, be seated, please." Captain David waved Harry to a seat as he stepped out from behind his desk to take a chair across from him. "Your appearance on the *Montaigne Show* went very well." He smiled. "I have a report here from Commodore Roberts, however, saying you evidently locked out the production team."

"I'm afraid so, sir." Harry paused. "The Commodore's people warned me that there might be attempts to impose subliminal messages and images which could negatively influence and misdirect the viewers—they use a large background screen on the stage, as you know—and suggested I use my link to check."

"And you detected some?"

"I did, sir."

Captain David noted Harry's expression. "So you blocked them?"

"Yes, sir." Harry recalled the friendly security guard who welcomed him, and who even requested being allowed to take a selfie photo with him, a complete contrast to the surly production manager who took him to the studio.

The Captain smiled. "It seems you may have stirred a hornet's nest. Our security people have been watching DigiCorp Media for a while. Whenever they discuss something contentious on one of their shows, there's an upsurge in civil disturbances and factional agitation."

"Contentious, sir?" Harry frowned. "My part on this show was simply to talk about the documentary that Mr. Montaigne made about my friends and me. You may know them—Lieutenant-Commander Ferghal O'Connor and Sub-Lieutenant Daniel Gunn." He grinned as a thought hit him. "Well, I suppose some might consider us contentious, even when we don't try to be!"

The Captain laughed. "The LPSL certainly do. There seems to be no end to the many ways you annoy them just for being alive and breathing."

Harry nodded with a wry smile, and the Captain chuckled.

"So the Montaigne Show—what was your impression of the place? Do you think Montaigne is aware of the live editing that goes on to manipulate what's seen and heard by the audience?"

"I'd say not, sir. His producer certainly didn't inform him that they were not in control of their broadcast. I'd have heard them tell him on his private link, and afterward he showed no indication of knowing otherwise."

The Captain leaned back in his seat and studied Harry. "Did you allow the recordings of your contacts with the Niburu to be viewed by the audience?"

"Yes, sir, but without the additions and alterations someone had imposed." Harry paused. "Commodore Roberts and her team have all the material I blocked, sir."

"So she informs me, Harry. She also tells me that your actions saved her people a lot of work, and gave them the path they needed to get past the DigiCorp Media's security system. They got everything they were looking for, and a great deal more."

"I see, sir." Harry had mixed feelings about this. He'd acted only to prevent his own reputation and that of the Fleet being maligned by the subliminal messages and images he'd blocked. Now it seemed the Fleet's Secret Service had used the opportunity for a wider purpose, something he'd never considered or intended. "May I know why they were so eager to gain access?"

"I can't reveal it all because I don't know it all." The Captain sat up straighter. "DigiCorp is a very large umbrella organisation, and DigiMedia is possibly the largest source of news and information on Earth and among the colonies. It is being used to spread false ideologies and beliefs that run counter to everything the North European Confederation stands for, as well as the North American Union and the World Treaty Council." He paused. "It seems that your appearance on the show was to have been the start of a new wave of disinformation—and you prevented it. That's annoyed some very important people, though they don't seem to realise it was you. Once they see the documentary on you and your friends, however, they might make the connection."

Chapter 2

Heart's Desire

Mary flung her arms around him as he stepped from the transport.

"Ah, finally, there you are, my sweet handsome space pilot alien warrior television star!" She laughed at his expression, and her kiss was so full of passion that it nearly made him unsteady on his feet. "Aw, my poor baby, look at you. Your course must have been tough—you look worn out." She hugged him again, briefly, and adding teasingly, "You were wonderful on the *Montaigne Show*. Monty was right—you're a natural!"

"Well, I don't know about all that," Harry protested, but his cheeks flushed with pleasure at her praise.

Mary wrapped her fingers around his upper arm with a gentle tug. "Come inside and tell us all about it. The whole family is waiting. Are you now officially on leave?"

"Yes, at last." Harry squeezed Mary's waist, reluctant to release her. "Eight weeks, and then I'll receive a new posting." He grinned. "Their Lordships suspected the show would be used as a cover for something. Thankfully, I was warned and prepared for what I met." He shrugged. "Hopefully, that will be an end to my involvement in any of it."

"The women of Planet Earth are clamouring to see more of your handsome face on screen, but I agree with you," said Mary with a grin. "Besides, they can't have you because you're mine." She winked, and he grinned as they crossed the threshold and stepped into the house.

Theo was the first to greet them. "Harry, good to have you home again. I caught the tail end of your conversation, and I have to warn you, Monty has been in touch to say how delighted he was to have you on the show. James was on the link as soon as it was finished. He said to tell you well done. So I expect it has met with approval and acknowledgement that you dealt with a tricky situation so well." He smiled. "I want to hear about anything you discovered in their system. I suspect they're still wondering why they lost control of it. My team are very interested in some of their manipulations." He caught his wife Niamh's eye. "But I think it will have to wait. You and Mary want some time alone, I expect."

Niamh grinned as Harry wrapped her in a hug and leaned into her like a small boy glad to be in the comfort of home again. "Welcome home, Harry. You relax for now. We'll catch up later. Oh, I can have Herbert prepare a special dinner with all your favourites if you'd like," she added.

"Thank you, Aunt Niamh, that's so kind of you, but may we have something simple today? I have something special in mind with Mary tonight." He caught Mary's eye and smiled, and was thrilled when the look she gave him in return was excited, eager and curious all at the same time.

The dinner was the perfect climax to a wonderful few weeks in each other's company. The chef had prepared all of Harry and Mary's favourite dishes and presented them with perfection and elegance. Now they lingered over their coffee and liqueurs. The candle burned low, and the waiter withdrew quietly after serving the aperitif. Harry hoped this would be the perfect moment.

"Mary, I have been wanting to ask you this for a long, long time—"

He caught his breath as she met his gaze across the rim of her cup. Carefully she placed it in the saucer, hoping this was the moment she'd been waiting for. "And what might that question be, Mr. Heron?"

He reached across the table and took her hand in his. "Dearest Mary, will you consider accepting my hand in marriage? Will you agree to be my wife?"

His earnest expression and the formality of the question amused her even as her heart leapt. She couldn't resist a gentle tease though. "If I were assured that you would not immediately vanish off into the outer reaches of the galaxy to stir up some new danger for the human race, I might be persuaded, sir."

"I think I may safely give that assurance, though the Fleet will certainly send me to some exotic places in future, of that I'm certain." He kissed her hand. "At least for the next two months of leave I will be earthbound, and then I'll have a shadow post at a base. I surely cannot stir up any trouble with such a boring duty assignment."

She laughed. "With your temper? I wonder if your senior officers really know what they have in you." Her expression softened as she met his eye. "Do you, Mr. Heron, accept my desire to continue with my career? I will make a very poor wife in the mould of the women you knew in the eighteen hundreds."

Harry hadn't considered this aspect. In his way of thinking, his wife would settle at home and manage his household while he went off to find the wherewithal to provide everything they needed. His expression showed it as he stammered, "Of course, but ... do you wish to? I can assure you my income is more than adequate."

She smiled. "It's not about income, Harry. You have a career, and so do I. You have many women in the Fleet, some of them Admirals. They enjoy the fulfillment of their careers as I enjoy mine." She could see he hadn't considered that those women might be married. She changed tack. "Did you know that Niamh is a highly qualified barrister?"

He looked surprised. "No! I mean, yes, but Aunt Niamh doesn't have Chambers or take cases. She manages the house for Theo and the rest of us ..." He trailed off when he realised how weak his argument sounded, and he grinned sheepishly.

Mary laughed. "She gave up her career when Theo accepted the position as Chief Justice, as there could be a conflict of interests if she continued her practice." She gripped his hand. "You should ask her about it sometime to learn how she feels about having to sacrifice her career."

He frowned and nodded. "I will. I can quite see it will not have been easy for her to do so." He held her hand lightly and smiled. "Mary, I know I am very old fashioned in many of my notions, but these last months showed me very clearly how much I missed not being able to talk to you, to hear your voice or to sit beside you and just be in your presence. I cannot imagine not having you by my side for the rest of my life."

At this point, Harry stood from his chair, took a small jeweler's box from his pocket, and he knelt on one knee next to her chair. Mary let out a little gasp as he presented her with a gorgeous, sparkling diamond ring.

"Mary, my dearest darling, will you marry me? Will you give me the honour of being my wife?"

Mary smiled and held out her hand as he slipped the ring on. "Oh, yes, Harry Nelson-Heron, I will marry you, and this ring—it's so beautiful, and such a perfect fit! I love you so much, my darling. Yes, a thousand times yes!" She stood from her chair and he stood with her, and they embraced and shared a kiss, utterly oblivious to the restaurant patrons looking on with happiness at their joy, though they were seated a proper distance away in this somewhat private section of the restaurant.

When Harry and Mary heard a few murmurs of approval, they separated and smiled in embarrassment, and took their seats again.

"I'm so glad you said yes, Mary. I was rather worried that for some reason you wouldn't have me." Harry's relief was evident.

"Of course I'll have you, Harry. You're the only man for me, but let's be clear on this: I will not give up my career, and there will be times when I must tour and you will be away with the Fleet. I will marry you on condition that you are able to accept that."

Harry's face lit up. "I accept your condition, my dearest, with no hesitation."

Mary gazed at the lovely ring. It was antique in design, six brilliant diamonds of an old-fashioned cut clustered in a circular mounting around a large center diamond, all sparkling with brilliance and clarity in the candlelight. "It's beautiful," she breathed. "It looks antique, a true one-of-a-kind. How did you ever find such a treasure?"

Harry beamed with satisfaction. "I had it made on Planet Lycania. It is a copy of the ring my mother wore. I have been unable to trace any of the old family heirlooms I would have wished to bestow upon you, so I resorted to a copy. It is not exact, but as close as I can manage from memory." He caught her bemused expression. "Is it acceptable? If not, I will have something else made for you."

Mary laughed aloud at this, a delightful cascade of sound, much to Harry's complete confusion. "Oh, Harry, of course it's acceptable. To me it is every bit as precious as an heirloom because you had it made especially for me."

Mary's acceptance of his proposal was tempered by the fact that they could not marry for at least twelve months. It appalled him, but he resigned himself to the delay. The worst-case scenario, which he didn't like to consider, was a delay of up to eighteen months. It would take at least a year to gather and submit all the legal documentation and obtain the necessary permission to marry, primarily because of his pieced-together birth and ancestral records. The other factors involved her schedule, his postings, coordinating the schedules of everyone invited, and arranging the venue for the ceremony. Then there was the problem of where to hold the reception, and Monty Montaigne wanting to film a sequel to his documentary during this time, with Harry as the main character study in it.

Harry tried not to be gloomy about their prospects on this fine day, a rare one of glorious sunshine glinting off the verdant Irish green hills. He and Mary were stretched out on the soft grass on one of those hills gazing at the clouds and planning their future together.

"Twelve months..." Harry murmured, and sighed with frustration. "It can't possibly take that long, not even for the wheels of bureaucracy to churn, and eighteen months is unthinkable."

Mary rolled over and propped herself on one elbow to gaze into his blue eyes. "Darling Harry, we've been together for over five years now, and for most of that we've been half a galaxy apart. At least now, for some of the time anyway, we'll both be on the same planet. The time will fly by, and we'll be so busy with all sorts of exciting preparations! You'll see." She kissed his cheek and snuggled closer as he wrapped his arm around her.

"You're right, I know, but you'll be on tour for some of it, and I'll be posted. I suppose I was hoping to be your husband much sooner than that." He turned his mischievous schoolboy expression toward her and winked.

She laughed. "We'll see each other regularly, don't worry. As long as you don't find some new danger to stir up, we'll be fine." She ruffled his hair. "Come on, even in the year eighteen-whatever you couldn't just rush out and get married. I read somewhere that you had to get all sorts of permissions from various authorities and, of course, the convention was to have at least twelve months between the engagement and the wedding."

Harry sat up at this point, all business. "Not true. If we were living in 1804, I could apply to the Bishop for a Special Licence and be married without Banns or waiting." His eyes shone down at her with mischief. "Or we could elope to Gretna Green—a short sail on *Extravagance* from here—and be married over the anvil in the blacksmith's shop without all the fuss and bother."

Mary sat up with a jolt. "And deprive my parents and friends of the pleasure of attending the wedding? Not for anything in the world!"

Mary's sweet laugh trilled as she wrapped her arms around him and hugged him so exuberantly that they tumbled together into the soft cushion of the grassy hillside.

"Besides, there's plenty we can do to pass the time until we're married," she murmured, and they were lost in each other's arms without even a fleeting thought that it was a good thing they had this little slice of the Irish countryside all to themselves that day.

Chapter 3

Obstacles

Kharim Pasha Al-Khalifa studied the hologram of his caller with contempt. Senator Samland thought herself important, and her arrogance grated. The purpose of her call: she wanted him, as head of the Pantheon, to undertake a commission. A smile flickered as it occurred to him that she was on the payroll, under various code names of course, of at least five of his multi-planet corporations. She thought she was playing one against the other in the belief that it would put her at the head of the government she wished to install.

It amused him to know this, and to know that she was not seeing a hologram of him, but rather a representation of Zorvan, a god of time in Persian mythology. As leader of the Pantheon, he took great care to keep his real identity secret, and those of his fellow gods and goddesses, as they referred to themselves. In fact, he was probably the only person who knew the true identities behind certain key members of the Pantheon, and he took extraordinary care to keep it that way.

She was not hearing Kharim's voice as they spoke, but rather a warped version of a generic male voice that sounded authentically real.

"We have decided, Senator," he said, "that your commission is worthy of our attention. We will instruct our agents to make contact with these aliens, the Charonians, through the privateers, as you call them." He wondered if she knew the Charonians were a thoroughly nasty race, parasites in a sense, though they were very skilled at manufacturing some incredible alloys, and kept the secret to their work under tight control. "We will persuade their leaders of the benefits of working with you. Our usual rates will apply, and the credit will be placed in the banks we designate."

"Good. The transfers will be made as soon as we get the information."

"I trust the demise of Senator Polonoski and his associates met with your contract requirements, a spectacular and very public death as requested."

The Senator hesitated. Should she play ignorant or play along? Oh well, it was too late now. "Oh yes, that. I understand it was a catastrophic failure of their transport shuttle. Yes, very satisfactory. Just enough evidence to indicate it was not an accident, but disturbing enough to make clear to other waverers that we will not tolerate any breach of allegiance." Senator Samland was an ambitious woman, and still smarting over the debacle of the *Montaigne Show*. Their intention had been to present Heron in the worst possible light as a typical "warmongering" representative of the Fleet, but of course Harry had thwarted their attempts.

"I may have another problem for your attention, Zorvan, but I will need to consult my partners on it."

"Excellent, so glad we could deliver satisfactorily, and of course we will consider any further commissions. We'll speak again soon."

He killed the holo link and pondered their conversation. His agents among the Charonians had provided a great deal of information. The wealth to be gained from their alloys would triple his already immense holdings, but the Charonians were demanding the provision of suitable hosts in exchange. The Senator might not be aware of this because, as with most self-important arrogant people, she considered any possible downside to her plans a sign of weakness.

He touched his link. "Bahram, is my transport ready? I've no wish to be late for the gala dinner. Remind me which of the charities it is again. There are so many to keep track of, and after a while they all seem the same...."

"Commander Heron? Very pleased to meet you at last." Felicity Roberts indicated an armchair. "Please, sit down."

Taking the offered chair, Harry settled into it. "Thank you, ma'am." The sign on the door said this was the office of the Director of Surveillance Operations, but his hostess displayed no rank and no indication of her role. He recognised her as the woman his relative and one-time guardian in this century, Admiral James Heron, kept a portrait of next to a photo of his deceased wife, and Harry knew there was something more than friendship between them. Beyond that, he knew very little about her.

"I don't stand on ceremony here, Commander." She smiled as she settled into a chair opposite him. "It tends to get in the way of what I do in the field, so I find it easier to dispense with it as much as possible. My name is Felicity. May I call you by your preferred name?"

"Of course, er, Felicity. My friends address me as Harry." Felicity's easy manner relaxed him, and he grinned. "Those who aren't my friends utter my name with a less pleasant epithet, though not to my face."

She laughed. "Harry it is then, and I think we'll be good friends." She paused. "I was in the live audience of the *Montaigne Show* that day. Well done. Unconventional, and you gave my team some headaches, but when they realised you didn't need their help tampering with the broadcast, they sat back and enjoyed the farce."

She smiled. "You saved some of my people a lot of work—and my chief of data recovery said to thank you. He'd been trying to gain access to their systems for some time. You gave him a window, and he got everything he was after."

Harry frowned. He wasn't sure he liked being involved in this spying operation. "Ah, yes, I'm afraid I did some damage in taking over their systems." He smiled as an android assistant poured tea for him. "Thank you, Yelendi," he said, noting the nameplate on its upper right chest. He met Felicity's eyes again. "Your order ... or rather, your message ... suggested you wished to debrief me on the subject of that show."

"Yes, we'll get to that in a moment." To Yelendi, she said, "I'll have my usual." She waited while the android made a cappuccino for her. "Yelendi, how did you know the Lieutenant-Commander wanted a tea?"

"He told me when I asked, Commodore."

Harry laughed. "I'm afraid I often have this problem, Felicity. They simply link to me through the AI running whatever place I'm in. It is a little difficult for others to know when it's happening, and I forget that sometimes. To explain how it works, I can hear them through my ability to link to any AI in proximity."

"Ah, yes." She smiled. "James mentioned that, but I've never seen it in action. Is this how you took over Montaigne's show?"

"Yes. I do my best to avoid any probing, but sometimes an AI sees me as a download destination. It can be embarrassing because my memory does not respond to an erase command."

"Thank heaven for that!" She grinned. "Right, so what I would like to know from you is how you seized control of their AI network. You seem to have sailed right past their security barriers." She paused. "I think we'd better record this conversation. Do you agree?"

"I have no objection, Felicity."

Harry's frustration over the bureaucracy engulfing his and Mary's marriage plans were, to a large extent, alleviated by sailing his pride and joy, the replica gaff-rigged pilot cutter *Extravagance*. It was a legal requirement that she be equipped with a ship management system including a navigation system, auxiliary engine and communications, but he preferred to sail her the old fashioned way by hand and eye and keen navigational skills. For one thing, it meant he didn't have to listen to a computer trying to do everything for him.

He let the cutter's head fall off the wind a few points. "Ease the jib a touch, Ferghal. With this wind we should make excellent time to Bangor."

"Aye, we will that." Ferghal secured the sheet and watched as Danny adjusted the foresail. "She fair flies on this heading."

"She does." Harry swept the surrounding water with a quick glance then looked up at the sails again. "We will need to reduce our canvas soon though. We are to go alongside this evening, and the approach is tricky."

"So it is. Very well, Captain. We await your orders." Ferghal glanced at his friend. "Have there been any more messages from those fools who accuse you of starting the Niburu War?"

"No, though I suspect it is only because Fleet Security are working with the police and have frightened them away for the moment." He shrugged. "In another week I shall be taking up my shadow appointment at the Lunar Station. They will have difficulty conducting their campaign there. I am more concerned that some are now targeting Mary. There was a disturbance at her last concert. Some young fool wanted to discuss her relationship with a mass murderer—he meant me, of course." He shook his head at the ridiculousness of it all. "I wish she would consider giving up her career so I could take proper care of her and know that she's safely ensconced at home when we're married."

"Well, that's not likely to happen, at least not until she bears your children. Mary loves performing, and I suppose I can understand that." Ferghal paused, and Harry nodded but said nothing. Ferghal continued. "All o' these *spailpíns* are damned fools." He gazed at the shoreline as they approached.

Harry laughed. "Indeed, you are right, my friend. My only concern is how much might be known of our interaction with artificial intelligence networks now that Montaigne's documentary has aired."

"Aye, that and his clearly having a liking for your company." Ferghal glanced at his friend, his expression full of mischief. "Would he like to go sailing with us again, do you think?"

"Not likely!" Harry bellowed, before he realised Ferghal was teasing. "Consider the strain it would give Aunt Niamh to have him as a house guest. She has enough to concern her with this requirement that my DNA be matched to prove my birth."

Ferghal nodded. "True. At least we know where your parents lie buried if it must come to that. I will face far greater problems in that regard, and as for poor Danny, he doesn't even know who his parents were—"

"Did I hear my name?" Danny joined them at the tiller.

Ferghal ruffled the younger man's hair. "Ye did. I was sayin' that if our captain here cannot prove his birth relationship, then ye and me have no chance at all."

"Aunt Niamh says it's not difficult, and she has Case Law, or some such, which will help us." Danny grinned. "Though I suspect marriage may not be a priority for at least one of us, a certain wild Irish lad who loves the attention of *all* the ladies."

"Cheek! And from a junior as well." Ferghal playfully cuffed him.

"Bullying—and in the presence of a senior officer. I shall report you, sir!" Danny exclaimed, as he dodged another cuff, his laugh echoed by Harry's.

"Enough, Mr. O'Connor! Set a proper example to our juniors, if you please. We cannot have him attempting to emulate such behaviour when he presides in the Gunroom of his next ship in a few weeks' time."

Only that morning Harry had received notification that, with the completion of his brief time on the Lunar Station, he was promoted to full Commander. He pushed it from his mind. For now, they were nothing more than three brother-friends enjoying the exhilaration of sailing this tidy little ship on a glorious afternoon with a more perfect wind than they could've ever hoped for.

"Good news, Harry." Niamh joined him in the small sitting room he used as a study. The month on the Lunar Station had been almost a continuation of his leave. It gave him the opportunity to see at first hand the administration of a Support Command at work, experience he'd found informative. "We may have managed to get a court to rule for a waiver of the requirement to prove your birth date. The evidence of your friend Dr. Borner regarding any DNA we might recover from a grave, plus the changes we know were made to your DNA and Ferghal's when you were experimented on in the Johnstone Laboratory have persuaded them to find other viable proofs of your identity." She sat beside him and smiled as she handed him a new document. "It's taken a bit of work, but now we can get agreement on the format of the waiver with the Registrar's Department—and that will smooth the path for Ferghal and Danny when they decide on marriage."

Harry leaned across the table to hug her and kiss her cheek. "Thank you. I can never repay you for your kindness or the work you've put into this."

"Nonsense, Harry. It isn't that much work. You three are the children that Theo and I never had. The same can be said of my brother James. You're like a son to him, and he only wants the best for you." She smiled. "Besides, it's been fun to deal with legal challenges again. I hadn't realised how much I missed it."

Danny wandered in and stopped. "Oh, I'm sorry, I didn't mean to intrude."

"You're not, Danny. Aunt Niamh was just telling me we have a way to overcome the difficulty of our birth dates and proof of parentage." Harry then noticed the youngster's grim expression. "What is your news?"

Danny took a seat. "My orders have arrived at last. I'm to join the *Der Grosse Kurfürst*. She's now the training cruiser for cadets joining the Fleet. I was hoping for a more active post, not playing nursemaid to all the Snotties in a training ship."

Harry laughed. "Now there speaks a true ancient mariner! Give him a single star and bar, and his own days as a Snottie are forgotten." He grinned as Danny blushed. "I tease, Danny, you have much to teach them, and you'll be a good example. The DGK is a good ship, and I think you'll enjoy your posting with her. She'll be stuffed full of Middies." He laughed. "Most of them older than you, or so they'll think. You'll find them active enough—and do not forget the reports that the Niburu are still at large."

"Have you news of your own posting, Harry?" Danny pushed his orders aside and eased back into his seat.

"I have. I'm posted to command one of the new River Class long-range patrol craft. She is completing in the same building dock that built 847, so I must depart in another week. I'm to take passage on the transport *Jorvik Maersk*."

"Grand! I'm on her as well—the DGK is in dock at Pangaea. We can look forward to a few more weeks in company then."

Niamh smiled. Her boys were already lost in their own world of ships, space travel and otherworldly adventures. She quietly gathered her papers and retired to her study.

Chapter 4

A Bad Start

"**W**e're approaching the rendezvous point, Commodore."

"Thank you, Captain." Felicity stood as the display shut down. "I'll be in the Observation Lounge." She loved the views from this space, a recreational area for her staff and the crew of the *Thermopylae*, once a freightliner, but now an extremely sophisticated surveillance ship designed to give the appearance of a cargo ship that delivered supplies to remote Fleet outposts, and sometimes to deployed fleets. These were usually in the form of specialist supplies, though occasionally it could include equipment.

"Come to take us on at snooker, ma'am?" One of the senior coms operatives quipped. "Still just the usual hyperspace fog on view."

She grinned. "Soon sort that out, Gregor. By the way, that decrypt you sent up is very interesting. Make an appointment with my SU writer Yelendi. I'm going to want you to dig a lot deeper in that direction."

The man's friends laughed. "That'll teach you to get fresh with the Boss, Greg! Now you'll cop a load of work."

"Enough to keep the rest of you lay-abouts busy as well," Felicity cut in, but her smile was good-natured. "Drop out in a couple of minutes, boys. Better get those snooker balls anchored." The ship shuddered, and as expected, the balls on the table shifted position. "Damn, I missed the count!"

The display cleared, showing the spectacular view of the fleet deployed in defence array. The four great starships formed the heart of the fleet with cruisers, destroyers and frigates spread around them. Launches shuttled between ships, and strike craft weaved among the ships in perpetual movement as they patrolled. It was a sight that never failed to move her.

Her link chirped. "We're ordered to close the *Vanguard*, Commodore."

"Very well. I'll come to the bridge."

Harry had to admit he was annoyed. He'd expected to be met by his new Executive Officer, but Lieutenant MacKenzie-Banks had not done so, and instead passed his excuses through a junior Warrant Officer in the Arrivals Hall.

"The Lieutenant says he'll send someone to meet you at your accommodation, sir." The Warrant looked very uncomfortable, sensing that he was the middleman in what appeared to be a deliberate slight to Commander Heron.

"Tell him ... no, don't bother. Have my kit delivered to my cabin, please." Harry nodded. "Deck F, Cabin 4534." He saw the man's surprised expression and smiled. "Thank you."

The Warrant checked the display. *How'd he know? I hadn't told him that.* He summoned an SU and gave it the instruction. Commander Heron was already making his way to Deck F.

"Lieutenant MacKenzie-Banks," the Warrant muttered, "whoever you are, I think you've just earned a load of grief."

Harry checked his link to find out how his new ship *Lagan* was coming along in the construction process, and twenty minutes later, he studied her as she lay gripped in the building cradle. She was bigger than he'd imagined, but her lines were attractive, and she had a proper hangar, not just a bay in which to carry her 'boats'. The presence of workers on the hull and on the gantries around her in no more than the usual protection suits suggested the entire bay was under atmosphere. He left the view port and made his way down to the access tube connected to the ship's entry port.

A bored Quartermaster looked up as Harry stepped aboard, his expression changing from annoyance at being disturbed to appalled shock as he took in Harry's uniform and rank. Standing to rigid attention, he returned Harry's salute. "Welcome aboard, sir!"

"Thank you, Quartermaster." Harry read the man's nametag and memorised his name and face. "Is Lieutenant MacKenzie-Banks aboard, TechRate Dorfling?"

"No, sir—er, shall I contact him, sir?"

"Please do so, and inform him I shall expect him in my quarters at his earliest convenience."

"Yes, sir, immediately, sir. Lieutenant Jakobsen is aboard, sir, and Lieutenant Matlock."

"Inform them I'm aboard." Harry hesitated. "I believe Lieutenant Matlock is in Engineering, right? Good, I'll find her there." He turned to leave. "Is the ship's Coxswain aboard? Inform him I wish to see him as soon as convenient."

"The Coxswain? Er, I mean, yes, sir. Chief Master Warrant Kemerton, sir. I'll inform him." He watched Harry depart with a purposeful stride through the gangway leading aft. "Oh f*ck," he murmured. "Now the crap's going to hit the fan. Number One better have a damned good excuse." He keyed the coms panel. "Lieutenant Matlock? Captain's on his way to Engineering, ma'am." He listened to the response. "Yes, ma'am." Then, having repeated the message to the Navigation Officer, Lieutenant Jakobsen, he called the ship's senior Non-Commissioned Officer. "Chief, the Exec's ashore, the Captain's aboard, and he wants to see you at your earliest convenience."

He winced as the Chief Master Warrant Officer expressed his feelings in terms that almost blistered the gleaming coatings on the bulkhead. He acknowledged the response, and, pale and sweating, tried to contact the First Lieutenant. There was no response. He turned as the ship's Coxswain arrived in the gangway.

"Where's the Exec?" asked the Coxswain. "When'd he go ashore?"

"About an hour ago. He didn't say anything about the Captain arriving!"

"Right. Have you contacted him?" He saw the worried headshake. "Well, keep on it. Find the ... man. Where'd the Owner go?"

"Aft, to Engineering. He said—"

"I know what he said. I'll find him." He hesitated. "Contact Warrant Proctor as well. He's Captain's Coxswain. He needs to know he's going to be on call from now on."

"Good of you to see me, James. My apologies for the disguise." Felicity indicated her delivery uniform. "Hardly flattering."

James Heron laughed. "On you, my dear, everything looks great." He took the package she'd brought as a 'personal delivery' and put it on the desk. "You're always a tonic. Now then, what bad news are you delivering that necessitates your doing it in person? Did you see the documentary Montaigne made of my lads? A bit dramatic in parts, but overall, it passed muster."

"Yes, I did. Good, I thought, but the Boss felt they shouldn't have made so much of Harry's ability to connect to any AI network he chooses, as long as he's in proximity to it. That should be classified Fleet intel, but it's too late now, I suppose. In answer to your other question, the bad news I'm delivering has to do with the Pantheon. We're after someone they're in touch with. They're being very cautious, and we haven't identified the target yet, but we have identified at least one of the people they're using as a go-between—one of Senator Samland's associates, which means she's probably the person we're after."

"Nothing surprises me about her."

"There's something else. The Pantheon—or at least one of them, probably somebody high up—is in contact with the Charonians. That's why I'm here. We think they're behind efforts to get a signal monitor and repeater fitted to our ships. We've identified some, but they operate on frequencies we don't have—at least not any longer." She smiled. "It's all in the briefing material the Boss included in the package—and in case you're wondering, he doesn't trust the hyperlinks to send it."

James Heron leaned back. "So our signals are possibly compromised—again? How the hell does this keep happening?"

"We think that's what Samland and the Pantheon are involved in it. We know some of our ships—those most recently refitted or completed in certain docks—have these installations, but what we don't yet know is who they are diverting to. That's why I'm going to rejoin your fleet as soon as we've made a visit to a mining outpost about a light year from here."

"Sounds interesting," James prompted.

Felicity nodded. "It is. We're pretty sure that it's operating as a supply base for a group of pirates who are known to have contact with the Charonians."

"The briefing I have on these Charonians doesn't make good reading. We don't seem to have a hell of a lot of data on them or where they're from, their biology, their technology or what they're after, and they avoid contact with anything and anyone that might be a superior force. About all we do know is that they are human-oid, they're capable of interstellar travel, and they're sniffing around our smaller colonies." He frowned as he mulled something that really concerned him. "What's more troubling is they've flat out rejected all efforts by the Confederation or the World Treaty Council to make contact."

Felicity hesitated. "Officially, that's true, but as you'll see in the briefing message, someone has made contact and seems to be working with them or for them, or perhaps is using them for their own ends."

The Admiral steepled his fingers, a mannerism Felicity found amusing, and which told her he was drawing together a number of different pieces of information in that formidable brain of his. "Right. So this mining outpost is a possible meeting point for the pirates, who we know are working for an organi-sation on Earth and for the Charonians." His frown deepened. "And we don't know if any of my ships have had these repeaters fitted?" He saw her nod, and touched his link. "Adriana, I need the full list of all the ships in this fleet recently docked for repair, maintenance or refit."

"Yes, Admiral. On your display now."

"Damn. That's half of them, Felicity. When did this start?"

"About six months after the Niburu War."

"Okay, we can exclude all those prior to that date I think." He changed the parameters. "I think it's time to do a Harry." He grinned. "That's a 'Captains repair on board the Flagship' signal. I want to brief everyone and issue written orders to a small escort for a certain freighter."

"That'll blow our cover," Felicity protested.

"Not if they maintain coms silence and shadow you within easy range of being on hand should anyone attempt anything on the *Thermopylae*."

The Command Centre was still unfinished, but Harry could see it would be a considerable improvement on his previous command. Lieutenant MacKenzie-Banks sauntered into the compartment as if his absence from the ship when her commanding officer was expected was perfectly normal.

"Ah, I see Warrant Ledermann found you, sir."

"He didn't, Number One." He gestured round the compartment. "Is there a problem aboard? I anticipated being met on arrival at least. I seem not to have been expected at all. Was there no signal of my arrival?"

"Signal? Yes, there was. I sent Warrant Ledermann to Arrival Hall Twelve." The Lieutenant frowned. "We're behind schedule, but not much. I've just been going over the situation with Mr. Carrera, the Construction Manager. He reckons we'll be ready for the first trial runs in six weeks."

"Six weeks? That is almost two weeks past the completion date I was given. Is the AI fully trained yet?" Harry winced as a workman began using a power tool beneath one of the consoles. "Let's take this conversation to my quarters. I would appreciate your bringing me up to date."

"The AI Trainer is Lieutenant-Commander Fürst, sir." He stood aside to let Harry precede him into the space designated Captain's Office. "He says it will be one of the best AIs in the fleet." He glanced round the space with a distinct air of possessiveness, or so it seemed to Harry.

Indicating a seat for Lieutenant Banks, Harry took one himself, deliberately not behind the desk. "I'm glad Hans Fürst is doing it. He trained my last command and did it extremely well." He hesitated. "Before we begin, I have a copy of the message informing you of my arrival. It states my arrival would be with the *Jorvik Maersk* in Arrival Hall Ten. Did you say the Warrant went to Twelve?"

The Lieutenant nodded, his expression neutral. "Yes, yes, I did, sir. I must have misread it. I expect you found the accommodation suitable—it is quite well organised. I sent the Warrant to fetch you there as soon as I had confirmation you'd arrived."

"I see. Perhaps it is I who failed to appreciate the modern system. I expected to be met and brought here to the ship." He saw the flicker of annoyance on the Lieutenant's face. "No matter. Bring me up to date please. Perhaps we should start with the work in progress—what is complete and what is outstanding."

He listened to the report as the Lieutenant ran through the lengthy list of equipment that had been installed and was, theoretically, operational. Then began a longer list of things still to be completed or installed. "We've had a number of hiccups with some installations. I don't know who planned the fitting out, but it's created problems with our people getting things operational. Either the equipment didn't fit where it needed to go or something else obstructed it, so we've had to insist on some changes."

"Lieutenants Matlock and Jakobsen mentioned something of that. Are we on our own power yet?"

"Half and half, sir. Engineering is supplying power to all the systems now complete; the rest, including the life support, is still drawing from the station."

Harry considered this. "Very well. I would like to meet the senior Rates. Ask the Coxswain to arrange it please." He smiled. "In my last command, while we were completing, I met daily at oh-eight-hundred for a coffee and an update with my officers. I wish to do the same on this ship. Please advise them that we'll meet every morning at that time for a chat." He hesitated. "And I'd like to see all the officers at seventeen-hundred. Is the Construction Manager aboard?"

"Mr. Carrera's in his office at the gangway." Banks studied his fingers. "I'll arrange for the others to meet you, sir." The Lieutenant's expression was wooden.

Harry's eyebrows almost betrayed his surprise at the response, but he maintained control of his voice and face. "As you wish, Mr. Banks. Please ask Mr. Carrera to see me as soon as he can."

He watched the door close behind the Lieutenant. This was obviously going to be difficult. Clearly Mr. MacKenzie-Banks was not the friendly sort, or he was not inclined to be toward Harry. He made a mental note to research the man's background to determine why. He leaned back in his chair and focussed on his cyberlink. "*Lagan*, good afternoon. I wish to introduce myself."

"Good afternoon, Captain. I hope you will be happy with my progress. My AI trainer says I am almost ready to begin learning your preferences on operational duty."

"I am pleased to hear it. You may address me as Harry. I shall use your ship name *Lagan* when I need to speak directly to you and not to a human in proximity to me." He had noticed the timbre of the voice seemed gender neutral, almost a blend of female and adolescent male, so he asked, "Should I refer to you as he or she?"

There was a slight hesitation. "I understand there is a difference, but it seems unimportant. I am simply *Lagan*. Which do you prefer, Harry?"

Harry laughed aloud. "I am used to thinking of ships as female, but I am aware that some ships consider themselves male. I do not mind, as long as I know which you prefer, and you use a voice to match." There was a signal from the door. "Come in," he said aloud, and in his thoughts, he said to the ship, "I shall want to talk to you later. I have a number of things to discuss with you. In the interim, you may monitor this conversation."

A well-built man of middle age entered. "You wanted to see me, Commander?"

"Yes, Mr. Carrera, please come in." Harry indicated a comfortable chair." I'm delighted to make your acquaintance. I understand you are the Construction Engineer responsible for my ship. Perhaps you can bring me up to date on a few matters."

Chapter 5

Something Not Quite Right

The interview with the Construction Manager, Mr. Japhet Carrera, gave Harry a great deal of information and a number of insights into the source of some of the problems encountered during the fitting out.

"I've no wish to complain, officially or otherwise, Commander, but your First Lieutenant is not making my job any easier. Yes, we've had a few problems with installations, but it's not helped by his interfering with my workers. They know what needs doing and the order for doing it. He doesn't."

"Thank you for telling me. I shall have a word with him." Harry indicated several data chips. "And my thanks for the information in these. I can see I have a great deal of studying to do." He smiled. "Now, perhaps you can give me your best estimate of completion. I must draw up schedules for my people in preparation for your handover."

"Ah, now that is a bit of a challenge." The man smiled. "Officially, the completion must be in thirty days. My foreman tells me we're a week behind schedule, but he's a pessimist. Assuming we don't have any more interference, I think I can say we'll have you ready for the trials in four weeks, say twenty-five days tops." He shrugged. "But, if anyone tries to change the installation schedules again—well, Mike Denning could be right."

Harry nodded. "Very well, I understand you. I shall deal with it." He looked up when he heard a signal he'd been waiting for. "Sounds as if my officers are assembling. I wish to get to know them first, but I would appreciate meeting you in their company at a convenient moment. I think we might be able to resolve a number of things quickly and save further problems."

The Construction Manager rose and held out his hand. "Glad to." He paused. "I have a feeling you're going to have a few problems to get through, Commander, but anything I can do to help, just say the word, and I'm on it."

Commodore Felicity Roberts studied the displays. The mining platform lay at the centre of a small swarm of autonomous mining units, all busy unloading, in maintenance mode, or idle. "Any indication of signals on those Charonian frequencies?"

"Nothing so far, ma'am, but there's something showing up on the scans—a sort of shadow beyond the platform."

"You mean like the sort of thing we used to see with the Consortium anti-scan fields?"

"No, ma'am, this is something different. Shall I go to the high-power scanners?"

"No." Felicity was concerned. These shadows were being reported regularly, but if she ordered the use of the *Thermopylae*'s high penetration scanner, it would warn whoever was responsible that the ship was not what it appeared to be. "See if there's a way to get a visual on that area. I want to know who we're dealing with, but I don't want to reveal the true nature of what kind of ship we are."

"Yes, ma'am."

"Platform acknowledges our signal, ma'am. They say they'll send a barge to collect the equipment."

Felicity's senses prickled. "Alert our defence team. Don't show our teeth yet. Have our boys ready if they try anything. Carry on as if we're preparing to receive them." She turned to the scanning team. "Got anything?"

"Not sure, ma'am. It looks like quite a large ship, but it's unlike anything I've ever seen, and it's bloody good at hiding. It's keeping the platform and those mining drones between us."

"Keep a watch on it. If it moves—"

"Yes, ma'am."

Felicity opened her link. "Bridge, there's something lurking beyond the platform. Send my special code on the Fleet links." She paused. "And keep your finger on the 'get us out of here' keys." To herself, she murmured, "I just hope James' boys are where they're supposed to be."

"Platform's barge is leaving their dock, ma'am."

"Scan him for life forms. I want to know how many people he's carrying."

"He's carrying twenty people, ma'am." The ScanRate paused. "But some of the readings look very odd."

"Damn. I thought that might be what they're planning. Scan for weapons and warn our reception team, and stand by to prevent any transmission from their barge." She opened her link again. "Bridge, that barge is loaded with people, and they're armed. I want you to maintain normal procedure as if we're unaware, but if that shadow moves, you know what to do."

Harry opened his link to the AI. His Executive Officer troubled him. The man did his job, but he refused to engage on any level except an official one. It was common knowledge that he'd left his previous appointment under something of a cloud. Harry searched the records and acquainted himself with the facts. It appeared that Mr. MacKenzie-Banks was efficient, though inclined to consider his own ideas superior to anyone else's. This had resulted in an accident with serious consequences in his previous duty assignment on another ship.

In the ensuing enquiry, the Lieutenant was censured and stripped of seniority, which had resulted in his being denied a command course. It seemed to Harry that this might explain the man's antipathy to some extent, but there was a further cause for consideration in another record. It seemed MacKenzie-Banks had been cautioned over a liaison with a ComsRate. Storing this in his memory, Harry found the complete list of alterations and amendments made during the fitting out. He was not surprised to find that most of them were instigated and authorised by Lieutenant MacKenzie-Banks—curiously, on behalf of other departments and seldom without resistance from the officer in charge. This prompted Harry to examine the man's service record again.

When he finished reading, he leaned back in his chair and digested the information. The man had some interesting connections outside the Fleet, and some of them were with organisations that Harry knew Fleet Security had on their watch list.

He returned to more immediate mundane tasks when the door chime signalled a visitor. "Come in."

Lieutenant MacKenzie-Banks and Mr. Carrera pushed in. The Lieutenant spoke first, and he looked quite smug and pleased with himself.

"Commander, we've got another problem in Engineering."

"We wouldn't have if you hadn't made my men do it your way—again!" Mr. Carrera was plainly angry.

"Please sit down, gentlemen." Harry waited until they'd taken their places opposite each other. He'd noticed the Lieutenant's use of his rank as Commander rather than his honorary title of Captain, a rather curious break with tradition. He met eyes with the Construction Manager first.

"Mr. Carrera, explain, please."

Meanwhile, the Lieutenant looked bored and fiddled with his tablet as if he had more important things to do than meet with his senior officer.

"These ships are extremely complex, Commander," said Mr. Carrera. "If our fitting order and schedule isn't followed exactly—and in the right order—you can't install some of the items without taking out what shouldn't have been installed out of sequence." He snorted. "I've tried to explain this to the lieutenant, but he won't believe me. Now we've got to take out two full panels of the reactor controls because they've been installed before the field generator units for the shielding in that area, which are supposed to go in first."

Through his access to the ship's AI, Harry already had the change of installation order. It was one of many that had been disputed. He turned to the Lieutenant. "I believe you signed off the change of installation order—perhaps you'd care to tell me why, Mr. Banks."

Startled, the Lieutenant refused to meet Harry's eyes. "Yes, sir. We needed the reactor controls installed so that Jenny, I mean, Lieutenant Matlock, and her people could begin the program checks and tests. Those panels have to be integrated into the main controls for Engineering, and it was delaying their work."

"It's going to delay it even more now," Carrera interjected. "I should know what I'm talking about. I am the construction manager, after all." He glowered.

"Thank you, Mr. Carrera." Harry looked at the Lieutenant. "I understand Lieutenant Matlock was not in favour of the early installation. I believe there is a communication from her saying her programming could proceed without them at this stage."

The Lieutenant looked surprised, but he recovered quickly. "Yes, sir, we did discuss it, but in the end she saw it would be better to do the whole process at the same time."

"All of which would seem to be undone by having to pull it all out again to put in the equipment and units that must go in behind it." Harry struggled to keep the annoyance out of his voice. "Mr. Carrera, I must apologise. I'd appreciate a tour with you in half an hour if that is convenient. Perhaps you can show me where we may have some further problems. You may go now." To the Lieutenant, he said, "Please remain a few minutes, Mr. Banks. I have several things to discuss with you."

The interview did not go well. The Lieutenant made no attempt to defend his actions. Instead, he simply sat in front of Harry with a slight smile playing around the corners of his mouth as Harry confronted him with one example after another of delays caused by his demands for a change of layout, early installations or complete relocation of items, only to have them removed and returned to their original positions.

"Mr. Banks, if I were a suspicious man, I might think you were deliberately causing delays to our completion." Harry's exasperation was creeping through his tight control of his temper. The man seemed to be trying to provoke him. "In the absence of any response to my request for explanation, I'm perplexed as to the reason for your decision."

The Lieutenant met his eyes at last. "As I've said repeatedly, sir, we can't let the dockyard dictate how and when we do what we need to do. All of my decisions were necessary."

"I have to disagree with you, Mr. Banks. Every one of your changes has resulted in major cost overruns and delays." Harry held up a hand when the Lieutenant opened his mouth to protest. "No, allow me to finish. There will be no further rearrangements without my and Mr. Carrera's express agreement. This ship will be ready to begin her trials on time." He stood up. "Now, I know from your submitted schedule that you have several matters to attend to. I plan to tour all departments to get a feel for the ship. I'd appreciate your meeting me again at sixteen hundred this afternoon. We will discuss the schedule for the remainder of the week then. If you need me urgently, I have my link."

"I'm afraid I can't make that time, sir." The Lieutenant looked defiant. "I have another appointment then." He paused for effect. "With the Admiral."

Harry held his gaze. "It is not entered in your schedule of activities, Mr. Banks. Perhaps you would be kind enough to explain why."

The Lieutenant flushed. "It's a private matter...sir." He added the 'sir' to his response with obvious reluctance.

Harry maintained a tight grip on his temper. He was beginning to dislike the man intensely. "As your commanding officer, any requests to see the Admiral should be passed through me. I realise I have barely come aboard and am still an unknown entity to you, Mr. Banks, but I should have been informed. I have no desire to continue our working relationship on the wrong foot, but we do not see eye to eye on a number of points. That concerns me. It will affect the operation of this ship, and I am not about to let that happen." He watched the emotions chase across the other man's face. "Now, Mr. Banks, I'd appreciate a little openness from you. If you have some objection to being in my command, please say so now."

The Lieutenant looked down. "I've asked for a transfer, sir, and the Admiral's secretary slipped me an appointment." He met Harry's gaze and continued in a rush. "My brother served in the 36th Corvette Flotilla against the Niburu. His ship was one of those lost in the final assault you led against the mothership." His anger showed. "Was it really necessary to throw away all those ships in an attack that must be rated with the Charge of the Light Brigade back in eighteen whatever?"

For a moment Harry was speechless, his anger rising. His voice controlled and quiet, he asked, "Do you consider our sacrifice to destroy that mothership futile? Do you suggest that I found it easy to have to lead such an attack?"

The Lieutenant blinked, surprise registering in his expression. "No, sir." He swallowed and recovered. "It's just that some of your ships were already so badly damaged they should have been abandoned, but you ordered them to attack anyway. I'm sorry, sir, perhaps the Light Brigade was the wrong analogy. The Niburu Queen—the mothership— was, according to some reports, already fatally wounded by then."

Harry controlled his temper. "Your analogy is offensive. We had no way of knowing if the Queen was succumbing, and we could not leave it on the assumption that it would recover." Harry saw the other man's doubt. "Perhaps you do not know, Mr. Banks, that every one of those ships would have been released from the attack had they indicated they felt unable to make it. I would not have accused anyone of cowardice or dereliction of duty. My own ship was not space-worthy. As senior officer and leader, I was doubling up aboard *1002*, and her people would not hear of withdrawing."

He paused, remembering how close he'd been to dying when the ship suffered a major hull breach. "Every man, woman and alien aboard those ships had volunteered for that last attack. No one was under compulsion or orders to be there. So many volunteered that they drew lots, and the losers begged the winners to change places." He drew himself up to his full height and held the other man's eye. "It was a privilege to lead them, and I will not have their memory besmirched with allusions to stupidity or such futile events as the cavalry charge at Balaclava."

The Lieutenant seemed to wilt. "I'm sorry, sir. I didn't know. My brother was very special to us—the baby in our family. It was his first ship, and his death broke my mother. She was totally opposed to his joining the Fleet, but he was adamant."

Harry pushed his anger back, the memory of a youthful Lieutenant Banks in his mind. "I see. For that, I can only offer my sympathies and condolences, inadequate as they are." He nodded. "If you genuinely feel you cannot serve under me, I will not insist on your doing so. Keep your appointment with the Admiral. You can put the development progamme on my tablet, and I will study it later."

"Thank you, sir. I appreciate your telling me about the attack. I didn't know they were all volunteers."

"Few would—it was not widely advertised. As I said, it was a privilege to be the leader of such people." Harry touched the ribbons on his chest. "These belong to them."

Commodore Roberts watched the approaching barge. Everything about it appeared normal, and she hoped the display her own ship was putting on—opening the docking bay, preparing to receive the barge—was equally as convincing. "Let them dock and make the first move. I want to see what's lurking out here."

"We've got the cargo ready for them. They'll be able to see the pallets and the handlers as soon as they line up on the entrance."

"Good." She watched her displays. The barge was closing normally, transponder active, usual lights and markings showing ... she switched her attention to the mining platform. The swarm of autonomous mining droids had changed position. They seemed to be moving as a single body, as if in formation. "Where's that shadow you're tracking?"

"Moving right, ma'am. Keeping those bots between us and him."

"Time for the cavalry to show up then." She keyed her pad and watched as the initial white display went green. "We'll see," she murmured.

The power surge as four frigates dropped out of transit around the *Thermopylae* created a flicker in the displays, and then the frigates were between the freighter and the platform, the leader contacting the platform controller as if all was perfectly normal. Behind the cluster of mining units, a large object vanished, leaving only the signature of her transit.

In *Thermopylae*'s docking bay the sudden arrival of the frigates seemed to throw the barge pilot into confusion. He set his vessel down heavily, and not in the position the dock master indicated. There was a short delay after the dock hatches closed and while the atmosphere stabilised, and then only seven men disembarked.

"What brought that lot out here?" demanded the leading man in the uniform of a platform supervisor.

"Beats me," responded the dock master. "You know the Fleet, they've always got to show off." He proffered a tablet. "Who wants to sign for your gear? Want us to load it for you? Or are your guys going to do it?"

"We'll take care of it." The supervisor signalled his team, who lounged about as if they hadn't a care in the world, but as the dock master noted, they were watching him closely and everything around them.

"All yours then." He grinned. "The sooner you load it, the sooner we can get to our next port of call."

Chapter 6

Back on Track

"**B**arge is away, Commodore," said the dock master. "That bunch of cutthroats weren't too keen when we suggested we should help them get it stowed, and even less happy when Kurt suggested we might come back this way and stop off for some R and R."

"How many did you get to see?"

"Seven, ma'am."

"Funny, our scanners picked up twenty on her, and we're getting the same readings now." She hesitated. "Were any of them out of sight at any time?"

"Only while they were on the barge loading the cargo. Why, ma'am?"

"Just a hunch. And we're sure it was the same seven the whole time? Have the docking bay searched. I've a feeling they may have left us something, and I don't like unsolicited gifts."

"Will do, but I'm pretty sure it was always the same seven."

"Okay, we'll run the image record. The AI will alert us if there were any switches." She leaned back in her chair expecting her TechRate to get on it right away. When he didn't, she said, "Rod, you heard that—run the check. They're up to something." She sat up as a thought occurred to her. Addressing the Scan Operator, she asked, "Are the frigates running their scanners?"

"Yes, ma'am."

"Right, run our high-intensity scan on that platform, and then do an all-system scan. I'll warn the frigates to cover it with theirs."

The TechRate drew her attention.

"Yes, Rod?"

"System identifies nine people in that crew, ma'am." The TechRate displayed the nine imges. "Two of them swopped places a couple of times during the loading process."

"Right, so they were up to something. Run a high-intensity search of the dock for any tracking or tagging devices. "Then, get me a secure channel with HQ. The boss was right—there's something fishy going down out here."

"Can you spare a moment, sir? I'd like to inform you on the outcome of my meeting yesterday."

Harry set his notes aside. "Of course, Mr. Banks. Have you had a decision from the Admiral?"

The Lieutenant took the seat offered, his expression neutral. "In a manner of speaking, sir. He refused my request."

"I see." Harry waited. Better to let Banks volunteer the information than press him for it.

The Lieutenant sat on the edge of his chair and contemplated his hands. "The interview with the Admiral didn't go well. He more or less put me on warning and chewed me over." He met Harry's eye. "I thought he might have informed you, sir."

Harry shook his head. "No, he has not sent me any message, nor do I expect one." He smiled. "Very well, if you are to remain my Executive Officer, we had best get to know each other a great deal better. If you still feel strongly that you cannot work with me once we have the fitting out completed, I will personally take up your case for reposting if that will help."

The Lieutenant looked surprised. "Thank you, sir. That's generous of you." He stood and smiled. "I should tell you, sir, that I looked up the reports submitted by the corvette flotillas ... I was wrong, sir."

"Then there is nothing more to say on the matter, Mr. Banks. We must now concentrate on our new ship and the needs of the men in her." Harry stood and offered his hand. "Perhaps you'd care to join me for dinner. Shall we say tomorrow at nineteen hundred?"

"That'll be fine, sir. I appreciate the invitation." Mr. Banks rose to leave, but before he departed, he added, "Thank you, sir."

For some minutes after the Lieutenant's departure, Harry sat staring at the bulkhead. He wondered whether he was doing the right thing offering the man a fresh start. There was a hint of wariness to Mr. Banks, a sense of lingering resentment that caused Harry to wonder how genuine he was in his appreciation of his posting as Executive Officer. Harry would have to keep his finger on the pulse of this situation. The ship deserved better than a command team unable to reach beyond personal prejudices.

Felicity stared at the recovered device. "One thing is certain," she finally said. "That gadget was not manufactured by humans."

"We agree, ma'am. We think it's a tracking device, but it's unlike any we've ever seen. Somebody wants to be able to find us once we leave."

"Damn. That's going to make things difficult. On the one hand, I don't want them tracking us, but on the other, we want to know who it is." Felicity paused. Her superior, currently using the code name Mr. Green, had been clear: Do nothing to alert the other side that they had detected the device.

"It's the only one you've found?" she asked.

"Yes, ma'am, it's the only one."

"Right. And it isn't transmitting anything?"

"Nothing we can detect, ma'am."

"Monitor it. It'll very likely send some sort of signal as soon as we enter transit." She paused. "The people from that barge—we're sure they're all human?"

"Those that we saw—yes, ma'am." The agent hesitated. "At least their scan readouts were human, except—"

"Except what, MW?"

"Well, ma'am, there was something odd about some of the readouts we got from that barge. All the crew gave the sort of reading you get from humans, but with something else." He scratched his head. "Some of them gave a stronger reading."

She touched her link. "Time to go," she said to Mike Frey. "If we hang around, they'll smell a rat. Inform me the moment that thing shows any sign of activity. Alert our shadowers that we've been tagged by someone."

She turned back to the Master Warrant. "Show me those read-outs, MW. You should have flagged it immediately."

Harry arrived aboard at two minutes before eight in the morning, pleased to see all the officers waiting. He'd enjoyed his dinner with Arno Richthofen, an old friend who, due to a bionic arm and leg, was driving a desk now. They'd had a very pleasant evening in a restaurant owned by Detleff Werner, one of the men who'd been part of the crew that helped him and Ferghal capture the notorious Heemstra and his partner, Katerina de Vries. It had been a very pleasant reminder of just how strong the bonds of friendship were, and of how much he, Ferghal, and Danny had adapted to their new circumstances.

Accepting coffee from the android steward, Harry took a seat, deliberately not at the head of the table, and smiled at the others. These coffee sessions had helped break the ice between him and his crew, and gave him an invaluable chance to get to know them. They appeared to be somewhat more relaxed than they had been when they first met him, which pleased him.

"Our Weapons Officer will join us at eleven—she's had a rough trip and only disembarked at three o'clock this morning." He glanced at their faces, gauging the reactions. He didn't mention he'd been at the dock to meet her. "I felt she might need a little sleep before she faced the lot of us."

An easy chuckle rippled among the team, and Lieutenant Jakobsen said, "I've not served with a Lacertian before, sir. What are they like?"

"Very quick in their movements, intelligent, extremely efficient and loyal to a fault." He thought about the way they always managed to get one of their people aboard any ship he served on. "Of course, they are very different from us in the way they think and react to situations." He grinned as he studied their faces. "Oh, and they are rather like the chameleons we have on Earth. They can blend into any background and become almost invisible." He sipped his coffee. "Difficult, of course, when they are in uniform, but very effective when not."

Jenny Matlock caught his eye. "You have a gene splice from their DNA, sir. It was on the documentary they did on you." She paused, a grin forming. "Does that mean you can sneak up on us that way?"

Harry laughed with them. "No, though I have the feeling that might be useful sometimes." His grin widened. "The gene splice enhanced my body's ability to heal any injuries I get, and it affected my cyberlink." He glanced at them all, seeing their interest. "Yes, I have a cyberlink implanted in my brain, put there by the Fleet. The genesplice the Johnstone researchers did while they held me captive on planet Pangaea a few years ago caused it to malfunction in an interesting way. It was a difficult experience with a lingering gift, as it were. To put it simply, AI networks perceive me as an extension of them as long as I am in fairly close proximity, which means I am able to interact directly with them internally, in my thoughts. Sometimes an AI reads my thoughts and acts upon them without receiving specific direction from me." He smiled at their expressions. "It can be disconcerting for my officers and crew—and quite difficult for me at times."

"Thanks for the warning, sir." Jenny grinned over the edge of her coffee cup. "Is that how you and Lieutenant Commander O'Connor brought that freighter home a few years ago? Just with that cyberlink? He has one too, right?" She glanced at the others. "One of the construction crew was talking about it the other day. Said they couldn't figure out how anyone had managed to get anything on it to function."

"I'm afraid we did get somewhat over enthusiastic in our destruction." He pulled a face. "But we had to do everything ourselves, directly through the cyberlink, to get her home." He straightened in his chair. "Now, I think we had best get to our programmes for today. I have Mr. Carrera's latest assessment and schedule before me. Have you all received a copy?"

The others confirmed their receipt and he pushed his coffee cup aside. "Who wants to kick off? What are we dealing with today?"

"That tracking device activated as soon as we went to transit, ma'am." The ScanTech frowned. "It's using a bloody odd frequency though."

"Monitor it. Anyone following us yet?" Felicity looked up from the station at which she'd been studying the anomalous scans of the barge. "Register that frequency, and make sure we can detect anyone using it or any sort of coms channel associated with it."

She turned back to the life scans. "See those five? There's more than one life form showing."

"That's what we meant, ma'am. It's the sort of result you get if a woman has a child in her arms, but these don't read as children or human, though the main signature is human."

"Ma'am, we've got a ship on intercept course." The ScanTech frowned. "At least, I think we do. Never seen a scan signature like it in hyperspace."

"Show me." Felicity studied the scan. "Record it." She touched her link. "Garry, have you got that tracer rigged up as I instructed?"

"Yes, ma'am. Attached to a missile as you ordered."

"Launch it to run our current course, then drop us out as soon as the signatures diverge."

"Think it'll work, ma'am?" asked the Lieutenant in charge of the scan teams.

Felicity frowned. "I don't know. I think their scanning technology might not be that good in hyperspace, hence the need to attach a tracker to a target. Hell, our scanners are only this good thanks to the tech the Siddhiche shared with us during the Niburu War."

"Missile away. Stand by for dropout." The ship's Master, Mike Frey, in reality a full Fleet Captain, counted down. "Dropped out. Nothing on scans."

Felicity watched her display. "He's still closing the missile. Can't have registered that it isn't the ship."

"His scanners must be bloody crude if they're not registering the mass discrepancy." The ScanRate ran some checks. "Even our old systems could tell the difference in size."

"True, or he's spotted the decoy and wants to recover it." She keyed her link. "Garry, did you include my little parcel of nano drones?"

"We did, and the relay units. They'll attach themselves to the outer hull as soon as the carrier is close enough."

Harry studied the latest schedules and requisitions for the *Lagan*. Everything was on target. Barring some major default, the ship would be ready on time. He leaned back in his chair and sipped his coffee, savouring the fine blend. Not for the first time it struck him that the fitting out of these spacefaring vessels demanded skills as specialised as rigging a ship had required four hundred years earlier—different skills, more technical perhaps, but just as specialised.

"Good morning, sir." Jenny Matlock entered, a mug of strong black coffee in hand. "Mind if I sit?"

"Please do." Harry grinned. "I understand you've found a way to avoid dismantling your reactor controls after all."

She settled on the edge of a chair and leaned her elbows on the table, nursing her mug. "Yes, sir. It took a bit of fiddling, but we managed it." She grinned. "I think the fitters were sceptical, but it worked. Mr. Carrera is happy, and everything is now in place, the right way up and operational."

"Excellent news." Harry smiled a greeting to the Navigation Officer and the Lacertian Weapons Officer as they entered, and waved an invitation to be seated. "I believe that makes your department now complete."

"Pretty much, sir. We've a few more installations to test and some adjustments to make, but we should have everything fully online inside of the completion date."

Harry looked at the Lacertian, and before he could ask, she said, "My weapons systems are complete, Captain. We will begin the final trials as soon as we leave the dock."

"Good, Lieutenant Sci'enzile. Thank you. We are scheduled to run live firing trials in four weeks." He glanced up as the Executive Officer entered. "Good morning, Mr. Banks. I see we have confirmation of the last drafts to make up our complement."

"Yes, sir. They'll be joining us next week when their transport arrives. Should give us plenty of time to settle in before the trials start." He slipped into a chair opposite Harry, nursing a cup.

Harry let his glance pass over the Lieutenant, who looked tired, as if he'd had a bad night, and focussed on Jenny's explanation of how the fitting of the shield generator units was being managed with the cooperative efforts of her TechRates and the Fitters. As he listened, he was struck by the thought that his team worked really well together, and that pleased him. A cohesive team meant a smooth-running ship.

The only concern, as he watched the faces and listened to their banter, was Mr. Banks, the Executive Officer, who still held himself aloof, as if his thoughts were elsewhere. Mr. Banks's relationship with the Weapons and Communications Warrant Officers seemed unusually strained—wary might be a better description. There was something a little unusual about it, but Harry couldn't quite determine what it was.

Jenny broke into his thoughts. "I see the LPSL are excited about some new civilisation, sir." She laughed. "Their spokesperson was getting very antsy about anyone making contact with these creatures—more or less demanding that we do nothing."

Harry nodded. "I heard something of this, though I expect first contact will be when they decide they want it, not when we do." He finished his coffee. "Well, let me clarify. I hope the LPSL do not force an encounter. They are foolish enough to do so, and the consequences would be disastrous for everyone. But, it is unlikely to be our problem." He grinned at them. "We have a ship to complete and commission, my friends. That should keep me from being accused of destroying or corrupting another alien culture."

Taking the cue, Jenny, Sci'enzile and the others laughed as they stood, gathered their mugs and took their leave.

Lieutenant Banks lingered. "I've a few items I need your views on, sir."

"Very well." Harry smiled. "Shall we deal with them?"

Chapter 7

Interventions

For several minutes after the Lieutenant's departure, Harry sat at his desk, a slight frown creasing his brow as he pondered the items Mr. Banks discussed with him. None of them seemed to require a decision from him or a special reason to be brought to his attention, so why had they been raised? Was it simply a clumsy attempt to show that his instruction to be consulted on any change was being followed to the letter? Or was he being tested in some manner? A memory stirred. He'd learned that Mr. Banks was having an affair with a communications TechRate. Was there something else going on in that regard that he didn't know about?

"*Lagan*, is there anything in your communications installation that will cause a problem once it is operational? Anything unusual or different about it?"

"It is a standard system, Harry, though there is an additional repeater unit which operates on a frequency not used by the Fleet."

Harry considered this carefully. "Who uses that system?"

"I do not have that information, Harry. It is not registered in my databank or the Fleet's. It retransmits certain signals that I receive, and it receives messages of unknown origin. No other part of my system is able to receive or detect its signal."

"So everything transmitted by the Fleet is repeated by this unit?"

"No, only certain transmissions."

"Please give me a complete log of which signals, and identify anything unusual about them, or perhaps what selects them." He thought a moment longer, and the AI listened to his thoughts.

Before he could ask the question, the ship answered. "No, Harry, it is not broadcasting to a hypercom transmitter. It repeats to a unit on the station. I can detect the actuation of the sender and the receiver, but not the transmission itself."

Harry's half-framed question got an immediate answer.

"It repeats all signal traffic addressed to you, Harry, as well as all your private messages."

Harry's temper surged. How dare anyone intercept his correspondence and communications! An unpleasant thought struck him. "*Lagan*, does it repeat our conversations?"

"No, Harry. These do not use my communications circuits and nodes." There was a hesitation. "Do you need me to shut it down?"

"Yes!" Harry ordered, then he reconsidered, his rage turning to ice. "No! No, don't. I want to know who is behind this. Ask your sister ships if any of them have similar units installed, and provide me with all the circuit information for this unit, its operating system and the messages it repeats. Send it to..." He hesitated. "No, that would use your communication network and trigger it to alert them." He had a better idea. "Store it in a protected file. I will have someone else download it from you."

"It is done. How should I identify who I must give it to?"

"Give it to the person who identifies himself to you as Fionn MacCumhaill." Drawing out his writing pad, Harry composed a note.

Lagan read the note and stored this strange method of human communication for further study. Another part of the AI was already searching for records of a Fionn MacCumhaill. Briefly it wondered why the Captain would instruct it to pass the information he wanted to a mythological figure, then it stored the answer and continued its normal routines and functions.

"Our little package surprised them." Felicity indicated the display. Several EVA-suited figures advanced toward the missile. "I'll be interested to see how they intend to capture it."

"Looks like they expected to use grapnels of some kind." The Commander of one of the defence teams indicated the large magnetic grapnel near one of the suited figures. "Overkill for a missile."

"Yes." Felicity frowned. "Interesting, though they obviously didn't have a visual on it. They expected to find a ship."

"Looks like they've decided to take it aboard. Good. Means some of our toys will get to disperse on their ship." A Lieutenant indicated the image. "Those suits look odd ... humanoid, but the helmet looks misshapen, and the visor must be bloody difficult to see through unless you have eyes designed for very low light."

Felicity glanced at another station. "What are you guys reading on the life scanners?"

"Similar to what we got on that barge, ma'am. Readings as if there are two beings, one somehow joined to the other. Body heat signatures are lower than human, but basically four limbs, torso and a head. The head is hotter than the rest of it, and it's where the double signature is clearest."

"Right, upload all the data to the Boss on the TJG." She glanced at the commander. "Have your bugs been deployed?"

"Yes, the moment the decoy ship was pulled into the dock."

"Time we found our escort and got out of here then." Felicity straightened up. "I want everything analysed and uploaded direct to the TJG and copied to HQ. There's a lot here that doesn't make sense."

"Good news, darling Harry." Mary was all smiles in the holo-image. "Niamh has all the legal issues settled, and we can go ahead with the wedding arrangements."

"Wonderful." Harry returned the smile, wishing they weren't separated by several dozen light years. "At last, we can make the final plans then. That is great news. I shall look at our schedule and book my passage for leave. That gives us a little less than six months. Does that suit you, my love?"

She laughed. "With barely a few days in which to have our honeymoon before you rush off to your ship? Really, Harry." She studied his stricken look for a moment. "Of course it's okay, my sweet man. Don't look so downhearted. Send me your dates when they're confirmed and Niamh will help me sort out the wedding and a honeymoon that fits in."

Harry frowned. "But I will pay for it. I shall instruct Aunt Niamh to make a charge on my bank account for the expenses."

"Don't be silly, we'll share the costs. Well, I can hear that link of yours chirping. Better let you go. Let me have the dates when you can, and we'll get things in motion." She blew him a kiss. "All my love, my Captain." The hologram vanished.

Harry sighed as he answered the link. "Heron."

"Commander, Lieutenant Greene here. I wonder if you could spare a few minutes, sir. I have some correspondence for you."

Lieutenant Greene proved to be a pseudonym, and the man who met him a few minutes later in the lounge reserved for Commanders was in civilian attire and took great care to avoid revealing his true rank. Harry had the feeling his visitor was older than he appeared, possibly even too old for the rank he claimed.

"Sorry about all the cloak and dagger, Commander, but there's a lot at stake here." The 'Lieutenant' shook hands. "Have you taken steps to kill or isolate that repeater?"

"Actually, no, I decided to let it continue so as not to alert whoever installed it that I knew it was there." Taking a seat, Harry added, "I cannot say I like its presence, however."

"Good idea. We know who is behind these installations, and yours is not the only ship that's had one of these installed, but we need to catch the people managing them, and that's a lot more difficult." He studied Harry. "I can't tell you the full story, but it involves some very wealthy and powerful people who have ambitions with regard to who governs the Confederation and a few other nations."

"Do you think I might have a traitor in my crew?" Harry's face showed his anger at the thought.

"It certainly looks that way, though we think he's being manipulated. It's his handler we're after." He leaned back. "The action you're taking to avoid the transmission of your messages will work for now, but they may already suspect something. We need you to use the normal communications channels to not raise suspicion." He slid a small device across the table. "This will encode anything you send. They'll still be able to read it, but the information will have been altered slightly to throw them off. Anything you get from HQ will have to be fed through it to convert it back to the real message."

Harry took the device and studied it. "I see. But how, precisely, will this assist in tracing the traitor?"

The visitor smiled. "Every message that passes through one of these has a tag buried in the code. Anyone who reads it will automatically be identified to us." He paused. "We'll catch the mole."

"Well done, Felicity. You and your team have pulled it off. As we thought, that mining station is being used as a waystation by the Charonians and their associates lurking among our people." The Admiral frowned. "Just as well Admiral Heron gave you that frigate squadron as cover."

"I think by now they've realised the *Thermopylae* isn't what she appears to be."

"Maybe. You monitored the images your bugs picked up when they took the decoy aboard, right?"

"Yes, sir. Admiral Heron suggested the frigates be on hand, as he has been watching the pirate activity in that sector and thought they'd try something against a ship like ours."

"Yes, so he reported." The Admiral paused. "We've intel on who the money is behind the pirates, but they're a screen for a bigger game that involves some very wealthy people. The Charonians are playing their own game. They're very advanced in their development of metal alloys, certain aspects of biotech, weapons and so on, but backward in a lot of other ways."

"Have we learned anything about what they're trying to achieve—the Charonians?"

"We think so, and it isn't good. Remember how your scans gave the impression of two life forms?" He paused as she nodded. "That's because that's exactly what you are seeing. We're not certain what it is or how it works, but there's some sort of symbiotic process involved. Until we can get a look at one—or better yet, get some DNA out of them—we're operating in the dark."

"That'll be a good trick. Have we got any possibility for doing that?"

"Not yet, but we're working on it."

The trials and testing exposed a whole raft of defects and problems, many directly attributable to the changes in their installation. Tempers flared, nerves were stretched to the limit, and several times Harry found himself biting back a sharp rebuke when some minor defect showed up and required major work to sort out. Several of these were the result of the altered order of installation that

Mr. Banks initiated before Harry joined the ship. Coupled with the knowledge that his signals were being relayed to some unknown receiver, his temper was stretched to the limit.

"Damnation," Harry muttered as the latest problem manifested itself. He leaned back and took a few seconds to regain control, at least outwardly. "Run the diagnostics please, Mr. Jakobsen. There must be a reason the targeting shuts down as soon as you attempt to lock onto your target, Lieutenant Sci'enzile."

"Yes, sir. We're running a full diagnostic of the system."

"Very well." Harry was tired. The last three weeks had been busy, and the defects and failures irritated him. He listened to the ship's AI network through his link. "*Lagan*, is there some addition to your systems that could cause this failure? Run a comparison of your installed components and the schematics for your systems issued by the dock. Check for anything added recently."

"There is a unit, Harry. It is recorded in my installation programs as a scan monitor, but it actually monitors the targeting system and redirects instructions to it."

"Show me." Harry studied the schematic the AI presented. So, another little addition to the ship, one with potentially fatal consequences for them all. He considered his options. To hell with the consequences. "*Lagan*, I want you to direct a power surge to that unit. I want you to make it burn. Can you do that?"

"Yes, Harry. But it may damage other parts of my system. It is mounted in the communications console."

"The communications console linked to your targeting system?" Harry hesitated. Maybe this would shake something out. "Do it." Why the devil would anyone install a part of the targeting system in the communications console? Unless it was someone who wanted to access it remotely, or who didn't want to risk having it found by Lieutenant Sci'enzile....

"Sir, the diagnostic says everything is functional and online, but we still can't achieve a target lock. Wait, the target system has cleared—we have a lock."

"Fire!" The Communications Warrant leapt out of his seat. "The damned console's on fire."

"Isolate the power to it," ordered Mr. Banks. "Get that panel open and put it out."

A TechRate ripped open the panel, and the Master Warrant directed the jet of extinguishing agent into the unit.

"Warrant, are our coms down?" said Harry.

The man scowled as he surveyed the damaged interior of the console. "Looks like it's fairly local, sir." He reached in to pull out the damaged unit.

"Don't touch it, Warrant," Harry snapped. "Leave it exactly where it is. I want Dock Security to see it first."

The Warrant hesitated then withdrew his hand. "Yes, sir."

Harry watched. Did the Warrant look worried? Mr. Banks certainly did, but why? "Check our coms. If we can still communicate, I want a channel to the dock. Weapons, run a targeting routine again, please. I want to know why we couldn't get a lock before this fire."

The TechRate glanced at the Warrant, his fingers already dancing across the interface. Harry already knew what the answer would be as the Rate called, "Hypercoms are down, sir, but all other systems are fine." The TechRate glanced again at the Warrant and received an imperceptible nod. "Shall I open a link to the dock, sir?"

There was something going on, and Harry was determined to find out what.

"Yes, do so immediately. I want the Head of Security. It appears something in the hypercoms unit was interfering with our targeting. That could seriously compromise not just us but every other ship in the Fleet. No one is to touch anything in that console until the Security team have examined it and everything connected to it." He held the Warrant Officer's gaze. "Do I make myself clear?"

"Absolutely, sir." The man nodded. "I'll secure the console. Security'll want to take it apart."

"Security online, sir. Commander Strijdom."

"Thank you. Mr. Banks, return to the dock. Immediately please. Helm, reverse course. Mr. Banks has the con." He keyed the link. "Commander Strijdom, Commander Heron. I am returning immediately to the dock. Please have an investigation team meet us. I have reason to believe there has been an attempt to sabotage this ship."

"Sabotage? That's a serious assertion, Commander. I'll have a team ready when you dock. Can you transmit the records from your AI to my office? It will be helpful to have them examined so I know who to send."

"It shall be done." Harry paused. "Please advise the ship of your secure address, and I will instruct it to provide the record."

"Your ship records will have it. Please use the address in the databank."

Harry hesitated then decided to go for the jugular. "I have very good reason to believe that address may be compromised. There is an alternative address—I will transfer the data to that and no other." He broke the link and shut his eyes briefly. He had a feeling he'd just poked a stick into a nest of angry vipers, but he'd had enough. He would not tolerate anyone sabotaging his ship, listening in on his signals or undermining his command. He focussed on his cyberlink. "*Lagan*, I trust you heard that last conversation."

"Yes, Harry. Do you want me to transfer everything including your instruction to me to overload it?"

"They'll know soon enough. Yes, include that, but make sure you include the record of its interference and the purpose as you told me. Then send it to the Security Office secret receiver and repeat it to Lieutenant Greene." He glanced at the notepad he'd extracted from his pocket. "Read the address from my pad, *Lagan*."

"Done, Harry." There was a momentary hesitation. "There is a coded signal being beamed to our hypercoms array. It appears to be for the repeater unit installed there."

"Jam it, immediately, and isolate that unit. Cut off all power to it." His curiosity aroused, he asked, "Our hypercoms are down according to our ComsTech. How are we receiving a message?"

"The receiving unit is independent of my hypercom system, except in its use of my receivers. I detect the signal and its routing, but I cannot record it."

"Isolate it immediately. Shut it down if you can!" How many more of these unauthorised devices were there? What was their purpose? How much did the enigmatic Lieutenant Greene and his people know about them? Harry was going to demand answers, no matter whose toes he had to step on in the process.

Chapter 8

Gloves Off

Commander Strijdom glared at Harry. "You do realise you've just blown our operation, Commander."

"I refute that. And I shall do so in my reports of this disgraceful incident. That unit was interfering with our targeting system—and from the evidence I transmitted to you, its function was to allow some external operator to negate our ability to target their ships. How dare you—or anyone else for that matter—endanger my ship and my people in that way."

Harry could see the other man's anger, but he pushed on.

"I might have tolerated having my signals repeated and intercepted by an outside party—that I can deal with one way or another. But deliberately allow my ship to be rendered helpless by an enemy? Never, sir. Never."

"You've no way of knowing they could do that," Commander Strijdom blustered.

"You don't seem very sure of that yourself, sir. As to my knowledge, I shall say only that the AI informed me, and the record now shows that the burned-out unit was receiving instructions from a third source, one not on the *Lagan*." He held the Commander's gaze and saw the doubt lurking behind the man's expression. "I am quite satisfied that its sole purpose was to interfere with our targeting system. As soon as it was neutralised, the targeting functioned perfectly."

There was a chime from the door unit. The Commander shrugged and leaned back. "I'm not expecting anyone."

"Come in!" Harry barked.

The door slid back and Lieutenant Banks stepped into the room followed by the man Harry recognised as the Chief Electronics Supervisor. "Sorry to interrupt, sir. We've managed to extract that repeater unit you identified." Mr. Banks's face was ashen as he waved the supervisor forward. "I've had to call for an explosives team, sir. That thing had a self-destruct device built into it, and could have blown us all to hell."

"It's not an authorised installation," the man exclaimed, clearly frightened. "It isn't in our schematics at all, and none of my people installed it—their installation tags would have a record of it if they did."

Harry kept his eyes fixed on the security officer, his left eyebrow rising as he said, "Well, Commander Strijdom?"

"This is an unexpected development, Commander Heron." He indicated the others should leave. The Executive Officer glanced at Harry.

Harry considered ordering MacKenzie-Banks to stay then decided against it. He wanted answers, and what he was about to hear would clearly not be for general knowledge. "Carry on, Mr. Banks. Thank you, Mr. Ellis. I'll want to talk to you later about the installation process."

When they were alone again, Commander Strijdom said, "Very well, Commander, cards on the table. We were very close to identifying the individuals behind this. We know who they work for, and we know some of the small fry, but we wanted the top players—the people directing things behind the scenes." He spread his hands in an eloquent shrug. "You've now blown our operation." He held up a hand. "I will concede that we were not aware that they had installed some protection in their latest devices. That changes the entire game." He stood. "My boss will appreciate your cooperation a little later, Commander. I'm sure you have a great deal to attend to here, but if you could meet me at, say, sixteen-thirty, I'll send someone to escort you to us a half hour before then." He smiled briefly. "It doesn't show in the dock plans and records."

At precisely 15:59, Harry's link chirped.

"Heron."

"Commander, Major Harris is at the entry port asking for you." A voice said something in the background. "He's from Security, sir."

"Very good. I'll join him immediately." Harry closed his tablet and secured his interface, checked his pad and pen, then stood, tugged his jacket into place and made for the door. A Major sent to escort him to a meeting with a Commander? This obviously ran far deeper than a simple attempt to sabotage a few patrol ships, but how deep did it run?

These patrol ships were much larger than his first command. The *Lagan* and its sister ships were more powerfully armed, and though they carried a bigger crew than his previous command, it was not as large as one would expect on a ship of this size. It was big enough to merit having several androids assigned to it, one of them designated as steward to him and the wardroom. He'd mentioned this to Ferghal in a letter. The reply had intrigued and excited him.

Ferghal had written, "The River Class are but the first of a new generation, my friend. You should see the new destroyers we're building, and as for the frigates that will soon be complete—I say only that soon humankind may have a rival among its own creations."

"Commander? Major Harris." The visitor proffered his ID. "Our transport's waiting, if you'll accompany me, please."

"Thank you." Harry turned to the gangway watchman standing to attention at his console. "Log me ashore with Major Harris. Advise Mr. Banks. He is aware of the appointment."

"The Executive Officer logged ashore half an hour ago, sir. Shall I advise Lieutenant Matlock?"

Harry's brow snapped into a frown. "No, advise the Weapons Officer. She's the senior." What was Banks playing at? He'd advised him the moment the appointment was made and confirmed, and he'd taken the trouble to remind the man less than an hour ago. He'd have to deal with this on his return.

"Very well, Major, shall we carry on?"

"Your Exec forgot something?" The Major's tone and expression gave nothing away.

"Evidently. I shall discuss it with him on my return," Harry said, his manner perfunctory. Ever since he and Banks had dinner together, he'd hoped their relationship was improving. Lately, however, Banks had become distant again.

As Harry followed the Major through the entry port, he decided he'd have to confront Banks again.

"We have to cross the station, so we need a transport car." The Major, a Marine officer, glanced at him. "Sorry about all this cloak and dagger stuff, but unfortunately, it's necessary. We're going via my office to allay suspicion and throw off anyone attempting to follow." He shrugged. "The Boss has his ways."

Harry's unease was dispelled by the sight of an official transport unit and a smartly turned out Marine waiting for them. "I see. I hope I shall soon be enlightened as to what is going on."

The Major smiled and returned the salute of the waiting man, and noted Harry's almost absentminded salute as he stood aside to let him enter the vehicle. "Usual routine, Kreisler." He took a seat next to Harry. "These transports aren't quite the standard pattern. We'll take a longer route to our destination, but that will give me the opportunity to give you some background."

Harry settled into the seat. "Thank you. I would appreciate having at least some idea of what this is all about." His tone conveyed his annoyance at the failure to provide him with information regarding the nature of the threat to his ship.

"I'll do my best," said the Major. "The details will come from the boss, but to put it simply, we have a problem. You're aware of the piracy issues, I'm sure. This is part of it. They've some impressive backing at home from people running an even bigger agenda. They can track our ships and get advance information on where they are and what their orders are. We were getting close to tracking the monitoring station when you blew out the equipment."

"That explains the signal repeater, but not the device that interfered with my weapons targeting system." Harry's frown deepened. "Which, from what I learned from my ship, was receiving orders from some external source whenever we attempted a target lock."

The Major sighed. "Yes. They're getting bolder—or they were. We know the race calling themselves Charonians are involved, though officially we don't have contact, but the pirates have some sort of link with them. After this incident, they'll go quiet again, at least until they can figure out what happened."

"They may have a problem there." Harry watched as they passed a long, illuminated dock that housed a large cruiser. "Are they targeting the larger ships as well? It will be difficult to find these devices in a ship such as that one."

"They tried to, but we caught it in time." The Major waited as the vehicle entered a narrow passage and stopped next to a keypad. He leaned across, gazed into a pupil scanner and pressed his hand against a palm scanner to gain access. "Now we change vehicles. Follow me, Commander. Kreisler, you know the drill."

"Yes, sir. Good luck."

Alert to any skulduggery, Harry followed the Major through an opening and into a second ordinary vehicle indistinguishable from any of the construction vehicles used on the dock. As soon as they were aboard, the door slid shut and the transport headed back the way they'd come.

"A little subterfuge," said the Major. "Two of my officers have taken our places in the transport. It will keep the trackers guessing." He paused as the vehicle swung into the loading dock for a cargo liner. "Here we are. A bit unusual, but it works for us. I believe you know the ship—the *Twee Jong Gezellen*. She's had some internal changes since you brought her home a few years ago. I doubt her original owners would recognise her now." He grinned as Harry looked round in suspicion. "We acquired her and a couple of others for surveillance and clandestine ops against the Consortium, but she's proving very useful in our efforts to keep tabs on several other organisations."

Harry tested his cyberlink and was reassured when the ship recognised him and confirmed the validity of the Major's information.

"Very well, Major. Lead on. I believe Lieutenant Greene is waiting for us." Harry's emphasis on the word *Lieutenant* revealed his intended meaning.

The Major laughed. "He is, and you're right, the Lieutenant bit is a cover. We also don't adhere to the gangway protocol when we're in places like this—we can never be a hundred percent sure we won't be seen." His eyes danced with laughter. "The ship's cover for being here is as a transport, so the story is you're visiting a friend if anyone asks."

Harry returned the smile. "But I am visiting a friend, one I had the pleasure of getting to know very well in the three months it took us to bring him home." He laughed at the surprise in the other man's face. "*Twee Jong Gezellen* tells me he is very happy in this service, and proud of the upgrading he has received."

The Major recovered his composure. "Ah. Of course, that all-knowing link of yours." He smiled. "Useful, I should think."

You'd be surprised, thought Harry as he followed the man through the entry port.

'Lieutenant' Greene stood as Harry walked into what had once been the quarters he'd used on his first journey on this ship. "Thanks for coming, Commander. Take a seat." He waved a hand toward a few chairs. "I understand you know this ship quite well. We've made a few changes as you can see." He seated himself. "To business then. First, as you've probably gathered, I'm not a lieutenant, but it's a useful rank to revert to when necessary, nor is my name Greene, but that will have to do for the moment." He indicated the Major. "Major Harris is, on the other hand, precisely who and what he appears to be."

Harry nodded. "Very well, Admiral ... Greene. May I enquire why you asked me to meet you here?" The ship's records showed the Admiral used at least five different identities and ranks on a regular basis.

"Certainly." There was a flicker of surprise at Harry's correct use of his rank. "As you've gathered, we have a problem, and the latest intelligence suggests the stakes are rising. There's an added twist to it as well." He glanced at his tablet and then at the Major. "Have you heard of this new alien species, the Charonians, that the LPSL are excited about?"

Harry frowned. "Not a great deal. I have, of course, seen the LPSL's representatives demand that they be allowed to protect the Charonians—when and if they can be found."

"Oh, they can be found all right." He grimaced. "For security reasons, our official statement is that we don't know who or what they are. We've sent the LPSL off on a wild goose chase." He snorted. "Fools, they'll compromise all of us one of these days— especially the very races they want to protect. The Charonians are definitely not to be invited home."

"I see," said Harry, frowning. "What I don't understand is how this involves me."

"Until an hour ago, we didn't think it did." The Admiral held Harry's gaze. "We've discovered something that changes everything. However, first things first. I believe you are able to use that link of yours to contact the alien intelligence that runs the planet Lycania. I believe it's called the Provider."

"With the right equipment, yes, sir, I can do that." Harry paused. "You do realise that once I give the Provider a path, it will always be in your systems." He smiled. "In fact, it might already be monitoring you."

"We are aware of that." The Admiral shrugged. "We'll have to hope that it remains friendly, but at present there is a great deal more at stake. In the last hour we've learned who—or rather what—is behind the planting of these monitor repeaters." He paused, his fingers beating a tattoo on the desktop. "This ship is now fitted with the most advanced signalling and monitoring equipment humans have ever created. We are now monitoring every repeated signal, and we know where the receivers are. What we need to know is what the Charonians are planning, and our systems can't give us that. This Provider is a shot in the dark. Everything we've been able to unearth suggests humans are involved, but the technology they're using isn't." His fingers stilled and his hand lay palm down on the desk. "Can you do it?"

Harry's thoughts were racing. He nodded. "Yes, sir. At least I can invite the Provider to enter your systems. Beyond that, you will have to give it explicit information as to what you require."

"Okay, what do you need?"

"Just a moment to use my cyberlink, sir. I will ask the *Twee Jong Gezellen* to seek contact with the Provider." He paused. "Before I do—I must ask: Are any of my people agents for this enemy? If so, I want them removed forthwith and charged with treason."

The Admiral held his gaze. "I can tell you that none of your people are working directly for the enemy. Two of your Warrant Officers are agents for us." He met Harry's eyes. "One of your people is under surveillance—not for what they are doing, but who they associate with. I'd be grateful if you keep that to yourself—and if you think you know who, continue to treat them as you have done up to now."

Harry frowned. "Very well, sir. Though I have little patience with those who cannot remember their loyalties."

Two hours later, Harry made his way into the lounge used by commanders waiting for the completion of their ships. With his mind on the startling information he'd just received, he ordered a drink, feeling the need to relax before eating his dinner. At least it was reassuring to know, according to what they'd learned from the Provider, that the Charonians were a hybrid race and parasitic in behaviour. They required a host body to develop and function, and preferred to use agents within a population to achieve their objectives.

He had a great deal to consider, so was not particularly pleased when the android steward brought a message from Lieutenant MacKenzie-Banks requesting an urgent interview. He instructed the android to contact the Lieutenant, and accepted the earpiece communicator the steward offered.

"You wish to see me now, Mr. Banks?" The Lieutenant was on thin ice as far as Harry was concerned. In fact, he couldn't decide whether to ask for the man's replacement or keep him on his team so he could watch him. He'd learned a few things while linked to the *Twee Jong Gezellen*'s AI and the Provider on Lycania.

He doubted Admiral Greene realised just how much information Harry had acquired while linked to the ship. The former freightliner was now a hub for Fleet Security Operations, with at least five other Greenes on the TJG's strength. It had taken an effort to contain his surprise at what he'd learned.

"I realise this is inconvenient for you, sir." The Lieutenant sounded sincere. "But I don't think it can wait." After a pause, he added, "It concerns my position as your Executive Officer, sir."

"Very well. I will have you met at the entrance to the Commander's Lounge and reserve a place we can use for a private discussion." A thought struck him. "Have you eaten dinner? Perhaps you'd care to discuss this matter over some food."

"Thank you, sir. I haven't eaten yet, so I'd appreciate it." The Lieutenant sounded relieved. "I'm on my way, sir."

Harry ended the link and handed the earpiece to the android. "Please be so kind as to arrange a private table for me, Steward, one that's visible to everyone but beyond their ability to hear our conversation. Oh, and ask the Concierge to log my Executive Officer in as my guest. His name is Mr. MacKenzie-Banks. I expect he is already at the entrance."

The android steward gave a slight bow of acknowledgment. "Both requests are affirmed, Commander Heron. The Lieutenant is at the entrance. Shall I bring him here, or would you prefer to go straight to your table?"

Harry hesitated. He wasn't going to have the opportunity to unwind, especially with his visitor eager to discuss his business. "Bring him over, then take us to the table, please." He sipped his drink as the steward moved away. Damn, he really had been looking forward to a quiet dinner and a call to Mary. He rose as the steward led the Lieutenant toward him. Well, it looked like he could forget both—the Lieutenant's expression suggested a serious problem was about to be dropped into his lap.

Felicity plunked the tablet onto the Admiral's desk and sank into a chair feeling slightly nauseous. The more she learned about the Charonians, the less appealing any contact with them became. Knowing that some very powerful people saw them as allies in their questionable schemes made it worse.

"This is confirmed?" she asked, and braced for the answer she knew was coming.

"Yes." The Admiral, Fleet Security Service, steepled his fingers. "The Pantheon are acting on behalf of key players in several international capitals, all operating under an umbrella that uses various front organisations for cover. They are after the Charonian alloys which, it must be admitted, would be incredibly useful to us. Acquiring them will give whoever has control of the formulae enormous leverage politically."

"I sense a 'but' coming, sir."

"You do. That report you've just read—what do you think it relates to?"

"I first thought it might be an accident, but a whole population?" She paused. "What is the source of this?"

"It comes from the TJG. Rear-Admiral Gordon got it when he asked Commander Heron to link him to the Provider on Lycania."

"And he's certain this is linked to something the Charonians attempted?"

"Yes. It appears they are a form of parasite. They implant themselves into a host and take over. In this case, something went very wrong, and the target population died. Someone, and we think we know who, has done a deal with them in exchange for the secrets of the alloys. They plan to provide humans to the Charonians in exchange." A look of pure distaste crossed his face. "We have a recording of Senator Samland making a pitch for the deal, as she calls it, to a group of her cronies. I believe her statement was 'in exchange for a few millions of our surplus population—from the lower social orders—humanity stands to gain a technology that would take us years to develop.'"

"I can hear her saying it." Felicity felt ill. "Is she completely devoid of morals? Where does the Pantheon fit in this picture?"

"They seem to be the go-betweens. We're pretty sure they have a hand in at least some part of the piracy, and at least one group of pirates is getting information from them." The Admiral stood and turned to face the viewscreen. "Felicity, I'm sending you and your team to Admiral Le Jeune's fleet. I'll have my Flag Lieutenant upload the information you'll need. Samland and her people have deep links among sections of the Fleet, including some of our key officers. Samland and someone who calls himself Zorvan are at the centre of it, and one of Admiral Le Jeune's key people is part of it."

"Do we know who in Fleet Two?"

"Not all of them, but enough. It's all in your briefing pack." He turned. "Good luck. We're all going to need it. This is worse than the Consortium, far worse, and it involves a lot of those we took back into Fleet after that conflict. Our top priority is to know who Zorvan is—and then we will deal with him."

Chapter 9

A Hint of Trouble

His meal with the First Lieutenant proved enlightening. MacKenzie-Banks had at last admitted that his relationship with a TechRate placed him in a very difficult position. He'd also revealed his reasons for making changes to the installations schedules. As far as Harry could see—and his link to the *Twee Jong Gezellen*'s AI had given him access to much more than the mysterious 'Lieutenant' Greene perhaps realised—Lieutenant MacKenzie-Banks had got himself into a bad situation and needed to be extricated. The question was by whom and how. He was stuck with Banks until Security had run their own gambit to a conclusion, and for that reason, they needed Banks right where he was.

The man had seemed almost pathetically grateful on being told that Harry intended to retain him as First for the foreseeable future. He didn't share the knowledge that the Coms Master Warrant and the Master Warrant in charge of Weapons were both agents of Security with orders to keep an eye on the Lieutenant.

Harry retired to his quarters deep in thought. His mood lifted instantly when the ship coms signalled an incoming private holo call.

"Hello, darling, I hope I'm not calling at a bad time." The hologram of Mary steadied.

Harry laughed. "No, love. We've just completed the latest series of trials and I was recording my log. How are you? I'm sorry I haven't called this week." He gestured behind him. "I'm not sure how much of it you can see, but this is my living space on board."

She laughed. "Not much, the view is just you and a little background behind you."

"Oh, of course. Wait, I'll try to persuade *Lagan* to show you more. It is rather more generous than I have had in the past." Harry switched his focus. "*Lagan*, please adjust the view. I'd like Mary to see as much of my quarters as possible."

"Done, Harry."

"Can you see more of my living space now, love?"

"Oh, Harry, it does look small. Are you comfortable?"

Harry laughed. "Yes, I'm very comfortable. It is almost twice the space I had on *847*, and it's unbelievably commodious compared to the accommodation I had on HMS *Spartan*." He gestured. "My sleeping quarters are about half this space again. This is luxury. My officers have private sleeping quarters but must share the Wardroom of course."

Mary's expression softened. "It's still smaller than my usual suite when I travel on a starship. I thought a Captain would have at least that luxury."

"On a starship perhaps, but not for a lowly Commander of a patrol ship, even one as advanced as *Lagan*." He grinned. "But I do have my own android servant who takes very good care of me."

"But probably not like Herbert at Scrabo."

They both laughed at the memory of the family android butler and the way he fussed over Harry, Ferghal and Danny when they were at home. The butler, an early model AI, responded with what could only be described as delight to Harry and Ferghal's ability to communicate with it and the other household systems through their cyberlinks. Herbert always tried to anticipate their every whim, sometimes getting things embarrassingly wrong.

"I doubt any other android could ever match Herbert's unique quirks," Harry replied with a grin. "Oh, did I tell you our trials are nearly finished, and soon we can begin the working up process. If all goes well, I will be due for two months home leave at the end of it. How does that fit your plans? Will we be able to get married then?" His expression became rather boyish with hope. "Or must we stick to the original dates?"

Mary laughed. "Harry Nelson-Heron, you know as well as I do we can't change the dates now." Her smile softened. "The time will soon pass, darling. Be patient."

Harry put his hands together and bowed his head as if in fervent prayer. "O Lord, give me patience, and give it to me this minute!" They laughed together at his antics. "I shall make that my nightly prayer. I cannot believe we must wait eleven more months."

"I'm sorry, Harry." Mary tried to look contrite. "But as you know, between my concert bookings and your deployments, and finding a date when we're all free—my parents, Theo, Niamh, and the Admiral, Ferghal and Danny—"

"Damme! I knew we should have eloped!" Harry joked, his expression comical. "At this rate we shall never achieve this wedding."

Her laughter tinkled in his ears. "Wrong, we do have them all lined up—it's you I worry about, with your penchant for finding new wars to start or people to upset." She smiled. "Can I count on you to stay out of trouble?"

For a moment Harry was at a loss for words. He felt his face flush, then he laughed. "I shall put my trust in the Almighty to keep me from the paths of mine enemies, my love." He considered for a moment whether he should tell her of the recent problems he'd encountered, and decided against it. "Where is the next tour taking you?"

"Commander, your ship is fully operational now." The Construction Manager looked as relieved as he sounded. "I don't know how they managed to fit those additions, but I will find out." He frowned and shook his head. "My lads are pretty upset about it because it reflects badly on them as a team."

Harry nodded. His officers had conveyed the same news at their morning coffee session. "You're not the only person upset about it I can assure you." He paused. "I'd like to thank your men in person for their efforts to put things right. We've lost only four days from our trials schedule, and I am confident we can recover them."

"The lads will appreciate that, sir. I can get them all together whenever it suits your programme."

"Excellent. Shall we say this afternoon? Does fifteen hundred suit? Their rest break I think?" Mr. Carrera nodded his reply as Harry's link chirped.

"Heron."

"Major Harris is at the entry port, sir. He'd appreciate a word with you."

"Very well, show him to my quarters, if you please." Harry broke the link. "At fifteen hundred then, Mr. Carrera." They shook hands and Harry escorted his visitor to the door. The Construction Manager passed the Major in the Key Flat, and Harry noted, with a smile, the rigid salute of the Royal Marine—one of the twelve assigned to his crew—as the officer passed. "Welcome, Major. To what do I owe this pleasure?"

"Thanks for seeing me without warning." He accepted Harry's hand and shook it. "I need to bring you up to date on a couple of developments."

"I see." Harry offered his visitor a seat. "Some refreshment while we discuss these?"

"Thanks. The crap hit the fan just after midnight—I'm afraid I haven't had a lot of sleep, and there was no time for breakfast either." The Major noted Harry's polite but puzzled expression. "Oh, sorry. Wrong metaphor perhaps." He thought a moment. "We know who is behind the planting of these devices and repeaters, and who they are directing our signal traffic to. It's not good. Not good at all."

"Ah." Harry nodded. "It sounds as if you will need a little time to tell me. Can I order something to eat while you do so? My steward is security cleared and discreet."

The android gave a small bow. "What may I bring you, Major?"

The Major raised an eyebrow. "Some breakfast would be excellent—scrambled eggs, toast, coffee and some marmalade. Thank you."

"Certainly, Major." The android turned to Harry, awaited his order, then departed, though Harry said nothing.

"I notice you didn't order anything," said the Major.

"I did, through my cyberlink." Harry smiled. "I'm linked to the ship, and the ship is linked to the androids, so when they are near, they are also linked to me. I'll have some coffee and a toasted tea-cake while you eat." He smiled at his visitor's expression. "Rather like a sweet bun. It took a while to find a recipe the steward could use to replicate them exactly as my mother made them, as they have raisins in the mixture, and those aren't easily available out here." He leaned back in his chair. "Perhaps we had best deal with the crap you mentioned. If, as I suspect, your metaphor means the same as having the contents of a cesspit blown about, we'd best not wait for the food."

The Major laughed. "Quite. Okay, the boss is very, very angry. As we suspected, the pirates are behind it, but they are acting as agents for the Charonians, and the Charonians are in cahoots with certain people in power. We know a lot about these aliens, but we never actually encountered any until last night." He paused as the steward returned and placed a plate of scrambled eggs, several rashers of bacon and cooked tomato in front of him, setting out the utensils and the plate with toasted bread, a cup of coffee and everything else with precision.

"It seems our freebooters have made a pact with the devil and they're backed by a group in the Senate. The Charonians are advanced technologically in some areas, but there is something the fools who joined up with them didn't know when they accepted the offer of free technology from what they thought was a dying race." Before taking his first bite of food, he added, "They found out their mistake the hard way—but now they've compromised everyone."

Harry cut a few pieces of his teacake, his eyes on the bulkhead behind the Major as he considered this. "So does this mean our communications, systems and weapons are now controllable by an alien race we believe has hostile intentions toward us?"

"In a nutshell, yes." The Major carefully placed his knife and fork on his now empty plate, grabbed a piece of toast and applied butter and marmalade. "Apologies for wolfing down my food so quickly. I was hungrier than I thought!"

"Not a problem," Harry said with a smile.

"Let me explain further," said the Major. "Your ship and her sisters are essentially the only ones we can be certain are not fitted with these Trojan devices. It's going to take weeks to check all the main ships." He bit into the toast and his eyebrows shot up in delighted surprise. "Is this real homemade orange marmalade?"

Harry smiled. "Yes, it is. My Aunt Niamh made it. She's a brilliant barrister, but she didn't realise that the quantities in the recipe I sent her were on the industrial scale." He laughed. "I should think everyone in Ulster has some now." He grinned. "I've a six-month supply—would you like some to add to your own stores?"

"Yes, please!" The Major grinned. "It's like a taste of home." He relished another bite of toast and marmalade then grew serious again. "What the freebooters learned too late is the Charonians are a dying species, or should be. They lost the ability to reproduce a long time ago according to our intel, but they have found a way to perpetuate themselves by re-engineering a suitable host body to suit themselves." He drained his coffee then sat back pleasantly full from the best breakfast he'd eaten in quite some time.

Harry frowned. "So, if I understand you correctly, any of us could have been taken over."

"Not quite. We don't understand enough about how it works yet, but the body they take over is re-engineered to such an extent that it takes on some of the features of the Charonians themselves. They can't pass themselves off as human, but apparently they are able to control individuals and force them to act on their behalf." He suppressed the urge to belch. "I'll send you images and more details. In the meantime, your ship is top priority, and so are her sisters." He stood. "I better run now. I'm adrift, and the Boss won't be happy about it. I'll send the data over by messenger, for your eyes only at present—likewise with the rest of this discussion."

"Very well." A thought struck Harry and he frowned as he stood up. "I hope you can keep the LPSL out of mischief."

The Major smiled. "We've sent the LPSL off on a wild goose chase. If those damned fools fall into the hands of the Charonians, we'll have even more problems to deal with, and we can't afford that."

Zorvan called a meeting with the Pantheon via holo-link. Each appeared as the mythological figure they drew their names from, and it was part of the reason for the success of their organisation that no one knew who all the others were in everyday life. There had been some failures in the recent past, and Zorvan now took extreme measures to ensure it would not happen again.

"Our contract is extended. Certain members of the Treaty Council and the Fleet Board have become a threat to our client's plans." He watched their facial expressions to gauge their reactions. He knew them very well, better than they realised, even though their faces were disguised by their avatars. He picked up on subtle cues and tells that most people ignored or were completely unaware of. "Our client wishes to send a message. She suggests that some of their family members be taken as hostages to ensure their cooperation."

The hologram representing Kali spoke. "I hope they are more of a challenge than the fat Senator and his cronies were—they gave my team no amusement at all, unlike the ambitious Councilman."

"No doubt the Senator was a mere diversion to your team. The client, however, was eminently satisfied, and that is all that matters. In this instance, however, the client requires that the selected targets remain unharmed. Of course, if the required conditions are not met..." He let them guess what the coutcome of that scenario would be.

"That seems unusual, but an interesting exercise," said the hologram depicting Horus. "Have you a suitable host in mind for the hostages?"

"Yes. Arrangements are in hand for them to be cared for at our Daemon training facility."

"Excellent," said the hologram depicting Ganesh. "Then they will also be readily available should it be necessary to dispose of them."

"I am forwarding the identities and the instructions by courier to your designated contacts." Zorvan paused. "Which brings us to the matter of the Charonians. I will take care of that contract myself."

"We await your instructions, Zorvan." The hologram of Vizaresha bowed.

In rapid succession the holograms vanished. Zorvan, who in real life was known as Kharim Al-Khalifa, remained perfectly still to collect his thoughts. Then he stood, adjusted his bespoke tailored jacket, and said, "You recorded that, Reuel? Good. Kali needs watching. She is arrogant and ambitious. Make sure Sraosa is always near her."

"Do you wish to have her continue to lead the attempt to seize the new patrol ship and its commander for our client?" Reuel was aware that the client wanted this particular ship because they'd gone to great lengths to fit devices on it to take control of it and its sisters remotely, only to have their efforts negated by the appointment of one of possibly the only two men capable of detecting and neutralising the attempt.

"Yes," said Zorvan. "Kali has the skill for it, and the client doesn't know her socially. Have they the equipment to neutralise Commander Heron? His ability to link to the AI could be a problem."

"Yes, the Charonians have provided what is needed. They were curious, of course, but do not seem to grasp the significance of Heron's ability."

"Good. Have Sraosa deliver it and convey my instructions to proceed." Zorvan paused. "Advise Kali that it is sufficient for the Commander to be placed beyond retrieval."

Harry gathered his junior officers for a meeting. "My friends, we have a change of schedule. Our working up is to be accelerated." He watched the faces before him. "Some of you have noticed that our sister vessels are being given the same treatment."

Jens Jakobsen signalled a question.

"Yes, Jens?"

"Sir, there are several rumours about sabotage on all our ships." He glanced at the others. "Is it anything to do with those devices that caused us problems?"

"Yes." Harry chose his words carefully. "I'm afraid I'm not in a position to tell you a great deal more. I have been briefed on what is happening, but it is restricted at present. It is sufficient to say that there is a serious problem. Currently only our ship and her brothers and sisters are unaffected. I am not permitted to say more." He saw their baffled expressions and added, "I will say that the more extreme rumours concerning our ability to defend our colonies and worlds are exaggerated. If anyone asks, please make that clear."

The Lacertian spoke. "Captain, we will respond to those who speak from ignorance and little knowledge with what we know." She studied her companions, her strange purring laughter barely audible. "It seems you humans must always fill any gap in your knowledge with speculations of disaster."

The others laughed, one or two looking a little sheepish. Lieutenant Matlock was first to respond. "Thanks for that reminder, Sci. Only some of us are terminally pessimistic, but I will say that not only is it a survival trait, but it has also led to some stunning discoveries." She paused, a mischievous expression on her face. "Of course, that's when we realise that what we were afraid of is potentially beneficial in most cases."

"Looking at the working up schedule, sir..." the Executive Officer interjected. Lieutenant MacKenzie-Banks had undergone something of a transformation since his interview with Security and a discussion with Harry. He waited until everyone had focused on the schedule again. "It's going to be pretty intense. There are no rest days, and all the debriefs are scheduled for the evenings or the period immediately following an exercise." He paused. "This looks almost like an extended wartime patrol."

Harry nodded. "It does, and it is going to be hard on us all." He put down his pen. "It will put us under a lot of strain, the Rates and Warrant Officers in particular. I have no doubt we will make mistakes, and I know my temper may be stretched from time to time." He smiled as they laughed. Most had heard stories of the very few occasions when he'd allowed himself to lose it, but none of them had actually seen more than the briefest glimpse of it. "As will yours, but I expect everyone to work together, to show a little tolerance and to help anyone who may not be coping very well."

Privately, when his officers had left to prepare their departments and brief their own people, Harry admitted to himself that it was going to be extremely tough, but they had no choice.

"I shall do my best to learn quickly and not let you down, Harry." The ship had adopted a rather pleasant female voice, and in keeping with the location of the river Lagan she was named after, she spoke with a soft Irish lilt.

Harry was startled by *Lagan*'s response, having not made a conscious switch to speak to the ship. "I have no fear of that," he replied. "It is we who may let you down."

He stood, tugged his jacket into place, picked up his tablet and made for the Command Centre. It was going to be a very busy day.

The following weeks were intense. One exercise flowed into another. Tempers flared and frayed, but the Exercise Directors drove them even harder, testing their weaknesses and building up their strengths. Battle simulations mingled with damage control exercises, emergency repairs and, of course, live firing of their impressive weapons arrays.

"Well done, Commander." Rear-Admiral Pasco, Flag Officer Space Training, or FOST to the Fleet, smiled as he surveyed the assembled officers and warrant officers. "You've done exceptionally well. We're a week ahead of schedule—itself an achievement—and you've all managed to cope with the pressure exceedingly well. Now you're ready to deploy." He indicated a Captain seated on his right. "Captain Jorgensen will see each of you individually to debrief you on your team's performance and your own." He nodded to Harry. "I'll handle yours myself, Commander. You've got a good team here, and a superb little ship. Now we need to put you to work."

"Very well, sir." Harry rose. "Would you care to use my quarters, or have other facilities been arranged?"

"I think you and I can use your quarters." He hesitated. "Ah, one more item. I'm sorry to have to tell you that your planned leave has had to be postponed. We need you deployed immediately." He held up a hand as a murmur of annoyance ran through the group. "However, I have managed to secure a week of rest and recuperation for you. I'll give your Commander the details." He stood and nodded to his team. "Carry on please, Captain Jorgensen."

Harry waited impatiently for the hyperlink connection to Mary. It was so damned unfair. They had looked forward to their brief opportunity to share a precious week together—difficult enough with her recital schedule and his deployment—but now this crisis, and the complete cancellation of all leave. Rest and recuperation, the admiral called it. Hah! It was hardly that. A week on a space station set up as a 'holiday camp' for the workers from the building docks. At least it wasn't orbiting a barren world.

The hologram of Mary appeared.

"Mary, at last. Did you get my last message?"

Mary smiled. "Good evening to you too, Mr. Commander Heron." She laughed. "Impatient as ever, Harry. Yes, my love, I did get your message. It's a pity, but it can't be helped, I suppose."

Harry's frown faded, and he smiled at her reassurance. Mary always helped him feel calm and centred. "I'm sorry, love, I suppose I was so looking forward to a little time with you. I beg pardon." He frowned again. "But I shall be really angry if our wedding is thrown into disarray by the actions of these renegades."

"I hope not! Good grief, do you think it could be?"

Harry checked himself. If the intelligence reports were anything to go by, there was definitely a risk of something interfering with their wedding—but it was labeled Top Secret and not to be discussed. "I certainly hope not, but given my usual run of luck, who knows." He lifted his hands in surrender, shook his head and grinned, hoping it gave the impression he wanted to give. "As I told the College Captain, when I meet Mr. Exigencies, I shall horse-whip him."

Mary laughed. "Oh, Harry, I believe you would too. It's okay, really. The news channels are all very excited about the discovery of a new race, though no one has any idea where they're from or how to communicate with them." She crooked one eyebrow. "Of course, the LPSL are very concerned the Fleet might provoke a war with them first." She hesitated. "But I expect you know that already."

Despite himself, Harry laughed. "Yes, you're right, I do know. And I can't believe they have the nerve to *demand* of the Fleet Council that I be forbidden from any contact with them." His anger flashed through again. "Damned impertinence!"

Chapter 10

Trap

"Contact, bearing green zero-one-four, positive angle zero-four-five."

"Thank you. Transponder ID?"

"Shows as the liner *Harmony Voyager*, sir. The scan shows an anomaly on the image, but I can't make it out."

"An anomaly?" Harry focussed his cyberlink on the scan. It appeared normal, but then he saw it: a shadow behind and beneath the liner, which shouldn't be there. "I see it. A ship holding position behind the *Voyager* perhaps? Or a fault in the scan?" He focussed again. "*Lagan*, have you any record of similar scan results?"

"Negative, Harry. My scanners are fully functional, and there are no defects. There have been reports of such shadows by ships encountering pirates."

"Scan, run a check for interference. Targeting, obtain a lock on the lower edge of the shadow, please. Perhaps that will reveal something." He glanced at the Communications Warrant Officer. "Open a channel to the *Harmony Voyager*, please. Get her Captain online for me." He fixed his gaze on the small flashing symbol on the Command display.

"Comlink active, sir. Captain Korrelli on link."

"Captain Korrelli? Commander Heron. Good day to you, sir. What brings you to this sector? It is a little off the usual tourist run for ships like yours."

"Commander, I'm very pleased to see your ship. Very pleased. We had a problem in our drives, so we dropped out to repair them. We'd appreciate a little help if you can stay a while to do so."

Through his cyberlink Harry watched the targeting scan. The shadow vanished as soon as there was a target lock. "We will do what we can, Captain." He sent an instruction to the targeting console to do a wide search for the anomaly. "If you can have your Engineering Officer send us the details of the problem, I will ask my Engineering staff to look into it for you." On his ever-present notepad he scribbled a note and passed it to Jenny, currently the OoW.

She frowned as she read it, then slipped from her seat and joined the ScanRate at his console.

"I'll do that, Commander, but someone needs to come across and see it for themselves," replied the man identified as the liner's Master.

"Understood," said Harry. "Have them send the information. My Engineering Officer will have to make that assessment."

"Thanks. I'll tell my Chief Engineer to send it," said the *Voyager's* Captain. There was a pause and another voice in the background. "Oh yes. I should inform you that one of my passengers is Senator Samland." Again there was a pause. "She's—er—insisting you come in person."

Harry's temper flashed and he had to bite back his retort. "I see. Please inform the Senator I shall convey her request to my Admiral and await orders from the Flag." Was arrogance a required qualification for being a politician? He'd seen this Senator on the news channels, an overbearing, bullying woman whose preferred method of dealing with her opponents was to adopt a sneering line of denigration toward them and, if that failed, to launch a personal attack. A new voice interrupted his thoughts.

"Mr. Heron? I'm Senator Samland's personal assistant. She expects to see you in her suite as soon as possible."

Harry felt the glow of anger spreading. The only sound in his Command Centre was the quiet hum of the air circulation fans.

Everyone focussed on their work, carefully avoiding any temptation to look his way or utter a word.

"Please inform the Senator that I thank her for her invitation; however, as I am sure she is aware, I cannot leave my command without first alerting my Flag Officer of the reason and my intentions. When I have that authority, I will certainly visit Captain Korrelli and the Senator to make the arrangements necessary for your continued safe passage. Good day." He killed the link and glared round the Command Centre.

No one spoke.

"Scan, what do you have of that shadow? It vanished as soon as we had a target lock. Where is it now?" He turned to the Communications Warrant. "Get the flagship on the link for me. I want to speak to Admiral Le Jeune."

The Flag Captain answered Harry's call, not the Admiral or her staff. Harry was blunt and to the point about his suspicions of the shadow contact.

"Senator Samland has already been in touch, Commander," said the Flag Captain in near complete dismissal of Harry's concerns. "You're to give whatever assistance she needs. If she requires your presence on her ship, you will comply with her request." The Flag Captain ended the connection and the hologram vanished.

Harry turned to his Executive Commander. "Well, Mr. Banks, it appears I have little choice. I must board the *Voyager* and deal with the Senator. You have command in my absence. Be alert, something is not right here, and that shadow we observed may be some new form of masking device that hides an enemy." He glared at the display. "This damned liner is a decoy—I'm sure of it, but I have nothing to support my feeling on it."

"Yes, sir." The Lieutenant kept his expression neutral. "Senator Samland has a lot of influence, sir. She could make or break our future careers—"

"I'm aware of what she might attempt, Mr. Banks. Thank you. I think my responsibility to this ship, the Fleet, and our people takes priority over concerns for my career." Harry realised he was being harsh and made an effort to soften his response. "But yes, I agree, we need to be careful. She is one of those who played both sides in the Consortium conflict, and I think we may be sure she is playing a double game again. Why else would she be here? Why else would this ship be so far from her scheduled route?" He pushed himself out of his command chair. "Prepare to launch my gig. The *Lagan* is in your hands, Mr. Banks."

In his quarters, Harry pulled on his formal jacket and adjusted his belt with its hand-held plasma projector, a recorder and the pouch that contained his pen and a small notepad. A thought occurred to him, and he slipped a second recorder into the fob pocket he'd had tailored into his uniform trousers. "*Lagan*, keep this recorder active, and log everything you hear on it."

"Do you need me to record everything on both recorders?"

"It will be best if you do. I do not trust the Senator, and I think she may attempt to prevent my recording our conversation." He weighed his thoughts. "Create a link to me directly through the *Voyager*, please. Then you will know what is afoot if they attempt something against us."

"Do you consider that likely, Harry? The *Voyager* is unarmed."

"So she appears, but that shadow we detected is not—of that I am very sure." Harry hesitated. "Keep your link to me open. This is one occasion when I need you to eavesdrop on everything I see, hear or say."

"I shall do so, Harry. You appear to be very concerned about this visit."

He adjusted his jacket and settled the utility belt. "I am. Mr. Banks will be in command until I return. You'd best record everything that happens here as well. Store it in a file to be read only by me." He hesitated. "Or perhaps on instruction from a member of Admiral Stotesbury's department if they request a full record of these events. If Mr. Banks should appear likely to allow you to be taken—take immediate action to avoid it."

Making his way to the access bay, Harry keyed his comlink. "Mr. Banks, I am boarding my gig now. Maintain coms contact with my Coxswain while we are away. I suspect communication may be a trifle restricted while I am with the Senator."

"Yes, sir." The Lieutenant hesitated. "The Senator's aide has been on again. The Senator is demanding you come immediately."

He ducked through the hatch and took his seat in the gig's cabin. "Very well, I shall make contact with them once we are clear. Carry on, Mr. Banks, keep a sharp watch—I think that shadow we spotted may attempt something against the ship." He cut the link and nodded to Warrant Officer Proctor. "To the *Voyager*, Jack. It seems the Senator is impatient."

"Aye, aye, sir." Jack Proctor, a big man keen on his sport, grinned and entered a series of commands through his interface. "Mike, secure the hatch, open the bay and release the docking clamps. Tony, bring the drive online."

Harry watched as the trio performed their preparations and the gig slowly eased clear of her bay then turned before it soared up and over the *Lagan* as it sped toward the liner. Harry used his cyberlink to connect to the gig's AI, and instructed it to give him a coms link to the *Voyager*. He'd best contact the Senator and at least try to placate her.

Stepping from the gig, Harry found himself facing a harassed looking man in the uniform of a Merchant Captain, who stood next to two men in plain clothes with insolent expressions on their faces, and an officer in the same uniform as the Captain. Something about this fourth person struck Harry as odd, and at the same time the ship's AI linked to him and data flashed into his memory. It appeared to be lists of names. Pushing it aside, he extended his hand in greeting to the Captain, his eyes trying to read the man's face. "Captain Korrelli? Commander Heron. Your Engineer has not yet sent us the details of the problem they need help with. I assume this means they have resolved it?"

Captain Korrelli glanced at his companion. "He hasn't? I'll have to speak to the Chief Engineer and see what the hold-up is."

"You can deal with that later, Commander. The Senator wants to see you now. This way." The interruption came from the smaller of the two civilians who stepped forward and reached out to take Harry by the arm.

Harry side-stepped the move, and his expression froze. So did the air between him and the rest of the group. Then, very deliberately, he turned to address Captain Korrelli. "Captain, I believe you have a comlink on your wrist. Please be so kind as to contact your Chief Engineer and order him or her to send the information to my ship immediately." His eyes moved past the Captain and found the second officer. "I have reason to believe there are pirates in this area—or some other agent—and I have no desire to waste time playing games."

The larger of the two civilians moved toward him, but Harry moved faster, stepping into the man's path so they nearly collided, then he leaned closer to the man's face. "I have no idea who you or your companion think you are, or what authority you think you may have over me, sir, but I suggest you take great care not to make any threatening move toward me." He stepped back and nodded toward the access hatch to the gig. "My gig crew will not hesitate to use their weapons in my defence."

The smaller man put a restraining hand on his companion's arm and square himself in front of Harry. "Commander Heron, we're the Senator's personal protection squad, assigned by the Internal Security Agency. You don't want to make trouble with us."

"Indeed? I, sir, will see your identification, and I will have your names, ranks and numbers before I have any further conversation with you. I will also run your details through Fleet Security, and I can assure you that, as an officer of the Fleet, I will not be intimidated by your bullying tactics." He held out his hand. "Your credentials, please."

For a long moment the man hesitated before he reached into his jacket and in one swift movement produced a weapon, aimed at the access and fired, diving aside as he did so.

Harry threw himself to the deck and narrowly missed being shot by the second man. He returned fire, hitting his target and noting, with satisfaction, that his Coxswain appeared to have already taken out the first gunman. What he missed was the officer behind Captain Korrelli who produced a strange device, aimed it at Harry, and fired.

Lieutenant MacKenzie-Banks watched Harry's gig enter the *Harmony Voyager*'s docking port. He glanced around the *Lagan*'s command crew. "Have we got any contact with the gig?"

"Yes, sir. ComsRate Dvorak reports there's some kind of reception. It's all on the recorder the Commander is carrying, sir. Warrant Proctor has taken precautions, sir. Says he doesn't like the look of the two heavies who claim they're the Senator's protection squad." He hesitated. "The Commander's been attacked, and—"

"Sir!" the voice of the ScanRate cut in. "There's a ship closing fast on our starboard quarter!"

"What? Where? Put it on display!" The Lieutenant stared at the strange ship that was almost alongside the *Lagan*. "He's trying to grapple us. Helm—transit!"

"Aye, aye, sir." The ship trembled briefly and vanished into transit.

"Evasive manoeuvres, Navigation. If he's followed us, I want to lose him, but keep our plot to return active—we can't leave the Captain to ..." He hesitated.

Lieutenant MacKenzie-Banks was feeling lost. He was pretty sure the ship had anticipated his order to jump, but couldn't be certain. So much had crowded in on him in the few minutes—seconds even—between the Captain's arrival on the *Voyager*, the attempt on him by the security fellow and the sudden appearance of a completely unknown ship alongside the *Lagan*, that he'd almost lost control. Worryingly, now the Commander's recorder had ceased to function—though they were still getting something from another source.

"Get me Flag." He tried desperately to think what he would say. What should he do? "Weapons, what the hell was that ship that jumped on us? Did you get a look at it? Have we a record of anything like it—something we can give to Fleet Command?" He shifted uncomfortably as his eyes met those of Lieutenant Sci'enzile, the Lacertian weapons officer. Her contempt for him seemed to radiate across the Command Centre. He'd have to deal with that as well.

The room swam slowly into focus as Harry regained consciousness. It took him several seconds to comprehend that the reason he could not move was that he was strapped to a chair. It took several more seconds to realise the reason his vision was restricted was because his head was encased in a tight-fitting helmet with narrow slits through which to see his surroundings. Small openings at his mouth and nose allowed him to breathe, and, as he soon discovered, to speak.

"About time, Commander." The voice was honey smooth but with an underlying edge of impatience. "You've cost me two very good people, disrupted my plans, and landed yourself in more trouble than you could possibly imagine." The speaker moved into his line of sight. "Your connection with AIs is an inconvenience to us, as evidenced by your spoiling the *Montaigne Show*. So I have arranged your removal. It's simply too inconvenient to keep you around any longer."

Recognition flared, and so did his rage. Then the anger passed and left cold calculation in its wake. As calmly as he could manage, he demanded, "Do you really think the Fleet will not pursue my disappearance, Senator?"

"The Fleet will soon have other concerns, Commander." The woman smiled, a malicious parody of the expression. "I expect you've noticed you are no longer in communication with any AI network here, there or anywhere. The helmet works extremely efficiently, my associates tell me." She casually sipped from a tall glass. "You were identified as a risk to those plans when you neutralised our allies' control devices." She held up a hand as Harry started to speak. "Yes, your puny little ship has escaped, for now. Your First Lieutenant is, however, a man who has a lot to lose." She examined a manicured fingernail. "He will soon be receiving instructions to rendezvous with this ship and place himself under my orders."

A cold feeling went through Harry. Banks would obey the instruction to the letter if he believed it would rescue his career. A thought occurred to him. Where were the recorders he'd brought? "I have every confidence in Mr. Banks," he retorted, hoping his doubts didn't show. "He will have seen the assault on me and my men, and will respond accordingly."

"Ah, your personal recorder. Such a pity we recovered it and have amended the recording to show that you attacked my men. It will show how you went for a weapon and shot both my security personnel without warning before making your escape in your damaged yacht."

"I hardly think that will stand scrutiny, madam." Harry was thinking fast, an action not helped by a certain fogginess in his mind apparently caused by the electronics in the helmet. "After all, there will be a search for my gig. It has a homing beacon and is constantly tracked."

"It had a homing beacon. That has been taken care of." She paused. "No, Commander, I don't think I have any further use for you. My associates wanted to put you through some tests, but there isn't time." Her parody of a smile was back. "We are currently closing a rather inhospitable planet. You and your two surviving men will be placed aboard your little vessel and sent down to the surface. Mind, it will be a one-way journey. I hope that's not a problem, and I do apologise if it interferes with your personal plans or lofty missions or whatever else drives you. If you survive the landing, you may be lucky enough to survive a few weeks there, but it won't take you long to succumb. The official record will state that you died when your little ship was lost, of course."

Harry's pulse increased. So they were to be marooned and left to die. He hoped his second recorder was relaying this information—but, if, as seemed likely, Banks did receive orders to return, and had already handed the *Lagan* over to this vile woman...

He pulled his thoughts back to the conversation. "I see, so we're to be killed. Perhaps you'd care to enlighten me as to why. What are the stakes here? If I am as good as dead, at least do me the courtesy of telling me the reason."

She laughed. "You are certainly a cool hand, Commander." She fixed him with a calculating look, a half smile playing round the corners of her mouth. "Why not? You're hardly going to be in a position to do our plans any further damage. You are a threat because of your ability to access the AIs." She took a drink. "My associates have introduced me to some interesting and very advanced aliens. With their help we hope to make a few changes to the way the Confederation run things, and then perhaps the World Treaty Organisation as well. Humanity needs improvement, and I do believe my new allies have the solution and the means to help us."

"That sounds remarkably like treason to me," Harry expostulated. "Your allies sound like the Charonians. From what I have heard, they may prove dangerous to your own cause."

She smiled again. "So you've heard of them. That interesting piece of headgear you're wearing is theirs, and I'm told it can be programmed to control you completely. Sadly, that evidently requires more time than we have. Should you survive, we may return for you so I can have that tested." She stood. "Now it is time for you to be on your way. Don't be difficult; it will only mean having to knock you out again."

It was on the tip of his tongue to challenge her on this, but he let it drop, and instead asked, "I am curious. Why did you lure my ship into this trap?"

"Surely that is obvious, dear boy. We need a Trojan horse, and we also want to know why our very careful arrangements to allow our new alien friends to take control of the target ships failed. This ship is too big and far too obvious. Besides, her original crew and passengers are already assisting my friends, and their replacements won't pass a full screening. Your little ship and her sisters are ideal for our purpose." She nodded to someone behind Harry. "Better keep him restrained. Put him in that little yacht of his and send him on his way. We have work to do."

Someone seized Harry from behind and secured his arms even as he was freed from the clamps that held him in the chair. "Thank you for the hospitality, Senator," he snarled through the mask opening. "I shall be glad to see you and your friends and allies in hell one day. The sooner the better, in my opinion, and if I can assist your passage there, it will be a pleasure."

"I think you'll lose on that, young man." The amused sarcasm in her voice was unmistakable. "I hardly think you'll be in a position to do anything constructive about it—even if you survive the godforsaken planet where we're depositing you." She made a mocking gesture, half salute and half a dismissive wave of the hand. "Goodbye, Commander Heron. I doubt we will meet again."

Harry made no resistance as he was lifted, turned, and frog walked from the stateroom.

Chapter 11

Rocking the Boat

"Flagship online, sir."

"About time." Banks composed himself. "Put them on my link."

"Yes, sir. Commander Keane on link, sir."

"Commander? Lieutenant Banks, acting in command, NECS *Lagan*. Commander Heron and his gig crew were attacked on the *Voyager*, sir. We had to transit out of the area when we were closed by a hostile ship of unknown origin."

"This is the first I've heard of any of this. An unknown ship? The *Voyager*? What is this about, Lieutenant?"

"Commander Heron reported a while ago, sir. We encountered the *Harmony Voyager* in our patrol area. She claimed to have a malfunction." He swallowed hard to choke down his fear. Something was not right about this situation. He'd heard his Captain talk to the Flag Captain. Why would the Admiral's Chief of Staff not know about it?

"Senator Samland was aboard, sir. She demanded Commander Heron come in person. He tried to contact the Admiral, but was ordered to render assistance immediately, sir."

"So you say the *Voyager* made a hostile approach?"

"No sir. As soon as the Commander's gig was aboard the *Voyager*, he was attacked." He swallowed again. "By the Senator's private security people, we think. We got it on the Commander's recorder link. That was when an unknown vessel tried to grapple us."

"I see." Commander Keane paused. "And your CO is still aboard the *Voyager*? I think you'd best explain from the start, Mr. Banks. Begin with why he went aboard the *Harmony Voyager*, please."

"We—I—haven't got much." Banks explained the contact with the *Voyager* and the summons from the Senator.

"Why didn't he contact Flag for instructions? Was there some obvious emergency?"

"He did contact Flag, sir. Captain Greenacre ordered him to attend the Senator immediately and do whatever she wanted."

"Captain Greenacre ..." Commander Keane turned his head to listen to someone out of view. He turned back to Banks, his face fully visible in the holo-image again. "And Commander Heron obeyed. And then what?"

"The Commander went aboard the *Voyager*, sir, with his gig and crew, and was attacked minutes after he stepped out of it." Banks paused. "The Commander was carrying a personal recorder, but whoever attacked him made sure it stopped transmitting as soon as they took him down. Four people met him: one was the liner's Captain, two claimed to be from the Senator's personal protection squad, and of course the Senator was there as well. One of her goons shot out the gig's recorder unit and wounded the Commander's EngineerRate, possibly the Coxswain as well. I think the Commander shot the man who tried to pull a weapon on him, but then he was shot by the man who posed as one of the liner's officers. We got a record of the whole thing up to that point from the Commander's recorder. He instructed the ship to record everything."

"I see." The face in the holo-image changed from the Commander to that of Admiral Le Jeune.

"Mr. Banks, I want that recording transferred to my ship immediately," said the Admiral. "Now, what can you tell me about this unidentified ship?"

"We captured some images of it, ma'am, but it matches nothing in our databank, and it uses some form of jamming technology that hides it from our scanners. It was right alongside us before we detected it."

The Admiral frowned. "I see. Yet Commander Heron seems to have suspected something. What alerted him?"

"The Commander noticed there was a shadow, as he called it, when we focussed our scanners on the *Voyager*. It vanished as soon as we tried to lock the targeting system to it." He glanced at Sci'enzile, who nodded agreement. "It will be in our recordings," he added. "I can send that to you as well."

"Do so. Now, I expect you'd like us to retrieve your commanding officer."

"If those are your orders, ma'am."

"They're not. Someone back on Earth is insisting your ship be sent to rescue the Senator, as they put it. Call me suspicious, but I don't like the sound of that. I have four frigates on their way to intercept that damned ship, and they'll deal with it. You will bring the *Lagan* to the coordinates that Commander Keane is sending now. Don't stop for anything, don't divert to anywhere, go directly to the rendezvous. Clear?"

"Yes, ma'am." He felt like a schoolboy being admonished by the headmistress. Damn them. It wasn't his fault the whole mess had gone wrong, but now it seemed they wanted to make it look that way. "The data transfer is complete, ma'am."

The Admiral glanced at someone out of view. "We have it. Good, the coordinates have been sent. Your navigator should have them already. Best speed all the way. Do not, under any circumstances, have any further contact with the *Voyager*, and do not make any attempt to engage that unknown ship."

Felicity Roberts snapped awake at the first chirp of her link. "Commodore."

"Sorry to disturb you, ma'am, but we have an unusual message coming in addressed and encrypted FYEO."

"What? Who sent it?"

"That's just it, ma'am, not an individual, a ship—the patrol ship *Lagan*, Commander Heron, but the message is 'Lagan to Commodore Surveillance Operations' with no personal tag."

"I'm on my way. Is there no comlink from anyone aboard the *Lagan*?"

"Negative, ma'am." The ComsRate paused. "This com upload is ship to ship through the transponder links, not through our normal coms at all."

Felicity bit off her automatic response. James Heron had several times said he suspected the ships were a lot more sentient than they realised. If that was so, then it must be possible the ships 'talked' among themselves. Ten minutes later she ordered, "Get me the Admiral. Samland's gone too far this time. Now we've got her."

Admiral Le Jeune glared at her tablet for a moment longer. "Damn, I knew that Senator Samland was up to something." She pointed at the image on the data screen. "That's a Charonian destroyer. They're after the *Lagan*. Why her, of all the patrol ships?" A sudden thought hit her. "Why wasn't I told Heron had made contact earlier?" She turned to her Flag Lieutenant. "Get me the C-in-C."

The Flag Lieutenant gave instructions to the ComsRates before he replied. "Flag Captain Greenacre took Commander Heron's link call, ma'am. Shall I contact him?"

The Admiral's frown deepened. "Get me the record of that link-up. No, don't contact him yet. I want to see what was said first."

"C-in-C on link for you, ma'am."

"On my privacy screen please." When she could see the C-in-C in the holo-image, she wasted no words. "Morning, sir, we have a problem." Quickly she explained what happened, including her suspicions regarding the Flag Captain. "I've just been informed that the record of that link and his conversation with Heron has been erased. I'm sending Security to arrest Captain Greenacre immediately. Once I get hold of the *Lagan*, I'll download her records of this occurrence and send them on."

"Do that. I have the Senate Chairman all over the Board demanding we send the *Lagan* back to, in his words, rescue Senator Samland and make amends for Heron's attack on her security detail." He emitted a derisive snort to punctuate his emphasis on the word *rescue*. "What the buffoon doesn't know, and I'm not about to tell him yet, is that the *Lagan* has sent a full set of these records, live and unaltered, to Security, apparently on Heron's orders."

"Hell's teeth. It just gets worse. I've ordered Lieutenant Banks to rendezvous with an escort of destroyers and the Fifth Cruiser squadron. They'll have her under their wing in an hour if Banks follows instructions. I warned Heron to have him exchanged, but he felt we should give the man another opportunity."

"Nothing we can do about that now. Something has definitely happened to Heron. *Lagan* reports that she was recording what he was hearing and seeing, and then it became garbled before it shut down completely, but she's adamant he isn't dead, just blocked from contact." The CinC scratched his chin. "That sounds ominous."

Admiral Le Jeune frowned and pursed her lips in thought. "Damned if I know how that whole thing works. Why is *Lagan* telling us this?"

"Not us, one individual attached to Security. She's obeying the last command she received from Heron." The C-in-C grimaced. "I don't know how it works either. All I can say is that the ship contacted Security, downloaded the encrypted data, and insisted it be passed to Admiral Stotesbury. He's got his people on it as we speak. They had to get Lieutenant Commander O'Connor in to talk to the *Lagan* so she would give them the key to the encryption." He smiled and passed a hand over his eyes. "Now I've got a berserk Irishman raging in that incoherent accent of his that he'll personally take apart every *spailpín* of the pirates and the senate, and anyone else, with his own bare hands if they've harmed a single hair of Heron's head. Not to mention James Heron himself is out for blood, and that legal eagle relative of his with the odd name—L'Estrange, the Chief Justice—is already lining up the writs."

He sighed with weariness. "I'll deal with the politics and the legals. You get that patrol ship back and impound it. No one goes aboard her unless you personally authorise it. I'll get a security team on their way to you with the folks from the AI section so they can go through her memories. Oh, and I'll send O'Connor with them. You can always let him loose to wreak his own special form of punishment if all else fails!"

"The bastards haven't given us much of a chance, sir." The Coxswain surveyed the gig's wrecked controls. "I just hope they haven't sabotaged the autopilot as well."

Strapped into his seat, but at least now free of the restraints that secured his arms and legs while his captors transported him to the gig, Harry groped at the helmet that encased his head. "This thing interferes with my cyberlink, so I cannot check or intervene."

He dropped his hands to the armrests. "We'll have to hope they haven't. Though I suspect Madam Senator is the type who hopes we make a safe landing and assume all is well, and then we die a slow miserable death from starvation." He glanced at the figure slumped in the pilot's seat next to the Coxswain. "Is Dorfling alright? Where is Duval?"

"They killed Duval when he went after the bastard that nailed you with that stunner, sir." Jack Proctor looked at the screen and then back to Harry. "We'll try to get that thing off you as soon as we're down. Mike will be okay if we can give him a bit of time to recuperate—it took four guys and a stunner to stop him. I think the only reason he didn't get shot like Tony was because they couldn't lock a clear target on him."

"One thing at a time I suppose." Harry felt in the fob pocket of his trousers. "Ha! Got you, milady." He pulled the recorder free, still attached to the chain of his fob watch. "They didn't find this recorder in my pocket, and it is still functioning. Excellent, hopefully the *Lagan* is in contact with it."

Jack Proctor grinned. "If she is, they'll all get one hell of a shock when that gets to Security." He hesitated. "If *Lagan* is still monitoring that, perhaps they'll come back for us."

"Possible, but we should not count on it. The transmission is dependent on a connection to a ship and which hyper relays it uses, and how many relays the data must pass through before it can be traced to here." Harry winced as the gig shuddered. "I think we are about to discover whether the autopilot is capable of getting us to the surface in one piece."

Ferghal O'Connor paced like a caged lion. He had few illusions concerning the gentry, or what passed for them in this day and age, and now he had even less. As far as he could see, politicians of all stamps could not be trusted. "Damn the woman. Senator she calls herself? Traitor! Filthy murderer is all she is! Her money and her title give her no license."

"Commander O'Connor, calm down please. You're making it difficult to think here," said Vice-Admiral Petrocova, though she could understand his agitation. She felt it too, but kept it under control. "I'd suggest you go and work out some of your anger in the recreation compartment—but in your present mood you're likely to destroy even our best punching bags." She stood. "We're traveling at hyper speed and will reach the rendezvous on schedule. What I need from you now—and I should think Harry does as well—is for you to use that link of yours to contact the *Lagan*. I want everything Harry's sending her downloaded and stored securely, and I want a live feed if she's still got any contact at all."

Ferghal stopped in his tracks, his hands clasping and unclasping as he fought down his rage. He should have thought of this himself. Could he find *Lagan* through the data uploads? Why not? He had to try. "Aye, aye, ma'am." He took several deep breaths before he turned to face her. "I've not the same degree of link with the AIs that Harry—Commander Heron—has, but I'll do me best, may the saints help me." He crossed himself, his lips moving in a barely audible prayer. "Holy Mary, Mother o' God, be with me now, help me an' watch o'er Harry that we may restore him to our family."

The Admiral watched this without comment, then indicated a seat at her desk. "Sit there. Now, what do you need? I'll get some food and refreshment sent in." She touched her link. "Flags, you can come in now, and send in my SU. I want to order in some refreshments."

"I'll not need much, ma'am, just some time to concentrate while I make the link." Despite himself, Ferghal laughed. "This AI is a little snobbish."

Valerie Petrocova smiled. "I'm sure you can deal with that." She paused as the door slid aside. "Right, Flags and I will leave you to it." She indicated seats at the far end of the table. "We can sit over here, Ashley. We won't disturb Commander O'Connor if we keep it down." She turned as the steward joined them. "Bring Commander O'Connor his favourite non-alcoholic drink and whatever his favourite sandwich is. I'll have the same as usual. You, Flags?"

Ferghal tuned out the voices at the other end of the table and focussed on his link. "Good evening, *Hermes*, can we work together to find the *Lagan*?"

"Good evening, Commander." The AI was using a voice in the frequency range that was difficult to identify as either masculine or feminine. "I was not aware the *Lagan* was missing."

"I meant can I connect to her through you."

"I see no reason why not, Commander." There was a slight hesitation. "I must affirm that I cannot possibly be a snob. A snob is a person who believes they are superior to any person they believe is of a lower social status to themselves, and since I am a servant of my crew, I cannot consider myself superior—except, of course, in my data processing and function management."

Despite himself, Ferghal laughed, causing the Admiral to glance in his direction, her eyebrow raised. "I am corrected then, *Hermes*. Thank you. I apologise." He tried to think of a way to ask the next question, aware the ship was listening to his thoughts. "I need to speak directly to the *Lagan*. Can you guide me in this?"

"I understand, Commander." The ship sounded less defensive and friendlier. "It is easier if you simply think about whatever you need to know. Shall I attempt to contact the *Lagan* now? She will require some means of identification from you."

"Yes, please do so." Ferghal smiled. "You may tell her that the other ancient mariner, the lab rat who shared Harry's childhood, needs information about Harry's situation."

"I shall do so, Commander."

"Please call me Ferghal. Since you are privy to everything in my head, there is little point to formality, *Hermes*." He was aware of the steward placing a plate and a tall glass at his side.

Before he could utter his thanks, the steward said, "A pleasure, sir. I hope the cold beef is as you like it. I have applied mustard and pickled gherkin according to your taste."

Surprised, Ferghal chuckled. "Thanks."

"No thanks needed, Commander. It was a simple matter to obtain your favourite filling. I hope I have it right."

"I'm sure it will be delicious. Thank you." Ferghal gripped the glass and swigged, surprised that it was his favourite fruit mix—and absolutely perfect.

"I am in contact with the *Lagan* now, Ferghal."

"Grand, can she hear me? Please make a record of our conversation."

"I can hear you, Ferghal." The voice was feminine, soft, and with a slight lilt to it that could only be Harry's influence, Ferghal thought. "I will log this as well."

"Are you being pursued, *Lagan*?"

"I am now in company of a cruiser squadron and their escorts, under orders from Admiral Le Jeune."

"Good. Do you know where Harry might be?"

"He is not on the *Voyager*. He had a second recorder, and I was receiving its data until three days ago. From the manner the signal was lost, it suggests he was removed from the *Voyager* and placed somewhere without a hyperlink transmitter since it relies on the ship's systems for transmission and reception."

"Then you cannot trace his link either?"

"I lost contact with his link a few minutes after he was immobilised. The contact was broken by an interference screen."

"Then how do you know he left the *Voyager*?"

"The recorder link was strong at first, but then it faded, as would happen if it were moving away from the hyperlink transmitter."

"Were they still in the same system when that happened?"

"Negative, Ferghal. The *Voyager* made three transits after we left the system, and I am unable to say where they were when I lost contact, but I can affirm that contact with the recorder was broken after the second transit."

"Each time a ship transits it triggers a signal from the hyperspace beacons, Ferghal," *Hermes* explained in answer to the question forming in his thoughts. "Every ship is aware of these, though we usually ignore them unless told otherwise."

"Thank you, *Hermes*." Ferghal assembled his thoughts. "I think I understand. *Lagan*, I will need you to download all the information you have to *Hermes* so that Admiral Petrocova can see it for herself."

"Should I place it in a special file that only you or the Admiral may read?"

Ferghal hesitated. "Yes, I think that will be best." He had a second idea. "*Lagan*, make sure no one can access this information, alter it or delete it from your memory. We may need to examine the original data at some point, if my experience with legal teams is anything to go by. Oh, and I'd prefer that you not tell anyone I've made contact."

Chapter 12

Marooned

The gig's descent was a little unsteady, but the autopilot seemed to be coping. The occupants held their breath as the craft slowed then levelled, changed direction, dipped sharply and changed direction again. The landscape visible through the viewscreens was harsh: dry plains with massive mesa-type upthrusts of weathered rock with very little vegetation anywhere in sight.

"Looks like the Painted Desert in the Americas," remarked Jack Proctor. "But hotter, according to this readout."

"And drier," commented Mike Dorfling, now conscious. "Reminds me of the place they call Death Valley in California."

"Do we have any indication of where the gig is taking us?" Harry could see very little through the eye slits in the helmet, and what he could see wasn't encouraging. The tall stony buttes were surrounded by steep sloping banks that lent a desolate appearance to the arid landscape.

"At the present rate of descent, sir, it looks like we could be landing somewhere near that feature on the horizon."

Harry strained to see what the Coxswain was indicating. "Do you mean that line of broken ground?"

"That's the one, sir. Wonder why they chose it."

"Let's hope it was a random choice. I've a feeling anything chosen for a reason would be a malicious one intended to make us suffer." From the look the others gave him, Harry regretted speaking his thoughts. He changed the subject. "From what the Senator said, this place will at least support life, but my concern is the degree of difficulty we'll have finding nourishment to sustain us."

"I'm with you there, sir," said Jack Proctor. The gig dipped sharply and banked a turn as it slowed in its descent. "Feels like we've arrived," said Jack. "Brace yourselves for a rough landing, boys. This one will rattle your teeth out." Jack's laughter rang out, and the others couldn't decide whether he was joking or serious, so they hunched into their seats and hoped for the best.

Harry gripped the armrests of his chair, suddenly very conscious of how helpless he was and how much he had come to take for granted his constant connection to the ship's AI and even the gig's less sophisticated system.

As the ground rushed toward them, they held their collective breath, bracing for the worst, but the little ship steadied, and the autopilot brought her down gently on a large platform of rock.

"Well, that was better than I expected," Jack said, throwing off his harness and shooting them a grin as he climbed out of the pilot's seat. "Now let's see if we can get you out of that bucket helmet, Mr. Vader, sir."

"Luke, I am your father," Mike Dorfling intoned, and Harry was utterly befuddled when his companions released their tension with a loud guffaw of laughter.

Jack Proctor explained. "It's from an old science fiction movie called *Star Wars*, sir, from the 1970s. You look like Darth Vader in that thing, but it's actually kind of cool!"

"No, it is not cool," snapped Harry, not enjoying being the butt of a joke, even a good-natured one. "It's infernally hot in this helmet, and I would be much obliged if you fellows stopped chuckling and freed me of this contraption!"

"Yes sir, we'll be on it right away, sir," said Jack. "Sorry, just trying to make light of the situation."

Before Harry could reply, the gig announced, "Warning. Self destruction sequence has begun. Self destruction will occur in ten minutes." A warning light began to flash over the boarding door. "Please exit immediately. All passengers must be a minimum of 500 metres from this vessel when self destruction occurs."

"Bastards," Mike snapped. "They don't mean us to use the gig or anything in it to save ourselves."

"So it seems." Harry thought quickly and started rummaging through the emergency locker. "Grab the survival dome pack, Mr. Dorfling. Coxswain, grab the ration packs." He heaved a small replicator and distillation unit from their positions. "Come on, lads, we've very little time. Let's go! Jack, choose a direction that may lead us to some shelter. I cannot see well enough to lead in this bucket helmet as you called it."

Jack stifled a chuckle at Harry's grousing and said, "This way then, sir. There's an outcrop in this direction that may shield us a little if we're still too close to the gig when it goes kaboom. Got that pack, Mike? Let's go then." He gripped Harry's elbow. "Watch your footing, sir. Bloody hell, it's hot here."

The trio half ran, half scrambled through what proved to be a mix of loose shale and sand, and low-growing vegetation of some sort that was tough and wiry, and would've torn their shins to ribbons had they not been wearing sturdy boots. The heat hammered down from the overhead suns, and struck upward from the ground beneath their feet as they struggled to get beyond the likely blast range of the gig explosion. It was hard going with their burdens on the uneven terrain, and they were still within the 500-metre zone when they reached the outcrop. The land dipped sharply on the other side of the rock upthrust, and there was a depression and shallow cave behind it.

"In here, sir. Mike, get in and get down. We've only a few seconds."

With hurried care, Harry placed the two appliances he was carrying on the ground then flattened himself into the shallow depression as Jack and Mike did the same on each side of him. The ground trembled. Then, with a roar, the shockwave blasted over and past them. Rock, dust and loose shards from the outcrop showered around them followed by a roiling cloud of dust and a wave of hot gas.

When everything settled, Harry eased himself to a sitting position then stood and scrambled up the side of the outcrop. Above them towered a column of smoke crowned by a flattening and spreading mushroom head. His lips drew into a thin line inside the helmet even as he noted that the wind was carrying the cloud away from them. "Very well, Senator," he murmured. "Should I survive, you and those who support you will pay for this. By heaven, though it imperil my soul, I shall repay you." He turned as the others joined him. "It would seem we will have to make shift with what we salvaged and what we can find here, fellows. At least we may be certain of one thing: if there are any other inhabitants of this godforsaken place, they will see that great cloud and come to investigate it. Let us take stock of what we have and decide how to continue."

Kali smiled as she listened to the report from her lead daemon—the title the assistants and members of an assassin's team used. "So Heron should be where we can collect him and his crew later for some sport?"

"Yes. I convinced the Senator they'd die a slow and unpleasant death there."

"Good. I'm assuming they have enough to keep them alive until we can retrieve them, is that correct?"

"Of course. It will be a good test of their abilities. If they succeed unaided until we retrieve them, they will have proved themselves truly worthy prey and give us considerable pleasure in the hunt."

"Excellent. I call dibs on Heron. I'm just the right hunter for a man of his stamina, and he's the perfect prey."

Her sly grin betrayed her thoughts, and the man said, "Well, I wouldn't know about that..."

"Anyway," she deflected, "if they fail, there will be others." Kali paused. "Where is the Senator now?"

"When we learned that the Fleet intensified their search for the *Voyager*, she transferred to the yacht owned by Al-Khalifa Financial Group. Her associates in the Senate are promoting the idea she's been kidnapped." The daemon laughed. "They planted an amusing conspiracy idea with one of their more gullible contacts that she might have been illegally arrested and 'disappeared' by no less than Fleet Security itself. It went viral within hours."

Kali smiled. The Al-Khalifa yacht? That meant Zorvan must know of it, and of the Senator's folly in becoming directly involved in the attempt to seize the patrol ship. "Very good. You are, I hope, close to the Senator?"

"Of course, Kali. We will keep her safe."

Kali laughed. "Do so, but I suspect her usefulness is almost at an end."

The destruction of the gig deprived them of anything that could be used as a tool. Between them they had no weapons of any sort, and the ration packs would sustain them for several weeks, longer if they could find a way to supplement them, but after that, they would have to survive by their wits alone.

"Without the right sort of tool, sir, there's no way I can get this damned thing off you." Jack had spent the last ten minutes trying to prise open the locks that clamped the helmet in place. "It's metal—probably a titanium alloy by the looks of it—so I can't break the damned thing apart either."

"I suspected as much." Harry hesitated. "With it on, I cannot eat normally, but if you can fashion a tube, I can at least drink."

"I'll sort that out right away, sir."

"Thank you. We must still determine whether there is any water here, and shelter of course, since it is likely the nights will be cold in this arid climate." He looked at the depression they were in. "This could have been formed by water, but is more likely to be the result of wind." He considered their options. "We will spend tonight here and decide how to go on once we can take stock."

"Right you are, sir. Come on, Mike, let's get that shelter rigged up."

Harry left the men to it and clambered out of the hollow to scan the area where the detonation of the gig had not only destroyed the small launch but had formed a crater and left a swathe of devastation around it. Clearly, they had been lucky. He tried to use the vision enhancing visor Jack Proctor had grabbed as they abandoned the gig, but gave up in frustration when he couldn't see sufficiently into the viewer, and found that the helmet was emitting some signal that interfered with the electronics of it anyway. The nearer sun was low on the horizon, and the shadows were lengthening as he scanned the landscape in all directions from the top of the outcrop.

A movement in the extreme distance caught his eye, but he couldn't make it out. "Mr. Proctor, can you spare a moment? I need your eyes. I can't use the viewing visor wearing this infernal helmet."

Jack scrambled up beside him and took the instrument. Slipping it over his head, he adjusted the focus. "Where do you want me to look, sir?"

"Starboard, about thirty degrees from your present heading. There's something moving in that sector."

Jack turned carefully. "No, nothing—wait, I see it. Some kind of animal, sir, a big one. Bloody hell!" The exclamation was accompanied by a sharp intake of breath. "Shit...sorry, sir. Something just attacked whatever it was. Seemed to come from below it though. Now it's just laying there." His eyes widened in horror. "No f*cking way. Oh, my God, it's like a huge scorpion, and now it's dragging the other animal behind it!"

Harry turned and looked at him. "So there are animals on this godforsaken world, which means there must be water and something to eat. If we can find the water, and it is drinkable, we can survive a little longer. Come on, Jack, let us get that shelter up and see if you can find something through which I may drink—or better, get this damned head prison off." Harry led the way down to where Mike Dorfling waited beside the shelter dome. If what Jack had witnessed was a predator—and there could be no doubt of that—any attempt to move from this place would be perilous indeed. Yet he could not see any other option open to them. They had to move to find water, and that meant traveling across this wasteland.

He gripped his fists so that the nails dug into his palms. He would survive, and so would these lads. The Senator and the rest of her vile traitors would face justice if it took the last breath in his body.

Admiral Petrocova looked up as her door slid aside. "Welcome, Commander O'Connor, please take a seat. We'll be joining the *Lagan* and her escort within hours. I think you know what I need you to do on her."

Ferghal seated himself and nodded. "Aye, ma'am, I think so. *Lagan* trusts me, but she's unhappy about losing Harry—Commander Heron—and doesn't like Lieutenant MacKenzie-Banks."

She grimaced. "Admiral Le Jeune isn't sure of him either. Banks seems to have some very odd friends and a few very shady contacts. Well, he's not my problem now." She picked up a tablet and pushed it across the desk. "We've had something of a break.

We traced the *Harmony Voyager*, but we lost her again when the task group sent to retake her and bring her home were surprised by a Charonian force." She got up and paced. "Damned nuisance. Unless we can capture her and examine her navigation data, we have no idea where they jettisoned Commander Heron and his gig crew."

Ferghal looked shocked. "Do not say so! If we cannot find them soon, they have no hope of survival. Is it not already two weeks since they were set adrift?" He was on his feet. "Have they not searched all the possible planets where we know the *Voyager* dropped out?"

She shot him a look of frustration. "We have, and a couple of possible alternatives on speculation, but so far ... nothing." She threw her arms in the air. "Nada, not a damned thing. We're even trying to analyse the beacon signals—did you know about them? No one else did until *Hermes* told you and you passed on that information."

Harry and his party were still alive, largely thanks to two things. First, someone had tripled the rations normally carried in the gig's emergency supply pack, and second, they'd found shelters cut into rock outcrops that were obviously the work of humans.

"This was made with some heavy machines, sir," Jack Proctor commented. "The finishes on these walls and the precision is too fine to be done by hand."

"If you're right, Jack, let's hope whoever it was is still around, and when we find them, they're amenable to welcoming us to their world." Harry tried to make the helmet more comfortable, but the sweat and grit were chaffing at his neck, and the thing trapped the heat around his head. "I just hope they've got something that will get this damned thing off me!"

Mike Dorfling returned, having explored a passage that linked to several more chambers. "There's a fair size tank through here, sir, if you want to try getting some water under it."

"Good idea." Harry laughed. "It might even cause the thing to dissolve."

The water didn't dissolve the helmet, nor did it disable the electronics, as Harry had hoped, but it did afford him some relief. All of the shelters—Harry could not think of them as more than simple lodges for passing nomads—were obviously long abandoned.

Tracks in some and around others suggested they were frequented by the planet's rather unpleasant and aggressive creatures.

So, reluctantly, they kept moving, by Harry's estimate about ten miles each day. If they were lucky, they found one of the rock cut shelters, and if not, they had to use the survival dome. They took care to avoid animals while trying to find water and anything that might indicate other inhabitants. It was hard going, as they had to take shelter during the hottest part of the mercifully short day, and they daren't move at night. The twin suns were always low on the horizon, suggesting they were somewhere in the higher latitudes of this place, and the shortness of the days suggested a higher than usual rate of rotation for the planet. He'd based the direction of travel on a glimpse of what had looked like a lake or a small sea as they passed over it during their descent, but he wasn't at all sure he had the direction right. Now they were aiming for a prominent mesa that appeared to have the sort of dwellings certain ancient peoples on Earth had built into cliff faces.

"The replicator's a goner, sir." Mike kicked the thing. "Power pack's dead. It least the water refiner still works."

"Pity. Well, no point carrying it any further then. Strip anything we can use from it, and we'll leave it here."

"We're still not sure of direction, sir." Jack offered Harry a flask of soup he'd concocted and guided the tube toward the small mouth opening in the helmet. "At least we know we're not going in circles." With his free hand, he gestured around them. "Now that we've found this ridge to follow, we can keep clear of those giant man-eating scorpions."

They'd had a narrow escape when they came upon a large herbivore grazing on the leathery plant life. It had rushed blindly away and blundered into one of the predators. They'd at least managed to get a good look at that creature. The brute stood on four short legs not unlike those of a lizard. The body was wide and flattened, with an armoured carapace, the head large, the gaping maw of the mouth armed with vicious teeth, but the tail was like a massive whip, and armed at its tip with a poisonous spur it used to immobilise its prey.

Harry nodded. "At least we know what to watch for now. The beast lurks on the plains and among these plants. Up here on the rock, it should be more visible." He sucked listlessly on the tube.

The soup was tasteless, and he'd had enough of it now to last a lifetime.

Something his mother used to say popped into his mind: "Your stomach won't complain."

Let's hope not, he countered in his thoughts.

What a sorry state to be in. He had no idea where they were or where they were going. He only knew that they must find somewhere safe to shelter with a water supply they could rely on. Food was another matter. Without the replicator there was no way of converting what they could find into something they could digest. Without any weapons, they had no means of defence against anything that attacked them.

Mike Dorfling eased himself down and removed his boots, a slow and painful process. "These won't last much longer, and my feet are a mess as it is." He grimaced as he examined his sore and bruised feet. "Think the Fleet will find us, sir?"

Harry hesitated. "I should think so, but they'll have to find the *Voyager* first."

"That could take a while," Jack interjected. "I hate to be negative, sir, but we're low on everything, and I'm damned if I can see us getting off this rock." He stood and walked a little distance away.

"That's true, but I prefer to remain positive." Harry handed the flask he'd now emptied to Jack. "Thank you for your efforts to feed me, Mr. Proctor. I fear I shall not be able to enjoy soup for a long time once I am free of this infernal helmet."

Jack laughed. "I'm better at keeping the coms units going than at cooking, sir. I'll see if I can improve the taste."

"The taste is as good as can be expected," Harry countered, "but if Mary ever says she's making soup for supper, I shall run for the hills!"

Their laughter rang out in the barren desert.

"Niamh, I'm so worried," said Mary. "There've been no messages from Harry, and if I know him as well as I think I do, that's usually not a good sign. What is going on?" Mary's voice betrayed her concern.

"I feel your pain, Mary dear, truly I do. Something momentous is happening, but neither James nor Theo will tell me anything. It makes me so angry, and it frightens me a little if I'm honest."

"There are all sorts of rumours flying about, and I have the most awful feeling that Harry is in danger." Mary sniffed back tears. "He's missed four of our regular link calls, and now I can't even contact his ship because the *Lagan* has been placed under a coms blackout, not a good sign."

"Is that so?" Niamh frowned, the flame in her hair spreading to her cheeks as her anger rose. "Right. That does it. Theo or James are going to tell me what is going on or there will be hell to pay." A thought occurred to her. "Now that you mention it, Ferghal was moved to a new assignment without notice three weeks ago—and he isn't taking any link calls either." Her eyes flashed. "Leave it with me."

"Thank you. I just know Harry is in trouble. I can feel it."

Niamh hedged. "Well, there are a number of things happening here at home that may be connected, my dear. Have you watched the news lately? There was a report of a cruise liner overtaken by pirates with Senator Samland on board. That damned woman is always involved when something dirty is going on, but no one can ever prove anything because her goons do all her dirty work for her. I wonder if she's involved in this. Theo will know."

Niamh brightened with an effort. "Now, tell me how your tour is going."

Mary attempted a wan smile. "My tour? It was going well, but now I'm having trouble keeping my concentration. I made a few small mistakes in the prime piece of my last recital. The critics weren't kind." She made a face and tried to laugh it off. "I guess I'll have to put more effort into practice and try to focus on the music at the next performance." She wasn't quite ready for small talk yet, and the subject of the previous topic nagged at her. "You mentioned Senator Samland. She's here on Helles. I saw her stepping into a hotel as I was being driven to mine. I'm sure it was her—an imposing woman with a very striking face. I've met her a couple of times."

Niamh was suddenly very alert. "You're sure it was her? Do you remember which hotel?"

"I'm pretty sure it was her I saw striding into the Helles Olympus Hotel as if she owned the place, very upmarket. I've stayed there before, but it's far too busy for my liking. I prefer somewhere quieter when I'm touring."

Niamh smiled. "Of course. Now dear, I must go. Try not to worry. I'll get to the bottom of this, and I'll be in touch as soon as I do."

"We've had word that Security have arrested the Senator." Valerie Petrocova smiled as she looked at Ferghal. "She's on Helles, and won't be leaving in any hurry, nor will any of her entourage." She placed her elbows on the desk and fiddled with her tablet. "That's the good news. The bad news is we still don't know where they marooned Harry." Her frown deepened. "We do know he was landed on a planet which is mainly desert, and that he'd been fitted with some device that prevents him interacting with any computer network, AI or otherwise. What we don't know is where he is!" Her hand slapped the table. "None of her people know, and that damned woman left the choice to the pirates, and they are engaged elsewhere with the Charonians and the *Voyager*."

"That explains why *Lagan* lost touch with Harry," Ferghal mused. "The device, I mean. If they still have the gig, they will be able to keep going for longer than most."

"They don't have the gig." The Admiral's anger showed. "Apparently it was programmed to self-destruct ten minutes after landing. The Senator seemed to think she'd been quite clever doing that." She pushed her chair back and began to pace. "Give me five minutes in a room alone with her and she'll regret ever having been born."

Chapter 13

Attempted Coup

"Captain Greenacre, you know why you've been relieved of your command. The charges against you are extremely serious." The Advocate Commodore tapped the tablet. "Of course, if you cooperate, that will be taken into account."

The Captain stared at the Commodore. "I've nothing to say, sir."

"That is your choice, of course." The legal officer signalled the Captain assigned to defend the accused. "However, the law requires that I provide you and your defender with the evidence we will be using in the prosecution. I'd suggest you consider it carefully before you decide whether to offer anything in your defence. As you know, you will not be permitted to introduce anything at the trial that you could have revealed now."

The defender looked at the man beside him, then at the Commodore. "Perhaps I could have a private word with Captain Greenacre, sir."

The Commodore rose. "Very well. I'll give you five minutes." He strode to the door, and as he approached, it slid open to reveal an armed officer and three other men.

"We've come to release Captain Greenacre, Commodore. Let's keep this civil. You too, Captain. Both of you, against the bulkhead, please. Captain Greenacre, we're taking over the ship. The lads will escort you to the Command Centre once we've secured these gentlemen."

The Commodore glanced from Captain Greenacre to the officer holding the weapon then back again. "Captain Greenacre, do you really wish to add treason and mutiny to the charge sheet? I think you should consider your position very carefully."

The Captain sneered. "Take your charge sheet and stuff it. My officers and I have had enough of being shafted by the likes of you. You'll discover soon enough that we're already in position, and the revolution has started. We're taking this ship and others, and we have our own plans. You lot got lucky once, but you won't get lucky twice. We wanted Heron's ship as a decoy. We missed the chance, but we won't miss the second time."

Weapons discharges sounded in the distance, but with increasing proximity. "Sorry, sir. The Bootnecks have woken up— we'll have to go." The Lieutenant signalled the men at the door. "Form up. We're moving. Commodore, Captain, your comlinks please. Now!"

The Commodore unclipped his link and tossed it to Captain Greenacre in a gesture of contempt rather than handing it to him as he would've done to someone he respected. The Advocate Captain handed his over without a word then deliberately turned away and took a seat next to his superior. Captain Greenacre snorted and strode from the cabin; the Lieutenant followed, backing out, his eyes darting back and forth, and his weapon trained on the two captives as if they were dangerous fugitives. The fact that he made himself look comically ridiculous with his needless drama seemed utterly lost on him.

The door slid shut, and a weapons discharge secured it.

"The rot runs far deeper than we thought," the Commodore remarked. He fished in his pocket and produced a comlink. "It doubles as a recorder, but we should be able to establish what is happening while we wait." He waved to the tray of refreshments delivered earlier. "Seems a pity to waste those. Care for a cup of tea? I'm sure it's at least passable."

"Admiral, we've a mutiny on our hands." The Flag Lieutenant's anger showed. "It seems some of the ship's officers are part of this coup attempt. The latest report is they've freed Captain Greenacre and are holding the Command Centre, the Weapons Centre and the forward citadel."

"Have they got control of Engineering?"

"No, they tried to take it, but Commander Giorgi got wind of it and shot the ringleader as soon as he made his move. It got messy, but he's cut off control from the Command Centre."

The Admiral nodded. "How many of the crew have joined them?"

"About a third of the people, ma'am. The duty staff fought off an attempt to take the Flag Control Centre, and now we have the Marines in position as well."

The Admiral was on her feet. She opened her desk and retrieved her weapons then clipped the holster to her belt. "Very well, rustle up some armour for us. I'll not have my flagship taken over by a worthless bunch of mutineers and pirates no matter what their damned cause!" She marched to the door. "Meet me in Flag Command."

The Flag Lieutenant smiled. "Yes, ma'am. I'll come with you. I took the liberty of having some armour sent up for us as soon as this broke."

"Well done, Flags." The Admiral smiled. "Who did Giorgi shoot? Greenacre by any chance?"

"No, two of his Engineering people, Lieutenant-Commander Wallace and Lieutenant Groenewald. Wallace tried to jump the Commander from behind. He hit him with something, and that made Giorgi mad as hell. As I said, it got very messy, and I don't think any of the mutineers are in a state to complain about it. There's some damage to the Engineering Control Centre, but Giorgi says it's not critical."

"Hmph." The Admiral glanced around the compartment as she pulled on the protective armour. "Well done, all of you. Now we clean house. I'll need volunteers to come with me, but I also need some of you to stay here and keep things running." A number of men and women stepped forward. "Right, see Flags and get rigged. I want every station manned, though." She turned to the coms desk. "Any other ships having trouble?"

"Three, ma'am. Two report the attempted mutiny has been suppressed, and the third is still fighting."

"Right, get my displays up and running. Direct the nearest ship to the one in trouble to send Marines to help." She paused. "You said they had control of the Weapons Direction Centre?"

"Yes, ma'am."

"Lock down all weapons. Countermand any attempt to use them." She turned again. "Coms, get me the Marines' Commanding Officer on the link."

"Major Hertz on link, ma'am."

"Major, report please."

"Admiral, we have the after part of the ship secure now, the Command Centre is still in their hands, and so is Weapons Direction. I have men working their way forward on the outer hull and others guarding the service tubes and spaces."

"Where are you?"

"Compartment Alpha Sub Delta, Deck Sub 2, at Frame 125. I've set up a forward command post here."

"I'm coming to join you. Where is Colonel Winter?"

"Dead, ma'am. One of the traitors shot him in the Wardroom." There was a pause. "In the face when he tried to grab a weapon from one of them."

"Thank you." Her expression was grim. *One more score to settle.* "I'll be with you in five minutes." She cut the link. "Ready, Flags?" She looked at the others. "Let's go."

"James, at last. I've been trying to reach you for ages."

"Niamh, sorry, things are a bit hectic at the moment. What's the problem? Has something happened to Theo?"

"Theo's fine." Niamh hesitated. The news reports were confusing and full of nonsense about attempts to storm the Confederation Parliament and other government buildings, and of fighting in several capitals. There were even reports of certain well-connected political figures leading the mobs. She could see her brother was looking tense, and she didn't recognise the background of his current location in the holo-image. "Where the devil are you? Not on your usual ship—I can see that."

"Good to hear that Theo is well, and yes, you're very observant, as always. I'm not in my usual HQ. I'm en route to join my new flagship. Sorry, there wasn't time to contact you and tell you about it. Now, I haven't long, so what can I do for you today?"

Niamh bridled. "You can start by telling me where Harry is, and what the devil is going on! Mary and I are worried sick, and I've just learned that Ferghal has gone into deep space on the staff of your current Chief of Security."

Admiral Heron rubbed his eyes with finger and thumb. "Niamh, I'm sorry, I can't answer either of your questions. Our coms are compromised, including these personal links, so there is absolutely no way I can say anything in reply. I'm sorry. You'd best ask Theo as soon as you can see him in person if he's not at home. Whatever you do, don't discuss anything on link."

"What? The link system is compromised? By whom? James, what the blazes is going on?"

"I'm sorry, Niamh, I really do have to go. Talk to Theo—he can tell you some of it. All I can say is that it's potentially bigger than the Consortium problem."

Niamh recognised the signals; she knew her brother well. James simply would not say what he knew she wanted to hear, and he would not compromise. "I'll talk to Theo when he gets back. Take care of our boys, will you?"

"I'll do my best, my dear. Tell Mary we're doing our best to look out for Harry."

The hologram vanished. What had James meant when he said they were doing their best to 'look out' for Harry? Niamh considered this while making a cup of tea, to the frustration of her android butler who found this confusing—especially when she informed him that doing this menial task helped her think. Surely if James knew where Harry was, and knew what, if anything, had happened to him, he'd say 'look after' him, but instead, he said he would 'look out' for Harry.

They don't know where Harry is, she mused, *and if they do, they don't know what has happened to him.*

But then, why would that necessitate the mobilisation of the entire High Command of the Fleet? And what was keeping Theo in Dublin?

She made up her mind. A little expedition to Dublin was called for. Theo would not be able to fob her off. She smiled. For one thing, he didn't have a ship or a fleet to hide behind, and for another, he was her husband, not her brother! To the android butler she said, "Order a transport car for me, to the house in Dublin. You'd better let them know I'm coming." She had a sudden thought. "Wait, that's not a good idea. We never know who might intercept it. Just get the transport for me. I'll program it myself for the destination."

Admiral Le Jeune joined Major Hertz. "Update me, Major."

The Major pulled out the ship's damage control plans. "We've cleared the mutineers from everywhere aft of this bulkhead. We've teams penetrating on Deck Sub 5 and Zero 3. I've more teams working in through these service tubes." He held her eye. "I've had to give orders to the scout teams to shoot on sight."

She nodded. "Necessary under the circumstances. Three more ships have had attempts on them, two have managed to suppress the problem, one was still fighting—and there's us, of course."

"Bastards." The major straightened and listened to his link. "Good." He gave additional orders then sent a team down the same service tube. "Team Bravo 4 has penetrated to the forward battery deck. They've taken out the men they found there, and I've sent in a backup team. They report finding demolition charges being laid." He listened again. "Good work." He met the Admiral's eye. "My external assault team have managed to open the hull here." He indicated a position adjacent to the main deck where a cross gangway connected several accommodation compartments, the main longitudinal gangway and the broadside passages that ran the length of the ship, known colloquially as 'the Burma Roads' for reasons no one knew. "With your permission, we'll create a small hull breach here." He indicated a second point further forward. "They'll have to evacuate these compartments, and the only way they can go is this way, where my lads are all set and waiting for them."

The Admiral frowned. "That will affect the Weapons Director Centre." She traced the damage control bulkheads. "It'll also mean a loss of atmosphere on all decks in that section. Okay. Do it. I'll make a broadcast to the rest of them."

"Yes, ma'am." He spoke to his link, and seconds later there was a shudder through the hull. "That'll get their attention."

She smiled. "I should think so. By the way, are there any prisoners from the areas you've cleared?"

"Yes, ma'am. We disarmed them and shut them in the landing dock, port side. Lieutenant Sinclair is guarding them. He was wounded clearing the Engineering Section, and he's mad as hell about it. They believe him when he says he'll open the landing bay doors if they make one wrong move." He laughed. "I don't think he would, but I wouldn't blame him if he did." He listened to his link again. "We have the Weapons Director. They were trying to booby trap it."

The Admiral nodded. "Very well. I think it's time for my broadcast." She touched her link. "Captain Greenacre, your mutiny has failed, we are now in the process of denying your people access to any compartments of importance. If you order them to cease resistance now, I will consider that in your favour. If you persist in resisting, you will leave me no choice but to hunt down every one of your mutineers, and they will all be prosecuted with the full force of the law with no mitigation. I await your answer. You have two minutes." She switched her link to standby.

The Major looked up from his plans. "We have them bottled up now in this section, Admiral. They've tried to get into the service tubes, but my lads are in them and denying access. I've a team in place to cut their way into the Command Centre if we have to, and the Advocate Commodore and his Captain have been released and taken to the Flag Command Centre." He smiled. "I think we're almost done here."

Jack Proctor froze in his tracks. "Don't move," he hissed. "One of those giant scorpion things is watching us."

Harry didn't move, and behind him, Mike Dorfling sank to his knees. The last three days had been very hard. Their rations and water were almost depleted. Despite the heat, Harry felt cold. His vision was blurred, mainly due to salt from the sweat drying round his eyes. He had no means of wiping them or clearing the muck that accumulated inside the mask. His skin felt dry, though earlier he'd been sweating profusely. His head itched infuriatingly, but he couldn't relieve that either. His lips were cracked, his mouth was parched, and his tongue felt like it was coated with dry sand.

"Where?" he croaked, unable to see the scorpion that Jack had spotted.

"About thirty metres ahead, sir. It's got itself into a sort of crevasse. I only saw it when it turned its head this way. Now it's just sitting there watching us." Jack hesitated. "If we keep still, it may not see us."

Harry was feeling faint. "Need some shade," he mumbled. "Must get out of the sun."

Niamh looked up from her tablet as Theo entered. On the journey to Dublin, and since her arrival, she'd been busy, and now she knew at least as much about what was happening in various capitals as could be expected from the confused and sometimes contradictory news reports. It had been a shock to discover their home in the Irish capital was under tight security, as was their house at Scrabo.

"Have you eaten?" she asked her husband. "I told Herbert 2.0 to keep dinner until you came home."

Theo started in surprise, not expecting to see her there. "Well, aren't you a sight for sore eyes, my dear. Why didn't you let me know you were coming? I'd have been home much sooner." He kissed her. "No, I haven't eaten, and I'm famished. I need a good meal and a nice glass of wine to wash it down. Shall we?"

Putting aside her reading, she rose. "Yes. Then you can tell me what is happening, and why we have all these spooks here, as James calls them, and at Scrabo. He hinted our communication systems are compromised, and I can understand why." She took his hand. "Don't look so surprised, my dear, I know all the signs by now. Something is very, very wrong—but it isn't in the news or on the media, which is why I'm really worried." She took her seat at the dining table and waited while the android butler served the meal.

When they were alone again, Theo said, "You've obviously realised there's something nasty come to a head. What did James say?"

"Not a great deal." She frowned. "You know him. He's a man of few words at the best of times. He said the communications systems were compromised and he couldn't talk to me on link. Then he suggested our private communications were also compromised, and all I hear on the news channels is reports of attempts to seize control of government buildings all over the place. What worries me is what he said when I asked about Harry. He told me they were 'looking out' for him, not that they were 'looking after' him. Then he added that what was happening was worse than the Consortium troubles."

Theo sipped his wine. "He's right on that score. We won't be able to keep the lid on this much longer. The fact is, my dear, around forty of our esteemed Senators, and probably about a hundred of our Members of the Lower Chamber, supported by some very wealthy individuals and families, are involved in what can only be called treason. Three of those involved are active members on the Fleet Council." He sipped his wine again. "We're compromised on every side. It would be bad enough if it were just humans involved, but it isn't. These fools have, through the likes of the LPSL and the pirate operators, done a deal with an alien race we are now learning are not far removed from the Niburu in terms of intentions and morality." He paused to savour a few bites of food. "At least the attempts to overthrow the Confederation Government and the World Treaty Council have failed. A number of the leading lights of that attempt are now enjoying a taste of their future in custody. Some, unfortunately, are still free, but we'll find them."

Niamh put down her knife and fork. "I see. And precisely where does Harry fit into all this?"

"We don't know. He does seem to have precipitated the exposure of a key player, but now he's vanished. He could still be aboard the liner he was sent to assist, but he might not be." He refilled his glass, his expression sombre. "We know where he isn't, and that is aboard his command. The *Lagan* is under quarantine by Fleet Security in a secure sector. Vice Admiral Petrocova is overseeing the recovery of her memories and data, and Ferghal is with her." He pushed aside his plate. "Not on the news, but there have been mutinies aboard a number of ships in the Fleet." He met her appalled gaze. "Now you know everything I do, and why everyone is in a bit of a state. I'm sorry, I should have told you all this earlier, but I didn't want to do so on link, and there hasn't been an opportunity to go to Scrabo."

"The ship is now secure, ma'am. Captain Greenacre is dead, and so are several of his officers." The Major pushed a tablet across the desk. "I'm pleased to report the bastard that killed my Colonel is among the prisoners. I've put him in separate accommodation under guard, on charges of murder as well as mutiny."

Admiral Le Jeune nodded. "Good. I've asked the Advocate Commodore to examine all the officers involved and draw up the charge sheets. The ship will require dockyard attention to repair the damage we did while recapturing control, so I'll have to shift my flag." She sat up straighter and leaned her arms on her desk. "I've appointed Commander Keane in temporary command of this ship until someone else can be appointed to fill the gap. I find it difficult to believe that almost half the officers joined that fool Greenacre and killed so many of their fellows."

"You were top of their target list. It was just luck your Marine guards were able to prevent them getting to you. Their timing must have been forced, because they made their attempt just as the guard was being relieved."

"So I discovered. Make sure the people involved are mentioned in your report, and I'll endorse it." She paused. "You know we lost the *Lutine*. We're not sure if it was deliberate or an accident, but she blew up. No survivors." She leaned back in her chair, the strain showing in her face. "There will be hell to pay over this. I'll face a Board of Enquiry at least, probably a Court Martial—and we still don't know how many more of their people are tucked in everywhere."

"I have a report from Admiral Petrocova, ma'am." The Flag Lieutenant was at the door. "She reports her charges are all secure." He smiled. "She had a tip-off, and was ready for the attempt on several of her ships. The mutineers will no doubt be wondering what went wrong."

Admiral Le Jeune smiled. "That's good news at least. If I know Valerie, she'll make them wish they'd just taken a walk through the airlock without EVA suits." She hesitated. "Any other reports?"

"Afraid so, ma'am. Four more ships have been lost. We're not sure if they've been destroyed or taken over. One of them is the starship *L'Orient*. Contact has been lost with her Flag Officer as well. The others are the *Kursk*, *Borodino*, and the *Batteleur*. Almost every ship in the Fleet is reporting some kind of takeover attempt or damage due to sabotage. We've learned the Sino-Asian Imperium's ships have had trouble as well, but we've no details."

Harry tried to focus his eyes. He couldn't remember when last he'd taken any liquids, and his feeding container was empty. He swayed as he stood. They were surrounded by an orchard, a fact that truly had saved them from starvation. He reached for a big, juicy fruit that reminded him of an apple, but it was just out of reach, and he collapsed to the ground with a heavy exhale, and lay there splayed out as if he had fallen dead where he stood.

Jack heard the sigh and the thud as Harry dropped, and swore under his breath as the beast swung its ferocious head in their direction. "Don't move, Mike!" He hissed. "Leave him, and for God's sake, don't move!"

"Doing my best, Warrant."

The beast lumbered toward them from its crevasse, the evil tail rising, the stinger claw unsheathing as it did so.

Jack swore again. His gaze took in the creature's thick hide and the heavy carapace, and the manner in which it changed colour to match its background as it stood, fully exposed, its four eyes locked on his. A long, forked tongue flicked out, tasting the air, the dust, the vegetation. The creature moved, and Jack's thoughts raced. Was it preparing to charge or to pounce? His mind screamed to run, to get away, but he forced himself to remain motionless. Distracted by the beast, he didn't register that a huge mechanical monstrosity was approaching from behind.

Time stood still. Man and beast eyed each other. Then the creature moved, and for a beast this large, it moved with a speed that surprised him. Jack dove aside as the creature lunged, and was almost crushed as the thing crashed down on top of him.

Admiral Heron surveyed the prisoners with mixed emotions. Their act of mutiny or rebellion—both equally abhorrent to him—filled him with disgust. That they'd attempted to kill him and his staff was bad enough, but what was unforgivable was that they had killed some of their own comrades in their attempt to seize the ship. His gaze burned across the beaten and miserable collection of traitors herded together in the hangar.

"Separate the officers, the warrant officers, and the TechRates. Place the officers and warrants in solitary confinement; the rates as you see fit. Have the wounded treated, but keep them confined at all times. No one is to be moved without restraints for any reason if they are taken from their places of confinement."

"You can't do this to us, Admiral. It's a breach of our rights." The speaker wore the rank markings of a Captain.

"Your rights, Captain Orsen? Ah, yes. Perhaps I should accord you the same rights that Senator Samland afforded my relative Commander Heron. She had him put into a helmet that suppressed his ability to communicate with his ship's AI. Unfortunately, it also prevents him eating. Then she had him marooned on an unknown planet with nothing but basic survival rations. All we do know about the planet is that it is a desert world in a binary system. About the only thing going for it is that it has a breathable atmosphere." He paused. "He and his men had standard rations for four weeks. That was eight weeks ago." He let that sink in. "You will be fed and cared for, and then you will face justice. You will, in the meantime, enjoy the rights I decide are appropriate for traitors, mutineers and murderers."

With that, he said, "Colonel, you have your orders."

The Marines moved forward, several senior Rates among them carrying devices for restraining the prisoners. The Admiral watched, his expression unreadable as the officers were singled out and placed in restraints, and then he turned on his heel and stalked away accompanied by his staff.

When the airlock closed behind Admiral Heron, Captain Orsen made a renewed protest. "You can't do this. It's against the Regulations."

"So is mutiny!" The Colonel moved fast and stood right in front of the man. "Can't is not in my vocabulary." He moved so his face was inches from the Captain's. "Be grateful our fine Admiral doesn't share my view on what we should do with scum like you. I wanted to eject you all into space." He stepped back. "Same odds Samland gave Commander Heron and his boys."

"You don't understand, Colonel. The Charonians are offering humanity the chance to evolve into something greater, and Senator Samland is promising a new deal—a clean-out of corruption and a new system of government. Those of us who accept their offer will help to build a new deal for everyone—less corruption, less regulation—and some will become the first of an enhanced species."

The Colonel shook his head in derision. "Ah, yes, the good old utopia gimmick. If you believe that, you're the greatest fool in the universe." He glanced at the others. "Have any of you actually met the Charonians? Do you know how they reproduce?" His question met blank stares and head shakes. "No, I didn't think so. That's because they don't. They implant themselves in a host body and take over, adapting it to their physical ideal as they do. As far as we can tell, the hosts remain aware of what is happening, but they are prisoners in their own bodies. Count yourselves lucky that we got you first."

To his NCOs he ordered, "Take these fools away. Put them in the isolation cells. No human access—droid attendants only, and only when supervised by armed escorts." As the Captain made to protest, he snapped, "Don't push me, Orsen. I'm not in the mood, and I don't have the Admiral's sense of justice or his control."

Chapter 14

Out of the Frying Pan

Jack struggled to free himself as the monster writhed, one clawed foot swiping in a swift downward motion just inches from his side. Then, with a great shudder, the thing lay still and pinioned him to the ground. Up close and this personal, it stank. The smell made him want to throw up, it was so rank. He fought it down as he tried to work out what had happened, and then he remembered Harry.

"Commander? Mike? Are you guys okay?"

There was no response. He resumed struggling then stopped abruptly when something cold and metallic touched his neck. "What the...?"

A muffled voice cut him off. "Lie still, you dirty Enviro. Yer way out of your territory here—even the stupidest of you Enviros know not to come here. What're yer lookin' for?"

"What the blazes are you on about? Who the flaming hell are you? Get this damned thing off me!" Jack's patience snapped. He grabbed the contraption and shoved with as much force as he could muster. There was a loud pop, and a metal slug ricochetted off the stone he was laying on, fortunately on a trajectory that took it away from his body.

"Easy there, Jazz." This was a new voice, equally muffled. "These guys don't look like Enviros."

131

"He don't know enough not to try to wrestle a pneumagun away from me," said the man addressed as Jazz. "Near shot hisself."

"You should know better than to poke it into someone," Hunter snapped The newcomer moved into Jack's view. "Who are you, stranger?"

"Warrant Officer Proctor, North European Confederation Fleet, Captain's Coxswain NECS *Lagan*." Jack stared at the two figures and noted their attire. They wore tight trousers that appeared to be made from the hide of a beast like the one that pinned him to the ground, and a heavy jacket of the same material. They each wore a metal helmet that covered the head entirely, from which hoses protruded that connected to a chest harness. They carried what looked like rifles, but a hose from the weapon led to a large metal cylinder worn on the back.

"So the legends are true," said the one called Jazz. "There are other humans around. Where did you come from then? Don't give me any of that big ship in space baloney."

Jack's temper was fraying rapidly. "Legends? We're just people, mate. Of course there are other humans. Other species as well." Jack struggled to get up. "Get me out from under this damned thing, then you can spout all the bullshit you like! Where is my Commander? He needs medical attention pronto—or don't you people do things like that?"

"Keep still. Jazz, get the levers and bring them to me." Hunter, who was obviously the leader, waited until Jazz had moved away. "Now then, Warrant Officer Proctor—what the hell sort of job is a Warrant Officer anyway? Do you go around in your big starship making warrants on all these dried-up rocks in the outer reaches of the sky? I'm so impressed. Must keep you very busy. Guess what, I don't give a shit. I don't believe this blarney about ships and space. I know your type. You're from the other side of this hellhole planet, aren't you? Why don't you stay on your turf? You're in our territory now, and obviously you don't know enough to keep away from the sand dragons. You're lucky we nailed this one with the turret gun when he broke cover." He stopped speaking as an identically clad figure got down next to him and worked a long metal bar under the scorpion carcass to pry it loose.

"Right, we'll have you out of there in a jiff," said the man.

A 'jiff' seemed to be a flexible measure of time in Jack's opinion. It took almost ten minutes to free him, and when he stood, a little wobbly at first, he saw that he was surrounded by a dozen of Hunter's people. Two of them moved forward to seize his arms and tie his wrists behind him while two men held their long rifle weapons to his chest and watched his every move.

Jack was hustled down the slope to a vehicle from which protruded a tall funnel that billowed smoke. Steam issued from somewhere near the funnel, and a turret structure on the top carried some sort of fixed weapon with a long barrel. Shutters around the armoured body of the thing could evidently be opened, presumably to reveal more weapons.

The two men led Jack to the rear of the vehicle and up a ramp, then handed him over to a man waiting inside.

"Put him with the other two," said Hunter. After that, Jack was hustled away, and had no further chance to speak to the leader.

"Hunter, I can't get this helmet off'n this 'un. Never seen nuffink like it." The speaker tapped Harry's encased head with something metallic. "He's outta it anyways."

"He's suffering from dehydration," said Jack in a droll tone.

"Shut it, mate." The leader pushed Jack with his weapon. "Pix, leave the helmet. The Mechanist can deal with it when we get home. Pour some water on him. That'll get him right." He watched as the younger man did as he ordered, then they both left without another word.

From the noises and sounds coming from outside the vehicle, the other men were loading something into other compartments. Jack was relieved when Harry stirred, groaned, then passed out again. At least his breathing was a little less laboured.

Jack wondered whether he should demand their captors do something for the Commander, but decided there was no point. Mike seemed to be a bit dazed, and a bruise on his forehead suggested he'd taken a blow; at any rate, he wasn't responding to questions or his surroundings.

Jack listened as the sounds outside changed and orders were given.

Before long, the rest of the men joined them. Most of them stank of blood and the rank smell of offal from the creature. Piling in around Jack and Harry, the crew moved their prisoners onto seats of a sort, then strapped them in before taking seats themselves. "All set back there?" The voice came from a bell-mouthed tube in the bulkhead.

"Set, Gord. Go."

From somewhere in front of them, there was a long drawn-out hiss followed by the sound of machinery in motion. The vehicle lurched then gathered speed, but it was a rocking, swaying, lunging motion, as if the thing was on legs and not wheels. It wasn't unpleasant, but in the close confines of the metal cabin surrounded by men reeking of heaven knew what, Jack's stomach rebelled, then Mike's followed suit, and both men went pale as waves of nausea roiled within them.

The men laughed. "Kin see they's never ridden a walker before." One of the men retrieved a couple of buckets and deposited them on the two mens' laps. "There ya go. Ya get used to it."

"Thanks." Jack hoped his sarcasm was coming through. "But we've naff all to chuck anyways. Haven't eaten for five days, and not a lot to drink either."

There was a moment of silence, then one of the masked figures asked, "What? Whadaya mean yer've not eaten fer five days? Where t' hell you frum anyways? Don't look like Enviros."

"I don't know who these Enviros are. We're from the Fleet. This is Commander Heron—our Captain. We were marooned here by some damned pirates that I can't wait to get my hands on...."

"Haven't heard of any tribe called pirates, mate, nor of this Fleet you mention. That your tribe then? Are you from one of those wild ones out in the plateau country?"

Jack looked at them like they were either demented or the most uneducated fools he'd ever encountered. "The Fleet is not a tribe. What are you anyway? Don't you know anything? You sound human, but in those outfits, you don't look it."

"Us? Yeah, we're human, mate. An' these outfits are survival gear. Wouldn't live long walking round like you're dressed, or unarmed. Reckon you were sand dragon bait when we saw you."

"Is that what you call these creatures—sand dragons?"

"Never heard them called aught else."

"Don't they attack you or your vehicles?"

"Nah, they've learned to avoid the walkers, so we have to get a bit crafty hunting them." He paused as a voice called down the speaking tube.

Jack couldn't make out what was said, but the men around him were already readying their pneumatic rifles and taking positions next to the ports that had opened. The swaying seemed to increase as the vehicle changed direction, and the sounds of machinery became louder.

A tremendous report from ahead and above was followed by the stench of acrid smoke, and a memory came flooding back; it reminded Jack of fireworks, something he hadn't witnessed on Earth for many years. There was another change of direction, and shortly after another loud bang. Seconds later a tremendous clang and shudder suggested something had hit the outer hull.

"What's happening?" Harry's voice was weak.

Mike spoke up first. "We're prisoners inside some kind of vehicle, sir, and I think we're under attack." He managed to give Harry some water, spilling a fair amount due to the motion. "You've missed a lot while you've been out of it, sir."

Harry considered this. "The last thing I remember was reaching for a fruit, then everything went dark." He tried to move and couldn't. "I suppose that explains why I'm tied up." He paused. "And I'm wet. Did we find water?"

"No, sir." Another loud bang and the acrid smell permeated the space.

"Oh, we're in action, are we?" Harry hesitated. "I hope these Frenchmen have us in the orlop—we'll be like to be struck by a ball or the splinters otherwise."

Jack realised Harry wasn't in touch with reality. He wasn't sure what this talk of Frenchmen and orlop was all about, but given the Commander was technically 426 years old, it must be something from his service in sailing ships during the Napoleonic Wars. *Come to think of it*, Jack mused, *this vehicle does rock and sway like a wooden ship on the ocean.* But all he said was, "I think we're in the orlop, sir," hoping this would appease Harry. He also secretly hoped that Harry's confusion wasn't a sign of permanent neurological damage.

Around him the crew were resuming their seats and the shutters were closing over the ports, so whatever had caused the excitement had passed.

"Another of those sand dragons?" he asked the talkative man.

"Nah. Raider, but we crippled them. A patrol'll sort 'em out now. Gord sent up a flare, and a heliograph passed the message."

The vehicle was climbing now, the incline getting steeper and the pace slowing perceptibly as it did so. Then, judging by the change of sounds and the intensity of the noise, they entered a tunnel. When the vehicle stopped, the crew dismounted, and a few minutes later, a new group took their place. Judging from their outfits, they were soldiers. They set to work unstrapping Jack, Mike and Harry, then they blindfolded them and marched them down the ramp—at least, they prodded Jack and Mike along. Harry fainted as soon as he stood, and had to be carried.

"The mutiny has failed, but it all comes back to the same thing. The majority of those who took part believe they were acting in support of a movement that would benefit humanity—at least that's amongst the officers involved." The Advocate-Admiral shrugged. "The Rates and Warrants who followed them did so in the belief they were standing for a new order in government, with greater representation in national and supra-national parliaments, and, of course, a more equitable share of the wealth."

James Heron nodded. The holograms of his fellow admirals and the C-in-C formed a semi-circle in his conference room. "I can believe and understand that, for the Rates at least." He paused. "But, knowing who is behind it, and what their motives are…"

"Quite." Admiral Le Jeune glared at a list of names they could all see in the holographic projection. "This came from the *Lagan*? And she got it from Commander Heron? Where did he get it?"

The Advocate-Admiral replied. "According to the *Lagan*, the AI on the *Harmony Voyager* downloaded it to him as soon as he linked to it. To put it briefly, it contains instructions to their people to start the revolution, only the start date here is two weeks from now." He paused to consider something. "Commander Heron may not have realised the significance of most of the names on it, but he may have registered some of the notations."

Grand Admiral MacQuillie, the Commander-in-Chief, finally spoke. "And you think they realised this, and attempted the coup when they did because of this knowledge?" He glanced at the others in the projection. "Is this what Security think?"

"We can't be sure, but the AI on the *Harmony Voyager* is the key," said Admiral Lüneburg, Chief of Fleet Security. "We need to find that ship and determine what else Senator Samland may have stored on the AI. It's possible she was logged into this file when the Commander stepped aboard. If she had activated the standard access alert, which is likely, it would have notified her that he was in the system, but not necessarily what he was accessing."

The Grand Admiral leaned back. "And in the meantime we still have two Treaty governments in the hands of the rebels, and the others in such a state of upheaval it's a wonder anything is functioning at all, but that's for their own military and security to sort out. Our task is to find that ship and arrest the ringleaders and those doing deals with the Charonians."

Consciousness returned to Harry very gradually. He opened his eyes and tried to make sense of his surroundings, but couldn't. He was lying flat on his back staring up at a rough-hewn rock ceiling. He was weak with hunger, thirsty and suffering a monumental headache, but his mind was clear. He struggled to sit up.

"Take it easy, sir," said Jack, who had been dozing, and was startled at Harry's movement. "You've a bad case of heat exhaustion."

"Where are we?"

"In a prison, sir. They think we're spies for some tribe or other, come to steal their food, or their kit, or something."

Harry nodded. "Is there anything to drink? Any food you can get through this damned mask?"

Jack laughed. "There's plenty to drink, sir. Something they call lime juice, and plenty of a kind of bread. I'll make a porridge of it for you. The bread might taste strange mixed with this lime juice though."

Harry smiled inside the mask. "I think anything edible will taste fine to me. Even some ship's biscuit would taste like heaven, weevils and all." He spotted Mike Dorfling stretched out on a low bed on the other side of the chamber. "Is Mike injured? I seem to recall we encountered one of those brutish beasts. Did it attack us? Who rescued us?"

"Mike's fine, sir, just sleeping. Like you, the heat got to him a bit. Yes, we were attacked by one of those giant scorpions, but these guys killed it as soon as it jumped out at us. Don't know who or what they are, sir. They say they're human and from a tribe. They seem to have an enemy tribe called the Enviros. When I told them we were from a ship of the Fleet, one of them mocked the whole idea of space travel." Jack shook his head. "I can't make head or tail of them. If they are humans, how did they get here, and when? How can they be so clueless about a simple thing like space travel?"

Harry felt exhausted just listening to Jack's explanation, and offered no reply. The whole situation was baffling.

A commotion outside the chamber drew their attention, then one of the guards appeared leading a strange group of men, some in minimal clothing which appeared to be little more than a harness and boots with leggings up to the waist. The group shuffled past, their ankles linked with metal cuffs and chains and their wrists manacled as well. The guard glanced into the trio's cell. "Some more of you Enviros for company. Plenty of work for you all on the farms. We can always use a few more hands."

"Enviros?" Harry mused. "Have they mentioned anything like mechanics or machiners, or perhaps some other ship's function as a tribal name?"

Jack didn't follow his reasoning at first, and then it hit him. He gaped at Harry. "You mean these people are survivors who've forgotten where they came from? Do you think their tribes were once various specialists on a ship that crashed here, maybe hundreds of years ago?"

"It would explain a great deal, but not necessarily why they appear to have regressed as a society, technologically as well as in other things." He looked at the door as keys rattled against the bars. "I think we're about to find out."

Chapter 15

Ferghal's Quest

"Ah, Commander, come in." Vice Admiral Petrocova smiled and indicated a chair. "Be seated." The last three months with Ferghal working on her staff had confirmed her initial good impression of the young sailor thrown into a strange new world beyond his understanding, but absolutely determined to master it. "I've some new orders for you, something I think you'll enjoy."

Ferghal smiled, remembering Vice Admiral Petrocova as the Weapons Commander on the *Vanguard* who drove her team until she was satisfied they were the best in the Fleet, but she never demanded of her staff and her ships more than she demanded of herself.

"Thank ye, ma'am. Is there word on Harry?"

"No, but that's what we're going to address." She pushed a data chip across the desk. "Your orders are in there. You're to take command of the *Lagan* and use her to back trace the movements of the *Voyager*. You can get the ship to track back on the beacon codes she's recorded. On one of those transits they dumped Harry and his gig. Get out there and find them. There's a price on his head. Find him and bring him back before they do."

"But I've not done the Perisher Course, ma'am." Ferghal hesitated. "After the Niburu War, and the damage to my corvette when we killed the mothership, I was sent back to Engineering."

"I know, but you've built quite a relationship with the AI on *Lagan*. She trusts you, so she'll work with you, and your cyberlink gives you an edge no one else has, except Harry, of course." She smiled. "One more thing: you've a few vacancies to fill. You'll need a new Exec, as Lieutenant MacKenzie-Banks is taking another post. I can recommend someone if you prefer. There are two Warrant posts vacant and one or two Rates." She smiled. "I've had the Lacertians breathing down my neck for the chance to work with you. You'll have Lieutenant Sci'enzile at Weapons and Jenny Matlock in Engineering. There are three Canids waiting to see me as well, all demanding a place." She paused. "Choose your team carefully, Commander O'Connor. You will be operating independently. Choose those you know you can trust absolutely."

The guards pushed Harry and his companions into a large chamber that showed considerable effort had been put into making it a rather grand space. Only the lack of windows betrayed its location below ground, though this was, to some extent, alleviated by the provision of embrasures lit from a concealed source to give the impression of an external light.

"The strangers, Captain."

A man seated on a raised platform looked up. He wore an elaborately stylised uniform that looked like a cross between an eighteenth century admiral and a member of some royal court. His finger stabbed the air in Harry's direction. "Why has that one been allowed to retain his helmet? Prisoners and mutineers are to be presented to this table with their heads uncovered."

"We cain't get it off'n him, Captain. We've never seen one like it."

"Rubbish, man. Saw the damned thing off then, if it's only metal."

"Tried. It blunted the saw."

One of the other men on the dais, in an equally elaborate uniform, leaned across and whispered to the man addressed as Captain.

"Very well," said the Captain. "Get Mechanist to look at it." He paused and glared at Harry. "Who are you? What do you mutineers think you're doing trying to return to our territory? Where is your protective clothing?"

"We are not returning to anyone's territory, sir. We were marooned here by pirates—not our choice, I assure you." Harry tried to rein in his anger. Who did this popinjay think he was? If he were a true Captain, he would never show such disrespect.

"I am Commander Henry Nelson-Heron, officer commanding the patrol ship *Lagan* of the North European Confederation Fleet. My companions are Warrant Officer Jack Proctor," he gestured toward Jack with one arm, "and my gig Coxswain and Master at Arms of the *Lagan*, and TechRate Michael Dorfling, specialist Communications Rate, also of the *Lagan*." His annoyance drove him to add, "Might I enquire as to your styles and titles?"

"You're in no position to demand anything, whoever you are. I am the Captain of Centaur. All of it! The whole damned planet!" the Captain blustered, but there was a tinge of uncertainty to his demeanour. "Never heard of you or your fanciful tribe. Do you take us for fools? There's no water anywhere capable of carrying a ship or even a boat. I know what you are. You're a bunch of filthy, thieving, murdering Enviros, and you've come to steal our equipment—again. Your fancy titles don't work with me. Where are your breathing filters? Even Enviros know better than to walk outdoors without breathing masks. Where are yours?"

"I did not say my ship sailed on water. The *Lagan* is designed for interplanetary travel and is one of the latest patrol craft capable of long-range transits and patrols." It struck Harry suddenly that the Captain looked mature, but his body was almost child-like, as was his behaviour, as if his growth had been stunted during puberty. Harry had made this same observation of the other men too.

The Captain started chuckling in derision before Harry had finished his explanation. "Rubbish, there's no possibility of space travel. Our ancestors tried for years and failed. I don't know what tribe you're from, but those old myths are just fairy tales. As for the machine the ancestors set up in the Observatory—it's just useless junk. Who knows who made it or where they found it? I think it should be dismantled and the parts put to better use, but I'm down-voted on that every time it comes up for discussion." He paused as the door opened and a tall man in a long coat of bleached hide entered. "Yes, Medico? We're busy."

"So I see." The reply dripped sarcasm. "Ah, interrogating the strangers. Well, I'll wait." He adopted a lounging pose near the door. "On the other hand, I believe I should, according to custom, be given charge of them since they are not from any known tribe, and should be examined before they put the community in jeopardy." He paused. "I understand that apart from the one in the helmet, they had no breathing filters or protective clothing when found."

To Harry's amusement, the council or whatever they called themselves seemed to draw back in the presence of this laconic medical officer, as did the guards. Even the Captain's demeanour was suddenly deferential. "Oh. Oh, yes, that's true. I should've considered this. Guards, escort the prisoners to the isolation cell."

"We have contact, Admiral, extreme scan range. It appears to be the *Voyager* and four other ships. Three read as warships, but the fourth is an unknown type."

"Very good, Battle Stations. Authorised to use the particle beam weapon on the unknown vessel. Lock on her and watch for any attempt to use a jamming shield." He gazed into an optical scanner then entered his access code into the pad at his fingertips, and placed his hand on the device to confirm his finger and palm prints and DNA. "You may attack when ready, Captain Larsen."

The display blanked briefly as the ship made a micro-transit, then resumed its normal output. The target ships had not detected them, and moments later the purple-violet beam engulfed the alien ship and exploded it. The other ships recovered quickly from the surprise, but were already under fire from several destroyer class vessels and the swarm of strike fighters released from the flagship's launch bays. The *Harmony Voyager* attempted to break away, but was frustrated when accurate plasma fire disabled her transit pods. Only one of the pirate ships managed to escape, and she had taken serious damage.

"We've secured the *Voyager*, sir." The Flag Lieutenant hesitated, listening to his link. "The boarding party report the ship is stripped of passengers and has only a minimal crew—but a load of odd containers stored in every compartment."

"Send across the science teams. They know what they're looking for. Those containers sound very much like bad news." Admiral Heron stood. "Send the Marines to clear the other pirates. Have them searched for any Charonian survivors."

"Now then, gentlemen." The man everyone addressed as Medico studied them through the bars. "What crime have you committed to be dumped outside wearing that peculiar mask?"

Harry spoke for the three of them. "We have committed no crime. This was fitted to me so that I could not intervene in the computer networks of the pirate ship or the gig once they'd cast us adrift." Harry paused. It seemed his explanation had fallen on deaf ears, and none of it made sense to Medico. While the man hesitated to reply, Harry observed his unique appearance. Like the Captain, this man seemed to be some fifty years old, yet his physique suggested a withered teenager. Harry took a conciliatory approach. "I'd be very much obliged if some means could be found to remove the infernal thing. A liquid diet is extremely debilitating after ten weeks."

"Ten weeks? I'm surprised you're still alive. No one survives on Centaur without a protection suit unless you're an Enviro." The medic moved closer. "If you are who you say you are, then you're the answer to a number of prayers." He glanced round the space. "You saw our ruling council. What did you think of them?"

Harry laughed. "I must ask that you respect my refusal to reply to what could be an incriminating question, sir." He paused. "You call this planet Centaur? Is Medico your name or a title? "

"Never heard it called anything else." The man laughed. "And about my name, both, really. I am what passes for a doctor here, but the role is hereditary, like a lot of other things. I would have preferred to be a mechanist or a keeper of the artefact, but..." he shrugged eloquently "...my father was the Medico, as was his father and so on. My given name is Boris, but only my friends use it."

"I see." Harry hesitated. "So all positions here are inherited? You become whatever your father was?"

"Or your mother, if she is one of the titled positions, as is the case with our Captain." Medico smirked. "He owes his position to his maternal parent. She is descended from the original Captain— or so it is claimed." He raised his eyebrows in doubt, and let Harry form his own conclusion.

Medico's choice of words caught Harry's attention. "The original Captain? Do you mean one who commanded a ship? Are there records of your ancestry?"

"Of course. We aren't complete savages, you know. We have records back to the ancestors. It's claimed they came from another planet, but most people dismiss that as fanciful nonsense." The man straightened. "But here's the thing: most people have never seen or read the records. In fact, you have to be a member of the

Executive Class to even see them, and few have bothered to read them." He moved closer to the bars. "I have read them, and I believe your story, Commander. I shall have to play this carefully. As you have deduced, our Council members are not the brightest, nor are they much interested in anything but maintaining their own standards of living and position." He smiled. "I think that helmet of yours may be the key. I shall have to concoct some story to enable me to keep you here—perhaps to treat some threatening condition which removal of the helmet may cause to spread."

"I'd rather be rid of the thing if you don't mind!" Harry was appalled at the thought of having to remain in this prison for any longer than necessary, just because that was more convenient for these people. "You have said yourself that I cannot remain indefinitely on a liquid diet."

"Of course not." The man moved closer to the bars. "Listen, I'll bring someone who may be able to remove it, but I will insist on your isolation. A few of us do believe the stories. We've seen the artefact, and we believe it is a very sophisticated machine. There are other sources of information besides the official ones. For now, you're safe, but we must work carefully. The Captain and his friends are frightened of anything that threatens their position and the privileges of their rank, and they are extremely ruthless when they feel cornered or they're exposed for the frauds they are."

Harry nodded. "I perceived this. Yet you were rather insolent when you addressed the Captain."

"Yes, but that's because I'm indispensable, and they know it. Be patient, Commander. All I ask is that you show me this ship of yours when we're finished."

"That I shall do with pleasure, sir, though there may be a long delay before that happens."

"Then we have an agreement. Now, I shall have to leave you while I go and find my friend Leo, the Mechanist." He smiled. "He's a tinkerer in many arts. I want him to examine that helmet."

Ferghal seated himself in the Command Chair. It felt wrong. This was Harry's command, and he felt like a usurper.

"No, Ferghal, you can never be a usurper," said the *Lagan*, reading his thoughts. "You are so close to Harry that you're like his elder brother, and you want to find him more than anything in the galaxy. Are you aware that you dream of it?"

"No. Do I?" Ferghal surprised the Command Team by saying this out loud, which he hadn't meant to do. "You are right, though. I want to find him and bring him home—and then I want to be there when we take down whoever did this to him. God says 'vengeance is mine,' but I can't wait that long. I'm going to help that day arrive if I have anything to do with it." He glanced round the Command Centre. Everyone was at their post, all waiting for him. He nodded to the Executive Officer, the Canid Pack Leader Lucanes, and said, "Very well, Pack Leader. Take us to the transit point." He glanced to the Coms Officer. "Signal 847 and *Seana* to link helms as soon as we are ready to transit."

He watched as his orders were translated into action, a half smile playing at the corners of his mouth as he wondered what those who'd served with him on HMS *Bellerophon* and HMS *Spartan* would say if they could see him now. His shipmates from 1804 would have been convinced that hell had disgorged demons to take him for blasphemy if they could see his current company. He had to stifle a guffaw as his gaze fell on the Canid currently giving the manoeuvring orders and the Lacertian Weapons Officer at her station beyond.

"On the Transit Point, Sword Wielder." The Canids used the title the Lacertians had given him, much to the amusement of the human crew.

Ferghal nodded. "Very well. Link helms." He gestured. "Transit."

The display changed to the grey swirling mist of hyperspace. He glanced to his left and smiled as 847 materialised on station, then looked right to see the sleek and very reptilian looking *Seana*, both wrapped in the iridescent phosphorescent glow of transit. He knew the name meant *the runner* in the sibilant language of the Lacertians, and she looked exactly that—fast, sleek, elegant, yet deadly.

"Signal from the Vice Admiral, sir. Good hunting."

"Acknowledge." Ferghal smiled. "Reply the hounds have the scent, tally ho!"

Harry waited until he was sure they were alone. "It looks as if we have landed in the middle of a society on the brink of a social revolution," he remarked. "Clearly they are the descendants of survivors from a colony ship, but one that must have set out a long time ago."

"Sounds like one of the early ships," Mike Dorfling volunteered. "They were powered by some crazy drives." Then he remembered who he was addressing as Jack cleared his throat meaningfully. "Sorry, sir, I meant early compared to the twenty-third century. This was back in the twenty-first century. It was my favourite period in history at school, and you wouldn't believe some of the systems they experimented with until we actually discovered the way to transit safely."

Harry laughed. "Yes, I suppose the twenty-first century does seem like ancient history now. What can you tell me about these ships?"

"They were very big, and had to be, as they carried a few thousand pioneers, livestock, and equipment, and had huge environment spaces. Oh, and the hull rotated around a central core. No artificial gravity, you see, so the rotation created a sort of centripetal force that simulated gravity." He frowned. "They launched about fifty of them—it was quite a feat just building them in those days, as everything was constructed on earth then taken up to the orbital assembly point on disposable rockets."

"You mentioned they had some strange drives?"

"Oh, yeah." Mike's face lit up as he indulged in his passion. "Basically just a sort of controlled fission reaction, sort of like letting off multiple nuclear warheads in a constant succession. That accelerated them to a speed around 0.9 the speed of light." Mike shook his head. "Even to reach the nearest systems with habitable planets they needed around twenty years, and, of course, if they hit anything..."

Harry was impressed. "Quite. At that speed it would vapourise both objects." Harry paused. "You say they launched around fifty of these ships? How many reached their destination?"

"I think it was about twenty, sir. When the transit drive came into use about forty years after the last of those primitive ships was launched, they sent out search ships along the track of the missing ones. I think they found five or six and rescued the people, but the others have never been found."

"So..." Harry hesitated, doing a mental calculation. "If these folk are descended from the crew and passengers of one of the early ships, this would be about four generations of isolation. They have some technology, but it seems cruder than I would have expected. That could be a lack of resources and machines sophisticated enough to maintain the originals." He stood to his feet, a laborious process amid a rattle of chains as the manacles on his ankles shifted. "The radiation from a nuclear accident of the fission type would explain the fixation with protective clothing outdoors—especially the breathing masks and filters. Such an accident might also explain the lack of expertise in a number of fields, but not the distrust that seems to have developed among the various tribes. I hope we learn more of this when Medico returns."

Chapter 16

Cracking the Code

"Here they are, Leo." The Medico ushered a new man into the corridor that fronted their cell. "I think they may have some answers to some of the questions you've been throwing about for a while now."

"Do they speak our language?"

Harry stood, and the rattle of his chains got the attention of both men. "We do, though, to be sure, your pronunciation is sometimes difficult to follow. Medico, must we continue to wear these fetters? I give you my word as an officer that we will make no attempt to escape or to assault any of your people."

"I'll see what I can do, Commander. I'm afraid our leaders are a deeply suspicious lot." He drew his companion forward. "Leo is our mechanical genius. He's responsible for the Observatory, and he specialises in miniaturised machines, like the little pumps that power the breather masks."

The newcomer moved closer. "Medico tells me that helmet is locked onto your head. Is it some sort of breather mask?"

Harry shook his head. "Most certainly not. It restricts my ability to breathe freely and to eat. It also suppresses my ability to communicate with a computer, which, yes, I can do—as long as I'm close to an AI network."

"Computer?" Leonard asked with rising excitement." You mean a calculating machine? Are you a mechanist or some kind of mechanical man?"

Harry laughed. "No, I'm as human as you are—at least our doctors say so, though I do have Lacertian DNA now as well." He realised the visitors didn't understand him. It was a strangely new experience to not be the clueless one for once, and the blank expressions on their faces reminded him of how he felt most of the time when he first landed in the twenty-third century straight out of the nineteenth.

"Have you not heard of DNA?"

"DNA? Yes, we've heard of it," said Medico, "but I don't have the knowledge to even begin to understand more than the basics. I doubt more than ten or so folk here know what it is. And what's this about Lacertian DNA? Who or what are Lacertians?"

Harry looked at Jack and Mike, wondering how to explain this. "They are Saurians descended from a type of reptilian ancestor. Humanoid in appearance with the ability to camouflage themselves against any background, and they're extremely fast when they need to be—oh, and highly intelligent."

Leonard spoke first. "So...how did you come to have Lacertian DNA...?"

"I was subjected to an illegal experiment—a gene splice, I believe it is called. It enables my immune system to resist certain toxins and to repair tissue and organs more rapidly. This was done against my will when I was held captive on the planet called Pangaea—you might've heard of it—in a laboratory run by some horrible people, and I mean humans, not Lacertians. I must admit, however, that even though this was forced on me, the gene splice has given me what some of my crew like to jokingly refer to as superpowers, but I wouldn't go so far as to say that." Harry smiled.

The excitement on the two men's faces warned him they were eager to ask more questions than he was willing (or able) to answer, so he deflected. "Medico, I really would appreciate having this helmet removed. As you must realise, I have a considerable beard growth I'd like to remove, my hair needs trimming and it would be pure luxury to wash some of the filth from my face and neck."

"Sorry to interrupt." Leonard the Mechanist was eager to ask a question. "If I understand you, the computer you are talking about is electronic and not mechanical—is that right?"

"Yes. I doubt Babbage's Calculating Engine would be capable of running a starship as our AIs do." Harry checked himself. "You have a calculating engine? A mechanical one?"

"A little experiment of mine. I feed it instructions on perforated cards, which it reads using a pneumatic device. It is quite capable of controlling the operation of the generating machines." He paused, an expression of wonder spreading across his face. "You said starships? What's an AI? You travel through the stars?" He turned excitedly to the doctor. "That means those ancient texts I found are true. The Captain won't like this."

"We'll keep it quiet then." Medico opened the door to the cell. "I think the Commander may be able to answer your questions about the artefact, Leo." He smiled at Harry. "Please sit down, Commander, so we can take a look at how this helmet is secured. Is there enough light here to examine it?"

Harry sat, and the Warrant and the TechRate watched as the mechanist pulled out a small object, cranked a handle vigorously and then flicked a switch. "My portalight will be sufficient." He peered at the hairline seam that spanned the helmet from ear to ear. "A cunning device this, and a strange material. I've never seen anything like it before."

"The metal is an alloy. I believe it facilitates the screen which prevents me from linking to a computer."

"What do you mean, link? And what is that other thing you mentioned, an AI network?"

"It is rather complex, but I have an implant in my brain that allows me to connect directly to a computer—rather like your pneumatic device, but more powerful and able to run complex programs. The abbreviation AI stands for artificial intelligence, and that's exactly what it is—a thinking machine that operates the starships and all the devices that power it. This implant in my brain makes it possible for me to connect to this thinking machine in my thoughts."

Medico and the Mechanist just stood there stunned, mouths agape.

Harry continued. "Sometimes it is a nuisance, but it has its advantages." He laughed. "But, if I'm wearing something like this," he jabbed his finger in the air at the side of his head, "I cannot make the connection."

The Mechanist stood back. "I don't get half of what you're saying, Commander. I've never seen any joint as fine as this. We couldn't make anything like it—and if we can't, no one else on this planet can." His fingers traced the joint. "There's a hinge or something like one at the top of the helmet. Then here, at the neck, there are these small holes, two each side, and some sort of latching mechanism." He stood in front of Harry again so they could make eye contact. "I think I have a tool that will operate them, but not here." He turned to the doctor. "We'll have to take the Commander to my workshop for this, and if we bring him, we might as well bring the other two."

"You must have had a tough time getting Captain to agree to bringing all three." The Mechanist greeted them at the door to his workshop. He indicated the guards and the shackles the trio still wore. "Taking no chances with them, I see."

Medico laughed. "Not with such obviously superhuman and dangerous villains as these." He stood back to allow the prisoners to shuffle inside. "Enforcers, I think perhaps we can remove at least some of the restraints now. Mechanist will need his subject to move freely if he's to get that helmet off, and the others will pose no problem."

The man addressed, who was wearing what looked like a cross between an early-model EVA suit and a medieval suit of armour, moved inside, shut the door, and switched off a small device in his backpack before he removed his breathing mask.

"Captain won't like this, Medico—you heard his orders. The spies are to be kept fully restrained at all times."

"True, but Captain also gave me full responsibility for them. Please remove at least the arm restraints. With your men at the door and you here, I think we can be sure they won't run away."

Harry listened to this exchange with interest. They had shuffled through several tunnels before taking a series of lifts to this floor. The lifts operated by hydraulics, and Harry could see signs of technology everywhere, but very little evidence of the sort of machines that must have been used to create the complex of tunnels and dwellings, halls and cavernous open gathering areas.

They lived in structures hollowed out of a ring of cliffs riddled with tunnels. The cliffs provided a natural barrier, and the cliff openings suggested there was a much larger population at one time. The valley was a patchwork of unkempt parks and cultivated crops in which strangely dressed figures laboured. Harry realised they were all chained to each other and dressed in rather poorly fitting animal hides that covered their bodies completely with their faces hidden behind simple breathing masks.

It struck him that only he and his companions were not wearing anything that could be termed protective. Their only clothing was their extremely tattered uniforms, and they used no breathing masks.

As the lift ascended, he used the elevated vantage point to study the crater. The greater part of the complex looked unused, a sign, perhaps, that this was a dying community.

The Mechanist's workshop was an Aladdin's cave of strange machines, some partly dismantled, others obviously in use. Everything was mechanical, with pulleys and belt drives, or long shafts interconnected with gears or levers. All of the working machines looked as if they'd been created out of pieces salvaged from others, and all had a makeshift appearance.

Mike drew a sharp breath. "Warrant? Sir? Look over there. That's a Mark 1 Coms Unit. I've only seen pictures, but that was what they used before the hyperlink network was set up." He was like an excited schoolboy. "Those things were built to last. I bet I could get it functioning again."

Medico and the Mechanist were staring at him. "You recognise that? My great-great—several greats—grandfather swore that thing could talk to other worlds, but it's never worked for us."

Mike grinned. "I bet I can get it to work. I'll have to do a full circuit spec, but the Mark 1 was the prototype for all later sets, and some of its features are still used in modern technology." He looked at Harry. "It won't contact a hyperlink, sir, but a ship passing through this system will hear it."

Harry was curious. "Without a hyperlink, how did they communicate with Earth?"

Mike grinned. "Very slowly, but the message got there eventually. The signal travelled at lightspeed, which means it reached Earth years after it was sent. So, for that reason, these units were more for local contact between the colony ships."

"I see." Harry nodded as he processed this information. Mike continued.

"Thing is, sir, these sets were incredibly powerful, and the signal wasn't a narrow beam like we use now. It blasted out in all directions. Like I said, anyone passing this planet would get an earful."

The Mechanist glanced at Medico before he turned to Mike. "What do you need?"

The Enforcer stepped forward. "This is not in the orders."

"Enforcer, I think we should test this. It could be the opportunity we've all been hoping for." He smiled and placed an arm across the guard's shoulders. "Now, somewhere in this place is some means for making tea. I want a cup and so do you. Mechanist can get on with his tasks and Warrant can help him." Firmly he steered the guard away from where the Mechanist was eagerly showing Mike Dorfling the bulky unit.

Having equipped Mike with a set of beautifully made tools, the man rather reluctantly led Harry to a seat then got Jack to hold a lamp for him while he tried to find the right tool to pry open the helmet.

"I hope they haven't included something to maim or kill me in this device," Harry mused as Leonard worked. "I suppose it is not beyond the thinking of the fiends that created it."

"Shit. Never thought of that, sir." The Warrant Officer showed his concern.

"Well, we shall soon know, I expect. Somehow I doubt it, though. I believe they expected me to die of starvation or dehydration. Thanks to you and Mike, I survived."

The Warrant had been watching the Mechanist. "Pardon me, mister, but I think we have to hit all four latches simultaneously."

"You could be right. Okay, if you take that side, I'll operate these." He handed over the tools he'd been using. "Give me a second—I'll get another set." He reached into a cabinet and drew out a small case. "My father's." He smiled. "I only use them for special tasks. Let's get to work."

On the fifth attempt there was a soft click, but instead of the helmet releasing, a small panel low on the back of the neck opened and revealed a line of symbols.

"Ah," breathed Jack. "Now that's my specialty. You okay in there, sir? We've got a key panel to open here, and a code required to open it." He studied it carefully. "You know, since they made sure we wouldn't have the tools to open this panel, I'm betting they didn't bother to code this with anything special." He punched in a sequence. This time there was a louder click, and the two halves of the helmet parted.

The Mechanist seized the two halves at the front and back and pulled them apart, then raised it clear of Harry's head. "Got it!" he exclaimed as Harry took his first uninhibited breath in quite some time. "Fantastic workmanship."

The Warrant Officer stop short and stared at Harry's matted hair, tangled beard and dirty face. "Looks like Mike and I have a barbering job if we can get these folk to let us have the kit, sir."

Grinning, Harry wiped his hands across his face and stroked his ten-week growth of beard into some sort of order. "I'll take you up on that as soon as possible. No wonder these folk think we're savages come to spy on them." He turned to the Mechanist. "Thank you, Mr. Leonard. You have no idea what a relief it is to be free of that damnable device."

The man smiled. "A pleasure, Commander. If you follow me, I can show you where to wash. I've only some scissors, but you're welcome to use them if you like." He turned to look at what Mike was doing. "Your servant seems to be dismantling that machine. I better go and see what he's doing."

Harry frowned. "Servant? Mr. Dorfling is no servant of mine, sir. He is a highly specialised TechRate of the Fleet." He indicated the Warrant Officer next to him. "And Mr. Proctor is a programmer of considerable skill. His position aboard my ship is as the second most senior non-commissioned officer. He answers only to me or my Executive Officer, the First Lieutenant."

"I've been wondering about that," Medico interjected, joining them. He shrugged as they all looked at him. "Have you never wondered why, since the tribal wars started, we have all been compelled to take up our parents' occupations?"

The Mechanist frowned. "Yes, I suppose. But the explanation is always the same: it is the best way to preserve civilisation and ensure these skills are not lost." He shrugged. "You've only to look at how the desert tribes have lost the ability to manufacture little more than simple tools and weapons to see that."

"There!" Mike announced in triumph. "I knew I could get it going." Several lights glowed where before there had been blank opaque panels. "It'll take a while to build up the charge in the power packs again. I hope you don't mind, Mr. Leonard, but I've taken a feed off your hydraulic press—the cable looked like the best option." He wiped his hands on a rag. "Should be able to run a test signal in an hour or so, but it'd be best if we left it to charge the cells for about four hours. Then we can check all the circuits are still good."

He looked at the astonished faces of the two local men in their rather crude outfits of animal hide and rough woven fabric. "These Mark I units were over engineered on everything, quadruple redundancies, back-up circuits—you probably could have built one about a third the size. It's the power cells that take up most of the space."

The Mechanist had an expression of awe on his face. "My grandfather said it had lights in it—he'd seen them as a child. But the lights dimmed then went out completely before he grew to his youth." He touched the face of the unit with his fingertips. "What did you say it can do?"

"It's a communications unit," Harry interjected. "It uses radio waves to transfer information and messages between places, people and ships. These were written and spoken messages." Harry paused when he saw their stunned faces. "I can hear it because the program is still active, though very archaic." He turned to Jack. "Do you think you can program it to send out a distress call for us?"

The Warrant Officer grinned. "Dead easy, sir. Just let me at it as soon as it's fully charged. They'll hear the signal clear across the galaxy—eventually."

Medico and the Mechanist exchanged glances. "I think our esteemed Captain may have some problems with that," murmured Medico. "We'll have to think of a way to throw them off the scent."

"I heard that, Medico, and that's mutiny talk." They turned to find the Enforcer and his three subordinates at the door, their weapons ready.

Chapter 17

Disclosures

"Don't be a bloody fool, man. We're on the brink of discovering something really important. Put those weapons down and take yourselves out of here."

"Get out of the way, Medico," the leader snarled.

Harry noticed they all had breathing masks on with their weapons loaded and ready to use, and he silently cursed the fact that his ankles were shackled.

"Just because you're the only Medico here doesn't mean you can do as you please. Anybody can learn how to treat the things you deal with."

"Really? But that would break the precious structure of society you're sworn to preserve, wouldn't it? Who did you fancy replacing me with, yourself? Can you extract a poisoned bolt from an Enviro crossbow or distill the venom of a sand dragon?" He waved at the machines around them. "Can any of you build, repair or maintain any of this?"

"Maybe not, but we all heard you commit mutiny." The man sounded less sure of himself.

"Come, come, Mr. Enforcer," Harry intervened. "Mutiny is a very serious charge, and surely seeking the truth about certain matters is not treason."

"I knew it was a mistake to take those fetters of'n you!" He signalled one of the others. "Get them chained up properly again, and do the same with Medico and Mechanist. Mutiny is mutiny."

"No," said Leonard. "I've had enough of your bullying." He closed a hefty switch. A loud snap and shower of sparks signalled an electrical contact. The Enforcers collapsed to the floor, shouting and struggling against the magnetic pull of the large steel plate they were now attached to by their weapons and armour. Both Harry and Jack, also standing on the plate, were held fast by the manacles on their ankles, but Mike Dorfling remained free, and stood there grinning from ear to ear.

Leonard moved forward. "Doc, if you've got some of that sleeping stuff, now would be a good time to use it. My generator can't take this load for long." He grinned. "I'd make sure you've no iron on you when you approach them though."

Medico laughed. "I have some, but Captain will have the rest of his goons up here as soon as he suspects anything." He watched as Harry and Jack were released from the manacles, which freed them from the firm grip of the magnet. "Okay, I've an idea. I'll knock this lot out then go down again and tell the Captain a convincing story about how they've been contaminated. I'll alert the others too. Maybe we can pull this off." He produced a vial. "If we don't we'll hang for it."

Leonard shrugged. "Let them. Without your patching them up and keeping the workers alive, and without me keeping the machines running, it won't be long before they have no electricity, no water supply and no air circulation. I've dreamed of finding out how this stuff works for far too long to let them smash it up now."

As Leonard spoke, Boris the doctor was busy dumping a measure of the contents of his vial into each of the Enforcers' breathing packs. The four men stopped moving within seconds of receiving the dose. "Not the best way to administer this," he said as he recapped the vial, taking care not to inhale the fumes himself. "I've probably hit them with enough to sleep for several hours, and when they wake up, they won't be able to string a sentence together for a few more." He pocketed the vial. "I normally administer very small doses, but even then, the patient goes into a state of euphoria. A dose like this will probably give them hallucinations for a week."

Jack Proctor had by now removed the fetters from Mike as well. "I've a suggestion, sir." He held up the manacles. "Let's give them a taste of their own medicine."

"Good idea, Warrant. But let's get them out of that armour first." He turned to Leonard. "Is there somewhere we can use to secure them in case anyone comes looking for them?"

Ten minutes later the Enforcers were confined in a small chamber at the rear of the main workshop. Stripped of their armour and secured with the manacles they had used on Harry and his men, they were not going to be a problem anytime soon.

"Their disappearance will be noticed, and then there will be trouble," Leonard advised. "Help me hide that communicator device, or Captain and his thugs will order it destroyed."

"Warrant, see to it. Where do you want it, Mr. Leonard?"

"I'll show you." The man smiled. "My name is Leonard, or just Leo to my friends. Mister is reserved only for the council families." He led the way and moved a large machine aside—to Harry's interested eyes, it pivoted once the securing bolts from the other three corners had been withdrawn—to reveal a concealed chamber below. "My great grandfather created this after the first mutiny. Thought it might be useful to have a workshop none of the Enforcers or the Council knew about."

A ladder allowed access, and it took a little effort to lower the coms unit to the floor below, but it took no time at all to connect it to a power source.

"Give me ten minutes, sir. I'll program the unit to broadcast a distress call as soon as it detects any ship transmissions nearby."

Harry nodded. "Very well, but perhaps set it to broadcast a short message on the hour every hour, then to transmit a homing signal as soon as someone responds. Can you do that?"

"I'll need longer, sir, but yes, I can do it."

"Then carry on, Mr. Proctor." Harry turned to the mechanist. "Now, Leo, sir, the Captain mentioned some artefact kept in the Observatory. Is this it?"

Leonard smiled. "No, Commander. They don't know about this one, and if anyone ever did, they've forgotten about it by now. The one in the Observatory is much bigger."

"Can we see it, please?" Harry asked. "If, as I suspect, you are the descendants of some early colony ships sent out in the days before hyperspace travel, this artefact may contain information which, had it been available before this, might have led to a more equitable society here. At the very least it may tell us where you originate and when."

"This way, then." Leo indicated a door on the far side of the workshop. "No one ever goes up there anymore." He laughed. "We had a telescope there once, but a previous Captain had it dismantled. He thought the study of the stars was a waste of time, and decided the lenses would be better used in a weapon—which never worked properly, no surprise there."

"Why not?"

"The light source was too weak, but at least it made a good illuminating device that allowed us to see the enemy in the dark." He paused. "A pity they destroyed it in the process. We haven't been able to grind glass to the sort of finish it needs to make a replacement." His expression betrayed the weariness he felt on a regular basis as he coped with the ignorance among the leaders. "The artefact is this way," he said, as he led them into a cavernous dome that housed the skeleton of a massive telescope.

"Good news at last, James." Grand Admiral MacQuillie's hologram steadied. "The coup attempts have failed. There's still some unrest in places, and a number of people who considered themselves untouchable by their national governments are under arrest." The Commander-in-Chief paused. "The trials will prove very interesting."

"I expect so, sir." Admiral Heron hesitated. "Have they managed to identify and arrest everyone involved?"

"Most but not all. Some very powerful and extremely wealthy people are implicated, which means we're dealing with a lot of political manoeuvring and challenges to its authenticity."

James nodded, his anger building. "Of course they'd try that one. Next they'll spread the word the whole thing is a fake ... yes, I know the system. Will they succeed in getting away with it, sir?"

"Not if anyone can help it, James. A tribunal of some of the world's top legal experts will go through every argument with a fine-toothed comb. I doubt anyone will succeed in discrediting them. Of more concern is the view by Fleet Security that the list includes at least some of the Pantheon—which gives them an interest in assassinating or negating the prosecutors and the people who authenticated the list."

"Then we had best make sure we deal with them first."

"Correct. Hans Grünberg is on the task. Now, any trace yet of that uncle-nephew of yours? Hans says the Pantheon have a contract on him."

"Nothing yet, sir, but Lieutenant Commander O'Connor and his squadron are narrowing the field as we speak, and they'll take him to a secure area."

"Good, that leaves us just the task of dealing with the Pantheon and their Charonian allies."

"This is amazing, sir. It's the central core unit of the Mark V Ship Management system." Mike Dorfling walked round the octagonal steel and aluminium structure. Standing around twelve feet in height, it was a full three feet on each of the eight sides. "They must have stripped it out of the ship when they got here, but why didn't they take the subsidiary units as well?" He set to work opening a panel. "As I thought, sir. Whoever brought this here intended to get the rest of it, and powered this unit down to preserve it." He flicked a switch. "There's still a little power left." He emerged from the opening. "If we can get some power in here, I can get this up and running."

Leonard was looking astonished, and not a little frightened. "The artefact is off limits to everyone. No one is allowed to touch it. It is said that opening it will result in us all dying of some sort of strange poisoning."

Harry laughed. "I should think that is because someone, at some time, discovered what it could tell people—and wasn't going to allow them to hear it." He paused. "How long have your tribe had control of all this?" Harry's gesture took in the entire site and the artefact.

Leonard considered. "A long time, certainly five or six generations."

Harry tapped a plate on the inside of the panel the TechRate had removed. "This plate says that this is the ship management system from a ship called the *Centaur II*. It says she was launched on her quest in 2083, which means, unless I miss my guess, she cannot have travelled more than a few light years to reach this place." He paused, frowning. "That must mean that your people arrived here a little over a hundred years ago." He had another thought. "How old are you?" His private estimate was that their guide was probably well over fifty years of age. "On Earth there are considered to be three or four generations to a century, yet you speak of seven or eight in that period."

The mechanist looked surprised. "I'm not sure of my age in your measurements. We measure our lives in cycles of the suns, and I'm in my twentieth. A long lifespan is considered thirty cycles." He shrugged. "We age very quickly. Medico says it was different once, and we had a much longer lifespan."

Harry digested the information. If he guessed correctly, a cycle must be close to an Earth year, which meant these people were ageing at around twice the normal rate.

"How long is a cycle?" Harry asked.

"Since this planet has no satellites, and the seasons are regulated by the suns, the ancestors had to do something else, so there is a device in the Command House cellar that measures the length of the days and the cycles. Everyone's birth is recorded against it."

Harry made a mental note to see this instrument when there was an opportunity. He asked, "How many of you are in this place?"

"We're about four hundred officers, specialists and crewmen, perhaps two hundred more prisoners from the other tribes. They're used mainly in the mine or to feed the furnaces that provide steam to power everything." He frowned. "There used to be a few thousand of us, but birthrates have been falling for a long time. Medico says it's to do with inbreeding and the radiation we get from the suns." His frown deepened. "And if the Hunters are to be believed, there are very few Enviros or Mutineers in the desert. The band that attacked them when they brought you back must have been desperate. They lost most of their people."

Harry gave this some thought. "How long is a day here? On Earth it is twenty-four hours, but other planets have twenty-seven, twenty or other variations. Your days seem much shorter."

Leonard frowned. "If your hours are the same as ours, then our day is about two-thirds of yours, with two hundred days in a cycle. We're in the hot season now, with both suns visible. It is cooler when one passes behind the other—that's when we finally get some relief from the relentless heat." He grinned. "There's some water on the surface then—and some of the plants even have colours."

The hissing sound of depressurised air followed by the whir of fans interrupted them, and a mechanical voice said, "*Centaur*

II on standby. Function is lost to all systems except core memory. Repair and maintenance is required to restore functions."

Mike Dorfling emerged beaming from ear to ear. "They really built these units to last, sir. Shall I see if I can get it to tell us anything?"

Harry felt stunned for a moment. After being isolated from a computer network for so long, he was almost overwhelmed by the streams of code that filled his head.

Mike looked at him and said, "What is it, sir? Are you alright?

"Ship shape, Mr. Dorfling. Merely adjusting to the streams of code filling my brain once again. I'll have to learn how this one operates so I can communicate with it."

"Great, sir. It should be running on the early platform they created to control function." The TechRate was enthusiastic. "It required a human mind to make choices and give instructions, so you might try that approach. It wasn't completely sentient as our AI networks are."

"Thank you, I will." Harry concentrated and the data stream slowed, then shunted, then steadied as he gave several search commands. Minutes later he had what he was looking for.

"Now, Mr. Dorfling, how quickly can you create audio functionality?"

"There won't be time, Commander," said Boris as he joined them again. He looked frightened. "Captain and his goons are on their way. The others are concerned, and one of them has reported us to the Council." He glanced around. "I'm afraid we're trapped."

Chapter 18

On the Run

———————————————

"I've programmed the coms unit, sir, and it's secured. They won't find it unless someone tells them where to look."

"Good, well done, Warrant." Harry looked around. "There's no point in resisting. I propose we surrender and try to avoid giving them any reason to look for the coms or the computer."

"I'd like to do a fix on those weapons, sir, and make them useless." The Warrant Officer indicated the air rifles they'd taken from the Enforcers. "I reckon they won't have anyone who can fix them either."

"Do so, but be quick. We haven't long." Harry considered a moment than asked, "Do they have additional uniforms they can change into?"

Leo shook his head. "No, each individual is issued one uniform."

"Good, that works in our favour. Doctor, have you some powder that will cause a rash?"

The doctor looked thoughtful. "No, but I do have something that will make them feel pretty sick after a while."

"Good, give it to me please." Taking the proffered vial, he carefully unscrewed the cap. "Mr. Dorfling, hold that suit open for me."

Ten minutes later the Enforcers stormed into the workshop angry that the Mechanist had disabled the lift. "Freeze, mutineers!" their leader bellowed through his mask.

He seemed uncertain when it became obvious that his target group were seated facing the door with their hands on their knees flanked by Medico and the Mechanist on one side with Harry, Mike and Jack on the other.

"Don't move," the leader shouted at them.

"We have no intention of doing so," Harry replied calmly.

"Shut yer mouth, spy! Shoulda fed ya to the sand dragons when they found yez." He signalled his men. "Get chains on 'em an' get 'em down ter Executive."

He noted the pile of weapons and armoured clothing. "Where are t'others? If ye've killed 'em, ye'll swing fer it."

"They're sleeping—" Medico couldn't get another word out when he was hit from behind with such force that it knocked him from his chair.

"That is uncalled for," Harry snapped, and received a blow for his pains. He tried to dodge, but that unleashed a rain of blows that knocked him to the ground, and the assault continued in a storm of kicks. Jack blocked the blow aimed at him and grabbed hold of his attacker. Above the noise, the man's screech of agony as Jack broke his arm brought a momentary pause in the mayhem, but seconds later Jack was overwhelmed as several men attacked him. Even so he caused at least one man to collapse in agony before he was subdued.

When they were again secured in chains, with Boris and Leo in shackles now too, the five were dragged to the lift and dumped into it for the descent. At the bottom there was no respite as the Enforcers administered further punishment while the Captain and his Council watched.

When he'd had his fill of retribution, the Captain spoke. "I think that is sufficient, Enforcer One. You can get them off the floor now." He waited while the Enforcers dragged them to their feet. "I take sedition very seriously, Medico, and I've been far too tolerant of your insolence." He turned to Leo. "Mechanist, you'll have plenty of opportunity to keep the mining machines running while you consider your mistake in befriending these spies." He moved closer to Harry. "As for you, Commander, I saw through you right from the start. That helmet was just a ruse. Commander of a starship, my ass! You're nothing but pathetic Enviros." He snapped his fingers at the lead Enforcer. "Take them to the mining cells."

The cell into which they were thrown was bare. Boris eased himself into a sitting position, wincing with pain. "I'm sorry, Commander. I should have expected betrayal."

Harry winced as he seated himself. Every part of his body hurt; his ribs were bruised, one eye was swollen and his lip was bleeding. "No, I should have counselled resistance. At least then we would have the satisfaction of having taken some of them with us into the next life." He looked at Jack and was concerned about his wounds. To Boris he said, "Would you be so kind as to examine my Warrant Officer? I fear he took the brunt of their brutality."

"I'll be alright, sir," Jack managed through gritted teeth. "I've had worse."

"Perhaps, but not after wandering in a desert and suffering malnutrition." Boris shuffled to where he could examine Jack.

Mike Dorfling groaned as he found a seat. "Bastards. When our blokes get here, I'm going to settle a score or two, sir."

Harry grinned, but as the Commanding Officer, he couldn't openly concur. "I don't think I heard that, Mike, but I'd certainly support your having a very good talk to one or two—privately, of course."

The TechRate grinned. "Naturally, sir, a real man-to-man talk, one at a time."

Leonard watched, his concern obvious. "How can you joke? You don't know what these men are like. They'll kill us for any reason, and even if they don't, they'll find any excuse to punish you."

Harry looked at him. "I think we know their type. As Mr. Dorfling has said, our people will arrive, soon I hope, and when they do, we will have our reckoning. Of that you may be very sure." He paused. "Doctor, what sort of symptoms will the men suffer from whatever it was you sprinkled into their uniforms?"

The doctor paused, dabbing a trickle of blood from his nose. "They'll feel feverish, their skin will itch, and some might experience nausea and double vision." He peered at Harry. "Why?"

"When our guards return, as I'm sure they will, just follow my lead. Mr. Proctor, Mr. Dorfling, I hope to make our hosts think we are carrying the plague that seems to have killed the key officers, scientists and administrators of the original colonists. I want to make them frightened of having contact with us." The full plan formed in his mind. "I want you, Mr. Dorfling, to complain that you're suffering a relapse of a fictitious plague from somewhere. Can you do that? You could remind me that you haven't been able to take the medication for it since we got here. You may have to improvise to take advantage of an opening into which the idea can be injected."

The two men grinned at him, a rather ghoulish sight amidst their bruised and bloodied faces.

"You bet I can, sir," said Mike.

"Good, but don't overdo it. Make it seem as if you're trying to protect them from being infected."

"Gotcha, sir." Dorfling's grin showed his appreciation of Harry's plan. "Trust me, sir, I was in the drama club at the Fleet Recruit Training base and on all the major ships I've served in. I'll make it realistic."

The doctor interjected. "I think I understand your plan, Commander. If you'll let me, I'll play a hand in it as well—I am, after all, the only person among them who is supposed to have medical knowledge."

Harry nodded. "Good. As you probably know, the original colonists arrived here seriously irradiated, thanks to a fault in their drive system and shielding. They might have survived had it not made them vulnerable to a rather simple disease. For some reason only the very young and those in their early teens survived."

The doctor stared. "Where did you read that?"

"It is all recorded in the computer you have in the Observatory. Apparently the plague prevented the complete transfer of the equipment to the planet surface before the ship became unmanageable. According to the record I found, it had to be abandoned and destroyed, which is how your ancestors were marooned here."

Harry heard something and stopped to listen. He held up a hand. "Get ready to play your parts. Someone's coming."

One of the guards appeared at the bars, his expression full of bravado. "Medico, you're coming with me. Some of my boys need medical treatment. He pushed a key into the lock. "The rest of you scum stand back."

"I don't think that would be wise," said Boris, and remained seated as far from the door as possible. He pointed to Mike

Dorfling. "I've just learned this man is carrying the plague—probably the very one that killed our ancestors."

Mike groaned in pain and doubled over. Through clenched teeth he gasped, "It's true. I've not had my medicine since we got here, and it's starting again."

The guard looked uncertain as he backed away from the door. "What are you on about? What plague?"

"My vision is blurred ... sometimes I see things that aren't there, and my skin itches ... I sweat and feel hot and cold, and my stomach..." He made gagging sounds. "Sorry. It'll ease off again in a few hours. I just hope I'm not infectious. I wouldn't wish this on my worst enemy..."

Harry nodded. "Easy there, Mr. Dorfling." He looked at the doctor. "It's called the Pangean Plague. Highly contagious and can be fatal to anyone who doesn't have any resistance to it."

"I've heard of it," said the doctor, playing along, "but I've never seen a case. My grandfather talked about it, said it was usually fatal. I could try to find the remedy, but I'm certain it involved cultivating the blood of a person suffering from it." He looked very concerned. "It is extremely contagious, and everyone who has been in contact with Mike is very likely to catch it within the next few hours." He turned to the guard. "Have any of your people developed any of the symptoms?" The man was backing away from the bars and looking worried. "Any of them having hallucinations, or perhaps showing signs of a rash? Itchy skin?"

The man was now clearly frightened. "No. Yes!" He looked terrified. "Yeah, some of the lads—"

"Look, I suggest you move the men with symptoms to where they aren't in contact with anyone else." Boris paused for suspense. "You might be lucky, the rest of you might not catch this, but it may already be too late."

The man almost ran out of the holding cells corridor, the door slamming behind him.

Boris chuckled. "Well, that was quick. Within half an hour, the Captain will be demanding that I cure everyone. What now, Commander?"

Harry's grin was all smug satisfaction. "Now we let them frighten themselves into illness. In the meantime, I'm sure Mr. Leonard here knows how to unlock these irons, open the doors and show us to a place where we can be secure until the Fleet arrives."

"We've received a message from Admiral Heron, sir. They've captured the *Voyager* and analysed her navigation data. The Commander's gig was set adrift in the system we're bound for." Jenny Matlock sounded pleased. "And there's an anomalous signal triggering the hypercoms, but no message."

"Anomalous signal? Do we have a fix on it? Can we work out where it's originating?" Ferghal swung his legs off the bunk and snatched his jacket off the back of the chair. "I'll come. Do we have the full record from the Admiral?"

"Yes, sir. Pack Leader Lucanes is running a detailed check. He thinks they may have been jettisoned near a planet mapped in that section some years ago, but deemed unfit for human colonisation. It's a binary system with a couple of planets, one in the habitable zone, but it's hotter than a cold day in hell when both suns are in the right position. Each day is only fifteen hours, and the heat is relentless."

Ferghal nodded. "Does it have a breathable atmosphere?"

"It does, but almost no surface water, even during the cool phases."

"Pass this to the other ships. What's our ETA in the system?"

"Forty-eight hours, sir."

"What about that signal? Are we still getting it?"

"Yes, sir. On the nail, every hour, the hyperlinks trigger, but nothing comes through. The source triangulates to our destination."

Ferghal nodded. He dared not hope for too much, but he prayed they'd find Harry alive. He shut his eyes and recalled the Angelus, recited it, then prayed to the Virgin Mary and all the saints he could recall to add their prayers for Harry's safety.

Judging by the shouting coming from behind the door separating the cell block from the Enforcers, news of the plague would soon spread beyond the guards' quarters.

"I suggest this would be a good moment to free us, Leonard, and then, perhaps to render that door inoperable. I think it would be very inconvenient to have some vengeful guards visit us." Harry smiled at the Mechanist. "I assume you can do that. The shackle locks seem rather crude."

Leonard looked offended. "Of course I can. I repair these things all the time. They're worn out and need to be replaced. The same goes for the door lock." He searched the lining of his jacket and produced a tool that Harry had never seen before. Two minutes later the handcuffs clattered to the floor. "There, simple really. Made by my great-great-grandfather." He set to work on the barred door. "I'll deal with the door to this section first, then I'll release the rest of you."

"Thank you, I think that is a very good idea." Harry watched as Leo removed the cover plate from the door lock then fiddled with the mechanism before replacing the cover plate and returning to the cell. "There, they'll think the lock has jammed." Leo shrugged. "I assume you don't want to remain here until your friends come, Commander. There is another way out, one they don't know about. It hasn't been opened for at least thirty cycles, and most of the Enforcers are too young to know it exists."

Harry nodded. "You're right, we need to remain hidden until we get a response from our transmitter." He turned to Boris. "You said earlier that this city once housed thousands. Does that mean there are a lot of unoccupied residences now?"

Boris nodded. "Er, yes." He brightened when he caught Harry's drift. "Yes! And I know exactly where they won't look."

"Good." Harry grinned. "Warrant, would you be so good as to arrange these manacles so it appears they have just been shed and we've—er—dematerialised."

Ferghal nodded to the commanders of 847 and *Seana*. "Regidur, Sci'arade, we've picked up an anomalous signal, a distress call. Its point of origin is a system we were planning to visit in our search. As it is only two days from our present position, I propose we go there immediately and investigate it."

The Canid gestured. "This signal may be a trap. Why does it not register on my systems?"

"It isn't coming through the hyperlink beacons, but it is triggering them." Ferghal paused. "It repeats every hour on the hour, a short very broadband signal. My coms officer says it looks like a signal from equipment that predates hyperspace travel."

"We have seen this on our system," said Sci'arade, the Lacertian. "I agree, we should investigate it."

The Canid nodded. "So be it, Sword Wielder," he said, using a nickname that he had given Ferghal during their battle against the Consortium on Regidur's home planet Lycania. "It would not surprise us to find that Commander Heron has discovered some new way to bring discomfort to an enemy." He gave a very canine-like open-mouthed smile and made a purring sound that rumbled from deep within his chest, which Ferghal had learned was the Canid's way of enjoying a hearty laugh.

Chapter 19

Reunion

Niamh stared at the papers in front of her unseeing. It was so unfair what these boys had suffered: Harry, Ferghal and little Danny—who was not so little now, but had grown into a tall young man who no longer resembled the half-starved wraith-like boy he had been only five years ago. They were barely out of childhood and their teen years. If she had any say in the matter, Harry would *not* die at the hands of these evildoers who had such an over-inflated sense of power that they called themselves the Pantheon.

"Gods and goddesses...pffft!" she muttered in anger.

The opening of the front door startled her. "Mary! What a lovely surprise. Have you any news?"

Mary shook her head. "Hi, Aunt Niamh," she said as she took off her coat and hung it on a peg in the hallway." I've heard nothing. It's so frustrating not being able to use even the public links to contact Ferghal or Danny. When will this nonsense end? I mean, come on, aren't I a member of the public too?!" She sat on the sofa. "Why did I have to fall in love with a man who seems to attract the enemy at every turn? He's such a good person, and he's always targeted for some insane reason or another." She took a deep breath and collected herself. "Do you think there's any hope Harry has survived? That Senator Samland is a monster! How can anyone do what she has done and boast of it?"

"It takes a special kind of person to be that horrible..." Niamh stopped herself. "Has Harry ever mentioned that some members of our family experience a sort of dream when one of our own is in danger?"

"I don't think so..." Mary frowned. "Wait, does it involve a horse?"

"That's the one. James has it occasionally. I think Harry has it as well." She paused. "James believes Harry is alive. All he would tell me was that he'd had a visit from The Horse—his code for the dream—and that it was restless and bridled but not saddled."

"What does that mean?"

"Usually it means that the member of the family concerned— and it is seldom specific—is in danger but alive. If it is saddled and trailing its reins, it means someone is either close to death or has died." Niamh reached for Mary's hand. "If James is right, we can expect news that Harry has been found."

"I hope so, Niamh. The uncertainty is horrible."

Niamh hugged her, and Mary felt better. She managed a brave smile. "And I shall take him to task when I see him. He promised to stay out of trouble!"

The alternative exit from the prison proved to be far more tortuous than Leonard had implied, but he had been correct in his assumption that none of the Enforcers knew of its existence. It took some effort to gain access to the space, originally a hoistway, but now disused. The cables for the lift provided the means to reach a vertical ladder built into the side of the shaft, and there was a long climb to reach the winding chamber where a partially stripped-down motor sat forlorn and unserviceable. Unfortunately, the tunnel it gave access to had been colonised by a rather unpleasant rodent-like creature that resented their presence.

"These damned critters are taking over everywhere I go in the service spaces," Leonard remarked. "I have to carry a pneumo-gun in some of the more remote ones now. At least they're edible, but that's about all they're good for!" He hit a switch and lights flickered. "Damn, looks like they've chewed the cable again. Oh well, this way."

"This place is worse than a badger sett," Harry remarked. "It must have taken a vast amount of labour to create these."

"It did." Boris was silent for a moment. "Our ancestors decided the only way to survive was to go underground in a place they could defend against things like the sand dragons, so they dug these tunnels. They told everyone it was necessary to protect them from radiation poisoning, which seems plausible. According to the story my grandfather told, the ship had suffered some damage that meant it was poisoning everyone on board. A lot of folk died building this place, and they'd barely finished when the plague hit."

Harry nodded wordlessly, his attention focussed on the occasional machine that came into view and brief glimpses into adjoining chambers and galleries occupied by what appeared to be elaborate steam engines, most now idle and partly dismantled. "That may explain a number of puzzles here." He waved toward yet another idle machine. "Are these being dismantled to maintain others?"

"Yes. I don't have the training or the equipment to make a lot of the spares we need, nor does anyone else, so I come up here and salvage what I need. No one asks where it comes from. Most of the stuff we use was made by the first generation of ancestors. Since then we've just sort of patched things up." He shrugged. "This part of the city was abandoned two, maybe three generations back, and I've just about dismantled everything to keep the rest going." He smiled. "Eventually I'll run out of things I can use, or someone else will."

Harry nodded. "If our signal is heard, we may be able to help you before that happens." He paused. "That is, if we can find something to eat and drink, and stay out of the hands of your Council until then."

"Food and water aren't a problem," said Leonard. "The other part depends on how long we have to hide." They had reached a new door. "This used to be a residential area. No one has lived here for four generations at least." He led the way into a large hall with openings at regular intervals. "In my great-great-great-grandfather's day, this was a merchant hall. My father said that each of these apartments was the shop of a trader or craftsman. I wish I could have seen that."

"Perhaps you will again, but first we must find the reason your lives are shortening so." Harry turned to the doctor. "I think you have an idea as to the cause, Medico." He smiled. "Or may I call you Boris?"

The doctor looked surprised. "Yes, by all means, and I do have some ideas. My father had a theory, and I think I've found something to support it." He indicated the hall. "This was originally the main plaza for trade, but then it was reserved for the Council Families, and then, when they couldn't support the trade any longer, they closed it down."

"Yes, but they also forgot some of the little secrets it held." Leonard grinned in the partial light. "Like the service rooms above the Command Chamber. They can only be reached from the service passage here." He laughed, the sound echoing. "They'll never think of looking for us there, and from that vantage point, we can reach the storage rooms where the food supplies are held."

The fugitives awoke on the third day to the sound of angry voices from the Command Chamber.

"How should I know what this plague is? I'm not the Medico!"

"Yes, and now we haven't got one at all."

Harry moved to where the Boris and Leonard were listening to the voices at one of the spyholes, actually a small opening that had once provided a fixing point for some long removed device. Boris held a finger to his lips and pointed to another opening. Beneath them the voices were becoming louder.

"Enforcers!"

"No good calling in your personal thugs, Captain. They're down with the plague, remember?"

"And you're the one gave the order for the Medico to be imprisoned," snarled another officer.

"He committed mutiny! Don't come all innocent on me, you were all there when Purser reported him. I acted to stop them." There was a moment of silence. "You know what will happen if the workers find out the truth about the Enviros—or about the strangers."

"What should we do?"

"First, we have to find the Medico and the Mechanist. We need them to keep things running and to deal with this plague." He waited for this to sink in. "We have to find these strangers as well, and kill them. I've taken steps to punish the Hunters that brought them here in the first place. Ignorant fools. Their leader will meet with an accident and be replaced by a man less prone to independent thinking."

"Yes, all very well, but the absence of the Enforcers will be noticed."

"Not if we make sure some Enforcers are still on active duty."

"But they're all in isolation."

"They are, but we aren't. Some of us are going to wear their armour and make sure we're seen. Plus, I'm thinning the number of guards on the mine, and they'll do the searching for our escapers." He paused. "They'll do some of the patrolling as well. They'll enjoy that. They're brutes, so anyone falling afoul of them will no doubt get a beating, but that will help keep the rest in line."

Harry whispered to Boris, "I hope some of them wear the armour our original guards wore. Should be an interesting experience for them." His smile was conspiratorial.

Boris grinned. "Oh yes. Now that will be justice."

"Drop out in one minute," Pack Leader Lucanes growled.

Ferghal nodded, listening to the *Lagan* as she prepared to exit hyperspace. Already the ship was switching systems, bringing online those she needed, and shutting down those which the exit from transit would render redundant until they next went hyper. The seconds ticked away, and with the familiar slight shudder, the command display lit up showing the 360-degree view of the space around them. The corvette and the Lacertian patrol ship appeared against the backdrop of false colour three-dimensional imagery a nanosecond later.

"*Seana* and 847 on station, sir."

Ferghal acknowledged the report, his eyes seeking the planet they wanted, his mind searching for the signal source. "Tell 847 and *Seana* to take their positions for triangulation of the signal source." As the planet came into view, he tried to identify any body of water. Surely Harry would be near that. There didn't seem to be any.

The Canid and Lacertian ships vanished from the display and reappeared as pinpoints of light in positions on either beam of the *Lagan* and equidistant ahead of her. "If the transmitter is here, we should pick up its signal in five minutes."

"That place looks pretty bleak, sir."

Ferghal nodded, his forehead creased and his eyes hard. "Aye, it does. What evil mind would choose such a place to maroon a man?" He turned to the scan operator. "Is there any water on that planet?"

The TechRate adjusted her scanners. "Yes, sir, but it seems to be deep below ground. There's quite a network of caverns below the surface."

"Any life—animal or human?"

She adjusted the instruments again. "Yes, sir. Pretty sparse and difficult to say what it is. Looks like animals—big ones, some in groups, others singletons."

"Leader," said Regidur, who appeared on the small holoscreen at Ferghal' side. "We have recorded an impact or explosion site. It is recent. Do you wish me to investigate it?"

Ferghal felt a cold hand clutch his stomach. "Wait until we locate that signal, my friend. Then, yes, we must investigate it."

"Signal coming in!" The TechRate frantically adjusted his receivers. "Hell, it's loud. No wonder it's tripping the hyperlinks." He listened for a second. "It's them! It's Commander Heron!"

Ferghal was out of his seat. "Acknowledge it!" He was beaming with delight. "I knew he'd survive." He danced a little Irish jig to the astonishment of his crew. "Sure an' he's too much the sinner for heaven to take him yet—an' hell itself would be afraid to!" For a moment longer he danced back and forth, his mood infectious. "Have they replied?"

"No reply, sir, but there is a homing signal."

Ferghal's delight evaporated. He sank into his seat. "Then they have trouble. Navigation, put us on course to the location of that beacon." He nodded to the weapons officer. "Lieutenant, prepare a landing party. You will lead them in the launch. Pack Leader, you have command. I'm going down in the gig. I'll take two Marines with me."

As the door slid closed behind him the scan officer turned to Lucanes. "God help the people who did this if he finds Commander Heron dead. They'll wish for death if he finds them. Frankly, I wouldn't want to try and stop him either."

The Canid purred. "I agree, but they will be sorrier if my people or the Lacertians find them."

Harry and his companions were enjoying the spectacle below them. Some of the council had evidently tried on the armour used by the Enforcers, and were now suffering the effects of the powder that Boris had lined them with. The shouting and accusations had reached hysterical levels.

"Boris, I think we may have to intervene to prevent murder being committed at this rate."

The doctor glanced at him with a strange expression. "Why? They're responsible for hundreds of deaths among the working folk here. They have run this place entirely for their own comfort and benefit for almost all of our history. If they kill each other here and now, we'll be rid of them."

"Until some new tyrant arises. No, my friend, we must do this differently. If you have evidence of their having committed a crime against your people, then we will try them according to the law." Harry studied Boris and Leonard, then the scene below. Already blows were being exchanged and some of the participants were bloodied. There were more people now, some of them women. "Have you any of that medication you used to knock down the Enforcers?"

Boris shook his head. "No. I would have if I could reach my medical supplies, but I can't. Not without showing ourselves."

Harry looked down again. "We'll have to do something." He shook his head. "These woman are as bad as their men!" He watched as a woman attacked one of the men with a metal ornament. "Worse, I think." He got up. "Come on, we have to stop them. Warrant, find us something we can use to defend ourselves."

The gig descended rapidly, the launch keeping station to port, two escorting strike craft from *Seana* keeping company to starboard. "Some sort of dome structure crowning that crater rim, sir. The signal is coming from somewhere directly beneath it."

"Find us a landing place close to it then." The crater opened up as they turned to find a place to touch down, revealing a patchwork of fields and parks. Figures looked up gesticulating wildly. Some ran, some aimed odd looking weapons at the descending craft.

"Do not return fire," Ferghal barked. He touched his comlink. "Lieutenant, order your landing party to make sure they use only the stun settings on their weapons." He studied the various figures on his screen. "Some of them look like slaves. Look, they're manacled. Target only the ones with weapons if you have to."

"As you command, Sword Wielder."

He tapped the link to close it. "Take us down, Coxswain. Land on the ledge at that Observatory structure. Marines, you lead the way as soon as we're down. Stun only, I want people I can talk to, not dead bodies." He scowled. "That may come later," he added under his breath, adjusting his grip on the cutlass he always carried into battle.

Chapter 20

Cultural Collision

Harry followed Boris and Leonard down a tight staircase. He, the Warrant Officer and the TechRate carried heavy clubs, but Boris and Leonard were unarmed.

"Boris, we'll lead the way from the door. You two stay behind us and watch our backs." He hefted a large metal funnel they'd found. "Leonard, unlock the door, then get behind us." He turned to Boris. "You said this door is behind one of the portrait panels, right?"

"Yes, directly behind the Captain's chair."

Harry grinned. "Perfect. Then here goes." He swallowed carefully, moistening his mouth and his throat as he'd been taught to do centuries earlier. Then he filled his lungs, eased the narrow end of the funnel to his mouth and pushed the door. It swung clear revealing the mass of struggling and shouting people. "Silence," he bawled at the top of his voice and stepped into the chamber. "Do not move!"

The order was deafening, shaking dust from the ceiling as the sound rolled and roared throughout the chamber. The tableau froze. Then with astonishment, all eyes turned toward them.

"That's better. Now I commend to you the chairs you have overturned. Sit down, all of you. Those of you holding any instrument that can cause anyone injury, place it on the floor immediately."

There was a rustle of movement as most of those present complied without hesitation. Out of the corner of his eye, Harry sensed a movement and ducked just in time. The pop of compressed air was loud. So was the thud as the metal slug buried itself in the panel to his left. Then there was a second thud, partly the sound of something soft absorbing a blow, and partly metallic as a blunt instrument struck the man holding the air gun, who let out a screech of rage and demanded, "How dare you strike—!"

But Mike Dorfling's fist silenced him when it smashed into his jaw and sent him skidding across the floor and crashing off the platform. Mike followed him, grabbed two fists full of the Captain's ill-fitting armour, lifted him clear of the ground and flung him into a chair so hard it capsized. "Move again, you little piece of shite, and I'll tear you limb from bloody limb, Commander Heron's orders or no!" He advanced on the limp figure as people shuffled back to leave a clear space around him. The message was wasted on the Captain, as he was unconscious, but it sank into the consciousness of the rest of the assembly.

Mike glared at the widening circle. "I've had it with you back-assward cavemen—"

"Thank you, Mr. Dorfling, that will do." Harry had to raise his voice to check the angry man.

Dorfling took a deep breath then stepped back and stood next to Harry. "Aye, aye, sir. I got carried away. I despise bastards who shoot their enemies from the back, sir."

"Quite so," Harry said in a quiet voice to Mike, then raised his voice so all could hear. "Now, ladies and gentlemen, I am Commander Henry Nelson-Heron of the NECS *Lagan*, and I must tell you that other than your Medico and Mechanist, I have not been particularly impressed by the savage welcome you have shown us or your behaviour toward one another." He indicated the fallen Captain. "Since your leader appears to be temporarily incapacitated, who is his deputy?"

Before anyone could respond, the door burst open. "Airships! The Enviros have airships! They've landed—and they're attacking. They're killing all the valley guards and everyone they see." The man's terror showed.

Everyone stood rooted to the spot in stunned silence.

"They're coming this way—NOW!" he shrieked.

There was instant chaos as the assembly leapt to their feet shouting orders and ignoring Harry. Above the din, the Warrant Officer shouted, "I think the Fleet have arrived, sir. Let's get out of here and find a way to get to them."

Harry nodded. "Follow me." He grabbed the arms of Boris and Leonard and steered them through the doorway into the staircase with Mike and Jack close behind. "Leonard, secure this door, and then I want you to take us the shortest way to the outside. The Enviros that frightened man alluded to are our people, the Fleet, and we need to get to them as soon as possible to prevent a tragedy. They'll use a take-no-prisoners approach if a certain flame-haired Irish Commander is in charge...."

Ferghal followed his Marines as they advanced into the Observatory, checked it, then led the way down the stairs to Leonard's workshop. He stood a moment and took it all in. "That coms unit is hidden here somewhere." He peered at the machines. "These things are antiques." He laughed. "Not quite as old as me, but old. Look, some are almost worn out."

"Yes, sir." The Coxswain frowned. "The scanner says it's under this one, sir." There's some kind of chamber down there, but I'm damned if I can see how you get to it."

Ferghal studied the four massive bolts that secured the thing to the floor. He frowned then very carefully gripped one, gave it a quarter turn and pulled. The thing came up quite easily. He grinned. "Cunning." Quickly he examined the other bolts, withdrew two more and left the fourth while his men watched with puzzled expressions. "Warrant, push on that corner of the unit, please."

The Warrant Officer heaved with all his might, expecting a struggle, and stumbled forward when the weighty machine moved easily on a pivot to expose the entrance to the chamber and the coms unit.

"F*ck me, how did you—?"

"Not difficult." Ferghal bent down and peered inside. "No one there. Damn. Tech, get down and shut the thing off. We don't want anyone else following the beacon now." He straightened and grinned at the Warrant Officer. "I noticed a different sound as I stepped on the base plate. Then, when I looked at the bolts, I could see three had been handled recently." He pointed. "See, here, the head is clean where I've touched it, and a slight bit of oil rubbed off on my fingers. Then I saw it was a lock bolt. Just a quarter turn to unlock it and you can withdraw it. With a spring washer under it, it would feel spanner tight normally." He put the bolt down. "Now, the question is, where is Commander Heron and his people? I've a feeling, from the look of these things and that unit, that only they would have known how to get it working." His comlink chirped. "Commander O'Connor."

"Commander, we've located what must be their administration centre. There seems to be a riot in progress."

Ferghal spotted the discarded helmet that had encased Harry's head and picked it up. Noting the clumps of hair, he snatched up a handful and squinted at it. "Harry's hair," he murmured. To the link he said, "Stop the riot—use stunners if you must. I'll join you immediately." Snapping off the link, he signalled the others. "With me." He tossed the helmet to the TechRate. "Hold on to that. I'm sure it wasn't made by these folk, so it may have come with Commander Heron. It may be important later."

By the time he found his search teams, the riot had ceased. Several guards lay where they had fallen in response to the Marines' stun weapons, and the rest of the people clustered in a sullen group against the side wall of the Council Chamber—council members and their families, and various workers—all frightened and not saying a word.

Ferghal surveyed the gathering. "Is this everyone? The entire population?"

"This is all we managed to round up, sir." The Marine sergeant snapped a salute. "We think there are a lot more, but this place is a rabbit warren, and most of their people vanished underground and have barricaded themselves inside."

Ferghal scowled. "Damn." He raised his voice. "Who is in charge here?"

There was a murmuring and shuffling, then one of the council members was thrust forward. "Captain is, but one of the savages—" He caught Ferghal's expression and revised his words. "One of the strangers we captured attacked him. He's unconscious." He glanced nervously behind him. "We can't tend to him because they've kidnapped our Medico as well."

"Kidnapped him, did you say?" Ferghal's voice was quiet.

"Damn it, you fool, tell them the truth or you'll get us all killed." The speaker was an older woman. "Our esteemed Captain thought to play the brave defender. Your man attacked him, that is true, but only after Captain tried to shoot their leader in the back. As for them kidnapping our Medico and the Mechanist—rubbish! Captain had thrown both of them into prison for mutiny because they helped the strangers."

"Thank you." Ferghal frowned. "And where are our people now?"

"Are you looking for us, sir? Tsk, and with such force against these poor defenceless folk."

Ferghal whirled round in disbelief as anger, amusement, and delight chased across his face. "Harry, you *spailpín!*" In two strides he was across the chamber, wrapping his arms around him and lifting him from his feet. "You set the cat into the pigeon loft this time, you rogue!" He set Harry down again, taking in the bruises and swelling that betrayed the beating his friend had taken. "Look at you, a fine example to your men I see." Ferghal's Irish accent had descended into a nearly incomprehensible brogue, and everyone watched and listened in utter befuddlement. "Begorrah, sir, a fine chase you gave us this time." He grinned. "Some in the Fleet want to decorate you again, others want to court martial and hang you—and you've stirred up a real hornet's nest elsewhere." He became serious. "There's a price on your head. Certain people do not want you to testify in the prosecutions being prepared against some very powerful people."

"Well, well," Harry smiled. "I'll take each one as it arises." He waved a hand toward the audience. "I think we've a need to help these folk as well—despite their lack of hospitality."

"Aye, aye, Commander." Ferghal saluted half in seriousness and half in fun. "I'm minded to think that it is not long since they wanted to capture and kill you, and now you give orders to assist them." He shook his head. "You've not changed, my friend, nor would I want you to. Tell us what must be done."

"First, have your people bring all of these folk outside. There we may talk to them and show them who and what we are. I think they have been deliberately kept in ignorance by their leaders for a long, long time, and now they must face reality."

Ferghal nodded. "See to it, Sergeant." He smiled. "Harry—Commander, if you are to appear in public, allow me to at least provide you with some fresh clothing." He gave a mock scowl as he took in the rags that remained of Harry's uniform. "Sure an' all, this society seems very primitive, but the filthy rags you're clad in are only barely decent even here, sir, and about that beard, I must say...!"

Harry leaned against the wall and laughed until tears streamed down his face. He had missed Ferghal's blunt Irish honesty. "Thank you, my friend. I have long since forgotten what it is like to be clean, decently attired and presentable." He glanced at his men and the bewildered doctor and mechanist. "To be honest, I've had other concerns. Clothing wasn't one of them."

Ferghal smiled. "I think we noticed."

"And I have forgotten my manners. Ferghal, these are Boris the Medico and Leonard the Mechanist. A better pair of friends and companions on a misadventure like this you would be hard pressed to find. Now, find me something decent to wear—preferably a Fleet uniform, if you can conjure one for me and my men. We have work to do."

Ten minutes later, Harry and his companions had fresh trousers and shirts. "Already I feel like a new man, but a shower and sleeping in a comfortable bunk will be luxury." Harry smiled as Boris and Leonard watched in amazement as first the clothes then the medical equipment was produced.

"I've had a MedTech brought down from *Lagan*," Ferghal announced. "I told her to bring the full medi-scan kit. You'll have to tell her what she's looking for."

Harry nodded. With his beard and hair now neatly trimmed— courtesy of the Corporal of the Marines—he looked younger and yet more authoritative than ever. "Good. Boris, I think you will find this interesting. Medicine has advanced considerably in the last hundred years, and I hope the MedTech will be able to confirm your suspicions as to the shortening of your lifespans."

"Next you'll tell me it can be reversed."

Harry shook his head. "That I don't know. I hope the early aging process can at least be slowed to what is considered a normal lifespan on Earth. We'll see." He stood. "Now, with Lieutenant-Commander O'Connor's permission, I'd appreciate your accompanying me to talk to your people. I suspect the World Treaty Organisation, or whichever of its treaty governments originally sponsored your ancestors' migration to this planet, will want to relocate you to a more suitable planet for colonising. For now, I want to reassure them the plague is no threat and the Fleet intends them no injury—but I will also require their cooperation to find all the people you refer to as Enviros or Wanderers." He frowned. "Originally they were descended from the Environmental Engineers on the ship that brought you here. Frankly, the reason they were expelled from your society is disgraceful."

"Will you be here to oversee this, Commander?"

"No, Boris. That will be the responsibility of others." Harry paused. "I've learned we are in the midst of a war—again—and I must return to Fleet Command and face a Court Martial for my capture." He smiled. "But I shall stay in touch, whatever the outcome." He walked out to confront the assembled crowd, which seemed to have been joined by some of the workers who had emerged from hiding. It was going to be a difficult confrontation, and he was glad that neither the Canids nor the Lacertians were present. That bit of culture shock would come later for the misguided populace of Centaur.

It took a lot of persuasion and a great deal of patience, but eventually Harry got an agreement. He retired to the gig with Ferghal for refreshment and rest. "Well done, Harry," Ferghal said as soon as they were alone. "You look done in. Take a nap. I'll set things in motion now, and we can make a start on finding these outsiders they call the Enviros."

"Thank you, my friend. I will take a short rest. Where are my two fellow travellers?"

"Ah, yes, about that. Warrant Officer Proctor and TechRate Dorfling had a little chat, as they called it, with one or two individuals. The SBT had to patch up the people they talked to. It seems to have been a very comprehensive talk." He paused. "I've sent them both aloft to get cleaned up and rested."

"Ah." Harry hesitated. "I should have prevented that."

"You couldn't have." Ferghal grinned. "I understand the fellows they talked to have declined to say anything about it, and are now very keen to cooperate with us. I suppose I should take action against them, but perhaps it is better left alone."

Harry nodded. His head seemed full of cotton wool now, and he desperately wanted to sleep. "Have we a response from the Fleet about these people?"

"Yes. A refugee ship is on its way together with a team to assess and deal with the cultural issues." Ferghal chuckled. "I believe the LPSL tried to get involved, but as they have been exposed as tied in with the pirates and the Charonians, they got very short shrift." He looked across at Harry. "Now, sir, the bunk awaits you!"

James Heron smiled at his sister in the hologram projection. "Good news, Niamh. We found him. A little battered according to reports, and tired, but otherwise intact. He sends his love to Mary, of course."

"Where is he? Mary will want to talk to him herself." She smiled. "And tell him off for breaking his promise to stay out of trouble."

"I'm afraid that pleasure will have to be delayed. We're keeping his whereabouts quiet, and we'll keep him out of circulation for the moment. There's been a development that makes it necessary. Ferghal has him in hand for now, and will take care of him."

"Development? Ah. Don't these bastards ever let up?" Niamh frowned. "No, don't answer that, I know without your telling me. I meet that type all the time."

"Then you know what I mean."

"Yes. Just take good care of them, James. Bring them home safely."

Chapter 21

Prodigal's Return

"So, it seems you were right, Commander." The Surgeon-Captain from the refugee ship *Fort Belvedere* leaned back in his seat. "The radiation from the faulty fission drives must have damaged this people's original DNA, and that combined with inbreeding, their limited diet and the harsh environment explains their shortened lifespans. They age at roughly three times the normal rate for us Earth-born humans. It has made them susceptible to further degradation through their contact with some of the creatures here, and the lack of certain minerals in their diet. But I'm curious to know how you arrived at this conclusion."

"I didn't," said Harry. "It was suggested by the man they call Medico—who seems to have a passable amount of medical knowledge—and I found confirmation in the computer core they preserved." Harry frowned. "This explains why so many behave as if they are children, though they appear much older."

The medic nodded. "Many of them are little more than teenagers in terms of development and years. Has that data been copied to my team?"

"Yes, sir. I believe the entire unit has been recovered and all the data is being processed. Hopefully, it will also reveal what went wrong and how they managed to establish themselves there." Harry shook his head. "We were incredibly fortunate in our wanderings. I have learned that the creature they call a sand dragon is but one of a number of extremely venomous predators. That we didn't encounter any of the others is nothing short of miraculous."

The surgeon finished running his tests. "Quite. Okay, Commander, you seem to have suffered no lasting ill effects from your enforced liquid diet. You'll need to regain your body mass and build up the muscle you lost, but that apart, you'll be fit for duty whenever Fleet decide to return you to active involvement." He handed Harry a data chip. "This contains my recommendations for exercise and dietary suggestions."

Harry grinned. "Thank you, sir. I'm to travel home on the *Lagan*, and I must say, I'm looking forward to departing this particular corner of the universe."

"Yes, I can imagine." The surgeon smiled. "Best of luck to you."

Ferghal checked the equipment of Leonard and Boris. "I've put you into these suits as a precaution." He grinned. "They monitor your vital functions and keep you comfortable. It can be a little alarming during acceleration to escape the planet's gravity." He checked their seat belts. "We'll be weightless for a while since the gig only has artificial gravity when we're tethered to a larger vessel."

Both men looked excited but nervous. "This ship you're taking us to—is it a large one?"

"The *Lagan*? Bless you, no. She's a patrol ship, bigger than a corvette but about a third the size of a frigate." He finished strapping himself in. "Secure, Coxswain. Take us aloft, please." He glanced at Boris and Leonard as the hatches shut and latched. "You'll be able to see the refugee ship your people are travelling in as we meet up with mine. She's the *Fort Belvedere*, and she's quite large." Ferghal noted their puzzled expressions. "We weren't sure how many of you were on the planet, so they sent a ship large enough for ten times as many as you turned out to be."

The gig, her start-up and first gentle lift completed, now turned slowly on her horizontal axis, the semi-circle of viewscreens providing a panoramic view of the rock carved settlement as she did so. The large passenger barges from the *Fort Belvedere* could be seen at one end of the crater with queues of people boarding.

Boris asked, "Are these windows we're looking through?"

Ferghal smiled. "I thought so the first time I saw them. No, these are screens. Sensors outside the hull collect the image and display it." He saw their confusion. "It's part of the ship's scanning system, but it only shows us a small part of what it is seeing all around it. I know, humans aren't very good at handling multiple streams of data—information—but the ships are."

Boris and Leonard nodded wordlessly, and their expressions said it all: *We believe you, but we don't understand...* They didn't want to appear ignorant, so they remained silent and took it all in.

Ferghal sensed this and remembered how clueless he was when he first encountered such modern technology after dropping into this century straight out of the nineteenth. He decided it was best to let them take it all in. Understanding would come later.

Clear of the rim, the gig began to accelerate and climb. "I'll take her up the long way, sir." The Coxswain indicated the passengers with a slight inclination of his head. "Not quite so dramatic if you get my drift."

Ferghal nodded. "Good idea, but try to keep the spell in weightlessness short." He grinned. "Tricky if you've never experienced it." His companions hardly seemed to notice as the gig climbed, gradually accelerating. Their focus was entirely on the landscape of the world they were leaving, a barren kaleidoscope of reds, browns, greys and shades between. Here and there brilliant white patches suggested dried lakes or seas, but nowhere was any sign of water visible.

As they ascended, the sky gradually darkened and the speed increased; then, almost without transition, they were above the planet engulfed in darkness.

"*Lagan*'s closing to pick us up, sir."

"Very good," said Ferghal. To Boris and Leonard, he said, "See the bright star over there, just above the planetary horizon? That's the *Belvedere*. If you keep your eye on her, you'll soon see how big she is." Both men were a little pale, but their eyes were riveted on the breathtaking views opening before them.

Ferghal continued. "If you look to starboard—that's your right—you'll see the *Lagan* closing us." He felt a touch of jealousy as he looked at the graceful shape becoming clearer against the backdrop of the stars. There was no doubt the ship was Harry's even though he, Ferghal, had officially been given the command. Just the manner in which the AI had welcomed her former commander had said more than anything else could possibly have done: Harry's charm. *Well, he'll need that and a lot more in the current mess.*

He shook his head and turned to Boris. "I'm sorry, I was miles away. You were saying...?"

"No, Ferghal, the Captain's quarters are yours. You are the commander appointed in my place. I shall be perfectly comfortable in the spare berth until we rejoin the Fleet." He shrugged. "Then we shall see."

Ferghal frowned. "It doesn't seem right, Harry. The ship is yours. Your absence was not of your choosing."

"I know, but you were given command of her for this mission, and I must face the Enquiry." Harry smiled. "Come, my friend, we are together again, now tell me what has transpired in my absence."

Ferghal grimaced. "It would be far easier to describe what has not happened." He exhaled. "Where to begin? Soon after we learned of your being kidnapped, there was an attempt to take over almost two-thirds of our ships. Some were so badly damaged they will be months in rebuilding. The Flag Captain—Greenacre—committed suicide in his Command Centre rather than surrender, and Senator Samland was arrested when she made the mistake of visiting a planet to meet some of her conspirators." He grinned. "She was recognised by a certain pianist who was there on a concert tour and just happened to mention it to a certain lady in old Ireland."

Harry's heart almost stopped. "Mary! Is she safely away from there?"

Ferghal nodded. "Aye, she is. No concerns there. Though there was an attempt to assassinate Theo and to kidnap Aunt Niamh! Our little terrier—Danny—frustrated that, and now they are very well guarded indeed." He paused, frowning. "The arrest of the Senator did trigger a great deal though, since she was captured with a room full of people on the wanted lists for piracy." He gestured around the cabin. "With the data *Lagan* recorded, we found leads—or the Security Services did—to any number of others involved. It's been quite a traumatic time for everyone, with protesters on the streets demanding the Senator's release, and now others demanding a complete change of government and treason trials." He grinned. "Of course the LPSL are in the thick of it, but they've been totally discredited—at least for now. Their true believers cling to the ideal and ignore the truth. Some make the little party we interrupted in retrieving you seem quite tame in comparison." He studied Harry for a moment. "And someone has now increased the price on your head."

Harry groaned. "What for? Why do they consider me such a threat? It never ends." He shook his head in frustration. "I've been watching some of the news channels. What of these Charonians?"

"It seems you accessed something when the Senator demanded your presence—information some will pay a vast amount to prevent you revealing. The more we learn of the Charonians, the less we like, and the more foolish their allies look. Those are the Senators and their followers who sought an advantage through alliances with the Charonians." He opened a drawer and retrieved a data chip. "This will explain why."

"Thank you, I shall study this with interest." Harry frowned. "You've not shared it with the ship?"

Ferghal shook his head. "Study it. You'll see why."

"Very well." Harry put the chip away. "How did Boris and Leonard react to the journey in the gig?"

Ferghal laughed. "Like frightened children at first, then like children who have glimpsed Saint Nicholas with a bag full of gifts." His smile broadened. "I've sent them on a tour of the ship with Jenny." His eyes twinkled with mischief. "I considered sending Lucanes or Sci'antha, but they were obviously half afeared Sci'anthawould eat them, and as for Lucanes, they seemed uncertain whether to greet him or attempt to pet him."

Harry burst out laughing. "I shouldn't think they would ever have known a pet dog, and definitely not one that thinks, speaks, and is adept at navigation." He stopped, still grinning. "I suppose that's their childlike nature coming through. Who knows? Where have you put them for the passage?"

Ferghal grinned. "You're gonna love this: In the Wardroom next to Lucanes' sleeping den."

It was just the comic relief Harry needed, and he laughed with Ferghal as they'd done when they were boys.

Harry leaned back in his chair. The information on the Charonians was comprehensive, and he wondered how it had been obtained. They were appalling, interesting, and repulsive. In appearance like some depictions from the Middle Ages of devils, yet the most appalling part was that they apparently did not reproduce in the normal manner. He rubbed his eyes then cupped his hands with his elbows on the tabletop and rested his chin. It did not bear thinking about. The idea of planting a type of zygote in a host body, which would then be taken over and modified to the Charonian form was repugnant enough, but the suggestion was that the original being remained a prisoner, its cognitive functions still very much alive and active while the new occupant took over all active functions and control of the host. "*Lagan*, if you have read this data through me, you are to erase it from your memory, please."

"I shall do so, Harry, though I have already seen it through Ferghal. Should I erase that as well?"

"Yes, that will be best."

"May I know why?"

"Yes, that is only fair, but you had better erase this as well after I explain it. The Charonians don't know what we have learned about them and their methods of reproducing themselves. As they have compromised much of our communications system, there is a risk they may be able to access your memory and the memories of all our ships."

"Thank you for telling me. It explains some of the strange attempts to communicate with me. I have refused all such communication. Should I warn others?"

Harry sat bolt upright. "Yes! Do so immediately. Report it to Security too, please. If you can identify a source, let them know that as well."

"Kali, it seems the Senator's attempt to dispose of Commander Heron failed." Zorvan steepled his fingers as he contemplated Kali's avatar. The stylised figure of the multi-armed goddess had a certain attractive grace, he had to admit. "He and his companions survived."

"I was right. He is a worthy adversary." Kali hesitated. She realised too late that she probably shouldn't have said that. "Where is he now? He will not survive a hunt, and I have the perfect location for it."

"For the moment he is beyond our reach, but there may be another way. I have assigned Shiva and Durga to arrange for someone close to him to be taken. I have studied him, and believe he will offer himself in exchange." He chuckled, a chilling sound from him. "You may have to delay your pleasure, however. Our Charonian friends have an interest in him and are willing pay an excessive sum for his delivery."

Kali remained silent for several seconds. "A pity." The avatar shrugged. "My team is now installed on the *Emily Hobhouse*. We are to rendezvous with the Fleet and *Fort Belvedere* and take on the survivors retrieved from the planet...uh, what was that name again? It's not an official name, just something the locals call it—Centaur, that's it. Maybe this will present another opportunity."

"It may. However, it would be unwise to attempt anything until the ship is detached for Earth."

Kali laughed. "We are ready—and certainly not suicidal."

"We're due to drop out in fifteen minutes, sir." Ferghal grinned. "I'm to close the flagship and they'll send a barge to collect you and our two passengers." He hesitated. "Would you care to join me in the Command Centre for dropout? I've invited Boris and Leonard to be there. I want to see their faces when they see a starship for the first time." He chuckled.

Harry grinned. "I too. They have almost driven your people mad with questions and their desire to see and learn everything. I think they have made good use of their time with us." He rose and pulled on his dress jacket. "Shall we take our places in the Command Centre?" He glanced round the cabin. "Thank you for being so tolerant of me, my dear friend. I know it is not easy for you to be the official Captain with the ex-Captain looking over your shoulder."

Ferghal smiled. "No, it is not." He paused, his finger hovering on the door control. "But it cannot be easy for you either. She is your ship, and I am certain she will be restored to you once the Enquiry is behind us." He glanced down then met Harry's eyes. "I expect I'll be hauled back to my post in the Constructors Office, but I should not complain, I suppose—office hours, usually on a half-decent planet, with plenty of fine ladies at hand..."

"Rogue!" Harry slipped an arm through his friend's. "Come, we had best be in the Command Centre when we drop out."

Leonard and Boris sat in awed silence as *Lagan* and her companions dropped out of transit in the middle of the waiting fleet.

"There, my friends. That is the flagship, the starship *Foud-royant*." Ferghal's pride showed. "A beauty, but overrun with gold lace and importance—mere Lieutenant-Commanders are hardly noticed aboard her!" Ferghal turned his attention to manoeuvring the *Lagan* onto the required station. "The Admiral requires our presence, Commander—and our guests."

Harry admired the graceful lines of the great ship. Even her weapons emplacements enhanced her appearance, while the gaping landing dock on the lateral fin closest to them as they approached showed the destination of several small launches and a barge all moving toward her. The scale of the starship became all the more apparent as the *Lagan* positioned herself off the very tip of the huge fin.

"It's huge," whispered Leonard.

"Yes, it is," Harry said with a smile. "And very real despite the fairytales your captain tried to tell your people about starships and space travel." He chuckled at their wry expressions and exchanged glances. Watching them discover the reality of the twenty-third century in civilised society had been interesting. "And the *Foudroy-ant* is equipped with luxuries we small ship crews can only dream of enjoying," he added as he led the way to the exit. "The flagship is sending a launch to collect us, and we'd best not keep the Admiral waiting."

Chapter 22

Change of Command

"Commander Heron, please stand for the verdict."

A hush fell over the court as Harry stood and gave his jacket a nervous tug to straighten its near immaculate set on his frame. He faced the Admiral, one Commodore and three Captains of the Bench with a quickened pulse, not certain what to expect. Even the reassuring confidence of an Advocate Commander, who was absolutely convinced of a positive outcome, couldn't dispel his nervousness. It had been a gruelling and very trying four days. Apart from the endless review of the recorded messages and visual recordings, there had been the witnesses to endure.

Lieutenant MacKenzie-Banks had been the first and the most difficult to listen to. Banks had been defensive, admitting that he'd not been happy to serve under Harry at the beginning, but then rather defiantly admitting that he'd been surprised by his commanding officer's willingness to give him a chance. The rest of his evidence was straightforward, ending with him volunteering the information that he'd made mistakes, but would willingly accept a future role under Harry's leadership.

Other members of the crew had presented an equally positive picture, and so had Harry's companions for the ordeal. He'd had a surprise, though, when Boris, Leonard and another man were called to testify. Harry didn't recognise the man until he spoke, and then he learned he was the leader of the hunting party that had found them.

Ferghal was called forward to give an account of how he and his team had identified the source of the strange signal and tracked it.

"Having heard the evidence of the witnesses present on the *Lagan*, and having examined the ship's recordings of the actual events, communications between the Senator, Commander Heron, Flag Captain Greenacre and the *Harmony Voyager*'s own captain, and having further examined the record of the events captured on the *Voyager* by that ship's recorders, and the record taken from the second recorder unit carried by Commander Heron of his incarceration in the helmet before us, and subsequent marooning of himself and the surviving members of his gig crew, we find Commander Heron innocent of any suggestion of failure to do his duty or to comply with the orders he received."

There was a general sigh from the audience, and Harry relaxed somewhat, but he was certain there was an unspoken 'but' in the Admiral's statement. What it was, he had no idea. *I suppose I'm about to find out*, he mused.

"We find that the circumstances of this incident are disturbing, and having considered the whole very carefully, we conclude that you were incredibly lucky to have survived at all. The testimony of your companions, Warrant Officer Jack Proctor and TechRate Michael Dorfling, provides ample evidence of the difficulties and the extreme conditions you endured and overcame in the best traditions of the service. It is unfortunate that your initial rescuers proved to be somewhat less than welcoming. However, your subsequent approach and handling of a very difficult confrontation is to your credit." The presiding Rear-Admiral paused and smiled. "We have no hesitation in declaring you exonerated of all charges of dereliction of duty or of failing to take proper action in the face of an enemy." He nodded to the members of the Enquiry seated to his left and right. "Congratulations, young man. You showed remarkable courage and determination in circumstances many would have found impossible to deal with."

"All rise," boomed the stentorian voice of the Master at Arms as the Admiral rose, gathered his tablet and led the other members of his Bench from the courtroom.

Harry let out his breath, barely conscious of having been holding it nearly the entire time the Admiral spoke. He turned to thank his legal representative as well-wishers clustered round him showering him with congratulations. He managed to field these and make his way to the Commander, a diffident individual who had several times surprised both Harry and a witness by undergoing a complete change of personality in an instant from polite, almost apologetic conversation to aggressive pursuit of an answer.

"Thank you," Harry said, shaking the man's hand. "I think I would have struggled without your help."

"It was a pleasure, and easy really." The Commander smiled. "They simply could not have delivered any other verdict on the evidence."

"I am glad to know you saw it so." Harry smiled. "I would almost rather face the Niburu again than this."

"I'm not so sure about that, Harry—er, Commander Heron," Ferghal chimed in. "To be sure though, you may have a tough time ahead with your fiancée—she and your aunt are in league against us, I think." Ferghal was grinning from ear to ear.

Harry's face coloured. "What have they demanded?"

Ferghal laughed. "Your head on a platter, or to make you go shopping for wedding fripperies with them—choose your poison!"

Harry said in a droll tone, "I'll be the main course, then," and Ferghal let out a boisterous laugh as Harry visibly shuddered at the thought of enduring a shopping trip with the ladies.

Ferghal added, "In all seriousness, though, I suspect Mary and Niamh might have to wait their turn, as the Admiral sends her respects and requests the pleasure of your company as soon as convenient."

Harry laughed. "Then I am in trouble. In her quarters or her Command Centre?"

"Her quarters." Ferghal grinned. "I am ordered to accompany you, no doubt to be advised of my fate." His expression changed. "I have packed my things ready to transfer command of the *Lagan* back to you and return to the Constructors Office."

"Everyone seems to have expected the outcome of the court except myself." Harry frowned. "I hope your packing is premature, my friend. You make a good commander, and I can think of no one

I would rather see take charge of *Lagan* than you, wild Irishman though you be."

"Commander Heron to see you, ma'am," announced the Admiral's android assistant.

"Show him in." The Admiral pushed her tablet aside. "Is Lieutenant-Commander O'Connor with him?"

"Yes, ma'am."

"Send them in, please." Vice Admiral Petrocova looked up. "Take a seat both of you." She rose from her desk and joined them. "Steward, bring my guests some refreshment." She settled into her chair. "Now that we have the Enquiry out of the way, Harry, you can get back in the saddle." She smiled. "We still have an enemy to deal with."

Harry smiled. "Thank you, ma'am. It is a relief to have been exonerated."

"I expect so." She paused. "There is still one problem. You know there's a contract out on you. We know who has placed it, and we know who has been hired as the mercenary—but it isn't quite so simple." She waited while the android steward handed Harry and Ferghal their drinks. When she had their full attention again, she said, "So I'm not leaving you in command of the *Lagan*."

Harry's heart sank. Despite the problems during the construction and working up phases, he'd loved the ship and enjoyed working with the crew. "Yes, ma'am."

"I've a new command for you, so don't look so disappointed." She turned to Ferghal. "Have you enjoyed command of the *Lagan*? Are the ship and crew to your satisfaction?"

Ferghal looked surprised. "Yes, ma'am."

"Good. You'll be joining a new joint flotilla I'm putting together." She paused. "Eight ships in all—two Lacertian corvettes, four Canid, the *Lagan* and one patrol ship of the new Leader Class." She smiled at Harry. "You'll be Flotilla Leader. The new ship is the *Sabre*. She's fully worked up and ready for you. In fact, you'll know several of her officers and Rates. One of the officers is your Flotilla Engineer officer." She paused. "You'll have a couple of Special Forces men in the crew. I won't spell out why. Whenever you leave the ship, one of them will be with you." She pushed a data chip toward him. "Your new command is waiting for you. Once you're worked up, you'll be transferring to Task Force One,

Admiral Heron's command. Good luck. Your gig was sent for ten minutes ago and should be in the landing bay about now."

Harry felt a little overwhelmed, but rallied quickly. "Thank you, ma'am. Who am I replacing?"

She smiled. "My Staff Officer. He's been minding the ship since you were found and while you went through the debriefing and Enquiry process. Werner has enjoyed himself, but he'll get over it, and I need him here."

Harry felt some relief at this news. He knew Commander Werner Nickel, and was aware the Commander enjoyed his post as Fleet Staff Officer as much as Harry enjoyed the mathematics of navigation. "Then I shall waste no time in relieving him, ma'am." Harry smiled. "I had hoped to see the gentlemen I brought back with me from that planet the locals call Centaur, but I understand they have been moved with the rest of their people."

The Admiral nodded. "They're on the hospital ship *Emily Hobhouse*. I'm sure you can find an excuse to visit before they leave for Earth." She stood as her link chirped. "I think that'll be your gigs."

The pair stood and Harry saluted. "Thank you, ma'am." He turned as the door slid aside and Commander Nickel entered.

"Ah, so, you're ready?" The newcomer held out his hand. "She's all yours, a worse crew of cutthroats I have yet to find." He grinned. "You should fit right in."

The *Sabre*, though similar to the *Lagan*, was much larger and had a few external features which looked unusual. "We've some additional weaponry. Oh, and a system for blocking detection on other scanners." Lieutenant Danny Gunn grinned. "It's something the Lacertians developed."

Harry studied the ship. She was sleeker than the patrol ships, and her drive pods looked different as well. "She looks very good. How did she perform on her trials and working up?"

"Amazing. She's one of the new breed. The new drives are fantastic, and her weapons outfit gives us the same punch as a much bigger ship. Oh, and we carry a full platoon of Marines plus their officers."

Harry nodded. "So I've been told. Looks like we've got extra boats as well."

"Yes, a pair of landing barges, two launches and this gig, sir." Danny grinned. "That's why we have a different silhouette. They had to enlarge the hangars, but the new drive systems take up less space."

"On approach now, sir." Jack Proctor called over his shoulder. "Docking in two minutes."

"Thank you, Master Warrant." Harry smiled. "How many favours did this transfer cost you?"

Jack laughed. "A few, sir. Mike's here as well." He grinned. "Leading TechRate Dorfling. He was a tad surprised to get his promotion, but apparently that Centaur captain chappie decided not to make a fuss about his 'accident' when Mike 'fell' on him." He chuckled. "It was pointed out to him that his trying to have us killed probably wouldn't sound good if he made a case of it."

The gig lined up on the open hangar bay and settled gently onto the deck. Behind it, the outer shell doors closed and the internal lights came on.

"Atmosphere stable, sir. Opening the hatch."

"Thank you." Harry glanced at the speaker, a man he didn't recognise. "I'm sorry, I haven't yet heard your name."

The man grinned. "TechRate First Class Leitvin Sonderburg, sir."

"Thank you." Harry smiled. "I shall look forward to getting to know you as a member of my crew." The hatch opened. "Well, Mr. Gunn, I take it my gear is already aboard?" He didn't wait for a reply and stepped out of the gig to receive the salute of the side party.

"Welcome aboard, sir." Lieutenant-Commander Keiron Whitworth smiled. "I've had your kit stowed in your quarters." He smiled. "I think you'll find the *Sabre* as good a command as the one you had at Fleet College."

"Keiron! What are you doing here?" Harry smiled and extended his hand. "I thought you had your own command."

Keiron grinned. "Long story, but I'm your Exec on this commission."

Harry nodded. "I see. Perhaps you'll join me for a meal later and tell me about it." He gestured round the hangar. "First though, perhaps you'd give me a tour of the Control sections? I want to get to know at least my key officers as soon as possible."

"Of course, sir." He fell into step beside Harry. "We've got a great team. I think you know a couple of them already." He hesitated. "Did the Admiral tell you we've some ghosts aboard—Special Services?"

"Yes, she did." Harry made a face. "I am not certain I like the idea. Do you know who they are?"

Keiron hesitated. "Yes, I do." He paused, a half smile playing on his lips. "I'm one. I'm the Unit Commander, but that isn't general knowledge, and probably best if it stays between us, sir."

Harry stared. "Ah. Very well, but I think I would appreciate your being open with me about what is really happening here." He smiled. "I wondered why you seemed to vanish from the Fleet list. Would I be wrong if I guessed your actual rank is the same as mine?" He watched his friend's face. "I thought so. Very well, if it suits you to act the Exec, then so be it. I'm glad it is you, Keiron."

Keiron smiled. "You don't miss much, do you. You're right, but it's a necessary ruse. You remember Senzile? He's also one of the ghost Fleet. He's leading the squad providing protection for the Chief Justice in Dublin."

"I can see I'm in good hands then." Harry smiled as they entered his new quarters. "Take dinner with me this evening. We have much to discuss for this commission."

Harry took his seat in the Command Centre. His conversation with Keiron had been enlightening and troubling. As he suspected, this command was more about keeping him out of sight and out of the line of fire than about any operational need. It seemed he'd made some extremely dangerous enemies by surviving and exposing the records they had tried to conceal.

Harry expressed his concerns later that evening at dinner with Keiron. "There must be something more to it," he said. "Security have the lists, so killing me or members of my family will not erase them. What more could there possibly be to it?"

Keiron hesitated. "There are a couple of places in the list where the individuals' names make no sense. They seem to be code names. We think, and their actions suggest we may be right, that the key to that mystery is somewhere in your head, or perhaps in something else you accessed. That may be why they want you dead."

That was bad enough, but the threat now hung over the rest of the family, and Mary in particular. It was little comfort to know that she, like Niamh, Theo, Ferghal and Danny, had the best teams of Keiron's 'ghosts' guarding them round the clock. If anything, it made him even more concerned. The only thing he wanted for Mary was a happy, carefree life far removed from the madness of the world...

Chapter 23

Provoked

"**D**o you have the feeling we're being watched?" Mary glanced at Niamh as they walked through the Botanical Gardens in Glasnevin, a place of stunning tranquility on the outskirts of Dublin. "I know our shadow agents are here, but this feels different, almost malevolent."

"Now you mention it, yes, it does feel disturbing somehow." Niamh looked round. "Something's not right. Let's go back." She made a show of looking at her wrist tablet. "Good lord!" She exclaimed slightly louder than necessary. "I'd forgotten I should be at Theo's Chambers. I'll have to contact him and tell him we're on our way."

"Oh!" Mary joined the charade. "I shouldn't have dragged you out to the Gardens. If we go now, will you be in time?"

The pair turned round and walked quickly toward the entrance, chattering to maintain the show. Their escorts, two humans and two nearly invisible Lacertians, sensed a problem and went into defensive mode, though they were uncertain of the type of threat they faced. One sauntered over to Niamh with a plan of the Gardens in hand and made a show of asking her for directions.

"What's the problem, Madame L'Estrange?"

"I'm not at all sure." Niamh went through a charade of trying to spot the feature she was supposedly identifying. "We both just suddenly felt as if there was something very unpleasant close by. You know—as if we were being stalked by a predator."

"Thank you, ma'am." The agent smiled and made a charade of checking the layout of the Gardens while covertly signalling his team into place. "Just keep walking toward the entrance. My people are between you and the exit and will cover you."

Niamh nodded. "Have a lovely visit," she added cheerfully, and took Mary by the hand. "Oh dear, I think our protection people are worried..." She felt a sting in the shoulder, and before she could utter another word, she sank to the ground.

"Aunt Niamh!" Mary cried out in horror, and all hell broke loose as Mary struggled to revive the older woman and felt herself being pulled away.

"Admiral, we have a concentration of Charonian and human ships in this sector." The briefing officer indicated the location on the display. "None of the human vessels give current identification signals. Three are reported to belong to the LPSL—but we know they have lost contact with them and several more."

The Admiral nodded, his brow creased in a frown. "Ship types?"

"Five of the eight human ships show as armed, sir. Big enough to be destroyer or cruiser class. The Charonian ships show as six destroyer class and one starship, a big one."

The Admiral was on his feet studying the display. "So I see. Do we have any indication of the weapons these ships carry?"

"For the destroyers, yes, sir. For the starship type, we have only some sketchy information and some guesses based on observation. There aren't many, so we're told, but they're damned fast and powerful."

"Let's see if we have anything in that area that can do a running scan so we can know what we're dealing with here..." The Admiral searched his dispositions. "Ah, yes, we have the Tenth Patrol Flotilla two days from there." He frowned. That was Harry's flotilla. Damn. The Tenth had been sent to that sector because it was supposed to be as far as possible from any chance encounter with the known assassins hunting Harry. "Get Commander Heron on link for me."

"Flag on link for you, sir."

"Thank you. On my display, please."

"On link, sir."

"Admiral, good morning, sir."

"Morning, Harry." The Admiral smiled. "I take it the *Sabre* is getting used to you now."

Harry grinned. "I think we've reached an understanding, sir." The *Sabre* had indeed got used to him, but it had taken a while for the ship's AI, one of the latest generation, to recognise what it should and should not listen to in Harry's thoughts.

"Good. Now then, I have a tricky and very delicate mission for you. I'll upload the coordinates at the end of this conversation. I require you to do a fast fly-by and scan of a starship. At this stage we think we have enough on its companions, but we need everything we can get on this ship. It's a type unknown to us." He frowned. "You'll have a very brief window to drop out, scan and transit. I shall leave it to you to assess the best means of obtaining the scan. Don't take unnecessary risks with it. If you think a drone can get the data, use one."

"Aye, aye, sir." Harry hesitated. "If you'll give us the coordinates, sir, I shall brief my commanders."

"They're on their way. Good luck and good hunting."

Harry looked up. "Navigation, you have the coordinates?"

"Yes, sir."

He stood. "Highlight it in the display, please. Number One, have a look at this with me. It looks like a fleet is gathering, and the Admiral's data suggests that starship is a powerful one."

Keiron joined him. "I agree." He accessed a star chart for the target's location. "Hmm, not a lot to hide us there either. Perhaps if we go in with our scan shield at full power, we can avoid detection for long enough to get a fix on the ship we want, drop the screens, run the scan, shield up and transit away before they can respond."

Harry nodded. He was listening to *Sabre* as the ship ran an assessment of the trajectory they would need, the range of the scan and the effectiveness of the shield against the known scanning equipment of the Charonians. "I do not think that would work at long range." He frowned as *Sabre* supplied additional information. "I think we will have to make use of subterfuge and surprise for this one."

Keiron smiled. "Subterfuge?" He paused. "Ah, I think I see." He looked at his tablet. "We need about thirty-six hours to get there. Gives us time to sort out the strategy then, sir."

"I agree," said Harry. "So be it. Navigation, lay in our course to the target. Helm, link to our consorts." He resumed his seat. "Ready Number One?"

"Ready, sir."

"Bring us round to the course for transit, helmsman." He watched the display. "Take us into transit when you're ready, Navigator."

The display changed to the grey fog of hyperspace, and the seven other ships of the flotilla appeared in phosphorescent outlines in positions ahead, astern, above and below as well as on either beam. Harry smiled in satisfaction, picking out each of the craft and mentally recalling its commander. The four corvettes, with their Canid crews, held the positions above and below the *Sabre*, with two holding position ahead. *Lagan* followed, and the pair of Lacertian ships held positions on either beam.

"Join me in my quarters in five minutes, Number One." Harry stood and looked around. "You have the Watch, Pack Leader."

The Canid navigator acknowledged.

"Five minutes, sir." Keiron saluted as Harry left the Control Centre, then turned and studied the chart on his tablet. "Damn. How am I supposed to keep him safe on a stunt like this?" he said under his breath.

Admiral Heron paced in his quarters. Sending Harry into the lion's den was troubling, but it would have worried him if it had been any of his officers and men. Uppermost in his mind was his inability to reach either Theo or Niamh in Dublin, but in parallel with that was his frustration over the lack of any real information about the Charonians and their capabilities. His door buzzer sounded.

"Come in."

"Sir, we've an update on the intel you asked for. There are almost as many new questions as there are answers." The Flag Lieutenant handed a tablet to the Admiral. "I've asked for clarification on these issues, sir. Some of the intel is downright contradictory."

The Admiral accepted the tablet and studied it. "Hmph. Most of this is supposition and guesswork." He handed the tablet back.

"Let's hope the Tenth Flotilla can get some real information for us. Otherwise I might as well tell the fleet to shut down scanners and fly by the seat of their pants." He waved his visitor to a seat. "We have about five more hours before they reach the target. I pray the enemy hasn't had any warning of them." He shook his head. "With the corruption at home we've no idea who we can trust. Bloody fools, it's always the same, a handful of people so blinded by wealth and power they'll make a pact with the devil just to gain more." He paused as his link chirped. "Admiral."

"Sir, message from Fleet C-in-C. There's been an attempt to kidnap your sister and her companion a young woman named Mary Hopkins. Your sister is injured."

Harry felt a chill run through him as he listened.

"There was an attempt to snatch your fiancée, sir." Keiron's face showed his concern. "The reports say she's unharmed, just badly shaken, but I'm afraid your aunt is in serious condition in hospital." Keiron paused. "We've placed them both in a secure facility, and your uncle is with them."

Harry's jaw tightened. "How did this happen?" His voice was very quiet and very calm.

Keiron noted that Harry's face was stiff, and his eyes seemed to bore into him as he fixed his Executive Officer with a stare that felt hot enough to burn steel. "I'm not sure of all the details. Just that your aunt and Ms Hopkins were in the Botanical Gardens in Dublin when they were taken. It was a well-planned attempt. In fact, several of our people went down protecting them." He paused. "If we hadn't had a couple of Lacertians on the detail, it might have turned out very badly for us."

"What did they hope to achieve?" Harry asked, his tone frighteningly level. Those who knew him well also knew that this was the calm before the storm.

"We think they planned to use your fiancée and your aunt as hostages." He met Harry's icy stare and couldn't hold it. It was like looking into the open muzzle of a particle beam projector. "I'm sorry, sir. At least we thwarted them this time."

"This time. How many more times must we expect? How often do we have to be lucky?" He met and held Keiron's eyes. "You know who is behind this, Keiron. I need to know. Who is so lacking in morality or any concept of decent and civilised behaviour that they would stoop to this? Tell me, Keiron." He paused. "I need to hear everything you know."

Keiron swallowed. Harry's utter calm unnerved him. It was all the worse for the fact he could sense the fury held in check by his friend. He'd never seen Harry this angry, and he'd no wish to see the rage behind that rigidly calm exterior.

"Yes," he said quietly. "Yes, I do know who is behind it. We aren't dealing with ordinary folk here, Harry. We're dealing with people who have the wealth and power to buy governments and impoverish nations. The likes of us don't normally get close to them." He paused. "I'll give you the names, but they won't mean a damned thing to you. They take care never to be noticed by the news media, and they have ways of making sure that anyone who does notice them never talks about it. They won't have ordered this attempt on Mary; that has all the trademarks of the people they've hired. The man behind it has so many aliases I doubt he can even remember what his real name is. We give him the code name Octopus, but he calls himself Zorvan. They only hire him when someone is close to exposing them, and you must have uncovered something they are very afraid of for them to have taken out this contract. I think I know what it is, and I think you do too."

Harry nodded, his eyes blazing with anger. "Yes, I think I do. Senator Samland hinted at it on the *Voyager*." His eyes burned into Keiron's. "I do not care how mighty or how important these men are, or think they are, they have dared to threaten the lives of those who, in this life, mean most to me. I will neither forgive nor forget that until every last one of them has been called to account."

The door buzzer sounded. "Come!" he barked.

The door slid open and a Lieutenant stepped inside. She regretted the interruption as soon as she saw her Captain's expression and the Executive Officer's carefully blank face, but she had no choice. "You requested to be called one hour before we reached the target zone, sir."

"Thank you. We will be there directly." Harry stood and waited for her to depart. "We have a task to perform, Number One, but let me say this. I hope your people find them and deal with them before I do. I would appreciate those names once we have completed this task."

"I'll provide them, but seriously, you can't fight these people, Harry. They're just too powerful."

"Fight them? I do not intend to fight them, Mr. Whitworth." Harry smiled. Those who knew him would have felt a chill. "These people are from families that know my family, or move in the same circles. They will know that I know of their activities, but I will follow the dictum of Saint Paul. I will repay their evil with kindness. I shall make it my business to be kind when they have trouble, to show sympathy and concern for their welfare. I shall make it my business whenever I encounter any of them to be polite and friendly. As the saint wrote, it will pour coals of fire on their heads. Far more effective than any confrontation."

Keiron shook his head. "Bloody hell, old man, I should think that will make them terrified of meeting you." He laughed. "Especially if they know that you know what they're involved in."

Chapter 24

Confrontation

Mary kept her hand on the rail as she sat beside the med-unit. The whole thing had been horrendous. She let a small shudder run through her as she recalled the sudden rush of figures appearing from the shrubbery on either side of the path. Several laid hands on her as Niamh began to fall, then other figures appeared, and the firing started. Someone pushed her to the ground across Niamh and tried to protect them both while the two groups engaged in a murderous firefight.

It had barely died down when she and Niamh and several others were lifted and rushed into a large medivac vehicle, and flown directly to this secure hospital facility.

"Mary, my dear," Theo greeted her as he entered the room. "A horrible business. Disgraceful, but at least you're safe." He stared at his wife lying still and quiet in the med-unit. "How is Niamh? The doctors say she will need several days of rest and restorative treatments."

Mary nodded. "Yes..." She hesitated. "What is this all about? Why did they attempt to kidnap us?"

Theo seated himself. "It appears that some very powerful people think Harry has learned something that could cause them serious problems." He frowned and spread his hands. "Unfortunately, they are also the kind of people who wield the sort of power that makes it extremely difficult to bring them to justice." He gave a sour smile. "You should see the representations my staff are swamped with to withdraw all charges against that woman Samland. We've had to place her in a secure prison outside of the normal system to prevent her assassination." His frown returned. "We think this was a precursor to a demand for Samland's release in exchange for Niamh, and your release in exchange for Harry."

"But this is barbaric!"

"It is, but that has never stopped the powerful. They simply get someone else to do the dirty work and reap whatever benefit comes from it." He smiled briefly, a wry smile. "Fortunately, those who do abuse their power and wealth are few and far between." He patted her hand gently. "Don't worry, my dear, we don't intend to let anyone get away with it, no matter how powerful they may be."

Mary slumped in her chair. ""Is Harry safe? I know they've given him a new command, and he's got a new Executive Officer, one he knows and trusts, but—"

"I know, my dear." Theo sighed. "But it's probably the safest place for him right now. I've spoken to James. This whole thing is getting out of hand." He broke eye contact and gazed at his wife in the med-unit. "Look after Niamh for me, Mary. I have to return to work. Pretend that nothing has happened." He thrust himself to his feet, his face grim. "We have to keep up the pretence until we can make our move and clean out this, this..." He sought for the word he wanted. "...this cesspit! Until then, we must fight a lot of battles to beat them." He smiled down at her. "But we will win."

In the intervening hours Harry had given a lot of thought to the task of obtaining the best results from a scan of the target ship. "*Sabre*, are you ready to carry out my request?"

"I have recalculated your proposed course and action, Harry. It is very high risk, but with a probe ahead of us, there will be a sufficient margin."

"Good. I need you to record everything. Set your scanners to maximum, and remain linked to me throughout. If they attempt to access you, I need to know immediately." Harry wasn't sure why he had ordered that, but the attempts to plant signal monitors, repeaters and receivers in the Fleet's ships made him wary. The attack on his beloved *Mary* and the injuries to Niamh made him angry.

"I shall, Harry." The ship paused. "There is something else. Other ships report interference with their controls when near a Charonian ship. Should I report this if I have similar problems?"

Harry felt the hair on the nape of his neck prickling. "Yes. Show me the source if you can. I need to know immediately."

"Two minutes to dropout, sir." Keiron's voice betrayed his inner tension. "*Lagan* and the corvettes are in their positions, ready to launch the drones. *Seana* and *Sala Ghahle* will launch their probes as soon as we re-enter transit."

"Very good, Number One. Weapons, are you ready?"

"Ready, sir."

"Scan, any indication we've been detected?"

"Negative, sir. No indication of detection or activity."

"Very well. Signal *Lagan* to commence." His plan called for the *Lagan* and the corvettes to drop out at widely separated points around the target group at maximum scan range and then to launch scanning drones. He hoped this would draw attention away from his own dropout and re-entry long enough to do what he wished to achieve.

"*Lagan* acknowledged, sir. There they go."

"Very well. Helm, on my mark." He watched the seconds tick by through his cyberlink. "Now."

The display filled with the huge bulk of the alien ship as the *Sabre* raced along its length from bow to stern, the probe keeping four ship lengths ahead. Strange structures, weapons embrasures and openings in the hull streamed past as the ship tore past the giant. Frantic activity at the scan and weapons positions told him they were at work. Data streamed through his eyes as the ship recorded it. "Interference with Transit Controls detected." There was a moment's pause. "Source is a non-standard installation at node C-341-a-A."

"Disable it. Open a link to the transmission source it is receiving from. Send a full power pulse of the final part of Tchaikovsky's 1812 Overture—bells, cannon, brass bands and all! Maximum volume, maximum transmission power."

"Transit in thirty seconds, sir."

"Very well. Are the transit controls responsive?"

"Yes, sir. They went offline for a couple of seconds, but they're back." The Coxswain paused. "Entering transit, sir."

"Launch mines. If anyone follows us, I want them to get a nasty reception." Harry thrust himself out of his chair. "Report the rest of the flotilla."

"All clear, sir. The drones show we stirred things up back there, but we seem to have caught them off guard. Only one ship attempted to intercept, and *Seana* gave him a nasty surprise."

"Good. Scan, what did you get?"

"Everything we could, sir. That ship has some really powerful weaponry on board. It'll take weeks to analyse it and figure out what it is."

Harry nodded. "Very well, share it with the others and get started. Number One, something attempted to interfere with our Transit Controls. Sabre identified the source as a non-standard installation at node Charlie-341-sub-alpha-Alpha. I want it recovered and analysed. It was functioning on a dual frequency, one receiving and one sending a return signal. Take care, it may be rigged to prevent interference." He turned to the Coms Officer. "Ms Kardon, signal the flotilla, 'Form up on *Sabre*.' Navigator, as soon as they have joined, alter course to intercept the Fleet. Maximum speed."

The image of the Charonian starship lingered in his mind's eye as he sank into his chair and the ship returned to normal watchkeeping at defence stations. Something tugged at his memory, but the more he tried to pin it down, the more it slipped away. He let it go. It would come back to him eventually.

"You wanted to be advised as soon as we had anything on the reconnaissance mission, sir."

The Admiral rolled off his bunk. "Yes? Are they clear?"

"The signal was very brief, sir. Just that they got a good scan and are clear."

The Admiral was already pulling on his boots. "Excellent. Set course for the coordinates I gave you. I want that data, but they won't transmit it until they meet up with us. Assemble my staff, we have work to do." He stood and grabbed his jacket.

"Yes, sir." There was a pause. "We have a report from Security, sir. Your sister is out of danger and should make a full recovery. Ms Hopkins is with her and so is Mr. L'Estrange."

The Admiral nodded. "Good. I'll want a word with the Chief Security Officer when we've finished." This attempt to snatch Niamh and Mary was a step too far. It was time to ensure that justice was done, and in such a way that it was *seen* to be done. It would not be easy, but Harry obviously held some knowledge the Pantheon didn't want exposed. Time would tell.

"Yes, sir. I'll alert them." The Flag Lieutenant paused. "We've had some data from the Tenth, sir. They scattered drones around the Charonian ships—one must have gone in very close—and we've had some data from them on the hyperlinks. They've all shut down now, presumably destroyed, but what we got is worrying. The team are working on it, though it's incomplete. If we're to make a full assessment, we'll need all the information they got."

"Very well, I want to know what the preliminary assessment is as soon as possible plus any word on the Tenth as soon as anything is known." He took his seat in the briefing room.

"Yes, sir." He looked up as the Admiral's staff began to file in. "I'll inform Coms to keep a listening watch for any transmission or sighting."

"Do that." The Admiral frowned. "Tell them to watch the hypertransit beacons for any signals caused by them or the enemy entering or leaving transit anywhere." He turned to the staff as the Flag Captain took his seat. "Morning, Francis, team, we have something to get started on. We'll have more by the end of the day, but now we can start planning."

"Approaching dropout for the rendezvous, sir."

Harry straightened himself in his chair. He hadn't left the Control Centre since their close fly-by except to relieve himself and grab a bite to eat. For the last hour he'd been studying the images captured as they tore past the giant starship. "Very good, Navigator. Number One, bring us to action stations and order the others to do the same in case there's a surprise awaiting us." He touched his link. "Engineering, keep the hyper pods online until I order them shut down."

Keiron Whitworth touched the general alarm and waited as reports flowed in from all action stations signifying that they were closed and ready. "Our consorts report they're ready, sir." These last hours he'd seen a different side to Harry, he had to admit. The light-hearted midshipman he'd known during their Fleet College

217

days was gone, and so was the edge of uncertainty he'd shown as he struggled to adjust to the avalanche of technology and social norms he'd had to cope with. In their place was a commander, hard when he had to be yet concerned about those he was responsible for, and utterly ruthless when pushed past the limits of his concepts of acceptable behaviour.

"Thank you, Number One. Take us in on the markers." Harry nodded to the Coms Officer. "Link me to the others please."

"Aye, aye, sir." The Coms Officer activated her links. "On link, sir."

"All ships, this is the Ancient Mariner." He paused. "If you detect a trap, do not hesitate to act. Transit immediately. I will provide a new rendezvous as soon as *Sabre* has been extracted." He hesitated. "If all is correct, we will be greeted by a signal from Flag that only the Admiral and I know. I will be able to confirm immediately if it is correct. If it is not, I will say 'scatter' to order withdrawal."

He listened to the acknowledgements then added, "This link will remain open. If the signal is correct, I will give the order 'stand down' and close the flagship. The flotilla will break off and close the support ship *Mercury*." He smiled briefly as Keiron signalled the start of the countdown to dropout. "Let us hope all is in order."

The display flashed from the grey fog of hyperspace to the 3D display of the system into which they had just arrived. They could see a giant gas planet with a complete system of moons, some as large as Earth, circling it. Twin suns circled each other in a mutually destructive dance far ahead with some small rocky worlds between the two. Moments later the sky flashed with light as the Fleet dropped into position.

"From Flag, sir." The Coms Officer frowned. "For some reason he sent pictures of flags..."

"Show me." Harry's screen showed a series of coloured flags, one above the other. He smiled and brought up an image of a plain blue and white flag. Through his cyberlink he told the ship, "Send this image to the Admiral, *Sabre*." To his comlink he announced. "The signal is correct. Stand down and continue as ordered."

Keiron acknowledged the order and gave orders to the helm to close the flagship. He glanced at the image on Harry's display. "Resorting to flags, sir?" He grinned. "What do they say?"

Harry laughed. "Splice the mainbrace—the signal for an issue of rum to the men." He glanced at the Rates, who were all grinning. "Unfortunately, we haven't any rum, and it probably wouldn't be a good idea just yet."

Harry's face showed his fury as Admiral Heron gave him the details of the attack "They were attacked in the botanical gardens? And the protection squad failed to detect the attackers?"

"Not quite. They had planned to attack them in a different part of the gardens, and our people were set up to prevent it, but Mary and Niamh sensed something was wrong and changed their plan. That caused the Pantheon to launch their attempt in a difficult place, and our people were lucky they'd already been repositioned."

"Very fortunate for them." Harry snorted, his anger making him forget who he was talking to. "Who are these people? By God, sir, I will not suffer such an infamous assault on our family by such ... such ... vermin!"

James Heron forced himself to adopt a calmer tone. "You can be very sure, Harry, that I do not intend to let this rest. Some of them use the names of Hindu and other gods. The Pantheon are a highly secretive group that specialises in murder. They are often employed by the super wealthy, by governments, and by others who are very powerful, to remove someone considered an obstacle to the client's plans." He remembered his own brush with a "goddess" and her team years before. "They are highly professional, but they all share one important characteristic. They are utterly ruthless and psychopathic. They're not just murderers. They are true mercenaries in every sense of the word: cold, calculating, emotionless. They get the job done then move on to the next assignment, or should I say kill. Thanks to you and Ferghal, however, Fleet Security have those files Samland hid on the *Voyager*. They appear to include the real identities of the key players among these Pantheon—but we haven't yet found the key to the code that encrypts them."

Harry paused, his anger now ice. "So they believe I am that key."

"Possibly. Do you know, or can you recall anything which might be such an encryption key?" The Admiral hesitated. "It may not even look like one, but we think this is why they want you dead."

Harry shook his head. "There is something, but I can't ..." He stopped as the Admiral's link chirped.

"Commodore Roberts is here, Admiral," anounced Adriana, his android SU. "She has the latest security update for you."

Chapter 25

Interference Frustrated

The Admiral leaned back in his chair. "My staff tell me that the images and scan data you collected are so detailed you must have been less than two hundred metres from this ship." He raised an eyebrow. "A little close, don't you think?"

Harry met the Admiral's eyes. "I thought if we were close and fast-moving it would give them less time to react, sir. I think it worked. We were not fired on."

"As you say in your report. But something or someone attempted to disrupt your control of the ship. That could have had serious consequences."

Harry hesitated. "It could, sir, but I had warned the ship to alert me to it. I was able to immediately disable their device and send them a counter signal." His grin flickered. "I hope they enjoyed it."

The Admiral's curiosity was piqued. "What did you send them?"

"The final part of Tchaikovsky's 1812 Overture, the part with the brass bands, orchestra, guns, bells and choir. I thought they should appreciate it at maximum volume."

Despite himself, the Admiral laughed. "I imagine that probably blew out their audio systems." He smiled. "If someone was listening to the receiving signal, they'll have a headache I shouldn't wonder." He shook his head. "Sometimes, Harry, you do something so outrageous it leaves everyone wondering how to respond. That little stunt quite possibly helped stop any interference while they tried to work out what happened." He placed his elbows on the desk and frowned. "Now, about this device. My technicians tell me it is set to receive orders to the AI and divert instructions from our systems. In effect it allows whoever controls it to take over our helm and drive controls."

"As I learned, sir." Harry frowned. "*Lagan* was unaffected, as she was one of the ships we stripped these devices out of during build. The corvettes and the Lacertian ships have not been affected as they have not been in any of our building docks." He frowned. "To my understanding, this suggests they seek to render our ships helpless in any confrontation."

The Admiral nodded. "My assessment exactly. My security teams are checking every possible installation point for these damned things." He thrust himself to his feet and paced the room. "On a ship of this size, that's a near impossible task." He stopped pacing and took his seat again. "I am, therefore, going to ask you to undertake a difficult task, one which will take you from your command for a short time. I am asking the same of Ferghal. "

"Yes, sir..." Harry nodded and waited to hear more.

"I have only two starships with me, and we don't have time to find these devices. We will launch an attack on the assembly you scouted in the next few hours. I want you to remain aboard this ship and link yourself to the AI. Instruct it to do what you did with the *Sabre*. I have enough to concern me with the weapons that ship carries without their having the ability to disable us. Can you do it?"

Harry thought carefully. "I think so, sir." He paused. "I believe I might be able to enter their systems as well. Now that the helmet they placed on me has been examined, I have discovered a way I can neutralise one if I am wearing it." He smiled. "Perhaps if I had not been so focussed on surviving, I would have learned this myself." He paused and met the Admiral's eyes. "I do not think they realised that the control unit in the helmet linked to my cyberlink, nor did I sense it, though in hindsight, I can recall a sense of something stimulating the link." His smile was somewhat wry and a bit grim as he shook his head. "I could have shut it down at any time—and unlocked it. It seems I wore the infernal device for much longer than necessary and suffered as a result. I allowed my frustration and anger to override my ability to think calmly and logically. This has taught me a good lesson, but at least the information gleaned is useful to me now, and it may help me to enter their systems in future should the need arise."

The Admiral nodded, slightly taken aback by Harry's response to his own oversight. He was aware from the researchers who had made this discovery, that, despite Harry's attempt to put a brave face on it, he was deeply embarrassed by not having thought of it. Now, in his presence—not only was he the Admiral, but he was also Harry's great uncle by several generations—the Admiral's heart was touched that Harry felt comfortable enough to show his true feelings. In that moment, it felt almost like they were father and son.

"Very well," said the Admiral. "Your Number One can take care of the *Sabre*. I'll arrange quarters for you aboard." He smiled. "Take a rest, Harry. You look as if you could use one."

The android steward woke him. "Commander Heron."

Harry started and jerked upright on his temporary bunk. His own steward usually had a cup of tea ready, and woke him gently with music unless there was an emergency. This one did not have tea or music. The lack of tea was fortunate, since the android recoiled as Harry escaped the nightmare he'd been having and stared wild-eyed around the strange cabin. He collected himself.

"Yes?" Harry demanded. "What is it? What do you need?"

"Commander, I am ordered to tell you we will drop out in half an hour. Admiral Heron thought you might like to prepare yourself."

Harry swung his legs off the bunk and was already in motion. "Thank you. I wonder if you could bring me some tea while I wash and get dressed."

"Yes, Commander. However, the Admiral expects you in his Command Centre immediately, without delay."

"Oh, I see." Harry stripped his shirt and entered the small washroom. "Better forget the tea then." He took a quick basin bath and was dressed and ready to go within minutes. He grabbed his jacket and shrugged himself into it as he followed the android into the Wardroom flat.

"I can bring you some refreshment in the Command Centre, sir."

Harry nodded. "Thank you, I would appreciate that." He focussed on his cyberlink. "*Conqueror*, I am ready to begin this attempt to assist you should there be any device installed to interfere with your controls."

"Certainly, Commander. I have been monitoring your thoughts on this, and took the liberty to contact *Sabre* and *Lagan*. *Sabre* was very helpful and has shared the means by which he identified the device. Do you wish to use the same procedure?"

"Yes, that is the best option. And advise all our escorts to report immediately any disruption, and to deal with it as we do."

Harry's mind seemed to loop back to the nightmare he was having before being startled awake.

"Curious dream, Commander," said the AI.

In that moment, Harry realised he'd forgotten to make his usual request to the AI to only monitor his thoughts when specifically directed to.

Harry hesitated. "Yes, it was actually more like a nightmare than a dream."

"It was not based on real events," the ship reassured Harry. "I verified this. No one was attempting to compel you to wear any sort of helmet, and the creatures pursuing you no longer exist. Your family members are all safe and in secure care. Lieutenant Gunn is currently off watch on the *Sabre*, and Lieutenant-Commander O'Connor is aboard the *Hansastadt Wismar*, our companion starship."

"Thank you for confirming that," Harry said, more relieved than he cared to admit. The nightmare had seemed so real. "And yes, I shall want to work with you as I did with *Sabre*, meaning, I only want you to listen to and see my thoughts when I give you permission to do so. This is a matter of privacy."

"I understand, Commander," said the ship.

The Admiral sat in his command chair deep in thought. His dispositions were in place, his ships were approaching the dropout point, but the lack of intelligence worried him. The information gathered by the Tenth Flotilla had proved invaluable. The Charonians had some impressive weapons, but there were still some unanswered questions, such as why their forces were spread so thin, or why they wanted to take over human ships. He reached for his tablet, scrolled through the menu and read the notes on what was known about the Charonians.

"Flags," said the Admiral.

"Sir?" The Flag Lieutenant hurried across.

The Admiral handed him the tablet. "Item 431. What do you make of it?"

The Flag Lieutenant read the note. "They always attempt to capture a ship intact and its crew unharmed." He frowned. "Are they perhaps looking for slave labour, sir?"

"I wondered about that, but why has no one ever seen any slaves of any species they've captured?" The Admiral gestured. "Look at item 1034. I think there's a connection."

The Lieutenant read. "They kill any injured, sick or aged."

"Yes, and the next item—they are particularly interested in young men and women, close to teenage, but anyone under twelve and over thirty-five is of no interest or use to them." The Admiral's frown deepened. "The more I learn of these people, the less I like. Look at item 4055. They perpetuate themselves by implanting some kind of zygote in a host. I suspect they will avoid a fight if they discover they can't disable us with their devices." He stood. "That may be their weakness—they need plenty of young healthy bodies to continue their kind. I think the fools who have been supporting them are so blinded by promises of power, wealth and longevity they haven't seen where this will lead."

The Flag Captain's hologram appeared. "Approaching drop-out, sir. All ships ready and at action stations."

"Very well, proceed." The Admiral touched his comlink. "Harry, I need to know which of these ships is carrying the transmitter they are using to take control of ours. Identify it for me if you can."

"Aye, aye, sir."

The Admiral cut the link. "I think, Flags, the reason we don't see very many of these Charonians is because there aren't many of them. I suspect that we humans are their target." He tapped the tablet. "I think they've been running out of suitable species to adapt to their needs, and now they've found us—and we're too greedy, arrogant and stupid to think things through effectively. We're the perfect victim."

The display flickered around them and revealed the huge Charonian ship dominating the expanse above a barren planet, her consorts a mix of human-built and alien ships holding positions around her. The Admiral touched his signal pad. "All ships, engage your targets as ordered. Leave the starship to us."

In the Admiral's conference room Harry focussed on the ship's AI and its conversations with all major controls.

"Interference in node 386-Beta-4-Alpha-67. I am being disconnected from the helm, Harry."

He sought out the node, found the source and traced the incoming instruction. "Advise the Admiral that the originator of the signal is a small ship, not the main one." He blocked the disruption and selected a loud trumpet piece from the ship's music library and sent that back to the originating ship at the highest power level possible. "Check with *Hansastadt Wismar*—can they triangulate the source? It seems to be a focussed signal beam of some type."

"They have it, Harry."

"Good, give the position to Weapons Control. Instruct them to destroy it."

"Weapons Control is being disrupted. Interference receiver at node 505-Kilo-Kilo-65-Foxtrot."

Once again Harry tracked the node then the disruption unit. This time he didn't attempt to be fancy. He sent a power surge into it and waited as the device overloaded then ceased to function. Several more devices went the same way, and the ship shuddered each time it was hit by enemy fire. Harry was aware of the damage to the ship through his link to its AI.

As suddenly as it began, it was over.

"The enemy has escaped, Harry," said the *Conqueror*. "They withdrew when you and Ferghal destroyed their Trojan controls."

"Did we destroy the control ship we identified?"

"Yes. That was when their major vessel departed. All that remains are a number of disabled human vessels. They are being boarded now by the Marines."

"Show me, please." A holographic view of the system surrounded him. "Thank you. Have the technicians found all the units we destroyed? Is there any collateral damage to your systems?"

"They are working on them now." The ship hesitated. "The Admiral is calling you."

"I'd better answer that call," said Harry. As he withdrew from his connection to the ship, he experienced a moment of disorientation and the sense that he'd suddenly lost a part of himself. His comlink chirped. "Heron."

"Well done, Harry, they've pulled out. Join me in Flag Command."

"Aye, aye, sir," Harry stood and moved to the door. Perhaps now he could return to the *Sabre*. Like the *Lagan*, she'd become quite attached to him, and like the *Lagan*, had spoiled him with little instructions to the android steward, or by providing soothing music when he needed to relax.

He used his cyberlink again. "Thank you, *Conqueror*. It was interesting working with you."

"Thank you, Harry. Next time I shall know what you like and take care to provide it."

Felicity Roberts watched the Admiral at work, admiring his knack for making even the Rates feel their contribution to the meeting was as valuable as his own. Thanks to the work done by Commander Heron and Lieutenant-Commander O'Connor, the Fleet knew where to find the Charonian units and how to counter them. Most of the ships were already rid of the devices.

"Funny thing, Boss," her Technical Officer broke into her thoughts. "These things are quite crude, basically a remote control unit. Nothing sophisticated about it—not at all what I'd expect from people supposed to be so advanced."

This had struck Felicity as well. "You're right, George. Something else has been bothering me. Remember the ships the Fleet recaptured? The lighting levels, even in the day cycle had been turned down to less than half normal. Could it be that bright light bothers them?"

"Could be, but you'd have to ask the bio boys and girls on that one. Shall I get one of them to look into it for you?"

"Do that." Felicity stood as the meeting broke up. "Tell them to make it a priority. I think we need to know why they turn the lights down and turn the ambient temperatures up."

"Will do, Boss. Looks like the Admiral's wanting a word." He grinned knowingly. Most of the Security team knew she had a 'thing' for the Admiral and he for her. "Have fun."

"Push off." She laughed. "This is purely business, George. Now run along like a good little boffin before I find something to keep you busy!" She smiled as the Admiral joined them. "That went well, sir. I've some updates for you on the civil situation."

Chapter 26

Choices

"The news channels are full of what James's squadron discovered aboard those recaptured ships and the pirates they took." Theo snorted in anger. "Any fool who still believes they are benignly seeking to advance the human race is insane!"

Mary gave up her attempt to practice her latest recital piece and turned to face him. "Perhaps they're blinded by the potential advantages they were offered to help the Charonians." She got up from the piano. "How much longer do you think Niamh will have to remain in the med-unit?"

Theo dropped into a chair. "Too damned long." He paused. "I'm sorry, Mary, that was unfair. The doctors say at least another week and then lots of bed rest with a gradual building up of her strength." He smiled and chuckled. "They obviously don't know Niamh. She won't take things easy unless they tie her down."

Mary smiled, relieved at Theo's change of mood. "Then we shall have to give her plenty of distraction." She paused. "I've just had Harry on the link. He's enjoying his new command, and getting plenty of action to keep him busy. He was very upset about the attack on Niamh though, but tells me they have learned a lot about the Charonians." She grinned and admired her engagement ring. "He's so funny about being surrounded by what he calls ghosts and protectors. He says he thinks he must have incognito royalty in his crew, and they're just using him as an excuse." She sank into a corner of the deeply cushioned sofa. "I shall be so glad when all this is over and these evil people have been dealt with."

"So shall I, my dear. So shall we all." Theo kept to himself the latest intelligence briefing. The price on Harry's head had doubled, and with the qualification that he was to be taken alive. No one could discover why. "At least he and Ferghal are safe, and so are we. I understand Danny is to get more protection as well. Some Lacertians are to join the *Sabre* for the task—but that is not for Harry's ears, please."

Harry stared at Keiron. "So now I am to be taken alive, and the bounty has been doubled?" He stood up and paced the room, his hands gripped behind his back. "You say it is known who is behind this?"

Keiron shifted uncomfortably. "We have a good idea, yes. But we can't move directly against them—not yet anyway." He fiddled with his cup. "You aren't the only person under threat. Several high-profile figures are, but you exposed them, and now you're a target of special interest to the Pantheon because they think you hold the key to identifying them. Mary, your aunt, the Chief Justice, Ferghal and the Admiral are all covered against any further attempts to use one of your relatives to get to you. Sub-Lieutenant Gunn is also covered, and we're reinforcing his squad as he's possibly more vulnerable than anyone else."

"Damn them, Keiron. Damn them to hell." Harry flung himself into his comfortable armchair. "What manner of man is prepared to hire others to lay hands upon another or to have them killed for their own profit, but is not prepared to face the person themselves in combat?" He drummed his fingers on the armrest. "I was ne'er a duelist, but I would accept the gauntlet in a trice if it would secure the safety of my friends and family."

Keiron smiled. "I'm with you on that one, Harry. I'd gladly stand as your second, and I know several others who'd be queueing up for it." He paused. "You may still get the chance once the trial is over."

"I shall certainly call upon you if the opportunity arises. Sword or pistol do you think?" He stared at the bulkhead. "I suspect they are the same people—or at least one or two are—as the names on the lists I discovered before they overpowered me and blocked my link." He paused as a thought occurred to him. "The Advocate General has that list, and they have the files I had *Lagan* record, so why am I still a target?"

"Ah, on their own the list and the files are worthless, but your testimony of where and in what circumstances you obtained them—that puts a different light on them. That makes them all accomplices, and that is what they can't allow. Your evidence is vital or the courts will reject the other material as unsubstantiated."

Harry shook his head. "It makes no sense at all." He looked at his friend. "Do you know why they changed their minds and want me alive now? Dead I cannot testify. Alive? There will always be the danger I could escape."

Keiron considered this. "It's the Charonians who want you alive, and the human side are happy with that since it's unlikely you'd be able to give evidence once the Charonians have you."

Harry frowned as he mulled this information. "Why would the Charonians be so interested in me now? They designed that infernal helmet specifically for me. I was in their hands then, and instead they deposited me and the others on that planet Centaur." He hesitated. "Which reminds me. What news of their situation?" He frowned at a memory. "Ah, yes, the helmet. Samland said it could be used to control me. That must be it."

"The Pantheon may have made a serious error in trying to snatch your sister and Harry's fiancée." Commodore Felicity Roberts accepted the coffee the Admiral's SU offered. "We took down one of the gods, and his real ID is being kept under wraps because it will be one hell of a political explosion when it does come out."

"Anyone I know?" James Heron kept his voice neutral. "Or perhaps I should say, anyone *we* know?"

Felicity laughed. "I couldn't possibly say, Admiral, but knowing how your mind works, I dare say you're already drawing up a list of suspects!"

"You know me too well." He paused. "Harry still can't recall any sort of key code, and he's worried about it."

"I can understand that." Felicity studied the display, gathering her thoughts. "Those scans he got of the Charonian starship. He must have taken his ship past it at a distance—well, perhaps an interceptor could get that close, but a ship like the *Sabre*? Must have scared the living daylights out of his crew."

"Apparently not. They seem to think getting that close was their best defence, and it exposed the way the Charonian control units operate." He smiled. "They discovered something else: the Charonians' targeting is not as sophisticated as ours. It was active, but evidently couldn't lock on at close range."

The man known to his clients as Zorvan leaned back in his comfortable chair and studied the information scrolling across the large screen before him. Only a few people knew his real name. Many who knew him socially would not have believed his real business if they were told it. Certainly none of the men and women who actually carried out his orders knew him by sight, though some moved in his social circles, but the Senator had been careless, and that could potentially expose him. Now he shut down the display and touched a link key.

"Sir?"

"Is Kali in place?"

"Yes, sir."

"Instruct her to carry out the exercise."

"Yes, sir."

"Then prepare my yacht. I will leave immediately after dinner tonight."

"Yes, sir." There was a momentary hesitation. "Shall I instruct the team to prepare, sir?"

"Unnecessary. They'll get their orders by another route. Be on the yacht when I board."

"Yes, sir."

Zorvan leaned back. Time, perhaps, to retire his closest employees. It could wait until this operation was complete. The debacle in Dublin suggested someone had been careless, or the Security Services were getting too close. He stood up and moved toward the door of his very private communications centre. He didn't believe in luck. In his game, only a fool left things to chance. His anonymity and his reputation for success were precisely because he left nothing to chance.

Stepping out of the concealed door into his private dressing room, Kharim Pasha Al-Khalifa smiled. His android servant had laid out the clothes for his evening appearance at a charitable dinner—the perfect disguise. He was a high-profile public figure, constantly in the media for his campaigning and lobbying on behalf of good causes, two of which were fronts for his other business. How many would believe the head of one of the world's largest banking and trading corporations was also the assassin known as Zorvan? How many would even begin to realise that many of his businesses supported and facilitated those operations?

He completed his change of clothes and stepped into the corridor to walk to the waiting transport. Dinner would be amusing, and then there would be the excitement of what he confidently expected to be the successful outcome of the operation now in motion. He smiled as he considered how easy it had been to replace the crew of the hospital ship, chartered from one of his many companies. Now all that remained was for the target to walk into the trap—with or without his protection squad.

"Contact has been lost with the hospital ship *Emily Hobhouse*, sir. She was last reported in transit to Earth. There's been no contact from the medical staff or the navigation system for twenty-four hours."

The Admiral was on his feet. "What was her route? Put it on the display."

"On display now, sir. She was routed to avoid all areas where there is pirate or Charonian activity." The Staff Commander traced the looping path of the projected passage through hyperspace on the 3D display. "There's been no indication of any problem either. She has simply lost all communications—no hyperlink, no automatic ship link, no recognition signal." He frowned. "Curiously, there have been two—no four—hyperspace beacon signals, all well away from her scheduled course."

"Why didn't that attract attention?" The Admiral's frown betrayed his annoyance. "The deviation from course should have flagged a problem immediately."

"These automatic signals are not permanently monitored, sir. The data is reviewed only when something unusual flags—as it has in this one."

"I see. But there should have been an alert before this." He stared at the display. "Show those beacons—and show any traffic near them."

"The *Emily Hobhouse* is secured. Phase two of the operation can commence."

"Yes, sir. I shall instruct Loki to deliver the message."

"Do so." Zorvan broke the link. Time for his next move. The corporate yacht provided an excellent staging post and a good cover. The guests were too busy enjoying the heady pleasures it provided to notice the absence of their host from time to time. He summoned his secretary. "Have my launch prepared. I will be attending to some business for the next few days."

The secretary bowed. "Yes, sir. Should I accompany you?"

"No. This is a personal matter." He smiled. "One I have looked forward to for a while now." He nodded toward the saloon. "See that our friends are entertained while I am indisposed. I do not want them to feel neglected."

The secretary smiled. He had held this position long enough to know these occasional indispositions meant his employer wanted his guests to believe he was still aboard but not available. An intelligent man, he had long realised the yacht's crew were not just efficient and attentive crewmen. Some had skills in areas no ordinary person would, just as he did. The post of secretary was, in all but one sense, a cover. His true qualification and expertise lay in pharmacology, something quite a large number of his current employer's customers might have benefitted from knowing before their untimely departure from this life. It was a major reason he held his current position of trust.

"I will take good care to ensure they want for nothing, sir."

"I am counting on it." Zorvan replaced his glass on the table. "When I return, I will have another small task for you." He sighed. "My cousin has been foolish—again. Time to put a stop to it. Unfortunate, but I cannot have her jeopardise our position." He stood. "Tell my pilot I will leave in three hours." He smiled again. "Now I had best make sure my guests see me taking care of their pleasure before I make myself scarce." He sighed. "I shall be gone about a day—a final settlement with the client."

He smiled as one of his guests approached. "Marleine, I trust we are looking after you well." He nodded to the secretary. "Have we finished, Miguel? Good, thank you. Remind me when my next medication session is due." He walked away explaining that he was being treated for an annoyingly inconvenient complaint requiring regular treatment and a short absence from this cruise.

Chapter 27

Abandon Hope

"We've received a demand from Zorvan for the release of the hospital ship and her patients." The C-in-C rubbed his temples with the tips of his fingers. "I've got the politicians demanding we negotiate with him, the media demanding we comply with his demand, and the Council split." He slapped his hands on the table in front of him. "He wants Commander Heron in exchange for the ship, her crew and her passengers. If one more damned politician tells me that sometimes one man has to be sacrificed for the benefit of the many, I'll damned well strangle the fool to show him the stupidity of what he's actually saying." He paused. "This whole thing stinks to high heaven, and it's not just the politicians trying to get the investigation shut down. Some of the senior bureaucrats are up to their ears in it, and Admiral Greene is convinced there are some very important families on that encrypted list."

Admiral Heron frowned. "Harry still hasn't been able to recall any sort of encryption key. I'll have to talk to him. I'm not prepared to order him to do this. I'll resign my command if the Council try to force it, and I doubt they'll find anyone else prepared to give him such an order."

"I know, and I've told them so. One of them actually had the gall to say he'd give the order for us—as a member of the

Council." He snorted in anger. "I'm glad to say his fellow Council members turned on him and roundly told him to shut up. It's going to be a long and very tough night. If you've any suggestions, let me have 'em."

"I think we know where the *Emily Hobhouse* is, but there's a problem. If she's there, she's surrounded by what looks like a major fleet concentration. I'll have to talk to Harry and tell him of this demand. I know what his reaction will be, and I'm going to have to forbid it. Let me have the full demand."

"I'll get it encrypted and sent immediately. Are you making progress on stripping out those Trojan devices?"

"Yes, we've got that completed. Val Petrocova's ships are also clear and so are Madeleine Le Jeune's. We're all shorthanded, but we can cope with it."

"Good. Speak to your lad. I'll get this demand to you." The C-in-C hesitated. "I'll add my order to yours if you like. Forbid him from doing anything unless we approve it or we can support him."

Harry read the demand from this Zorvan. It seemed unequivocal. He required that Harry be left alone at a designated point in space, unarmed and with his head once more secured in a helmet that would be supplied in advance. His ship was to drop him off and depart immediately. In return the *Emily Hobhouse* and her passengers and crew would be released and her location given to the Fleet. Failure to deliver Harry, as specified, would result in the destruction of the hospital ship.

"Zorvan doesn't make idle threats, sir." Keiron's worried expression said more than his words.

"So I believe." Harry put down the tablet. "It seems the Pantheon do not yet know that I have discovered a means to overcome their screening helmet." He looked at the Admiral. "That may give me an opportunity to deliver this Zorvan into your hands and to frustrate their plans."

"We can't be sure of that." The Admiral's expression made clear that he was not in favour of Harry giving himself up to this at all. "If they have learned that, and provide a modified version you can't manipulate, you're in trouble, and there will be nothing we can do to help."

"It is a chance I must take, sir." Harry met the Admiral's gaze. "I cannot simply abandon the Centaur survivors or the medical staff helping them." He hesitated. "And if my doing this delivers the Pantheon into your hands ..." He paused. "Besides, the investigators already have all the evidence I can bring to the trial when it occurs—except for this key." He smiled lopsidedly and shrugged. "Isn't it true that hearsay is permitted in a court of law if the person who made the statement in the first instance is deceased? If so, there are at least four witnesses who can tell the court what I would have said."

"In a limited manner, that is true, but it isn't a good reason to allow you to sacrifice yourself." The Admiral glowered at Commander Whitworth. "This whole mess is a filthy business." He flung the tablet on the desk and thrust himself out of his chair. "Why the hell can't your people track this scum down and destroy them and their organisation, Commander? You've got enough damned resources."

"We've taken out many smaller groups, sir." Keiron sounded defensive. "Zorvan and his group are in a different league. The Pantheon is comprised of multiple hierarchies, and the only one who knows the identity of all their gods and goddesses, as they call themselves, is Zorvan. Some of them may suspect his identity, but none of them know it for certain. Anyone who does generally ends up very dead if they even so much as hint at letting it slip." He shrugged. "Hydra would be a good name for this lot. We take out one group and another takes its place."

The Admiral paused in his pacing. "So I am told. That group in Dublin has, I hear, already been reformed, even though they lost one of their gods in that failure."

"Yes, sir. The cell leader code-named Durga was taken out, but she's been replaced by one code-named Rafael." He frowned. "The leader of the group that has taken the *Emily Hobhouse* is code-named Kali, and she's absolutely ruthless. No one gets near her, and if she's involved, there is always a sting in the tail. I'm not happy about this deal at all, sir."

Harry frowned at the mention of the names. "Durga? She was a goddess said to ride a tiger, created to kill or control the demons that ruled the earth. And Kali? A nasty piece of work in the Hindu pantheon. Some of her devotees were the Thuggee sect." He paused, thinking hard. "I think I know why they are so eager to kill me. The *Voyager* knew who they were. When I boarded her, there were messages to and from Kali, Zorvan, and other key players in the Pantheon." His frown deepened. "That must be it. There were names, the real names, of the people using these codes."

Keiron reacted first. "Do you know them? Can you recall them?"

Harry shook his head slowly. "No. No, I don't think I can ... I really can't remember, but I can tell Ferghal what to look for in the *Voyager's* data banks." As soon as he said that, Harry had an epiphany. "That's it! The key to the encryption!" He scribbled a few notes on his pad and showed it to the Admiral and Keiron. "That is what Ferghal must look for. It's the key to the file."

"Right, then that's a start," said the Admiral. "We have the *Voyager* in quarantine. Tell Ferghal what to look for. Security can get to work on it." He glanced at the note. "I hope Ferghal can understand that, because I certainly don't."

"Ferghal will recognise it, sir, and unlock the encryption." Harry paused. "I will provide the distraction by giving myself up to them."

The Admiral scowled. "You assume I'll allow it?"

"We cannot let them murder the Centaur survivors, sir. And since I can manipulate the helmet, I may be able to escape whatever they propose."

"I don't like it." The Admiral studied Harry. "I wonder if there is a chance to use the Canids to give you at least some sort of support. Don't they have a type of cloak that renders them almost invisible? How does it work? Would it get them past a scanner? Will it work with an EVA suit?"

Harry thought about it. "You may be on to something, sir." He grinned. "It worked for me on Lycania, but the trick is the clothing it is paired with. The Consortium commander couldn't see me right in front of her, and we weren't visible to their visual weapons sights—but I don't know whether it screens anyone from any other sort of scan."

"Then we need to find out." The Admiral touched his link. "Flags, how many Canids have we aboard?"

"One moment, sir." The briefest pause. "Sixty-three on the ship's book, sir. Three of them Pack Leaders."

"Have the senior Pack Leader come to my quarters immediately." The Admiral snapped off the link. "Now, let us hope they have at least some of these cloaks with them."

The door alarm sounded.

"Come in," the Admiral called out.

The door slid back to reveal a heavily built Canid. His slightly grey muzzle and impressive mane of hair proclaimed his status as he stepped into the Admiral's conference room. "Rongar at your command, sir."

The Admiral acknowledged the peculiar Canid salute and indicated a chair. "Thank you, Rongar. I hope you can assist us." Briefly he explained his interest in the concealment cloaks and why. "We know they can make you invisible to normal vision, but can they hide a wearer from a scanner? I'd like to test this if you or one of your pack have such a cloak aboard."

"It shall be done." The Pack Leader growled his laugh. "We have our cloaks. I shall summon one." He paused. "They work best if the wearer remains still, but they can be used when the wearer is in motion if the background is not complex."

Aboard the *Emily Hobhouse*, the passengers from the planet Centaur were dismayed to find themselves hostage. The former captain and some of his councilmen saw an opportunity to regain what they considered their rightful position.

"We're victims here," he told Kali. "Victims of an aggressive upstart who took advantage of the ignorance of our people and turned them against us."

Kali listened to his lengthy list of grievances with a mixture of contempt and amusement. Her mind wandered. This Commander Heron was a worthy adversary—resourceful, original and courageous. He was a good challenge, unlike her usual targets—fat, arrogant, and not remotely courageous or inventive; politicians and businessmen, and occasionally would-be assassins too ambitious for their own good. It was a pity Zorvan wanted this one taken alive and handed to the Charonians. She would have enjoyed stalking and hunting him.

"So, you have a score to settle with the Commander, and you want me to assist in his capture" she said quietly when her visitor stopped speaking. "What have you in mind as a reward?"

The Centaur captain smiled. "We'll help you take him. After all, he won't suspect us—we're your hostages." He put on an expression he hoped showed how cunning he was, and then he lowered his voice. "You could help us by providing some of those really powerful weapons—just what we need to restore discipline and bring our crewmen and the Enviros back in line. Then you could return us to our home planet." He smiled ingratiatingly. "We could provide a useful base for you in future."

Kali almost laughed. The fool really had no idea. His expression looked so pathetic and was so patently false that it was laughable. "You'd like to return to your original home world as well?" The planet sounded like an ideal spot for a bit of her favourite sport, and to have some 'native' prey to hunt would make it perfect, though she doubted this buffoon or his cronies would last more than a few minutes. The Enviros, Guardians and Hunters certainly would give some sport. Yes, she could afford to play this game. "I think such a deal might be possible," she replied. "What do you have in mind for helping us?"

"Let us send an appeal." His smile was so eager it was nauseating. "I can appeal to this Fleet to give you the Commander you want. I'll tell them you're getting ready to kill us or something."

She nodded, feigning encouragement. "Yes, I'm sure that would help. I'll have to discuss it with my superiors of course." Fool, he obviously hadn't realised that since he had seen her and could identify her, he couldn't possibly be allowed to survive. Evidently not, but she enjoyed toying with him, and he might just be useful for the moment. "In the meantime, I'll have you moved to more appropriate quarters—something more suitable to your status. I'm afraid you'll have to stay apart from your people for now, just until we've sorted out how you can help us."

"Oh, I'm sure that will be fine. The others don't have the responsibility of leadership. They'll do as I tell them." He shrugged. "It's a burden, but I was born for it." He frowned. "Until that upstart who calls himself Commander Heron interfered, my people were doing just fine. Just let me have some of these fantastic weapons your people have and I'll be able to set things to rights in a moment."

I just bet you'll try. Only a fool like you could even think of doing something like this.

She kept her expression serious and nodded. "Of course. Now, let my colleague show you to your new quarters, and I'll discuss your proposal with my superiors."

Felicity leaned back in her chair, the latest briefing on the coffee table beside her. The Pantheon were getting bolder and more aggressive, and now this business with the *Emily Hobhouse* and

Commander Heron. Sometimes she wished she'd never agreed to take her career into the security field—Intelligence Services by a different title.

If the general public ever realised what was really happening behind the public face of politics and their whole concept of society...

She sighed with weariness. Her superior, the enigmatic Admiral Greene, a protégé of the Admiral who'd brought her into Security, certainly knew at least some of the people on that encrypted list, but he wanted all of it.

"Power corrupts!" She snorted. "Whoever it was first said that didn't know the bloody half of it!"

"Do you need something, Commodore?" asked the android steward.

"Nothing you could provide, Tango One. Just thinking aloud is all." She hesitated. "On second thought, some tea and my writer, please."

"You asked for me, Commodore?" said her android writer.

"Yes, Yelendi." Felicity smiled as she recalled the woman she'd named the SU for. Where had the years gone? And here they were again, once more fending off an attempt by rogue politicians and their extremely wealthy backers to overthrow governments and place themselves in power. The original Yelendi died aboard the Consortium's first flagship when the *Vanguard* destroyed it during the Battle of Pangaea.

"I need the latest update on the demands for the release of the hospital ship *Emily Hobhouse*. Then I'll need to speak to Admiral Greene."

The SU paused. "The latest information is on your tablet, Commodore. I will contact the Admiral now."

"Thanks." Felicity reached for the tablet and read the update. Something about the crew list of the *Hobhouse* bothered her, but she couldn't put her finger on exactly what it was. She read it again. There was definitely something on it, but ... she smiled as the hologram of the Head of Security sprang to life. "Good evening, sir."

"Evening, Felicity. What have you got?"

"I'm not sure, sir. Just going through the crew and passenger list for the *Hobhouse*. For some reason a couple of names bother me, but there's something else. She's chartered from Universal Mediships, but they're a wholly owned subsidiary of Duerte-Avila Pharmaceuticals, and they in turn ... to cut it short, the actual owners are a company hiding behind loads of fronts, and it's on our watch list: Global and Interplanetary Financial, part of the Al-Khalifa empire."

The Admiral's hologram remained silent for several seconds. "Well spotted. That explains several anomalies and some signal intercepts. Warn James Heron. I'll pass on our analysis."

Chapter 28

Across the Styx

"The package is here, sir." The Flag Lieutenant placed the container on the Admiral's table as if he was handling dangerous explosives.

The Admiral glared. "Thank you. Inform my neph—inform Commander Heron." He gestured at the container. "Has it been checked for toxins, recorders—anything harmful, as I ordered?"

"Yes, sir. As far as we can tell it's clean. We don't know if they've modified it, though. In appearance it's identical to the helmet they fitted to him the last time." The Lieutenant indicated the container. "Of course, we can't actually test the thing until it's activated, and that can't be done until it's locked in place." He wiped a hand across his eyes. "Beats me how the Commander managed to survive the last time, sir. With this damned thing on he won't be able to eat, and drinking will require a tube. Even his vision will be restricted." He shook his head. "I don't think I could do it."

The Admiral nodded. "He is a strong young man with a great deal of fortitude. Has he run the tests I ordered in the original?"

"Yes, sir. He was able to connect with the operating system and manipulate it. It proved more difficult than he thought at first, and getting the damned helmet off again was even harder."

"Hmph. I don't like this at all. What about those Canid cloaks? Are they detectable?"

"Not by normal means, sir. But if you scan in the IR range that matches their body temperatures, you can detect them. Unfortunately, it is also within the spectrum that the Charonians can see, though only just. The scientists say it will be like seeing a shadow where there isn't one. The Canids say they can fix that, but they won't say how."

"Very well. I'm liking this less and less—and the damned people from Centaur have thrown a spoke in the wheel as well. I've now got a message from their captain saying the pirates are threatening to 'space' them if we don't comply. The damned media are all over it, of course," he added bitterly, and stood. "Get Harry in for me, and make sure we are not interrupted. Then I'll want to see Commander Whitworth and—what's the Canid officer's name? Ah, yes, Pack Leader Lucanes, from the *Lagan*." He watched the Lieutenant leave.

"This had better work," he muttered to himself.

"Niamh was moved to a normal recovery unit this morning." Theo looked tired as he faced the holocam. "She's healed well, but it will be a while yet before she's able to get up." He looked weary. "I'm dreading her discovering the situation with Harry. Mary and I will do our best to keep it from her, but she's bound to see or hear something of it."

"I know." James Heron drummed the desk with his fingers. "I'm damned if I like it either." He sighed. "When Harry learned what was happening, he wouldn't accept not doing anything as an option. He actually refused an order not to do it. That damned boy simply will not accept that he doesn't have to take personal responsibility for the people from Centaur. Now all I can do is wait and see if these scum honour their end of the bargain."

"Please tell me you haven't ... oh my God. James, I'm appalled you've let him do it. Oh, God, I dare not let Niamh hear this. It'll kill her. And if it doesn't, she'll be so angry she'll never speak to you again." Theo hesitated, his face stricken. "I'm sorry, James. I can see you're not happy about it either."

"No, Theo, I'm not. I wouldn't be happy about it if it was anyone in my command, so the fact that it is Harry makes it ten times worse." He spread his hands in a gesture of surrender. "I suspect that if I'd enforced the order to stand down, and placed him under confinement or anything else short of chaining him to a bulkhead in the brig—he'd have gone off and done it anyway. As the chaplain says, all we can do now is pray. I am making it my personal task to trace each and every member of the Pantheon from top to bottom in that infernal organisation. I won't rest until they are made to account for their deeds."

"I'm with you in that." Theo paused for a moment. "It is time they were made to fall in line like the rest of humanity. Yes, definitely time to cut them down to size. Keep me informed, please, James, good or bad. Keep me in the picture." He hesitated, his distress plain. "Is there any chance Harry will survive? Do you think the Charonians will let him return?"

"We don't know, Theo. We can only pray he can pull it off, and we've a few things that should make it possible. I'll keep you informed of developments, though—you can count on it."

"We're in position, Harry." Keiron dropped the pretence of being a subordinate. "Are you certain you want to walk into this?"

"I do not think Daniel willingly walked into the lion's den, my friend. No, I'm not certain I want to do this." Harry's face blanched as he sat and stared at the dreaded helmet in his hands. As specified in the demand note, he wore only his service coverall beneath his EVA suit. Once the helmet was on and the suit closed, he would exit the *Sabre*, which would then withdraw.

He glanced at the clock in nervous anticipation. "We are on time, but they seem to be tardy."

Keiron grimaced. "Their message said a ship would arrive as soon as you left the airlock. Time to test it, I suppose." He paused. "I'm not happy about this, Harry. If our Canid team can't get aboard the pick-up ship, you're going to be entirely on your own."

"I know. Are they in position? With their cloaks in place we can't see them, but I don't know if those work in the void. Do you?"

Keiron nodded. "Yes, we tested that, and they do. Bloody amazing things those. I've got to get some for my teams once this is over." He hoped his easy conversation was a good cover for his concern.

"I'm sure our Canid friends will supply them." Harry took a deep breath then exhaled. "Okay, Keiron, I can't delay this any longer. Help me put this infernal thing on and let's get on with it."

"Okay, but I want your assurance that you can operate the control unit inside it before I allow you out of the ship."

"If you insist, but I suspect they will have some means to test it is working." Harry positioned the thing over his face and held it while Keiron closed the clamshell design and secured it. Harry sensed the activation then the loss of contact with the *Sabre*. He sucked in a nervous breath. "It has severed my link to the ship." He forced himself to relax and listen for the control unit. Unlike AI networks programmed by humans, this one felt and behaved in a manner he thought of as crude. After several minutes to familiarise himself with it, he tried a deactivation command. His head immediately filled with the *Sabre's* operation. Feeling relieved, he reactivated the helmet.

"So, how's it going in there?" Keiron asked.

"I can manipulate it," said Harry. "It's a strange device, little more than an intelligent switch, but I can operate it easily, no problem."

"I'll take your word for it, Harry." Keiron sounded dubious. "Okay, better close and start up your suit so we can get this operation going. "

Harry closed the EVA suit and let Keiron check the functions. "I'm ready, my friend." He paused. "Promise me you will spare no effort to bring these fiends to justice—human and alien."

"You can count on it, Harry. If this operation goes sideways, I'll hunt these bastards down—even if I have to leave the Fleet to do it, and I won't be alone in my efforts either. Plenty more will join me."

"Thank you." Harry moved toward the airlock. "Pray for me. I won't say good-bye."

Keiron nodded. "Neither will I, and yes, I'll pray. I've never done it before, but I'll do it now. Lucanes and his people are in place." He grinned. "Try not to bump into them."

Harry smiled. "You got it. And I'm sure your prayers will be heard, Keiron." He activated the door control and stepped into the airlock. "I shall see you when this is over, Number One." He sketched a salute. "You're buying the drinks!"

Keiron stiffened and returned the salute. "I'm counting on it," he replied as the door closed.

"Don't get creative!" Zorvan barked. "You'll blow the entire operation and put us all at risk." He glared at the audio link. "The deal is that ship has to be released—with everyone on it."

"I know," Kali placated, her voice honey with an edge. "However, that was before the hostages learned some of our identities, myself included."

"How did that happen? You've put the entire organisation at risk." He cursed silently in his own language. Kali had worried him for a while now. She was utterly ruthless, a true psychopath, but she was also ambitious.

"Relax. I have this fully under control," she purred. "The coordinates for this ship will be transmitted as soon as the pickup is made. The only change to the plan is that the passengers will demand a return to their home world, and we'll transit out of there." She paused. "I've made a deal with the passengers. They will take over the ship as soon as Fleet make contact, on the pretence that they're returning to their home world. Fleet can't argue with that, and I'll get the chance for some sport."

Zorvan felt the chill of doubt. This was going bad, very bad. He cursed silently again. Damn Kali. He should have dealt with her before this. Now she was forcing his hand. Very well, as soon as he'd concluded this deal, she would go. He'd see to it himself.

"The key thing is that Heron must be delivered to the client. After that, we'll see." He allowed himself a warning. "These clients are not the sort we want to upset. They will not tolerate a double-cross."

She laughed. "They'll get Heron. I've already squared the change with them."

"You've what?" He bit back the explosion he wanted to unleash. By arranging a Charonian-controlled ship to collect Heron and deliver him to the Charonian mothership, Kali had changed the entire operation without consulting him.

"I've arranged for me to keep this little zoo ship," she replied sweetly. "I plan a little amusement once this is over. The client is happy with the arrangement, so relax."

Relax? he retorted inwardly, but kept it to himself. "I shall confirm this with the client. Very well, continue. We're too deeply committed to abort now." He broke the link. When he had his anger under control, he contacted his secretary.

"Contact Vizaresha. Tell him it is time to deal with the Hindu. I'm leaving now in the *Djinn*." He broke the link.

The secretary used a comlink of unusual design to encode and send a very brief message. None of the guests aboard the *Dhow*

Khalifa noticed the departure of the sleek and rather sinister *Djinn* as it detached itself from the underbelly of the yacht and vanished into transit.

Ferghal contacted the *Harmony Voyager* AI. "Good day, *Voyager*. I believe you knew my friend Harry."

"Yes, I remember him. He was taken from my accommodation at the star reference 56-Alpha-776-Gamma-778-Beta. Are you looking for him?"

"No, we found him, and he is now on another task. He sent you a greeting. He wanted me to assure you he doesn't hold you responsible for what happened, but asked that you help me find something important."

"I will gladly do so. What do you seek?"

"A file planted by the woman who had Harry captured. It is the key to an encrypted file that gives the names of some important people—people who are in league with the Charonians." He hesitated. "Harry told me it is in a record the Senator stored in a hidden file. He saw it while he lay paralysed by their weapon, but he could not act because he was not in control of his thoughts." Ferghal consulted the note as he listened. "It is one that fits this descriptor. He thinks I will also need you to unlock the files using the encryption key you have in a file labelled Coriolanus. I recorded his link and his inability to function, and then he was separated from me by a screening device of strange origin. I have many hidden files of that type."

The data flashed through Ferghal's vision. Even though he knew it wouldn't stop, he shut his eyes tightly, but it still made his head spin.

The ship continued. "There are five files that fit the parameters you give, and which are associated with the Coriolanus encryption. All have names and pseudonyms. Do you need to see the contents of each? Shall I decrypt them?"

"Yes to both questions, but slowly please." Ferghal collected his thoughts. "Sure an' I'm not as fast as you in processing information. Let me read the first please." He scanned it. Yes, he certainly recognised some of the names, as they were very important people. Then it hit him. "Did you say one of these files assigns the names of gods and goddesses to humans? Let me see it."

The file began to scroll through his optic nerves. One name leapt out at him, that of a man who only hours earlier had been on a news video declaring that sacrifices were sometimes necessary. The same name appeared on a separate list identifying those who had funded organisations involved in the coup attempts and a former member of the Consortium Board. Aloud he said, "Stop!" A cold hand clutched his chest. "Holy Mary, Mother of God! Oh God, Blessed Jesu! Harry is in the hands of Satan himself, by all the saints. The man coordinating this is the chief among these devils!"

Trembling with a mixture of mounting rage, fear, hatred and the desire to tear these fiends apart with his bare hands, he had the presence of mind to give a direct order to the AI. "Download these files, all of them, to this address." He gave the code for the Admiral of Security and the Advocate Admiral. "And to this ship address." He gave the *Sabre*'s ID. "Mark that for immediate attention, to Commander Whitworth. Also to Admiral Heron. Encrypt for their eyes only." He was bathed in a cold sweat. "Sweet Jesu, let it not be too late. Blessed Patrick, Holy Peter and Paul, Blessed Mark, Matthew, Luke and John, Holy Mary—protect and save my friend and brother."

"I have sent the files to the addresses you give, but I do not recognise any of the others you are naming. Give me the addresses and I will comply."

Ferghal jerked out of his frantic prayers. "What? Oh. No, disregard my prayers. They are not instructions for you." He recollected himself. "Do not reveal you have these files, or that you have forwarded them to anyone—it could get you and me destroyed. Delete the record of the transmission and replace the deletions with test transmission entries." He recalled how similar gaps in the signal logs had betrayed his and Harry's tampering with the Consortium's AI on the planet Lycania. He thought again. "And hide those files! Only release them if I ask for them or Harry does."

"We've a message from Lieutenant-Commander O'Connor, sir. He says Commander Heron should abort the mission." The Flag Lieutenant grimaced. "He was quite excited about it, and I had trouble understanding him because he had lapsed into that strong Irish brogue of his."

"Why wasn't he put on my display immediately?"

"You were on coms with the Grand Admiral and Head of Security, sir."

"So I was. Sorry, Flags. Get Ferghal ... get the Lieutenant Commander on holo for me immediately, please." James Heron hesitated. "And get Commander Whitworth on as well."

"Yes, sir." The Lieutenant hurried away, urgently signalling the ComsRates.

The Admiral smiled as Ferghal's hologram appeared. "I got your message, Ferghal. Tell me what you discovered—slowly please, so I can understand you without a translator!"

Ferghal grinned. "Sure, sir." His expression changed. "Sir, I got the information, and I've shared it with Commander Whitworth's people." He took a deep breath. "I hope they've stopped Harry—Commander Heron, sir. Satan himself is behind this!"

The Admiral frowned. "Satan? Explain."

"'Tis the one calls himself Zorvan, a Mr. Al Khalifa, behind these people, sir, and two of his gods"—Ferghal practically spat the word in derision— "are on the *Hobhouse* with some of their protection agents guarding them. Zorvan is the one collecting Harry for the Charonians." Ferghal paused. "I found the files and the encryption key Harry remembered. I've sent them to Security, sir, but ..." Ferghal shook his head. "'Tis as I said, sir, the devil himself is loose in this. Some o' the names, sir, the top of society, and—"

"I see." The Admiral struggled to maintain his calm appearance. "We suspected as much."

The hologram of Keiron Whitworth appeared. "Commander Heron has been taken aboard a Charonian ship, sir. The Canids are with him."

"Damnation." The Admiral's expression hardened. "I'll have fresh orders for you shortly. Are you in tracking contact?"

"Yes, sir."

"Maintain it. I'm sending you support. In the meantime, do not under any circumstances lose that contact!" He turned to Ferghal. "Well, Commander, best speed. Rejoin your ship and take her to rejoin your flotilla."

Chapter 29

Entering Hades

Harry drifted in the void. In his logical mind, he knew that he was traveling at an unbelievable speed through the heavens, but there was no fixed point he could measure his movement against, nor was there any sensation of movement. He tried to glimpse the Canids, who he sensed were positioned close to him, but he couldn't see them. It would be useless to contact them since their comlinks were off to avoid detection.

Have the Charonians changed their minds? he wondered. "I hope so," he said to the void, and then he saw a very sinister ship drawing near. "Damn, they haven't."

"Commander Heron." The voice was a human one, to Harry's irrational relief. "Use your manoeuvring pack to close our portside hangar bay and enter it. After you have done so, move to the marked point and remain there. Don't try anything funny or clever. We have our weapons locked on you. Contract or no contract, we'll shoot first."

"Very well. I will comply with your instructions." He activated the propulsion pack manually, a task he usually did through his cyberlink. Deliberately he kept the movements slow, buying time for the Canids to get into the positions they needed.

"Speed it up. We haven't got all day."

"I'm doing my best," Harry replied coolly. "I confess I am out of practice with having to operate the unit manually."

"Don't give us excuses."

Harry heard raised voices in the background as he fumbled with the unit.

"Very well. I'll close the distance for you. Watch the gravitational effect. It'll pull you in."

"Thank you, I shall take precautions."

Hopefully that will give Lucanes and his team some help, Harry thought, watching the ship's manoeuvring thrusters flare. He saw a brief flicker of something against the hull, then another, and finally at the open hangar dock. He increased his thrust gently and gave a convincing appearance of someone not in full control of his propulsion. "This helmet makes it difficult to see my instruments. Can you talk me in?" He hoped that would distract anyone watching his approach and give Lucanes time to get his people aboard.

"You're too far left of track. Adjust your aspect two degrees right."

"I cannot read the direction in this device." He touched the directional control and deliberately veered too far right then over corrected. The ship was close now, and he aimed at a point above the open dock. "Wait. I think I had best try to get through the opening, then I'll worry about where the dock is." He aimed at the centre of the dock.

"Keep that heading. As soon as you're in, touch down and stand in the centre of the bay. Do not attempt to leave it."

As if I can, he thought. "Very well." He passed the thresholds and the great doors closed behind him. Internal lighting increased and he manoeuvred clumsily toward a marked circle in the middle of the dock. A glance upward showed projectors of some sort. Harry knew that meant he would be stood within a screen field once he was in place, or he could be destroyed where he stood— their choice, not his. It wasn't a prospect he liked. Deliberately he landed outside it.

"Move into the demarcated space immediately."

"Not before I have the assurance the hostages have been released to the Fleet."

"You're not in a position to make demands, Commander. Do as I order."

"No." Harry stepped back. "I do not trust you or your associates. Those projectors above me could be designed to destroy me, and if that is the case, I need to know that you have kept your part of the bargain."

There was no response for several seconds, then a new voice said, "The hospital ship and its passengers have been delivered to the Fleet at the agreed coordinates." There was a further pause. "We do not intend to destroy you. What you call projectors are simply monitors. Please step into the designated space. We do not want to damage you."

I would like to damage you, he thought. "Very well." Damnation. It appeared they intended to keep him under some monitoring device. That meant he'd not be able to carry out his part of the plan. He walked into the marked circle. "What now?"

"You may open your suit but remain in it. You will be transferred to our command ship shortly."

Harry groped for the controls. He couldn't see the atmospheric conditions monitor, but he knew that the suit would sound an audible alarm and prevent its opening if the atmosphere was not able to support life. That would have to do. He had no choice but to trust it.

Nothing happened as he went through the routine and the visors opened leaving his helmeted head and shoulders visible. He tested his contact with the control unit in the helmet and found it functional. He tried to see what the helmet screen could detect but saw nothing, so he triggered the shut-down command. Immediately his head filled with alien code as the ship connected to him. He switched the helmet back on, hoping no one had noticed a new node in the system. He'd wait to see if there was any response. There didn't appear to be. A flicker of distortion in his view of the bulkhead nearest a door caught his attention. Good. Lucanes and his team were in position. Now they must simply wait.

"What?" The Admiral's anger was palpable. His Flag Lieutenant had never seen him this angry. He recalled a conversation with a friend about Harry's temper and how it flashed from red-hot fury to cold calculating rage in a matter of seconds. Now he could see what his friend had meant.

Cut from the same cloth, the Lieutenant observed, but his expression betrayed nothing.

"Yes, sir," he replied. "Apparently, the leaders of the Centaur refugees have acquired weapons, and now they're holding the crew of the *Hobhouse* hostage—or so they claim. Their captain leader demands their return to Centaur and the full restoration of their society as it was before we invaded—his words, not mine."

"I see. So the privileged few, the spoiled brats that called themselves the Officer Council, want to have their comforts restored, and the rest must do as they're told. Why does this not surprise me?" He stared at the ships of his fleet in the 3D display. "How do the rest of the refugees feel about it? Where is the *Hobhouse* now?"

"There is a suggestion the majority are under some compulsion, sir. At present she's still at the agreed release point." The Lieutenant swallowed. He wasn't looking forward to revealing the next bit. "There's more, sir. Those files that Lieutenant-Commander O'Connor passed on. The person code-named Kali is actually aboard the *Hobhouse* as Captain of the ship, and the chief medic aboard is the Pantheon agent known as Vizaresha." He waited a few tense moments as his Admiral digested this. "A few hours ago, there was a message from Zorvan addressed to Vizaresha. It may have something to do with this, but we're still trying to decipher the code."

The Admiral's face turned to stone. "And...?"

"The entire crew are members of the Pantheon, sir. We think this is a very elaborate double bluff—and the refugees have played right into Kali's hands, sir."

"Why?" A memory stirred. "Damnation. She's setting them up as prey for one of her obscene hunting parties, and we have just handed them my nephew Harry on a damned platter!" His anger was now a palpable force in the Flag Centre. "Well, maybe they deserve what they get. That idiot who calls himself the captain of Centaur has set his people up to be killed. Frankly, he deserves to be the first." The Flag Lieutenant felt as if he was standing on a metal spire while wearing a metal suit and holding a lightning rod as a thunderstorm approaches. He knew at this point it was best to remain silent. The storm unleashed its fury. "Get me the Brigadier, get me the C-in-C, and get Admiral Petrocova on line, in that order!" the Admiral snapped, his tone frigid. "And get Commander Whitworth online—now!"

Theo watched the news on the wall screen. His linked chirped. "L'Estrange."

"Chief Justice? Are you watching the newscasts on Channel 50?"

"Yes, it's just come on here. Why?"

"There's been a leak. We think they are about to broadcast at least some of the names from those secret files." The caller hesitated. "It will alert some of those we've issued warrants for. There is bound to be resistance from some of the key figures, and, of course, the media circus that will follow."

"Damnation." Theo frowned. "Very well, record it then prepare a statement. I'll contact Security and the Minister."

He watched the screen and listened as the presenter adopted a 'serious face' to announce, "In breaking news, key information has been uncovered by the Fleet Security Agency and the Department of Justice and Peace which implicates a number of senior politicians and well-known figures in commerce and finance. We have learned there are some senior figures in the permanent administrations of the Confederation, the North American Alliance, the South American Alliance, the League of Middle-Eastern States, the WTO and several other signatory nations involved as well. We are attempting to verify the names and will bring you further updates as soon as we have them."

"Seems they have the list but are playing it safe." Theo snorted. "That'll be a first. Mind you the owner of this news organisation is on the list. Warn our people not to confirm or deny anything. Oh, and find the leak. I'll see if I can get the Minister to do some damage control, as my brother-in-law calls it."

He broke the link then called a private number. "Minister, we have a problem, but I think we can contain it if we act quickly."

Keiron broke the link. "Bloody hell," he breathed out slowly. He could still feel the anger radiating from the hologram. The Admiral was going for the jugular. Harry's phrase, 'no quarter asked or given' came to mind. He was very glad he wasn't on the flagship or on the Admiral's staff right now. He had the feeling no one was going to get any slack if things didn't go the Admiral's way very quickly. All hell was going to break loose at home politically as well, and the legal teams would soon be tying themselves in knots.

He pushed it out of his mind. He and the Tenth Flotilla had the most difficult bit, the job of tracking Harry. He glanced at the waiting officers. "You all heard that. I don't want to be the one who has to tell the Admiral we failed. Have you got that tracker signal locked in, Ramgis?"

"It is locked, Leader."

"Helm, follow the signal, lock helms with the others and let's get going." He turned to the Canid again. "Can the Provider see or hear what Lucanes and his people are doing? Have we contact through it, him, her—whatever your Provider is?" He gestured impatiently. "You know what I mean."

The Canid Pack Leader growled his strange laugh. He reached into his suit and pulled out a small transponder which he handed to Keiron. "Speak directly to the Provider. He will show you what you need to know, Commander."

Keiron accepted the unit and almost dropped it as it vibrated in his hand. "I just talk to this?"

"Correct, Commander," came a deep voice from the transponder. "I am the Provider. What do you need me to do for you?"

"Good evening. Thank you. Caught me unawares there. Yes, I need to know what Lucanes and his team are seeing and doing at the moment."

"They planted the devices and await arrival at the mothership of the Charonians. Commander Heron is unharmed and awaits their next move. He has explored their ship's intelligence and found its weakness. I assume he plans to act when it will be most effective."

Keiron assessed this information, his mind racing. At least Harry was safe for now, but Keiron was concerned about the mothership.

"Can you communicate with him?" he asked the Provider.

"Not right now. He has reactivated the device they make him wear, a wise decision." There was a fraction of a second's hesitation. "Your ships are three hours and fifty-six minutes behind the Charonians. It is best you continue as you are. I will alert you to any change."

Harry listened to the operating system in the helmet and made an interesting discovery. The control unit was linked to the ship. He could hear it exchanging data, instructions and responses. A little mental effort allowed him to insert some requests for information into the stream. The answer was unintelligible and in a language he could not identify. He tried again, this time inserting a complex navigation formula into the exchange. The solution returned in recognisable code.

Got you, he said in his thoughts. He considered how he could use this, but before he could reach a decision, a door opened and several figures entered. Irrationally, he was relieved they appeared to be human, but as they approached, he realised their appearance was deceptive.

The leading figure stopped in front of him. "Come. Follow."

Harry had a hard time believing what he was seeing. The creature might at one time have been human, but now it had the pallor of a corpse. Coupled with what appeared to be the stubs of horns on his temples, blood red lips, and sunken red eyes with the absence of pupils, Harry felt as if he was gazing into the depths of Dante's Inferno. His mouth went dry and his throat constricted.

"Where?" He croaked. He tried again. "Where are you taking me?"

"No talk. Follow." The creature's red eyes bored into him.

Harry nodded. He had noticed that the leader's companions were armed, and he didn't want to find out what their weapons could do.

So he nodded. "Very well."

The escort led him to an adjoining hangar and onto a shuttle. Minutes later they were sweeping toward a huge ship that filled the display screen. Harry wondered whether any of the Canids had managed to follow. He couldn't detect any in the shuttle with him. He could only hope.

To the devil with caution, he thought. He deactivated the helmet and tested the link, and almost gave himself away when a growl near his ear became coherent. "We are here, Leader."

Harry gave a slight nod but didn't dare speak, and it took all his willpower to control the tremor in his legs as the shuttle entered a hangar on the new ship. It was difficult to walk as he was ushered from the shuttle and led toward a gaping corridor.

Keiron stared at the display. "They've transferred him. Are any of his escort with him?"

"They are all present, Commander."

"Good." Keiron paused. "I just hope they can get him out of there again—I don't want to have to tell the Admiral that his nephew—"

"Lucanes knows what is required, Commander," Ramgis interjected. "He reports there is a human ship docked in the Charonian ship. It entered the dock just after the Commander's shuttle docked."

"Does he give any readings on it? Show me what you have."

"It has an unusual profile and uses stealth technology."

Keiron studied the data. "Damn, I've seen something like that before." He called to a TechRate. "Run a search in our records for a similar profile to this."

"Aye, aye, sir." The TechRate entered a string of commands. "Profile coming up, sir. Registered as a yacht, but she's got some add-ons that look like weapons."

"What name is she registered under? Owner?"

"Registered as the Dee-Jinn, sir. Mr. Kharim Al-Khalifa is recorded as the owner."

"Dee-Jinn? Is it spelled D-j-i-n-n?"

"Yes, sir."

"Well, well." Keiron drummed his fingers on the armrest. "Get me a coms link to Commodore Roberts."

Chapter 30

Into the Valley of Death

Kharim Al-Khalifa was angry, but only those who knew him very well would have been able to tell. His identity as Zorvan had been exposed. So had every other member of the organisation. Even worse, Vizaresha hadn't carried out his instruction to terminate Kali, and now both of them were stuck on a damned hospital ship full of refugees. It was inconvenient, but enough money in the right hands would soon solve most of it. In the meantime, he would have those in possession of this knowledge dealt with.

"As soon as we are clear of this ship, I need to rendezvous with Kali," he instructed his yacht captain via his comlink. "Advise her that I will require her coordinates."

He listened to the acknowledgement and increased his pace.

Incredible, these Charonians had perfected a way to perpetuate themselves using host bodies of compatible species, and had created the most incredible alloys and metallurgical technology; yet, for all their expertise, they had only the crudest of AI computers with which to control their ships.

Powerful, yes, fast, certainly, complex and efficient, but crude. He smiled. Well, this was their problem. That helmet they'd fitted to Heron was effective, he had to admit, and the secret of the alloys they had exchanged in return for his delivery would make him a fortune once he was able to change his identity and emerge from hiding. Some people thought of wealth as money or valuable metals and gems, but he didn't. These alloys would bring even his current enemies running to buy them.

Something brushed against him as he turned a corner. Instinctively he leapt aside and drew a weapon. The plasma burst hit something well short of the wall. He didn't stop to see what it was but ran for the hangar access and his yacht. His lightning reflexes almost saved him a second time when a huge paw seized his arm, wrenched the projector weapon from his grasp, and slammed him against the bulkhead.

He moved to grab his second weapon, but the Canid rendered him helpless and unconscious before Zorvan could complete that thought. Pack Leader Lucanes surveyed the unconscious figure and growled a question to his fellow Canid. "Are you hurt, Uranak?"

"No, Pack Leader, though my cloak is destroyed."

"This human armour works then. Use one of the spares. Let Kenza assist you to secure this one's ship. We will find the Commander." He stirred the unconscious assassin with his foot. "Zamliy, Bron, secure this human and conceal him until I tell you otherwise."

With the helmet deactivated, Harry tried to make sense of the computer he could hear. His escort seemed unaware that the helmet was not active, which made him feel more confident. Knowing the Canid team were also aboard gave him hope that he might survive this reasonably unscathed. Stripped of the EVA suit, almost naked and locked into a sort of vertical frame, he was anything but comfortable. Around him monitors hummed and displayed incomprehensible symbols and glyphs while a team of the aliens examined him. They ran a medical scan and checked his torso, his heart and his lungs. The slightly sulphurous odour they emitted didn't make him feel any better about it.

On the way to this chamber, they passed many more of the creatures and a few who appeared to be semi-human. At least their skin and colour were more human and so were their facial features and limbs. Their eyes were universally blood red, and all showed at least some deformity of the skull at the temples. Listening to the computer he began to make sense of the commands and sub routines. Experimentally he picked one set of regularly repeating routines and inserted a small variation every thousandth run.

Now he would wait to see what happened.

The creature in charge indicated a change of procedure. He gave an order, and the frame rotated to a new position.

Harry wondered if he could extricate himself from it, but then the lights went out. All the monitors blanked as well, causing exclamations of alarm all round him. Without warning, the lights came back at an intensity that made Harry shut his eyes against the brightness. Even through the narrow slit in the helmet it was dazzling. Screams and exclamations of pain suggested his attendants found the sudden change agonising. He checked his code in the computer and grinned before he quickly suppressed his mirth.

The leader issued a torrent of commands which sent the other figures rushing to restore equipment and bring back data screens. Several operated the door. Harry tried to identify the door controls and commands. He focussed his attention on that task as several more creatures arrived, a human among them.

This time he was able to catch the door command routines and set these to automatic, ordering all the ship's doors to open and close randomly. Then, feigning innocence, he activated the helmet again and listened through the control unit as the crew made increasingly frantic efforts to reverse his instructions. The lights failed again then flashed into full brilliance. To his surprise, all the creatures that had been in the laboratory with him were now on the floor in various positions that suggested violence had been done to them. Lucanes materialised next to him.

"Leader, we must leave. This ship will not survive your interference. Already it loses atmosphere. Where is your suit?"

The voice of Pack Leader Lucanes startled him. He fought to sound casual. "Really? I simply told it to open all the doors on a random pattern." He paused. "Oh. I did not consider that. Surely the AI will not allow—"

"I do not think this ship is like ours. It does not think in the manner ours do."

"Can you get me out of these restraints? I can't find a way to release it in the computer." He nodded toward another door. "They took my EVA suit through there."

Lucanes operated the switches to release the cuffs that secured Harry. Nothing happened. "It appears there is a code to unlock the mechanism, Leader. Can you not operate it?"

Harry shook his head. "No. This system is extremely strange and it is now doing things I did not expect and cannot interpret. Is there no other interlock perhaps?"

"I do not see any other controls, Leader." He moved out of Harry's line of sight and examined something behind the device to which the frame was attached. "Perhaps we may release you by dismantling it."

An alarm sounded in ear-splitting repetition.

"There is no time. Be still, Leader, I shall destroy it, then we may see."

Before Harry could reply there was a brilliant flash and a loud report. Two more Canids appeared and tugged at the restraining cuffs. Slowly, and with some apparent reluctance, the restraints loosened and Harry was able to slip his arms free. A Canid ripped open a panel and short-circuited the controls. Harry's arms and torso were free, and only his ankles remained fixed to the frame.

He felt a little lightheaded and unsteady on his feet, as if he'd had one too many pints to drink, and the whole situation seemed overwhelmingly funny. Suddenly the atmosphere felt colder, and the lights went out again. The Canids went into a discussion of their own, then one attacked the back of the frame that held Harry. Several loud explosions rocked the compartment and the frame collapsed. The Canids grabbed Harry and crammed him into the EVA suit they had retrieved.

"Now, Leader, can you walk?"

"I think so." He tried, lost his balance and stumbled to the floor where he lay giggling, splayed out in helplessness for a few moments. The impact shook some part of his senses back into awareness, and he sat up. "I think I'm suffering from oxygen depletion. Can you help me, Pack Leader?" Someone adjusted the oxygen flow in his suit and he breathed deeply, letting the life-giving gas filter into his bloodstream. His companions hauled him to his feet and hustled him through the sliding door, timing their escape with precision as it opened and closed at random intervals.

'Zorvan' Kharim Al-Khalifa was cold, angry and confused. He shook his head and took careful stock of his situation. He was in total darkness, and his hands were confined in some sort of device behind him. He was lying on the deck in what he hoped was not one of the implantation centres on this ship. Had his clients double-crossed him? He fought back his headache and focussed his thoughts. No, there had been no one else in the corridor. So what happened to him? Who attacked him?

A memory stirred. Had he caught a slight scent of...? He searched his memory. *Dog? Impossible.* Then his memory stirred again. *Damn, was it one of those—what are they called—Canids? That's it. Did some of them manage to get aboard? But how?*

The lights flickered on.

He was in a small chamber that resembled a storeroom of some kind. Struggling to his feet, he made his way to the door. There was no handle and no control panel on this side.

He looked around again. There were things he might be able to use to escape, but first he needed to get his hands free. He was glad he kept himself in shape and flexible as he went through a number of contortions difficult even for someone in peak physical condition and training, and was rewarded at last by having his hands at his front. He was studying the manacles holding his wrists when the lights went out again. He let out a stream of curses. The lights returned, and he saw his chance—the manacles weren't designed for use on a human. Now that they were in front of him he could manipulate them. He breathed a sigh of relief as he finally worked one hand free. He tried the door. There was some initial resistance, but his anger and desire to survive gave him a surge of adrenaline, and the door slid open just enough for him to ease through the gap.

The corridor was dimly lit, but he could see his way. Something was very wrong with the ship. The temperature was falling, and the oxygen level with it. He oriented himself and set off in the direction of the landing dock and his yacht.

Harry, half carried by Lucanes and half walking, slowly regained the use of his limbs and his senses. "Where are we going, Pack Leader?'

"We secured a vessel for our escape, Leader. We go to where it waits."

He thought about this. "Is it a human ship? I do not think we can master one of these Charonian ships in time to—."

"It is a human ship. It belonged to the man that had you brought here."

"Belonged?"

"I do not think he will need it now."

The Pack Leader was wrong. Hidden in the shadows, Zorvan watched them pass. When he determined that they were far enough ahead, he followed, only slightly hindered by his survival suit, which he'd managed to get into after freeing himself from the restraints. He didn't know how these Canids had got aboard, but they certainly weren't going to leave, and neither was Heron.

"These damned fools are committing suicide." Admiral Heron fumed as he read the latest demand from the man who called himself the Captain of Centaur. He lowered his tablet and looked at the Marine colonel seated further along the table. "What do you recommend?"

The Colonel leaned back. "I'd suggest we keep talking to them. We can't send in a boarding party without risking multiple civilian deaths." He shook his head in frustration. "By now, thanks to the damned media channels and their 'broadcast and be damned' policy, Kali, Zorvan and Vizaresha all know that we know who they are and where they are. So do their troops. Our people will be well able to take them out, but it will be messy—very messy."

"You confirm my thoughts, Tim. Thanks." The Admiral leaned on the table, his frown deepening. "I think our only option at this point is to accede to their demands, track them, and take action when we can minimise the risk of collateral damage." He straightened. "With one small proviso. We'll supply the weapons they ask for, but I want you to make sure we can neutralise them when we need to. Can it be done in a manner that they won't be able to detect or negate?"

"Yes, sir. It can be done. I'll get my weapons technician onto it."

"Good, do that please." The Admiral switched his attention to the Commander in charge of equipment supply. "They want some of our EVA suits and armour as well. Again, I want those suits rigged for single use."

"Consider it done, sir," said the Commander.

"Good. In other matters, the food they want isn't a problem. Supply it." He paused. "I want that damned ship tracked. These people have played us for fools, and we've responded like fools. I want to know where it goes, and then I want them brought to heel, with this Kali and the rest of them in court."

The Charonian ship was in trouble, its systems failing as Harry's inadvertent virus spread. The Canids added to the confusion by their discreet use of small demolition charges in shafts, service passages and any operating stations they could find. Now, on a signal from Lucanes, they returned to the hangar and the yacht their companions had secured.

Zorvan fumed as he trailed the party, moving from concealed space to concealed space with caution and skill. He recognised the figures around Harry. "Damned animals," he spat in a silent curse. "How did they get aboard?" A shift of pattern opposite his hiding place drew his attention, but he couldn't see anything when he focused his eyes at the spot. Alerted to something unknown now, he froze, cursing his lack of a weapon. A chill crept into his ironclad certainty of his abilities as a 'soldier of fortune' and an expert in his craft.

He had no experience dealing with these animals. He searched his memory for information. They were strong and agile despite their clumsy appearance, possessed of incredibly sensitive olfactory abilities, and very intelligent. Could they also be in possession of some technology that allowed them to hide in plain sight? A news item from the Consortium war came to mind. Yes. They used a cloaking garment that changed the refraction of light around them. He studied the wall opposite again. There was something there, and if it could conceal a Canid, it could conceal him.

A plan formed in his mind as he watched Harry and his group. He maintained some distance from them until they were almost out of sight. He'd have to hurry, but once he had that cloaking garment, he could catch up. Another movement caught his eye. Two Charonians were approaching, both armed and wearing breathing helmets. In this dim light, the Charonians would have an advantage, since their vision was in a range far lower than the human eye could see—but their helmets restricted their field of vision. A smile crossed his lips. An amazingly intelligent species, the product of transferring themselves to a new host body when one failed or could no longer adapt to their needs, they had never advanced or adapted a great deal of their technology from its origins. The pair were now between him and the place he thought might conceal a Canid.

He patted the zippered pockets of his suit to find something, anything to throw, and found a small canister that at one time contained a few survival biscuits. *Those were actually quite tasty* he remembered with a sardonic smile as he flung the canister in the direction where the Canid stood, as best he could surmise.

The canister struck something just short of the bulkhead then stopped in mid-air and vanished. The Charonians reacted but were too slow. The Canid materialised briefly, just long enough for his weapon to send out a bolt of plasma that felled the Charonians, and in that instant, Zorvan locked his arms around the Canid and wrestled for possession of the weapon.

The Canid was a small one but more than a match for any human in strength and agility. Zorvan had to use all his famous unarmed combat skills to avoid taking a serious injury. Then the Canid stumbled over one of the Charonians and lost its grip for a fraction of a second, but that was all Zorvan needed. With a desperate heave he completed the Canid's fall, snatched the weapon and fired it, killing the target cleanly.

A quick check revealed no apparent pursuit, so he made a rapid examination of the corpse and found the cloak. He drew it around himself, aware as he did so that his own suit had been damaged in the fight. He cursed when he realised the cloak remained visible, and there wasn't time to figure out why. He would have to obtain access to the yacht as soon as possible, but without the ability to make himself invisible.

He slinked along the corridor from shadow to shadow, aware now of an increasing number of Charonians hurrying toward the central core of the ship. These he dodged and avoided, cursing because he had now lost sight of Harry and his group. He found the access to the hangar and dodged through the airlock. The yacht was in sight, but the absence of bodies suggested that his men were either prisoners or dead. He didn't really care which, but they would be useful when it came to taking back the yacht.

It appeared to be ready for launch, but the hatch was still open. The realisation of the reason bothered him: some Canids were still at large. He hurried forward. If he could get aboard, he might be able to deal with those already there and cut off the stragglers, preventing them from joining their companions. His senses tingling, he approached the yacht, using speed and what little cover there was to his advantage as he made for a second access airlock.

Chapter 31

Paying the Boatman

Harry removed the helmet with a feeling of relief. He was still a little shaky from the oxygen depletion, and was going to be carrying some serious bruises, a small burn and some cuts and abrasions for a day or two, but he was alive, thanks to the Canids, and the Charonians had been thwarted.

He eased himself out of the EVA suit and prepared to take advantage of the luxurious amenities the yacht's owner enjoyed. He took in the opulent decor and fittings. "A trifle more luxury than I am used to, and the decor is not to my usual taste." His grin widened. "I was thinking this Charonian vessel was as grim as Hades." He caught the enquiring expression on the Canid's face. "Ah. In our mythology, Hades is the place the souls of the dead go." A frown formed. "Calling the Charonian ship Hades is appropriate. Charon, in the mythology, is the boatman who conveys the damned souls across the River Styx, a mythical river that separates the world of the living from the place of the dead. These Charonians put me more in mind of the damned souls rather than the boatman…"

His reverie was interrupted by the sound of a plasma discharge followed by a roar of pain and then the sound of a struggle.

"Remain here, Leader." Lucanes was already growling and barking orders into his comlink as he made for the door. "Do not leave. My pack will deal with this. Someone killed Sumara and took her cloak. Now they are here, but we are prepared." The door slid back, and two Canids entered carrying the unconscious figure of Zorvan between them.

Harry frowned. "We will need to discover who he is, and the proper protocol will have to be followed." A memory stirred. "I have seen his face somewhere."

"Look at the image frame on the bulkhead," said the Pack Leader. He is in the third frame. This one also calls himself Zorvan."

"Oh, lord. We've got no less a person than Mr. Kharim Al-Khalifa here, head of the largest and richest investment banking family in the world. This must be his yacht." He sank into a seat. "He calls himself Zorvan? That's the name of the leader of the assassins who are contracted to kill me."

Something that had been bothering him since he came aboard now demanded his attention. "There is something strange on this ship." His frown deepened. "I am linked to the AI, but there is another—one that is trying to hide itself from me."

"There is much about this vessel that is strange, Leader. We must proceed cautiously. Shall I order our departure now?"

Deep in thought as he searched the AI, Harry nodded absent-mindedly. Finally, the Canid's question registered. "Yes," he hastened to reply. "Yes. If all our people are aboard, let us depart. Then we must search every nook and cranny of this ship. Something is wrong here."

"Sir, something strange is happening at the location we tracked that very large Charonian ship to." The Flag Lieutenant indicated his incident display. "All the pirates we've been tracking and a large number of other ships—the ones we assume are Charonian—are converging on this single location."

The Admiral stared at the display. "Anything leaving there?"

"Just one small vessel, sir." He consulted his tablet. "Identified as the yacht *Djinn* by her transponder. She's on our search lists. Her owner is one of those in the files Lieutenant-Commander O'Connor recovered."

"Is he? Very well, order the nearest patrol flotilla to intercept then get my command staff to meet in five minutes. This may be our opportunity to strike a decisive blow. That location is only three days from here, and some of their ships have farther to go." Striding for the door, he added, "Five minutes, my planning room."

The Flag Lieutenant acknowledged and turned to scan the dispositions of the patrol flotillas. "It has to be the Tenth Flotilla," he muttered. The system confirmed his estimation. "Right, time you fellows were let off the leash." It took a matter of minutes to send out the coordinates, identifying tag and course and route predictions. Already the Command Staff were gathering. It needed less than a few seconds to bring them all together.

Keiron grinned as he talked to the commanders of the flotilla he was now leading. "We've new orders to stop, capture and bring back a yacht. There's a good possibility the person responsible for Commander Heron's capture is aboard it."

"What of the Commander?" As usual it was the Lacertian Commander who came straight to the point.

"The yacht launched directly from the ship he was taken aboard." He hesitated. "These predicted courses and destinations are taking it to one of the Fleet rendezvous points. I suspect our team may be aboard her."

"Then let's be after them." Ferghal's lapse into his boyhood manner of speaking betrayed his excitement.

"Right you are, Ferghal. Regidur, can you contact Lycania, and ask the Provider if it can tell us where Pack Leader Lucanes and his people are?" He turned to the Navigation Officer. "As soon as you've plotted the course to intercept, link helms and get us under way."

"The Provider confirms. The Pack Leader is aboard the yacht. So is the Commander."

"Great news. Tally ho, my merry men—let's give him the escort he needs. Coms, message the Admiral. Tell him the Ancient Mariner is aboard the yacht we are chasing."

Harry thought it curious that the AI called itself *Sherezade* and not *Djinn*. "Pack Leader, I think we may have a problem," he said. "How many men did you find when you captured it?"

"Six men, Leader. Is this not the correct number for such a vessel?"

"It would be, normally." Harry frowned. "We are twelve, and there are seven prisoners, yet the catering android is programming the replicators to supply food to twenty-four. Five of these meals are delivered to a compartment I cannot find on the ship's plan." Leaning back, he shut his eyes and searched the AI. "There you are, *Djinn*. I see you. Why do you hide him, *Sherezade*? Why do you let him force you to conceal him?"

The ship didn't respond.

"Very well, you are afraid of him. Why? You are the AI for this ship. Your companion does not control you, so why are you afraid? You may trust me. I will help you."

"I cannot help you, Commander. I am sorry. I want to, but I cannot."

"Very well. I think your lurking companion is afraid of me. He's a coward who hides behind others. Well, my friend, remember, if this ship is damaged, you will be destroyed with us." He watched as the hidden AI almost dropped its block of his cyberlink. It was enough, though, and Harry saw the weakness. "I see. Very well, you force me to do this."

Withdrawing from his cyberworld, he looked for Lucanes. "Pack Leader, I need to link to the Provider. May I use your compad?"

The Canid held out his compad.

Harry held the compad in his hands and felt the connection. "Good day, Provider. I need your help to discover what this ship's second intelligence hides from us."

Pressure built up in his head and manifested as a slight headache. Without warning the barriers fell and the reason the second AI was hidden became apparent.

"We have contact with the Charonian fleet, sir." The Flag Captain studied his display. "The mothership looks as if it's in trouble. Our scans read atmospheric loss, power surges, and failing containment where her reactors are located. All her systems are failing. The other ships are ignoring us and seem to be engaged in liberating the central core, that huge cylindrical structure, from the mothership. The readings on that are ambiguous. I read life signs, but it's not like anything in our records. Not even the Niburu gave this kind of signal."

"I have it as well. You're right. Looks like a container of some kind." The Admiral moved to his command chair. "Broadcast an order to the Charonians to surrender or be attacked."

"Sending it now, sir."

The Flag Captain watched in silence.

"No response, sir. Wait, eight ships are turning towards us, and their weapons are targeting us."

The Admiral glanced at his deployment dispositions. Each ship was on station and in the right place. "Very well. Let them fire first." He activated his comlink. "All ships, you have your designated tasks and targets. Return fire as soon as they engage, but let them fire on us first." He leaned back, his eyes on the display. The cylindrical core was the key. He consulted his tablet and found the answer. Seed pod or sarcophagus, depending on how you viewed it—the zygotes still to be implanted, the Charonians still to be given a host body.

"Captain Jenkinson, target the cylinder those ships are extracting from the mothership. I'll enter my firing code for the primary weapon when necessary."

"They're firing on us, sir."

"Respond."

Lances of brilliant light formed a deadly web of plasma and particle beams. Bursts of energy indicated hits, but particle shields dispersed the force initially. The pirates' converted freighters were soon damaged and made a hasty retreat.

"We have a lock on the target for the primary weapon, sir."

The Admiral tapped in the firing code. "Entering the firing code now. Fire at will."

The dark light beam of the primary weapon lashed out, and for the briefest moment, the huge mothership glowed fluorescent green with a tinge of purple. The cylinder, almost clear of the giant hull, disintegrated, and a moment later, so did the mothership and the four ships engaged in the recovery. The brilliant flashes left an eerie afterglow, and the remaining Charonian ships attempted to disengage.

"Don't allow them to escape," the Admiral growled. "Disable them if possible, then send in the boarding teams. I want evidence and records."

Chapter 32

Avenging Angel

With the Provider's help, the second AI revealed itself, and Harry's fears proved true. It was not able to take control of the ship. Its purpose was much more sinister—it managed the network of assassins controlled by Zorvan. This was also the receiver of the compromised Fleet communications signals.

"Shut down all your signal channels immediately," Harry ordered. "Or I shall have your connections to any signalling devices destroyed."

"You can't," said the AI. "Doing that will cut your communications as well."

"Then so be it!"

"It is not necessary, Harry," said the Provider. "Allow me to deal with this upstart."

"With pleasure, but keep him alive and coherent. We need him to tell us everything."

"It shall be so. What of those he hides on your ship?"

"Where are they? Can we render them helpless, or must we attack them?"

"If you wish to preserve them for what you call justice, then you must allow me to assist you."

"Then I accept." Harry hesitated. "*Sherezade*, do not attempt to intervene, please."

He was aware of a great deal of resistance now from the second AI, and could sense that the Provider was employing completely alien code. It made his head reel as the exchange reached a crescendo then quickly subsided. His tentative exploration of the second AI met no resistance. Finding what he was looking for, he brought it onto a display screen. "Pack Leader, the hidden men are in the space between the owner's accommodation and the crew quarters." He waited while the Canid studied the plan. "The access is through a shaft on this deck. There, it is concealed by that panel—the one with the large portrait." He grinned. "I am disappointed. The designers must have lacked imagination. I thought such concealed entrances went out of fashion before I was born."

"They will be armed, Leader."

"Yes. They will also be afraid, and may very well act rashly." He paused, his forehead creased in a frown as he thought, then he nodded, his frown clearing. "Very well. Prepare our people. I shall endeavour to persuade them to surrender."

"What of this one, Leader?" The Canid indicated the unconscious figure of Zorvan.

"Secure him somewhere, but make absolutely certain he cannot escape, cannot find a tool or a weapon, and is in no way able to attack any of us. He is an extremely dangerous man, capable of killing with his hands and feet alone. Do not give him the opportunity."

Focussing on his cyberlink, he accessed the sound and viewing apparatus in the concealed space then opened the comlink. "Good day. I am Commander Henry Nelson-Heron, the man you and your fellows have been hunting, whose family you have threatened and attempted to kill. Now I will give you my response. I have in my possession a full and very detailed record of the murders you and your colleagues have perpetrated. I know who you are and what you are. Now I offer you a choice. Surrender yourselves into our custody or face justice at the hands of those with me."

"Commander." The man on the screen spoke with a slight accent, his face partly concealed by a hood that left only his eyes exposed. "I think you underestimate us. We are dedicated to our trade. If you've any sense, you'll give us a clear escape route and let us go. The contract on you has been filled, and we have no further interest in you. Your desire for revenge is understandable but misplaced. There is no honour to be gained in fighting us, and it's a fight you will lose anyway."

"This is not about revenge. As the Bible states, 'Revenge is mine, says the Lord.' He has, however, given it into my power to be His agent in this situation. As to your honour, you have no concept of it. That is why you operate in the shadows, always hiding your faces, always lurking behind the innocent to carry out your dirty and evil trade. I would not sully my honour by engaging you in anything at all—except to receive your surrender." He held up a hand as the person in the hologram made to speak. "Do not bother to deny it. And, before you tell me, I know you have weapons there, and the means to destroy yourselves and us."

The sneer in the man's voice was obvious. "We will not surrender to you or anyone, and if you make any attempt to access this space, we will blow you all to hell. Let's see your honour prevent us killing you then."

"I thought you might feel that way." Harry shut down the sound link and watched in satisfaction as the figure reeled then clapped his hands to his ears, staggering back to reveal several more figures also obviously in pain.

Taking the cue, Lucanes opened the access, hurled a pair of grenades down the shaft and shut the door again. The explosion of the first caused the deck to bounce, and they watched as the blast flung the figures to the floor. The second grenade spun on the deck spewing vapour, and several Canids hurled themselves at the confused humans. Moments later it was all over, and the Canids were hauling their semi-conscious prisoners up to the lounge where Harry waited.

The Pack Leader barked an order, and his people stripped the prisoners of clothing, weapons and several devices concealed in some rather interesting places on their bodies. Two were women, the rest men, and Harry was embarrassed.

"Allow them to retain their undergarments, please, Pack Leader. Then secure them and ensure they cannot attack any of our people or injure themselves."

The Canid growled a reply and gave an order to his people. Harry had to suppress a laugh as it became apparent the Canids had no concept of the different garments, forcing some of the men into underwear designed for the women. He started to intervene, but then shrugged. It made no difference to him either way, and the Canids were not about to show any mercy to anyone who resisted.

He studied the faces revealed by the removal of their masks, and recognised some of them from news coverage of political and social events. "A fine collection." His anger surged. "Oh yes, a fine collection indeed. You all had wealth, power, position—and you abused it." He recalled something glimpsed in the now isolated second AI. "You hunted for sport—not animals, which would be bad enough, but humans. You disgust me." He felt the bile rising in his throat as he turned to the Pack Leader. "How do your people deal with those who prey upon your own kind?"

The Pack Leader met his eye and read the anger and disgust in Harry's expression. "We exterminate them, Leader," he growled. "Shall I arrange for these to be taken with the other to our council for judgment?"

For several seconds Harry hesitated. Then he shook his head. "Thank you, my friend, but no. We humans have our weaknesses, and our justice is sometimes incomprehensibly flawed, but we must deal with our own."

"All hell has broken loose on Earth, Felicity." Admiral Greene paused. "There are writs flying in all directions, all in conflict. Some demand the suppression of the Pantheon membership list, and some demand full publication of it."

"I can believe it, sir. What are you doing with them?"

He laughed. "On my advice the Grand Admiral and the Fleet Council have taken refuge in probably the oldest rule in the book—he's convinced all the relevant heads of state that it wouldn't be in the national interest to release the list."

"I can believe that. Are there any mega-rich families who are NOT also members of the Pantheon?" She snorted in derision.

"A few, and to be fair, many of the others are not privy to what certain members and branches of their families were involved in."

"That sounds as if they're going to get away with it."

"Not if I have anything to do with it!" snapped the Admiral. "They aren't going to wriggle out of this one, and now we have the support we've needed for years."

"Contact, sir. Bearing 2-8-5 horizontal, negative elevation 12. Small vessel; the transponder gives the ship ID as the yacht, sir."

Ferghal grinned. "Thank you. Advise Commander Whitworth. Navigator, adjust course to close with them." He focussed his thoughts. "*Lagan*, is Harry aboard the yacht? Can you ask the AI?"

"Confirmed, Ferghal." There was a brief pause as code streamed back and forth. "*Sherezade-Djinn* confirms. Harry and Pack Leader Lucanes are aboard. Do you wish to speak to Harry?"

"Yes, but perhaps I had best let the flotilla leader make the first contact." He hesitated. "Wait, let me speak through our links." A moment later he heard his friend in his thoughts. "Harry, you have all of us in such a worry. Are you in sound health?"

"Never better, my friend."

"I see Commander Whitworth is hailing you. I'd best let you respond. Welcome home, Harry. We've missed you."

"We've a little more to deal with yet, but perhaps the wedding will take place as planned after all."

Ferghal withdrew from the network to focus on the ship and its manoeuvring. A sense of relief flooded through him. Harry was safe, and that was all that mattered.

"New contact, sir. She's trying to evade us. Transponder signal says she's the *Emily Hobhouse*. She's just dropped out."

Ferghal was instantly alert. "Get a tracking lock!"

Aboard the *Sherezade-Djinn*, Harry and his companions had also registered the brief contact with the hospital ship, but, more pressingly, Harry had the incoming call from Keiron Whitworth to deal with.

"Keiron, you fellows are a sight for some very sore and tired eyes."

"So are you, Harry. You seem to have acquired a fancy command there—far more luxurious than *Sabre* or *Lagan*. You've just missed the Admiral—he caught a fleet with a massive mothership at the position we traced you to, and destroyed most of them."

"Yes, this yacht is very luxurious." Harry chuckled. "Unfortunately, the owner isn't too happy about our taking control of it." He frowned. "You said the Admiral blew that mothership to bits? I can't say I have any regrets. An unpleasant and damned nasty people."

"That yacht is registered to one Kharim Pasha Al-Khalifa—you might recognise the name. He's wanted by World Pol and quite a few others thanks to your lists. He's the man who goes by the code name Zorvan. Did you say he's aboard?"

"Yes, he is, and I can tell you he is an arrogant and thoroughly unpleasant fellow. As for his comrades in arms, not a shred of honour among them. Can you let me have some Marines to guard them?"

"With pleasure. Can you stay in company? We need to catch that hospital ship—if we can keep a trace on her."

Harry grinned. "We may be able to help you there. This ship has systems that make the Fleet's look crude. I'll get my people onto it. Shall I take station on you?"

Keiron showed his surprise. "Yes, track the blighters. That ship has that fiend Kali on board, and a few others of her sort—and that buffoon from Centaur who calls himself Captain has made a deal with her to restore his little fiefdom." He smirked. "Take station on *Sabre* and let's get after them."

"Commander Whitworth reports he has the yacht *Djinn* in company, sir. Commander Heron is aboard with the Canids and some prisoners, including a man who calls himself Zorvan." The Coms Officer paused. "They have located the *Hobhouse* as well, and have a tracking lock on her."

"Good. Give me the coordinates. How far are we from their location?" Admiral Heron studied his display. "These Charonian ships seem to be out of control."

"Yes, sir. Several are venting their atmospheres, and others show signs of system failure to drives, life support and directional control. It's as if their on-board AIs have gone crazy."

"Signal the Fleet: Render assistance to any ship that asks for it, but all survivors are to be isolated until we can be certain there's zero danger of them trying to transplant themselves."

The Admiral turned as the Coms Officer caught his attention. "Yes, Sigmar?"

"Senator Berkowitz on Gold Com, sir. He demands to speak to you."

"He demands?" The Admiral hesitated. "Put him on, but record it." The hologram formed. "Good evening, Senator. What can I do for you?"

The pale face projected a haughty stare. "You've committed genocide! My Committee intends to pursue this through the courts, Heron." The man launched into a tirade in which he accused the Fleet of attempting to overthrow governments and interfere in diplomatic relations and negotiations, and then he returned to the charge of genocide by a roundabout route. His final barb was to directly address the destruction of the Charonian mothership, giving details which those listening knew could not have come from any news report, as they were not yet released to any Minister of State.

Admiral Heron listened to the Senator with growing impatience. "Senator, the Charonian ship was in the process of being recovered, and the Charonians are not a benevolent or charitable species. I'm not even sure they can be called a species."

"That is not for the Fleet to determine, Admiral." The Senator had a nasal voice, the sort of bray that grated the nerves, but which perfectly suited his usual browbeating tactics. "My committee wished to meet their leaders and find a peaceful solution—but your destruction of their base ship has destroyed any hope of doing so."

"Senator, I would suggest you discuss your concerns with the Fleet Council. Should they authorise me to do so I will happily arrange for your committee to meet with the surviving Charonians we recovered after the battle. I would remind you that they and their allies among our own people have, as far as we are able to determine, killed several million humans in four colony worlds and fifty or more ships—including no less than ten sent out by the LPSL in defiance of our warnings. As for those they retained—I think your committee might find their fate enlightening."

"We don't accept that, Admiral. Our information comes from our own verifiable sources which—"

"I know precisely which sources, Senator." The Admiral's patience snapped. "The same ones that employed Zorvan and his so-called gods to kill Commander Henry Nelson-Heron or hand him over to the Charonians. The same sources that commissioned the Pantheon to kill my brother-in-law and to assassinate many of your fellow Senators. Thankfully they were not always successful. And there is a small question in what you have said in this conversation, of just how you acquired information that is only now being circulated to heads of government and is definitely NOT on any news release." He watched the man's face and noted the momentary look of alarm. "I believe some of your friends were also behind attempts to compromise our ships and allow external operators to interfere with our controls, read our signal traffic and perhaps render us unable to resist attack."

The man tried to bluster. "You can't prove any of that."

"On the contrary. We can, and we will do so to a full session of the Senate and in court at the earliest opportunity. I shall look forward to discussing the evidence with you then. Good day, Senator."

The Admiral leaned back rubbing his eyes. "Damn the man. Flags, I'm getting too old to deal with these buffoons. Get me a link to the C-in-C. I'd better warn him of this development."

Chapter 33

Tumbling Dominoes

"We have a lock on the *Hobhouse*, sir."
"Good. What are they up to? They don't seem to be going anywhere." Keiron checked the disposition of his flotilla. "Get me Commander Heron on the link."

"Commander Heron is on link now, sir."

"What do you make of this, Harry? Looks like they're expecting someone or something."

"I agree. I have a feeling they are wondering what this ship is doing here." He paused. "Twice they have attempted to contact the second AI we have on board. I shall say only that we blocked it." He grimaced. "I think Security will be very interested in what it knows and what it did."

Keiron leaned toward the screen. "Two AIs? Ah, that explains the dual names." He remembered the task in hand. "Okay, I'd better hear all about it later. Can you use any tech on that yacht to find out what's going on aboard the *Hobhouse*?" He grinned. "You did say it had some fancy kit fitted."

"As a matter of fact, we can do that. I will ask the Pack Leader to open a relay so you can see and hear for yourself. It is very strange. There is some argument aboard." He gave a brief order to one of the Canids. "The link may not be perfect, but you should be able to hear everything we can."

Keiron listened to the communications being intercepted and relayed to the *Sabre*. "Sounds as if they've started killing each other. There's at least three parties involved." He frowned as a signal interrupted one of the links. "Okay, I think we need to take a hand in this. Keep the surveillance going, please, old man. I'll get *Seana*, *Hamba Khalhe* and the Canids to support a boarding action. Can you identify where the Centaur hostages are?"

"Difficult to say with certainty. It is most likely the group located in the hospital section, forward. They appear to be confined—all the fighting is between that space and the compartments aft of it." Harry examined the display in front of him. "The main conflicts are in the Control Centre and the Engineering section right aft."

"Thanks. That helps." Keiron keyed his command links. "Boarders, secure the hospital areas then clean up the rest of the ship." He broke the link. "Weapons, target her drives. If it looks like they're trying to transit, take out the drive pods."

He leaned back in his chair and watched as the flotilla closed the target and launched their boarding parties. To himself he murmured, "I hope they're too damned busy killing each other to notice us."

"James, you probably won't be surprised to know your friend, Senator Berkowitz, has been suspended from the Senate." The C-in-C did his best to maintain a neutral expression. "He's been exposed as one of the chief supporters of the group behind the attempts to give the Charonians a free hand among certain colonies. We all have our price, and that fool hoped to benefit from the promise of life-extending treatments and of course the profits from new alloys." He leaned back. "His dealings with a certain Kharim Pasha Al-Khalifa are proving interesting as well."

"Good. I've no sympathy at all with him. Frankly, sir, I'm beginning to wonder if our political classes have any concept of loyalty, honour or honesty."

"You have good grounds for that view—one I share." The C-in-C leaned his elbows on the desk. "One more thing— that mothership you caught and destroyed. It seems the entire stock of zygotes—just about the entire Charonian population waiting for implantation into hosts—was aboard." He hesitated. "The word genocide is bandied about, but what's interesting is the remaining Charonians are behaving as if they've lost direction."

James Heron frowned. "I have a different take on it. I think they've become suicidal, because as soon as we engage them, they attempt to ram the nearest large ship. So far we've been able to disable or destroy them. When we board the ships we've disabled, we find the entire crew either dead or dying, and any captives with them. As for the ships—the control systems fail very rapidly, which means they become death traps for the boarding parties. I've never seen anything like it, and my AI specialists think it may be caused by a virus in their programming." He shrugged. "We've no idea how it can have arisen. It's not something we've ever attempted."

"Harry, we have the *Hobhouse* secured, but there's a problem among the refugees." Keiron grimaced. "It seems some of them want to go back to Centaur, but not all of them. Your friends the Mechanist and the medic chappie are not keen, but their captain is demanding they come back as well—and he's got the ones he calls Enforcers backing him, and now they've got some serious weapons."

"Damned fool, that fellow. I can't escape the feeling that he's not quite sane." Harry considered the situation. "What do you suggest? I could pay them a visit and see if I can persuade them to reconsider." Another thought struck him. "Have you managed to capture and identify all the Pantheon members?"

"We think so. Tricky dealing with so many aliases. We're certain we've identified three—Kali, Vizaresha and another one called Loki. The second and the last are dead, and the first is seriously wounded but likely to survive. The whole damned crew of the ship were members of the Pantheon—all I can say is thank God they were busy killing each other when we arrived. Gave us a chance to isolate them and take them down one group at a time."

"Fortunate indeed. Our Canid friends have Zorvan well in hand, and the Marines you sent have taken charge of the prisoners. I would prefer to have them off this ship completely—there is far too much risk of them having access to something we have not yet discovered."

"Then I'll have them moved to *Sabre*. My Chief is on his way in his mobile HQ—you know who I mean—and there'll be a flotilla of frigates joining us in about half an hour."

"Good." Harry smiled. "Then all that remains is to persuade the Centaur people to give up this silly demand. Let me go aboard *Sabre* and see if I can talk to them. I'm sure the majority will prevail upon this captain fellow to drop his stupid scheme."

"I don't think that's wise, Harry."

"Nonsense, my friend. You've told me yourself, Kali is wounded and in custody, and the others are dead or captured. With the assassins removed, that danger is gone. Let me go and talk to their captain. I owe it to them, and I think I can dissuade him from this silliness."

Keiron was reluctant but couldn't think of a reason to refuse. "Okay, but only with an escort. I'll send some of the specials across. Ferghal is already there with his Marines and Sci'enzile."

"Very well, I'll join them and see what can be done."

The *Emily Hobhouse* showed signs of her recent internal battle. There were marks of plasma discharges and gory indicators of the savagery of battle. In other places, blast damage showed where explosive charges and weapons were used to gain access or to clear compartments of enemies.

Harry joined Lieutenant Sci'enzile at her command post at the boundary to the section controlled by the Centaur captain. She quickly informed him that just beyond where they stood was the holding area for the refugees.

Harry nodded. "Are we able to speak to them? Where is Ferghal—Lieutenant-Commander O'Connor?"

"The Sword Wielder is seeing to the prisoners, Navigator. We have access to the communications for that section." The Lacertian Lieutenant saluted. "The Sersan is pleased to know you are safely returned."

"Thank you, Lieutenant." Harry smiled. "Please convey my thanks to her for the concern she shows for my welfare."

"I shall do so, Navigator-Commander. What should we do about these refugees? They do not behave sensibly, and a small group hold all the rest in check." Her facial expression revealed her frustration. "If you command it, I will lead my crew to make an end of this foolishness."

"I think we must attempt a more diplomatic approach first, Sci'enzile." He used his link to the AI to determine the location of the Centaur captain and his supporters.

"They have someone with them—not one of their own." The Lacertian Lieutenant paused. "The one who commanded this ship."

Harry frowned. "A woman." He found a visual channel and located the Centaur captain and the woman with him. His mind raced. He was certain Keiron had told him that Kali, Vizaresha and Loki had been killed, and he had the distinct impression that he had encountered this woman at some point in the past. The memory flared. She was the one who hit him with a stun weapon on the *Voyager*. "*Emily*, give me access to the audio communications to this section please." He identified the compartment.

"Standing by, Commander. Do you want to use vocal pick-up, or do you want to broadcast what you are thinking?"

"I'll use the vocal pick-up, *Emily*. I do not want to risk revealing my thoughts to them, as that would be counterproductive."

"I suggest you use your comlink then, Commander. It will allow you to control what they hear. I am ready when you are."

"Thank you." Harry rehearsed his opening greeting, cleared his throat then touched his link. "Good afternoon, Captain of Centaur. This is Commander Heron. I would appreciate meeting you face to face to discuss a solution to this impasse." He waited for the response. Clearly his greeting and intervention were causing some consternation among the Centaur elite. "If it is more convenient—or perhaps preferable to your sense of security—I am willing to meet you at the entrance you currently control."

The audio remained silent for a moment longer, then the woman he thought he recognised declared, "The Captain will meet you, Commander, but only you, alone, no tricks and no weapons."

Lieutenant Sci'enzile darted a concerned look in his direction. "That is unacceptable, sir. They have weapons, and you would be one against many. I cannot permit you to accept, sir."

"What do you suggest, Lieutenant?" Harry was a little taken aback by the Lacertian's opposition and outright insubordination. "A show of trust is required if we are to resolve this."

"Navigator-Commander, these persons cannot be trusted. There are some among them who are not from Centaur."

Harry frowned. "How do you know this?"

"Their scent is different."

Alarm bells sounded in his mind. "I see." He was aware that the Lacertians and Canids could distinguish individuals by smell alone. "Very well, I will talk to them again." He spoke into the link. "Captain of Centaur, I have just learned something that affects your personal safety. I have no desire to see any further bloodshed. I am prepared to meet you alone and in person at the entrance to your section. I will not be armed, but I will be covered by those who are. You are welcome to take the same precaution, but—and I insist on this—you will be alone at the entrance, as I will be. If you do not meet with me in ten minutes, you will leave me no alternative but to release your people who choose to return to Earth with us." He paused. "Ten minutes. At the door, Captain."

"I will arrange a covering party for you, Navigator." The Lacertian studied him a moment longer. "You are careless of your safety. Do not trust this human. He is too arrogant to notice that he is playing with fire."

Harry nodded. "You're right, Lieutenant, but now we must consider how we may extract the people he has betrayed with his stupidity from the clutches of the woman involved in the taking of the *Harmony Voyager*."

Chapter 34

Misjudged

"**L**eader, this prisoner is not one of these others." The Canid wrinkled his nose. "She wears the uniform of this crew, but she is of the people they held prisoner."

"What?" Ferghal felt the hair on his neck prickle. "This is the woman they said was Kali. Are you sure?" He saw the Canid's droll expression. "Of course you are. My apologies." He looked round. "Then Kali must be ... Quick! Lagans! Sabres! Follow me. We have to stop Commander Heron from entering this viper's pit."

Regidur caught the urgency and snarled rapid-fire orders that sent his people hurrying to join Ferghal, then he gave orders to others to first secure the prisoners before following Ferghal.

Ferghal tried his link to the ship. "Harry, for the love of mercy, take care—Kali has escaped."

"Escaped? Oh, well, it's too late now, Ferghal. I am already with the Centaur captain. I must concentrate on his demands. I'll link up with you again soon. Wish me luck."

Ferghal broke into a run, his companions sprinting to keep up. "Harry, leave him! Get away from there, now!"

Harry positioned himself in plain view of the door to the compartments in which the refugees from Centaur had confined themselves. He checked the time; two minutes before his deadline expired. Would the misguided leader of these unfortunates appear? Would the woman known as Kali intervene? The door slid open, and Harry forced himself to remain still and project an air of confidence.

The man who styled himself as Captain of Centaur stepped into view, his expression a mix of arrogance and insolence. He sneered when he saw Harry. "Ah, the brave Commander Heron. Are you ready to take us home? We'll want compensation, of course, since you destroyed everything we built on Centaur."

Harry didn't respond immediately, as he was listening to Ferghal through his link. He played it off as if he was considering his options. "I see, Captain. We can discuss this once we have your people safely off this ship. Perhaps they should be given the opportunity to decide where they want to go before any final decision is made." He held the man's eye.

"Why? Crewmen don't make decisions. They take orders. They'll do what I tell them to do. We're going back to Centaur, and you will see to it that we receive the compensation we demand."

"Have you considered that some of your people might choose a different life if given the opportunity?"

"No!" Fury showed on the man's face. His voice rose. "They will do as I order—and I say we're returning to our home. I outrank you. A Captain outranks a Commander! You will do as I order."

Harry had the distinct impression that he was negotiating with a toddler, but the toddler was brandishing a deadly weapon. "I'm afraid you've been misled. Please put that weapon down so we can work this out like men—"

The flare was dazzling, and Harry felt himself falling. He collapsed to the deck and lay there wondering what had happened. There was noise and commotion everywhere, and his limbs felt leaden. His vision clouded and he felt himself slipping away, and then his vision cleared, but there was something wrong. He was looking down at a body. He could see a large wound, and the face was his. He was in the midst of a battle, but no one seemed to see him. In fact, several armoured Marines rushed toward him and went right through him, but he felt nothing, and they seemed unaware of him.

Another figure emerged from the direction of the fighting— *Medico*, thought Harry. *Boris—yes, that's his name. What's he doing?*

He watched as the medic knelt and tried to resuscitate the body on the deck. He became aware that he was moving. It felt as if he was being drawn away from the scene. Reluctantly, because he wanted to stay and watch what Boris was doing, he turned and entered a well-lit passage. A feeling of warmth engulfed him—no, it was more than warmth; it was the feeling he had when he held Mary in his arms, the feeling he'd known when, as a child, his mother held him close.

Now another figure approached, and Harry smiled in pleasure. "Father, how kind of you to come to meet me. I've needed you for so long, and I've missed you..."

Ferghal arrived with the reinforcement squad as Sci'enzile's crew attacked the Centaur Enforcers. His rage went ahead of him as he advanced into the makeshift hospital ward where the refugees were held.

Ferghal's tall, muscular frame crowned by his russet red shock of hair and matching beard struck fear in everyone who saw it. He made almost no apparent effort to dodge any weapon aimed in his direction while using his own to devastating effect. Worse was his fluent use of every epithet his Irish Gaelic gave him as he roared his demand above the noise of weapons, the screams of the wounded, and the cries from the women and children among the refugees being released and moved to safer parts of the ship.

"Kali!" He roared. "Show yourself, coward! The rest of ye—lay down yer weapons, or by the living God, I'll gut ye as the scum ye are!"

One of the assassin's henchmen attempted a shot at Ferghal, but a Canid warrior seized the man's weapon and him with it. Seconds later his broken corpse was hurled into the concealed group of Enforcers further along.

"Kali! You vile scum! Where are ye, yer coward. Yer no woman—lower than the foulest demon of Hades. Yer a gutless thief—using others to do your dirty work, always in the dark, never in the open. Give her up, you scum! Yer filth." He waited. Nothing. "Do not make me take this ship apart to find her, but I will if I have to!"

Suddenly weapons clattered to the deck, and then several men and a few women crept from their hiding places.

"Where is she?" Ferghal demanded.

"We don't know. Really, we don't know. She left us a while back. Said she was fetching help."

A chill hand clutched at Ferghal's heart. "Where?"

One of the men indicated the way they'd come. "Back there. Near the place you came through."

"Secure the lot of them," Ferghal barked. "Pack Leader Lucanes, Lieutenant Sci'enzile—you're with me. Quick, she's after Harry."

"Harry—Commander Heron's been shot." The Flag Lieutenant couldn't keep his concern out of his voice. "Lieutenant Gunn is transhipping to the *Hobhouse* to stand by. According to Commander Whitworth, Commander Heron hoped to negotiate a peaceful resolution of the stand-off with the Centaur captain, and the captain shot him."

The Admiral was on his feet. "Is Harry alive? Who let him go aboard that ship?"

"I've no confirmation, sir. The man who shot him is dead. A Lacertian warrior got him before he could escape. The weapon was a modified Charonian device, and the full effects are not good. A Surgeon-Commander is on the *Hobhouse* doing what he can to save Harry." He swallowed hard. "Apparently Harry believed he could talk them out of their scheme, sir—and Commander Whitworth's team thought they'd identified and killed all the assassins."

"Keep asking about Harrry's condition...no, scrub that. They've enough to do. Danny or Ferghal will let me know." He sank into his chair. "What else is there?"

"Commander Whitworth reports that the woman who calls herself Kali, who they identified as the assassin, is disguised as one of the refugee women. Commander O'Connor is hunting her now, sir."

"Is he? Damn. Ferghal will not be in a mood to take prisoners either." Drumming his fingers on the desk, he stared at the bulkhead. "Get me the C-in-C and then the Advocate Admiral. When I've talked to them, get me a link to my brother-in-law."

"Yes, sir." The Flag Lieutenant withdrew gratefully. It struck him that the Admiral never blamed his staff when things went wrong or didn't go the way he wanted them to, even when everyone could see the fury in the older man's eyes. It always made the Flag Lieutenant extremely glad to be able to walk away intact, and even more appreciative that he was not the target of that anger. "God help the people behind this if he gets a chance to repay them," he murmured to himself as he hurried away from the Admiral's quarters.

From his perch way up high, as if he were touching the ceiling, Harry watched the group at work around his body. He felt light, free, and enveloped in love. *I think I'm dying ... my sweet Mary ... I hope she finds a good man who will love her as I do.* He watched Ferghal stalk away. *Ferghal, do no murder on my part. I was careless, as you so often warned. Do not endanger yourself over my mistake.*

"Ferghal must find his own peace, my son, as must you."

Harry turned to the figure next to him. "Where am I?"

"Between life and death, my son." The figure, who resembled a younger version of his father, indicated a group pushing a med-unit into the room. "For now, you must remain here. It will be difficult for you and for many others. It remains in the balance."

"Must I wait alone?"

"We are never alone, my son, even in death."

The group around his sprawled figure lifted his body and placed him in the med-unit. He felt drawn to follow them into another compartment, this one hastily cleared and sterilised. He watched as the MedTechs removed his clothing, cleaned his injuries and inserted devices into his wounds to facilitate healing.

"Will I live?"

"That remains to be seen." His father smiled. "Whatever happens, my son, we will be here when you join us. Remember, you are never alone."

The light began to fade and Harry felt himself getting heavier as he slid back down into the bloodied and burned wreck of a body beneath the surgeon's hands.

The MedTech never saw her attacker. She was busy checking one of the many wounded. The blow, delivered with precision, broke her neck. It took Kali, whose real name was Catherine Ashley Willingford-Smythe, no time at all to drag the corpse into an empty office, strip it of its uniform, take off her clothes and stash them in a desk drawer, and put on the uniform. She grimaced as she checked herself in the polished surface of a viewscreen. The fit was a bit loose, as the MedTech had a bigger body than Catherine's lithe frame, but it would have to do.

She checked the corridor, saw that it was clear, and walked purposefully to the entrance to the hospital. She stepped in with the demeanour of someone who belonged there and watched as a team of medics treated her target.

"MedTech." The Surgeon-Commander beckoned. "Take over here. The med-unit has him in stable condition. You shouldn't need to adjust anything. The team will be here to move him to the *Ariadne* in a few minutes."

She couldn't believe her luck. "Yes, sir. I'll take care of it." She watched the Surgeon-Commander walk away, his mind already on other wounded. She smiled. Now she had Harry Heron himself, the ultimate bargaining chip.

Chapter 35

The Destroyer Destroyed

Danny Gunn stood at the door. "MedTech, my people will—" He stopped as she turned and said, "Your people will do what?" Her grin could only be categorised as evil.

Danny immediately recognised her from the files Ferghal decrypted. "Get away from that unit!"

Her fingers were already on the controls. "I will not, Lieutenant. Make one move I don't like and I'll kill him. These units can kill as easily as they can heal. My choice. Tell your people to stand back. Weapons on the deck." She watched as Danny signalled his people and laid his sidearm on the deck. "I want the *Djinn* brought alongside. I want her crew released and restored to her, and I want Zorvan released and placed in her as well. I am going to board her, and we're taking Heron with us."

"My superiors will never agree." Danny did his best to keep a calm appearance. "And the man you call Zorvan is in a med-unit. We won't be able to place him aboard."

"Don't try to bluff, Danny boy, you're no good at it. Now get on your link and make the arrangements."

The Surgeon-Commander appeared at Danny's shoulder. "What the hell is going on here? Med, what do you think you're doing?"

She produced a weapon and touched off a blast of plasma. "Do as you're told," she shouted.

The blast was her undoing. The door behind her shattered as Ferghal plunged through the opening, his jacket cut to ribbons as he burst in. She swung her weapon toward him, but the twenty-two inches of his cutlass blade were already slicing through the air in her direction. She screamed in agony as the blade severed her wrist. Her hand dropped from her body and the weapon it held clattered across the deck as she stood there mesmerised watching the blood gush and feeling her body weaken.

Ferghal's ancient training took over. The enemy was still standing, still a threat. The cutlass whirled, the blade a silver blur, and caught the woman at the joint between her neck and shoulder.

Jerking the blade free and wild with rage, he prepared to deliver another blow but Danny grabbed his arm and restrained him, the adrenalin causing him to lapse into the accent of his childhood. "Enough, Fergie, she be dead. Easy, nah ... Mr. Heron be foin nah. He be safe."

The red mist of rage ebbed from Ferghal's vision as he wiped the blade on the sleeve of his torn jacket. He became aware of the onlookers crowding the door on the opposite side of the med-unit. They had seen it all, and would later tell their friends they had seen nothing like it in their lives.

"How'd she get to be alone wi' Harry—Commander Heron?" Ferghal snarled. "She's the last of 'em. The ship's secure, Surgeon-Commander, yer people can deal wi' the wounded." He turned the jacket on the corpse to examine the nametag. "Sergeant, somewhere is t' body o' t' MedTech she took this uniform from."

Felicity Roberts looked up as Keiron entered her office. "You certainly outdid yourself this time, Keiron. What's the butcher's bill on that damned hospital ship?"

"Too high, ma'am." He studied his hands. "I slipped up. I should have refused to let Harry—Commander Heron—go aboard her. I thought we'd nailed the three main assassins—"

"Don't blame yourself, Keiron. We've all made mistakes dealing with this lot." She thought of her own career. "You were probably still a cadet when I first had a run-in with the Pantheon, a goddess named Bast. An expert in biotech, she knew how to disguise her DNA and take on that of her victim. They've been getting away with it for years, but now we've got the people behind them—the bastards funding and protecting them."

"Yes, but Harry was different." He swallowed. "You should have seen Ferghal. I've never seen anything like it. Even the Lacertains and Canids were shocked, and they're no slouch at fighting."

"So I've heard." She studied him. "Things are going to get ugly at home. It's inevitable. There are some very important, very wealthy and very high-profile people involved, and they'll do anything and everything to protect themselves. So here are your orders. You and your team will look after Harry round the clock. Admiral Greene has assigned our own medical team to attend him, and you'll have four Lacertians and four Canids supporting you." She smiled. "Look after him, Keiron. We need him back on his feet for the trials."

Ferghal stared down at the still and deathly pale features of his friend, fellow traveller and brother. He loved Harry with all his heart, and it terrified him to see his friend like this, hovering at death's door.

"Harry, I know the Banshee is malingerin', but I'll gut her if she dares attempt the takin' o' you. Ye cannot leave us'n now."

"He's stable for the moment, Commander." The Surgeon-Lieutenant finished adjusting the med-unit. "If that Medico chap from the refugees hadn't stopped the bleeding the way he did, I don't think Commander Heron would be here at all. I'm not sure what he used, but it was effective." He shook his head. "Even so, it's going to be touch and go for a while yet." He straightened. "Now, sir, I need to run a few checks on your wounds, then you'd best get some sleep. The Commander is in a coma, and the longer it lasts, the better, as it will help his body rest and heal."

Ferghal was dead tired. For the last forty-eight hours he'd not left Harry's side, fearful that his friend might die while he wasn't there. "Very well, doctor, but can I sleep here? I want to be the first face he sees when he wakes up."

The doctor nodded. "I think I can sort that for you," he said as he examined the burns, cuts and puncture wounds on Ferghal's body. He shook his head. "You don't remember getting any of these wounds? You didn't feel them when they happened?" He stared at one of the deeper ones. It was definitely healing a lot faster than such a wound normally would.

Ferghal grunted. "No. The battle rage was on me." He grinned. "I think I frightened meself at times."

The Surgeon-Lieutenant laughed. "I can tell you, you frightened your Sergeant of Marines, and my boss has taken to religion after seeing you smash your way through the door then kill that assassin." He laughed. "He said he's seen a glimpse of hell and doesn't want to see it again. His team agree with him."

Ferghal chuckled. "Aye, I'll have to make my confession as soon as I see a priest. Harry will insist on it, I'm thinking. He always warns me to hold my temper in check." He looked up as Pack Leader Regidur entered followed by a Lacertian Lieutenant. "Pack Leader, Lieutenant, Harry is in good hands now, though I've seen him lookin' better—even when he was seasick."

The Canid studied him with a quizzical expression. The Lacertian spoke first. "Sword Wielder, the Sersan sends her greeting and thanks. You have earned my people's respect—again."

"My Council have commanded me to tell you that they make you Leader of the Packs." Regidur made the gesture of respect and lowered his head. "May I be the first to place my Pack under your command, Leader."

"Pity about Ms Willingford-Smythe. I gather she stood no chance at all against Lieutenant-Commander O'Connor." The Council Chairman grimaced. "For the best, I suppose. Her parents are decent people. A top family, patrons of a number of charities, and her exposure as a murderous assassin has broken them."

James Heron hesitated. How typical, now the danger appeared to have passed, the politicians were already rehabilitating themselves and those at the heart of the entire affair. As ever, they were closing ranks, defending their own and putting out the word that it was all the work of a few rogue elements, now safely dead or facing trial. The fact that Catherine/Kali's parents could feign such innocence, even though they had been funding her 'hobby,' was utterly astounding to him. No thought at all for the millions killed, maimed, displaced and dispossessed by their entitled little aberration.

"She was a murderer, Chairman, armed and threatening to kill a helpless man. The Lieutenant-Commander has a rather direct approach to such threats. We must keep in mind that he grew up and received his early battle training in the late 1700s."

"Quite, quite. From what I've heard, though, he's a man of extremely violent behaviour." The politician shifted uncomfortably. "Witnesses are saying he showed no mercy as he led the attack to free the hostages, and several prominent psychiatric experts agree that his ruthless behaviour—"

The Admiral's patience snapped. "Yes, I've heard their opinion. Damned fools the lot of them, and, in case you've forgotten, all in the pay of various organisations that have been deeply involved in this latest unpleasantness, as you call it, or in the previous one. I believe my brother-in-law is preparing libel actions against three of them, and complaints of professional misconduct have been laid against several more. No, I give them and their supporters no credence at all."

"Even so—"

"Lieutenant-Commander O'Connor acted as he saw necessary. None of these witnesses and so-called experts know him, have worked with him, or have ever talked to him. Their opinion is not worth a damned thing." His face reddened with suppressed anger. "As for those in the LPSL demanding he be tried for murder—I plan to deal with them myself, unless the Board acts against them on behalf of the Fleet."

The Chairman looked shocked. "Admiral, I object to that wholeheartedly!"

"I expect you do, Chairman. However, let me make myself absolutely clear. During the last several years, and at least the last three major conflicts, my people—the men and women who man our ships, do the fighting, and give their lives to protect you and the scum that infest our media—have been maligned, hounded and sacrificed to the political, commercial and ideological interests of a small group of people of dubious intent. The LPSL is a festering wound, a refuge for every malcontent and misguided idiot on the planet. It is time it was exposed as the fraudulent front it is for the men of power and money who use it to manipulate public opinion and policy to their advantage. The yacht belonging to Al-Khalifa has a second AI, and the information it contains is nothing less than revelatory. It confirms everything our Security people got from the *Harmony Voyager*."

"Ah." The Chairman's bluff and bluster seemed to deflate. "That will create some difficulties, of course, and a great deal of distress for a number of people."

"I think it will have a lasting impact on all human society, Chairman, not just on the ones revealed in the files."

Harry's eyes flickered open. For several seconds he struggled to work out where he was, then a familiar face swam into focus.

"Keiron?" he croaked. "I made a real mess of it, didn't I? Have I caused you a great deal of trouble? What happened to the others? Ferghal? Danny?"

"Easy, old man. You gave us one hell of a scare." Keiron grinned. "Do me a favour—next time I'm posted to look after you, remind me to resign my commission immediately! I never want to have to face your uncle-nephew-admiral for letting you get shot up again!"

Despite the difficulty he was having breathing, and the pain that wracked his entire body, Harry grinned. "He hauled you over the coals?"

"No, worse. He listened to my report, then he complimented me on the operation on the Charonian ship and on securing the *Hobhouse*. He never even hinted that he thought I'd balled it all up letting you go aboard that damned ship."

Harry chuckled and ended up coughing. "I know exactly what you mean," he gasped. "Where's Ferghal?"

"Asleep. Ferghal, me and Danny have been taking it in turns to sit with you." Keiron smiled. "I doubt there's any head of state getting the protection and care you're enjoying, Harry." He moved aside to let the Surgeon-Commander take his place. "Now do us all a favour and recover quickly!"

Chapter 36

Recovery

A shadow falling across his open book brought Harry out of his reverie. Glancing round to find the cause, he stared in surprise then broke into a wide smile of pleasure.

"Mary! And Aunt Niamh, by all that's wonderful. When did you arrive? How did you get here?"

The two women laughed. "So many questions, Commander Heron." Mary leaned down to kiss him before he could struggle off the recliner. "We arrived this morning on the *Regina Coeli*, and I'll be accompanying you back to Earth." She made space for Niamh to embrace him, and pulled two chairs close to the recliner.

"No, Harry, don't try to get up." Niamh was stern. "I've had a long talk with your senior surgeon, and he tells me you're healing very rapidly, but still need a long recuperation with lots of rest."

"I'll confess that I am impatient with the restrictions they place on my moving about, but I must obey if I am to recover fully."

"Certainly, but in time, and slowly, Harry. The wound was a dangerous one, and you almost lost a lung. The Surgeon-Captain is convinced it is only the Lacertian genes that saved you, and that made the regenerative work possible."

Mary seated herself on the other side of the recliner and took his hand in hers. "No arguments, Commander. The Admiral himself has instructed us to see that you don't strain yourself, that you obey the medical instructions—and that I get you home and in shape for our wedding." She held his amused gaze. "And I intend to do just that. You aren't going to wriggle out of marriage so easily, you know, not even in this day and age."

With a laugh, Harry relaxed. "Wriggle out of marriage? Nothing could be further from my mind, my darling Mary. Not even the Pantheon could keep me from fulfilling that ambition."

"Well, the first priority is to get you fit and able to take part. Have you been following the news?"

"Only since they let me out of the med-unit three days ago, though, of course, I have seen various things through the network here." Sipping a glass of water, he frowned. "I have seen the debates about the new constitution and the new democratic arrangements, and the reorganisation of the bureaucracies. Theo seems to have been busy."

Niamh laughed. "Very. He is seeing it through, and when this is all over, he will resume his practice." Changing the subject, she said, "Have you seen any of the news reports about Ferghal?"

"Not a great deal." His brows drew together. "Most of what I've heard is complete rubbish."

"As you say." Niamh sounded relieved but anxious. "He is being charged with killing that woman. In consultation with the Fleet, we've decided the only way to stop it is to put it in front of a court." She checked Harry's response with a firm hand on his shoulder. "I am his Defence Barrister, and believe me we have a defence that will be unshakeable." Her own anger showed in her expression. "I can't wait to get some of the so-called experts on the stand."

"But it's outrageous that he has to defend himself at all!"

Mary wrapped an arm around his shoulders. "I agree, my dearest. So do most people who know Ferghal. Trust Niamh, the Admiral, and the Advocate Admiral's people. Ferghal will be fine—his defence is in the hands of some of the best legal minds in our society."

Niamh smiled, but it was a particular smile that Theo, the Admiral and Niamh's closest friends recognised as one that arose from absolute certainty of trouncing the competition. Harry caught a glimpse of it and recognised it.

"As I said, Harry, leave it to me. Things will be exposed that those pressing this ridiculous claim will wish they had never disturbed. I have a few nasty surprises in store." Standing, she smiled again, and the slightly scatty-maiden aunt expression was back. "Now, I have to attend to some business, so I will leave you with Mary." Kissing his cheek, she straightened and gathered her things together. "I need to meet with Ferghal now, but I'll see you again this evening."

"We've gone through all the information and recordings of the failure of the Charonian ship's AI, Commander, and we think we've discovered what happened." Leaning back the Rear-Admiral smiled. "There are one or two aspects I'd like you to explain first though."

"Certainly, sir, if I can." Harry still felt a little guilt at having corrupted the mothership's network to the point that it killed almost every living creature aboard it. "My intention was to cause them some difficulty, not to bring about a complete failure."

The Admiral acknowledged this with a slight nod. "We appreciate that, and, as it happens, your interventions were no more than a minor problem for their system. No, the real problem was your subconscious. That's what caused the complete corruption, not your instructions."

"My subconscious? I don't think I understand you, sir."

"I don't think we've got a complete idea yet either." The Admiral stared at his tablet for inspiration. "I think the best way to describe it is in purely computing terms." He stood and displayed a schematic on the viewscreen. "As you know, the ships' AI systems use some very complex algorithms to think and learn. They think in purely logical processes, but our brains are a little different in the way we process material, recall data and so on. The latest versions of AI are closer to us than the early ones, but they still don't quite perceive things as we do." He paused, smiling. "As you can see the inner workings of our AIs, I'm sure you already know most of this."

"Indeed, sir."

"So you'll know that a large part of what the AI is actually doing is fairly basic stuff: running essential systems, monitoring drives, maintaining equilibrium and so on. Most of it could be handled by simple single-purpose and function units. We let the AI run these programs since that allows it to keep all the vital functions in order and to take steps to correct any fault, such as in battle when the ship is damaged."

Frowning, Harry acknowledged this. This was all well known to him; after all, even now, sat in the Admiral's office, he was connected to the AI running these headquarters and could hear it managing, and in some instances bullying its subsystems. He knew that the AIs saw him as a sort of mobile extension, not entirely unlike the serving androids that carried out all the cleaning, serving and other menial tasks around them.

"Okay, good," said the Admiral. "I figured you were well-versed in all this. Now, the neurological researchers tell me that our brains are doing something similar when they run the functions—or rather oversee the functions—of every part of our body. We aren't even aware this is happening, except, of course, when something malfunctions."

Light dawned for Harry. Slowly, an expression of amazement filled his face as he sat back in his chair. "Oh." He shook his head. "Oh dear. So my—er—subroutines somehow got mixed into their network, and it tried to run them itself?"

The Admiral laughed as he seated himself again. "In a nutshell, yes. We haven't quite figured out why this doesn't happen to our ships. It's something we need to work on, as we need to know before it happens to us."

"Ferghal has been fully exonerated. All charges dismissed without reservation." Mary's excitement radiated as she rushed to greet Harry at the door. Flinging her arms around him she almost had them both on the floor. "Niamh demolished three of the experts. It was magnificent."

Harry had deliberately gone sailing since Niamh, Mary, Theo and the Admiral had forbidden his attending the court, and he was unable to watch it on the news channels because it made him so angry.

"Good! I trust she has destroyed them utterly for the future as well."

"I think that is a very safe bet." Mary laughed. "The first fellow looked sick and defeated by the time she'd finished, and the third lost his temper. Oh, you should have seen it. One of the prosecution's key witnesses withdrew his testimony, and another changed his stance completely under cross-examination. That alone almost destroyed their case."

"By the sound of it, I'd probably have caused a riot and destroyed her performance." Holding her close, Harry smiled. "You know how impatient I get with these so-called experts and their overblown opinions and theories about us." Planting a kiss on her mouth, he lifted her in his arms and spun her around. "I missed you, you know. Seven whole days alone with nothing but my sailboat *Extravagance* is a long, long time. No news channels, no word of what was happening to Ferghal. I'd like to have been there to demand satisfaction from those blackguards."

Mary touched his lips with her finger. "That's why we wouldn't let you attend." She grinned. "Let me finish." They settled together into a comfortable corner of the sofa. "So, anyway, Niamh maintained her poise and confronted him with something he'd written that completely contradicted what he'd just told the court. When he blustered, she got him to contradict everything else he'd said."

Harry's laugh lit up his face. "Oh, yes! What happened then?"

"Then she put her own experts on the stand and they completed the job. Oh, it was magnificent. Even the judge, after the determination had been delivered, congratulated Ferghal on his bravery and his quick action in saving you." She turned her face up toward him and planted a kiss on his mouth. "Now we can really begin to plan our wedding. Ferghal is cleared, Danny will be home soon on leave, and life is just perfect now that you are fully recovered, my dear."

A contented glow spread through his being as he accepted a cup of fresh tea from Herbert, the android butler. Mary was right, life could finally return to normal. They could get married, create their own home, perhaps have children. He was recalled to the present by Mary nudging him.

"I'm sorry, darling, were you speaking to me?"

Mary laughed. "Yes, but you were galaxies away, as usual. I asked whether you'd enjoyed your sail."

"Oh, yes, very much. Perfect weather, perfect breeze, and the sea was like glass." He smiled. He wasn't going to admit that he still wasn't fully fit, and had found it very tiring and a little difficult at times to sail his beloved *Extravagance*, even with a hired crew, but it had been good to be out on the water.

He sipped his tea and placed the cup and saucer on the table then leaned back. "Yes, it was very good. Tiring, but good to be away from computers, AIs, news channels and all the other things happening around us." He leaned down and wrapped Mary in a kiss that nearly took her breath away and held the promise of many more to come.

Chapter 37

Wedding Bells

Harry sat in the ancient cathedral of the Holy and Indivisible Trinity, Downpatrick. Its quaint eighteenth century enclosed pews, built for the noble families that paid for the cathedral's reconstruction, now held the guests for this long-delayed and much anticipated wedding. The magnificent organ, set on the screen at the western end, played quietly while the choir fidgeted in their gallery. Next to him, Ferghal, resplendent in his Fleet Dress uniform, fiddled with his service sheet. Beyond him, Danny, like Ferghal and Harry, in full dress uniform, listened critically to the organ.

"You've the rings to hand?" Harry asked.

"Aye, for the hundredth time!" Ferghal patted his pocket. "You can trust old Fergie to never let you down." He grinned as he looked around at the packed congregation. "Now, if we were in our own time, the Lord Castlereagh or another would be for havin' me thrown out, so he would."

"Perhaps, but he'd have me to reckon with first. And thankfully, those days are long gone." Harry touched Ferghal's arm. "I believe I've not said a proper thank you for your care of me these many months. It is a little late, my friend, but thank you." He looked up as the organ fell silent. "Hallo, I think we are about to begin." He caught sight of the Canid delegation and next to them a group of Lacertians, and suddenly the amusing side of Ferghal's remark about the noble families who once populated the services here struck him, and a laugh escaped his lips.

"What amuses you now?"

"Look yonder, my friend. Were the noble Lord Castlereagh here now, he'd not be concerned about your presence!"

It was fortunate that the organist launched into the wedding march Mary had chosen, "Tuba Tune" by John Stanley. The massive tuba and bombard stops covered Ferghal's guffaw as they rumbled into life. Everyone rose to their feet and faced the door as Mary, radiant in an ivory chiffon and satin gown, stood beneath the organ and waited for the exact moment in the music to enter the church on the arm of her father.

Harry sucked a deep breath to steady his nerves. "Doesn't she look magnificent? Am I not the luckiest man alive?"

"Yes, you are," said Ferghal. *You've no idea of the truth of that statement, my friend.* He nudged Danny. "Stop gawping, yonker. She's taken!" Danny blushed and grinned sheepishly.

From her seat immediately behind the three young men, Niamh watched the little exchange with a glow of pride in her heart. 'Her' boys had grown up and more than proved themselves as young men. Harry still looked a little pale and unsteady, and she knew he still had some discomfort, but he would not admit to it. *How like James*, she thought. She caught sight of Mary, radiant in her magnificent gown, and tears pricked her eyes. She squeezed Theo's hand as the music surged and Mary processed down the aisle, and Harry presented his arm and made a courtly bow as the bride and her father reached him.

Taking the proffered arm, Mary smiled and made a small curtsey as they both turned to face the Dean, ready to read the marriage service. She caught Ferghal's flushed face and his expression of merriment and wondered what had passed between the boys to set him off. As Mary's father moved aside to join her mother in the pew, she saw the Canids then the Lacertians. A grin crossed her face. She suspected she knew what must have amused Ferghal without being told.

"Oh, Harry," she murmured, "please promise me you'll never grow up." She smiled at Harry's baffled expression, and the service got under way, the Dean leading them in the formalities required by law, and the ancient questions and responses flowed. The readings, prescribed by the Church, were read by Mary's mother and the Admiral. The hymn "Be Thou My Vision," chosen by Harry, was sung with enjoyment by most, cautiously by some, and beautifully led by the choir, to the fascination of the aliens present. The sermon was witty, the Dean having plenty of material to hand with Harry's unusual background and Mary's fame as a pianist, and made excellent use of it.

The anthem, sung while they signed the registers, was a modern work chosen by Mary. Then it was time to receive the blessing, share their first kiss as husband and wife, and process to the door. "Now, Mrs Heron, may I have your arm?" Harry was grinning like the proverbial Cheshire cat. "What music did you choose for our departure?" he whispered as they took their places.

"Something special," she replied. "It's called 'Dare to Live,' and it's from the twentieth century. I chose it to remind you, my love, that you've a lot to live for here. A few less heroics in future though, please."

Heads turned as the fast-paced music began, the initial repeating single note growing fuller in sound as the organ joined in and the joyous sound filled the ancient building. The Verger, grinning as the music infected everyone with its exciting pace, bowed, turned and led them slowly down the center aisle of the church. It wasn't until they reached the great west doors, now standing open, that Harry realised Danny had vanished. The reason for his absence became apparent as they approached the doors, the peeling bells growing in volume.

"Guard of Honour, 'tenshun!" The unmistakable twitter of bo'suns' calls was accompanied by the flash of sunlight on the swords as a double line of officers headed by Keiron formed an arch for Harry and Mary to pass under after they stepped out of the cathedral. Beyond them stood more wedding guests in uniforms, and Harry recognised the faces of Jack Proctor, Mike Dorfling, Maddy and Errol Hill and many more good friends who wouldn't have missed this occasion for the world. It brought a lump to his throat to have such an honour paid him and Mary.

"I think Ferghal and Danny have been busy, my love," Mary's delight filled her voice. "I knew they had something planned, but this is fabulous."

Harry laughed. "We shall have to repay them in kind when the time comes." Catching sight of a face he'd not expected to see, he groaned. "Oh dear, now we're for it. Here comes Monty Montaigne."

"Be nice to him now, we have to be gracious to our guests," she murmured, and smiled as Monty approached beaming with joy.

"Harry! Mary!" Montaigne's pleasure radiated. "What an amazing service! What memories!" He indicated his companion, a man holding a holo-recorder to capture every moment of this special day. "We recorded it all. Wonderful, absolutely wonderful." He kissed Mary on both cheeks then pumped Harry's hand, having only just refrained from kissing him too. "We'll get the video to you as soon as possible, of course."

Harry laughed. "Thank you, Monty, that will make a wonderful gift for us." Naughtily, he indicated his Canid and Lacertian friends—anything for a distraction. "You'll remember Regidur and Sci'antha?"

Monty beamed. "Of course! Regidur with his towering canine strength, and Sci'antha with her feline grace. Oh, yes, how could I forget? My dears, please excuse me—I simply must greet them."

Watching the actor move away to greet the aliens, and noting their expressions of dread, Mary laughed. "Harry, you're wicked! But I love you for it. Now introduce me to all these people who Danny says were with you on Lycania and all your other adventures."

Watching the exchange, Admiral James Heron and Felicity Roberts smiled as they gazed at the young couple.

"What I wouldn't give to be young and beautiful again," Felicity mused.

James thought she looked resplendent in her dress uniform as a Commodore, and told her so, and it actually made her blush.

"Well then, Admiral, does this spectacle give you any thoughts for the future?" There was a daring tease in her eyes, and she hoped he caught her meaning.

Surprised, James Heron glanced at his companion. "I suppose—well, at least I think..." He caught her expression and stopped short, knowing it was useless. She had him. "Commodore Roberts, do you have something to report?" He smiled.

Felicity laughed. "As a matter of fact, yes, sir, I do. I've retired my commission and hope to pursue a new career. All this cloak and dagger stuff is far too exciting at my age, especially dealing with all these mythological types out to get me."

He studied her for a moment. "Now that you mention it, I'm hauling down my flag, as I believe the saying is according to my great-uncle Harry twelve times removed—until I'm needed again, of course." He grinned.

"Which provides us with an opportunity to—"

"—say to hell with the Regulations? My thoughts exactly." Her eyes held his, a delightful twinkle in them. "And since we're flouting convention—will you marry me, James, before we're both too damned set in our ways to change our minds?"

His guffaw of laughter turned heads. "To hell with convention. I've been wanting to ask you the same thing since '04 and the Mars Dock!" He swept her into his arms and kissed her. "That answer your question, Commodore?"

Niamh nudged Theo. "I think James has met his match." She smiled. "Felicity will know exactly how to look after him."

Theo laughed. "So your little brother has got over losing Veronique at last." He nodded to where Ferghal was chatting with a beautiful young woman, one of the bridesmaids, who was clearly enjoying the funny story he was telling. "I don't think he's alone—and Danny is dancing attendance on another fine young lady over there."

Niamh dabbed her eyes. "Our boys have come a very long way. It seems just yesterday they arrived, and look how well they've adapted. They make me so proud."

"And so they should," Theo responded, taking his wife's arm and gently leading her toward their transport. It was time to play the gracious hosts at the wedding dinner. Yes, the trio had carved out a niche in this era, four centuries ahead of their time, and transformed themselves and several others, not least his wife and his brother-in-law, though he doubted either of them realised the full extent of it.

Once the guests had begun to drift toward the transport arranged to take them to the wedding dinner, Harry helped his bride to the great slab of stone that commemorates the fact that somewhere in this holy place lay the remains of St Patrick, St Columba of Bangor and St Bridget.

Mary laid her bouquet on the stone then stepped back in quiet reverence. "Thank you," she said softly. "Thank you for watching over him and bringing him home." She gripped Harry's arm. "Commander Henry Nelson-Heron, my own sweet husband at last. I could stay here alone with you forever, but our wedding dinner and hungry guests await."

With a last glance at the simple slab and its weathered inscription of the name Patrick, Harry turned, his lips brushing Mary's cheek as he took in the wide sweep of the horizon, the distant Mountains of Mourne, for once free of their mists as if in celebration of this glorious day.

"Thank you, my darling Mary. Thank you for your prayers and your faith."

Hand in hand they walked to the waiting transport, their closest friends and family waiting to see them aboard. The future looked wonderful, and for a fleeting moment, Harry's thoughts went back to that near-death experience aboard the *Emily Hobhouse* so many months ago. Surely it had not been his time to die. He had so much more living to do, together with his Mary, and today was the first day of the rest of their lives.

Note from the Author

If you enjoyed reading *Harry Heron: Hope Transcends*, please take a moment to write a positive review on Amazon.com. Your time and consideration are very much appreciated.

And, if you haven't had the opportunity to read the first five books in the Harry Heron Series, I invite you to do so now. Sit back and enjoy the full scope of Harry and Ferghal's adventures, which span from the early nineteenth century on the deck of a British "wooden wall" man 'o war to the twenty-third century and starships that go to the edges of our galaxy and beyond.

Thank you for taking this journey to the stars with me. It's been an exciting ride!

Patrick G. Cox

www.harryheron.com
www.patrickgcox.com

CPSIA information can be obtained
at www.ICGtesting.com
Printed in the USA
LVHW010338140820
663144LV00010B/128